"Your mother was simply at the wrong place at the wrong time."

"You're the one who said that something about this site worried you," she reminded him.

"This site, not Philadelphia. Your mother's death has nothing to do with this dig."

"We'll see, won't we?" Images of her mother's face rose behind her burning eyelids. How could Anati be lying still and cold on a steel table in a medical examiner's lab?

Abbie swallowed, trying to breathe normally, trying to ignore the pain in her chest. Buck might be a good cop, but he was wrong if he believed this was just a crazed druggie out to make a quick hit. Her mother had died because of this project—because of what someone was afraid she'd discover. Abbie was as certain of it as she was that none of the authorities would listen to anything she said.

If the murderer had killed her mother with an Indian axe, he'd done it deliberately to make a statement, and he'd been the one to carry the weapon to the scene... Which meant he'd intended to commit murder. The place to start the investigation wasn't in the city where her mother had died. It was right here on Tawes.

Other books by Judith E. French:

BLOOD KIN
THE WARRIOR
AT RISK
THE BARBARIAN
THE CONQUEROR

BLOOD
TIES

JUDITH E.
FRENCH

LOVE SPELL NEW YORK CITY

For Forrest with love...

LOVE SPELL®

April 2007

Published by

Dorchester Publishing Co., Inc.
200 Madison Avenue
New York, NY 10016

ISBN-10: 0-505-52714-6
ISBN-13: 978-0-505-52714-1

The name "Love Spell" and its logo are trademarks of Dorchester
Publishing Co., Inc.

Printed in the United States of America.

Visit us on the web at www.dorchesterpub.com.

BLOOD TIES

July . . .
Tawes Island
Chesapeake Bay Country

Ears pricked, the fox stepped out of the tangle of tall phragmites and sniffed the air. Only the whisper of swaying marsh grass, the drone of insects, and the mournful cry of a dove broke the stillness of the misty morning. The vixen was young and her sleek red-gold coat glistened in the ribbons of dappled sunlight that filtered through the wisps of remaining fog.

The fox froze, coiled muscles tensed, inquisitive eyes scanning the beach. From a pine bough overhead, a squirrel chattered, but the vixen gave no indication that she heard. She leaped gracefully over a mossy log and trotted down the slope to the narrow strip of beach framing the salt water pond.

The fox raised her head, inhaling the sweet stench of carrion. She crossed the damp sand, her gaze locked on the prize that her keen nose had already located.

A few yards off the shore, the body of a grotesquely swollen man bobbed in the shallow brackish water. He floated face down and naked, except for the monstrous garment formed of multitudes of feeding crabs. Above and below the surface of the brackish water, Chesapeake Blue Claws feasted on the sun-baked corpse.

Craters gaped in the ruined flesh. Crabs gnawed at the pale, bloated buttocks. White bone gleamed through the ruins of the left shoulder. The dead man's hair had been close-cropped, and the back of his head and neck was a squirming mass of crustaceans.

The fox stood quivering at the water's edge, waves lapping her dainty front paws. Her nostrils flared as each breath brought her the delicious scent of ripe flesh. Every instinct urged her to leap into the water and partake of the bounty, but she hesitated.

Something troubled her.

Her hackles rose and her ears flicked nervously. Somewhere over the salt marsh an osprey shrieked, but the vixen never turned her gaze toward the sky. Glancing back at the body, she salivated, and licked her lips. The cloying odor of decaying flesh hung heavy on the air.

The vixen lifted her head and sniffed the salt breeze drifting off the marsh. Abruptly, she whirled and fled across the beach, vanishing into the trees. The crabs continued to feast, oblivious to the watching eyes.

Unaware of the human watching . . . unaware of the presence of pure evil.

CHAPTER ONE

Emma Parks stood with her hands on her hips and her mouth open as the candy-apple-red helicopter circled the open field, swooped, and hovered over her mother's cow pasture before landing. The pilot gradually reduced the engine speed and shut it down. Once the rotors came to a full stop, the pilot and sole occupant, female, climbed out onto the field. She wore jeans and a tank top, canvas athletic shoes with a green leaf design, and dark sunglasses. Slung over one shoulder was a worn leather backpack.

"That your girl?" Emma asked the woman standing beside her.

Karen Knight grinned and waved. "Abigail Chingwe Night Horse, soon to be Dr. Night Horse. Sounds pretentious, doesn't it?"

"Ching what?"

"Chingwe. It means *bobcat* in the Lenape. Her grandfather named her. He still spoke a little of the old language. He's dead now, but he was insistent that she carry his mother's name."

"Why is she Night Horse and you're Knight with a K?"

"Long story." Karen hurried forward to give her daughter a hug. "We expected you an hour ago."

The young woman removed her glasses. "Indian time, Ànati."

"That's Lenape for Mom," Karen explained. She was shorter than her daughter by a head, but it was easy to tell they were blood kin. They shared the same dark hair and eyes, copper skin, and high cheek bones. At least Emma supposed that Karen's hair had once been as glossy black as the girl's. Now, age had seasoned Karen's with feathers of pure white. Her daughter's tan was darker, but Emma knew she'd just gotten back from three months in Phaistos, in Crete, where she'd been working on an archaeological dig.

"Welcome to Tawes, Abigail." Emma offered a callused hand. "I'm Emma Parks. You two will be staying with me while you investigate the Indian burial ground on the far side of the island."

The young woman's serious expression dissolved into a genuine smile. Her teeth were white and even, as perfect as any movie star's. "Please, call me Abbie."

The young woman's hand was lean and strong, and she looked Emma in the eyes. Emma liked that. She never trusted a creature that wouldn't look you straight on, neither human nor animal. These two seemed like good folks, even if they were from the mainland. And they were Bailey's friends. Emma put a heap of faith in Bailey's good sense.

"The site is an ideal spot for archaic hunter-gatherers to make camp. Possibly early Algonquin." Karen said. "Bailey Tawes took me out there yesterday."

"I can't wait to see it," Abbie answered.

Emma shrugged. "Just as well you weren't here yesterday."

Karen shot her a warning look. "Later," she mouthed behind Abbie's back, and then asked, "How's your dad?" as the three of them walked away from the red helicopter toward the pasture fence.

"Same as always. Excited over a new Andalusian mare he just bought from Spain. Feathers ruffled that I wouldn't stay for the powwow."

"You could have. I could have managed for a few days."

Abbie shook her head. "It's not until next weekend, and if I agreed to stay, he would have wanted me to dance. He always wants me to dance. The last time I wore that regalia, my buckskins were too tight."

Emma arched a graying eyebrow. To her way of thinking, Karen's girl Abbie was thin as a rail and needed feeding. Karen said she didn't have a beau, and it was no wonder. Most men would rather have something soft to cuddle up to on a cold night than hug a broom stick. "I can't tell you how much it means to all of us on the island, your being here. Volunteering to see what's out there in the marsh. We wanted to get the state archaeological people in, but you know what dealing with bureaucracy is like."

Karen laughed. "Don't we just."

"Glad to help," Abbie said.

"Abbie's been in Crete this summer," Karen explained. "What with my project in Canyon de Chelly, we haven't seen much of each other this year."

"I hope you both like chicken and dumplings," Emma said. "I've got fresh corn on the cob, and my mother—everybody calls her Aunt Birdy—sent over a blueberry pie."

Karen groaned. "I warned you. Emma's meals are to die for, but I'll be twice my size in a week."

"You look great, *Ànati*. If anything, you've slimmed down since you were in Athens."

"Right. Isn't that what your father's been saying for twenty years?" Karen rolled her eyes.

"So, maybe it's true. I like you fine, just the way you are."

Emma climbed over the split-rail fence and motioned for them to follow. "There's a gate up near Mama's house, but this is quicker."

"Obviously, there's no airstrip on Tawes," Abbie said.

Emma chuckled. "No stop signs, no cars, no traffic lights or taverns, and not much in the way of roads. I bought myself a four-wheel 'gator last fall, but most folks walk or go by water."

"And Bailey offered us the use of her horses," Karen said. "After walking that marsh trail, I'm ready to saddle up."

"You'd be welcome to borrow my skiff," Emma offered, "but the water's shallow in that marsh. Takes a flat-bottomed pram or a little aluminum to get through the guts and into the beach. I've got one of those, but I need it to check my crab traps every day."

"You're a crabber?" Abbie asked.

"Used to call myself one. Started on my daddy's workboat when I was knee-high to a duck. Time I was fourteen, I had thirty pots of my own. Used to tend them before school. But it's a hard life, scratching a life out of the bay. Up at four, out on the water by five, rain or shine. Some days you come back loaded with jimmies; other days, you don't catch enough to pay for gas." Emma grimaced. "Too old and not enough ambition to do it anymore."

"I'd assumed we'd rent a boat here on Tawes to go back and forth to the dig. If there's no good place to set the R22 down near there, we could reach it by water."

"Bailey has open pasturage," Karen said. "We hiked in to the site from her house yesterday. There's a Mr.

Williams who lives closer. I met him yesterday, but I don't know if any of his property is clear enough to land safely."

Emma frowned. "George has let the place get over-run with trees. Used to be good farmland, but George is getting long in the tooth. Now he mostly crabs. Elizabeth's"—she corrected herself— "Bailey's, that's your closest access. And nobody on Tawes rents out their boats. You might find a skiff in Crisfield by the week. Won't come cheap, though."

"How do people get back and forth to the mainland? To Annapolis? Or to Maryland's Eastern Shore? Isn't there a ferry?"

Emma shook her head. "During the school year, there's one that carries the kids to high school in Crisfield. Some folks take it to do their dealin' at one of the big supermarkets. But, it don't run in summer."

"And you fussed when I said I was bringing the heli-copter?" Abbie threw her mother an *I told you so* look.

"What's the cost of fuel for that thing?" Karen countered.

"Dad offered, and I took him up on it. It will come in handy for flying to Philly."

"You know I worry about you in small planes."

"Safer than driving to the airport."

"I know. You've told me that often enough."

"I want to warn you, Abbie. You can't always depend on phones here on the island. Half the time there's no signal."

"That's the truth," Karen agreed. "Yesterday, when Bailey and I . . ." She trailed off. "Let's just say that when we needed the cell phone to work, it was as dead as a log." Emma's mother's farm wasn't far from the village. A ten-minute walk took them down a dusty lane and past a cluster of tidy nineteenth century homes, interspersed with large two-story farmhouses. Most had barns and carriage houses, picket fences, and brick chimneys.

"You won't get lost in Tawes, once you get your bearings." Emma pointed. "Up there's the main street. Hang a left, you pass the church. Keep walking, you come to the town dock. Turn right, you'll see Dori's, the town's only market. There used to be more stores when the oyster shucking house and the canning factory were open."

"Reminds me of Cape May," Abbie said. "That green house is definitely early Victorian, and the mustard-colored one on the other side of the street is a Greek Revival."

"Closer to the dock is the old part of town. A few homes stood here since before the Revolution. Wait until you see Forest McCready's mansion."

"I never expected to find anything like this on the East Coast," Abbie said. "Rural charm without commercialization."

"Things don't change much on Tawes. Folks like it that way. We Parkses have been here since the 1600s."

Karen admired a grape arbor that arched over a log bench in the nearest yard. "So a lot of the old families must be related."

"True enough," Emma said. "I've got so many cousins and cousins twice-removed livin' on this island, I never rightly counted them all. As a matter of fact, you might say we're woodpile cousins."

"How's that?" Abbie asked.

"According to Mama, her grandmother on her daddy's side was pure Nanticoke. We sure all got the dark hair. Leastways, mine was black when I was a sprout."

"I'm familiar with the Nanticoke tribe," Karen said. "One of the grad students at Penn was from Lewes,

Delaware, and she said she was Nanticoke."

"Mama always said the Nanticokes and the Powhatan were cousins to the Lenape over on Delaware Bay. Used to speak the same talk."

"I wonder," Abbie said, "why it was always Grandmom who was an Indian and not Grandpop."

Karen wrinkled her nose and gave Abbie that secret look that mothers do when they want their daughters to hush up, but Emma didn't take offense.

"Can't say about folks in other parts, "Emma said," but here on the Chesapeake, when the first settlers came from the old country, white men outnumbered the white women twenty to one for more than a hundred years. Guess it was natural some would take Indian wives. And who would make a better partner than a girl who was used to living off the land?"

"I think you're right," Karen agreed.

Emma quickened her step. "There's my boarding-house on the left. The white two-story with the blue shutters." She stopped and shaded her eyes with a broad hand. "Unless my sight's goin' the way of my knees, I believe that's our new police chief."

A tall, sandy-haired man in his late thirties rose from the porch swing and ambled down the front steps. "Afternoon, ladies."

"Is this a social visit, or is it official?" Emma asked.

"I needed to ask Dr. Knight a few more questions."

"Certainly, Chief Davis, "Karen said." I hope you haven't been waiting long. My daughter just flew in from Philadelphia to assist with the preliminary site evaluation. She's a doctorate student at the University of Pennsylvania."

The girl introduced herself. "Abbie Night Horse."

"Is that Miss or Mrs.?"

"Single, if that's what you want to know."

He nodded. "Ms. Night Horse. Pleased to meet you."

Emma could hardly hide her amusement. Abbie was inspecting the police chief with the appetite of a starving woman who'd just stumbled onto a hot chicken-and-dumpling dinner, and the Davis boy was eyeing her with equal enthusiasm.

"Hmmm." Emma cleared her throat. "It was Karen you came to question, wasn't it, Chief? Abbie hasn't been on Tawes twenty minutes."

His grin widened as his eyes sparked mischief. "It was, Miss Emma. Thank you for reminding me." He nodded to Abbie again. "A pleasure, ma'am." His wit was sharp, but his words were slow and lazy, his voice laced with the island way of talking. Emma was glad that all those years in Delaware hadn't made him sound like a mainlander.

"You already said that." Abbie's gaze lingered on the width of his shoulders, then moved down over his tight gray T-shirt to his flat stomach. She stared—just a few seconds too long for good manners—at his jeans-clad hips and then took in his worn cowboy boots. "You ride, Chief Davis?"

"Any chance I get."

Emma had the distinct feeling they were not talking about horses. It was heating up fast on this porch. "I'll just put some ice in the glasses and get that chicken on the table," she said. "Buck? You're not too busy to eat, I hope." Emma glanced at Karen. "He's been staying with his brother Nate, but Nate's wife Faith isn't the best cook on Tawes."

"Will you be staying for dinner, Ms. Night Horse?" Buck asked.

" 'Course, she will," Emma said. "She and Karen are rooming with me here while they poke around the Indian site. Where else would they eat?"

"I see." He took a pen and notepad out of his back

pocket. "And are these your only guests at present?"

"Yep," Emma said. "Just the two of them."

"So you still have that room vacant you mentioned last week?"

"Hasn't been used since Christmas when Daniel left."

"Would it suit you if I moved in tomorrow? Nate's house is getting a little crowded for the six of us."

"Suits me fine." Emma put her hand on the screen door. "I could use some help in the kitchen. Abbie?"

"Certainly. But I'm curious. My mother's only been here two days, Chief Davis. What's she done that merits police interrogation?"

"I was waiting to tell you when you got here," Karen explained. "Bailey and I discovered a drowning victim out at the site. It was pretty gruesome."

"You found a body?"

Yesterday morning. One that had been in the water awhile. We attempted to call the authorities, but I couldn't get a signal on my cell. We went to Mr. Williams's house and he was kind enough to help." Karen looked at Buck. "Has the victim been identified?"

"Not officially, but—"

"Roger Gilbert's boy, Sean," Emma said, "from over on Deal Island."

"That's not public information yet," Buck interjected.

"His uncle's boat." Emma rested her palm on the door frame. "The dead boy's the right age, and Sean's been missing. He's a midshipman at the Academy in Annapolis, second year. Was," she corrected. "His parents called the undertaker, and neighbors are bringing funeral hams. It's Sean Gilbert, right enough."

"Thanks, Miss Emma. I can finish this up without your help."

She pursed her mouth. "Just stating facts. Wish it

was some stranger instead of a Deal boy." Emma motioned to Abbie. "We may as well get the food on, since it's obvious we're in the way here."

Abbie stepped into the entrance hall; Emma followed and let the door bang behind her. A fat tabby cat mewed a welcome from the wide staircase. "You can go up and get unpacked if you want. Mind you don't tread on Linus there. He's a good mouser, but he's always underfoot. The doors are all marked. I put you in the Carolina Wren room. Your mother's in the Robin's Nest, across the hall. There's just one bathroom upstairs for the guests."

"It will be fine. You should see the conditions on some of the sites I've worked at in the Greek Islands." Abbie slipped her backpack off her shoulder. "So Mom and Bailey found a body yesterday?"

"That they did. Best let her tell you about it. Crabs had been at the boy."

Abbie shuddered. "I think I'm glad I stayed in Oklahoma a few days longer."

"Yeah, it was a sight folks are better off not seeing. For certain, something Bailey didn't need to see." Emma lowered her voice. "I think she's in the family way. She's not said anything to Daniel—he's her intended. . . . Or to me, for that matter. But Bailey's fillin' out, and she's got that shine about her. I'd be willing to lay hard money that Daniel will be bouncing a baby on his knee by the first of next year."

"I hope it works out for them. Mom and Bailey have been friends for years. She's always been good to me."

"Good to everybody. Good blood in her. She's got the Tawes eyes, you know. Just like her Uncle Will. Daniel's lucky to have her."

Abbie carried her backpack up the stairs, and Emma continued on into the parlor. She'd already set

the table in the dining room, so all she had to do was
bring the food out of the kitchen. All the windows
were open and there was a nice breeze off the bay,
making the downstairs cool despite the July heat. Outside on the porch, Emma heard Buck ask about the
exact time the two women had discovered Sean's body.
Emma moved a little closer to the window, not really
eavesdropping, but curious. Karen's reply was too low
to catch.

"Is there time for me to take a shower?" Abbie
called down.

"Sure," Emma answered. That would give her a few
minutes to get the food on the table. She hurried into
the kitchen to mix up the batch of iced tea she'd
started earlier.

Everything she'd put together for Abbie's first dinner on the island looked good. There was a fresh-
baked blueberry pie for dessert, and she had her first
ripe garden tomato to add to the salad. But something
kept gnawing at the corners of her mind like an eel
chewing a chicken neck.

It had to be that Indian burial ground where Bailey
and Karen had found the drowned boy. Old-time people stayed clear of that stretch of shoreline, and Emma
saw no reason to argue with common sense. Maybe
the Gilbert kid had just had bad luck, but maybe it was
something else.

Once, hunting, she'd followed a wounded deer out
there. She'd tramped the marsh until twilight before
she'd finally found the animal and finished it off. That
swamp was a queer place with strange sounds and
something Emma couldn't put words to . . . something
that raised the hairs on the nape of her neck just to
think about it.

She liked Karen Knight and her girl Abbie. Emma

enjoyed hearing tales about far-off places and the pyramids and such. She damned certain wanted Karen to find reason to keep the marina people off Tawes. But she didn't favor the idea of those two poking around on that cursed section of the island. The way Emma saw it, no good could come out of it, and a lot of bad.

Buck pushed his chair back from Emma's dining-room table. "If you ladies will excuse me, duty calls."

"Don't forget the meeting at the church at seven. Matthew said he'd keep it short, just fill folks in on what's happening and introduce them to Karen and Abbie."

"I'd like to join you, but I can't. As police chief, it wouldn't be right for me to take sides."

Emma shrugged. "I told Matthew that's what you'd say. Certain you won't have another piece of pie?"

"Thanks, but no. That third helping of potato salad and the first slice of blueberry pie will probably hold me until breakfast. Tell Aunt Birdy she's outdone herself." He glanced at Abbie, hoping he'd read the signals right. "I'd be glad to show you some of Tawes, Ms. Night Horse. If you're interested?"

Almond-shaped dark eyes appraised him. Taut silence stretched between them. He waited.

"Business, Chief Davis? Or pleasure?"

"Strictly pleasure."

Her lips curved into a smile. "About eight?"

"Eight it is. And, Ms. Night Horse? Wear something you can ride in."

He headed for the back door before Emma or Karen could notice the sudden fullness that had swelled the front of his jeans. Abbie had an edge. She not only intrigued him, she sizzled like a steak on a hot grill. And a man didn't live on potato salad and blueberry pie alone.

By the time he reached the back porch, he'd startled humming to himself, and when he'd covered the three blocks to the old seed store that served as the town's police station, it was hard to push Abbie Night Horse out of his mind long enough to finish the paperwork on the Gilbert boy's drowning.

The hands on the wall clock pointed to 6:45 when Buck switched off the light and locked the office door. This was probably one of the few locked doors on the island, but if the real estate people bought the property they'd taken an option on and built the marina project, Tawes would have to change.

He hoped Forest McCready could find good reason to stop the developers at Onicox Realty in their tracks. After years on the Delaware State Police, Buck had looked forward to coming home, to having things the way he remembered them. He wanted Tawes to remain isolated from the mainland madness, and he'd do anything in his power to keep it unspoiled.

His sister-in-law was finishing up the supper dishes when he entered his brother's cottage on the far side of town. Faith raised a soapy hand as he opened the screen door. "Wondering when you were going to get home."

"Paperwork to finish on that drowning. You or Nate going to the meeting tonight?"

"Not a chance," Faith said. "Matthew Catlin and Forest McCready would probably burn me at the stake. I'm all for the marina. It's bound to bring jobs." She returned to scrubbing her frying pan.

"How about Nate?"

"It's a free country. You ask him."

In the living room, Buck's brother was lounging in his easy chair, watching the news out of Salisbury and drinking a Bud. "You look comfortable," Buck said. "Going to tonight's meeting?"

"Nope." Nate raised his beer can. "A cold one left in the fridge." Five-year-old Sammy was busy painting her father's toenails hot pink, while Johnny, three, drove a racecar through the tunnel formed by Nate's legs. The house was relatively quiet, which meant Baby Joel must be sleeping.

"No, thanks. Just want to grab a quick shower; then I'm going to show the archaeologist's daughter some of the finer points of Tawes."

"I'll bet you will. If you're hungry, Faith made clam chowder and her special cornbread."

"Are you being a smart-ass about my cooking again?" she called from the kitchen.

"No, honey." Nate rolled his eyes. "Just, next time, no need to add so much salt."

Buck paused in the archway that led to the narrow hallway and the windowless bedroom he'd been sharing with Sammy and Johnny. "I'm moving into Emma's place."

"Can't get Daniel's cabin yet?" Faith dried her hands on a kitchen towel. She'd pinned her blond ponytail up into a knot, and pieces were falling down. "You know there's no need to move out. You're always welcome here."

He grinned. "I appreciate your putting up with me, but it's time I let Johnny have his bottom bunk back."

"I'm going to get the attic wired for a third bedroom next month," Nate said. "Honest to God. We can make out until then."

"Right," Faith said. "Three years you've been promising to do it."

"I came home to Tawes to stay," Buck said. "I can afford my own place. I'll talk to Daniel. Bailey's still dodging a wedding date, but maybe he can convince her to let him move in with her."

"Too bad about Sherwood's farmhouse. Right on

the water." Nate drained the last drops of his beer. "Brick house. And the barn's solid. You could have fixed that place up nice."

"Yeah. I would have liked to buy the house and ten acres, but it's out of my price range now. If the realtors get it, they'll bulldoze everything and throw up condos that start at a half-mil apiece."

"Shame on you two," Faith put in. "Neither of you have said a word about that drowned boy. I went to high school with his older sister. Funny, isn't it? Sheila always bragged about Sean's swimming."

"Anybody can drown." Nate handed the empty can to Sammy. "Throw this in the trash for Daddy, will you, princess?" He settled back in the chair. "Maybe the kid was drunk or high."

Buck shook his head. "No sign of it. No reason to think it was anything but a freak accident. Of course, the coroner's report hasn't come in. That will be weeks—if we're lucky."

"If you want a shower, you'd best wait a little," Faith said. "Nate had one before supper. I'm not sure how much hot water is—"

"No problem," Buck said.

"Oh, yeah," Nate chimed in. "With the hot date he's got lined up, he needs a cold shower to keep hisself under control until the time is right."

CHAPTER TWO

The tree-shaded brick church was three-quarters full
when Abbie and her mother followed Emma through
a side entrance to a front pew designated reserved by a
line of hymnals. Emma gathered the books and
stacked them at the end of the bench. "This is for us.
You two go up and take a look at Matthew's collection.
That's just some of the Indian stuff from the site." She
waved toward a long table with an array of stone and
ceramic artifacts.

A goodly crowd surrounded the table but people
stepped back politely to allow the newcomers a clear
view. Abbie scanned the display, noting a number of
fine quartz and chert points, a hematite celt, two sand-
stone axes, incised ceramics, an intact drill that might
be made of flint, an obsidian pipe, and a five-inch section of a soapstone bowl. North America wasn't her
area of expertise, but she had followed her mother
from site to site since she was five, and this was Native
American Archaeology 101.

It was evident that the pieces represented a time pe-

riod ranging from prehistoric up to European contact. If the items had been recovered from the area
they'd come to investigate, there was no doubt in Abbie's mind that the spot had been occupied for thousands of years. Not that that made a solid case for
preventing development of private property, but it did
prove an urgent need for further investigation.

A tall, angular man with wire-framed glasses and a
gray mustache strode purposefully to the table.
"Thank you all for coming. If you'll just be seated, we
can start." Since he spoke with authority and was one
of the few males in the church wearing a tie, Abbie assumed this must be the minister, Matthew Catlin, the
amateur archaeologist who'd been instrumental in
bringing them there. She tapped her mother's shoulder and they took their seats beside Emma.

"Is there anything new, Matthew?" called out an
older woman sitting directly behind Emma. Abbie
glanced back. She was thin, with an unusually smooth
complexion and few wrinkles, despite her white hair.

"I don't see the Squire." A man across the aisle
stood and peered around the church. "You told us that
Forest McCready would be here."

"Shhh." His female companion—Abbie guessed it
was his wife—tugged at his shirt. "For the love of God,
Phillip!" she scolded. "How can Matthew tell us anything, with you runnin' your mouth?"

The accents that filled the church were as distinctive
as Emma's, but more Old English than Old South to
Abbie's ear. The words and phrases were quaint and
old-fashioned, but she had no trouble understanding
them. The island fascinated her, and not just because
of the potential archaeological site.

"Will Tawes saw surveyors out there yesterday," reported the white-haired matron, standing and raising
her voice. "Way I hear, the sale's not gone through yet.

So the mainlanders are trespassing. What good is the law if they can run roughshod over our land when they please?"

"Money talks!" came from the back of the church. "I told ye all this truck would come to nuthin'."

Matthew raised his hands and motioned his flock to calm. "Friends, neighbors . . . illustrious guests . . ."

"There's Bailey," Abbie's mother whispered. "Over there. That's her uncle Will with her. I don't see her fiancé, Daniel. He's the minister's brother."

"Ah-hem." Matthew Catlin cleared his throat pointedly. A hush fell over the church. "Thank you. Thank you. First of all, I'd like to introduce our archaeologist, Dr. Karen Knight, and her daughter Abigail. Please stand." He offered a professional smile. "Everyone! Give them a big Tawes welcome!"

"Where's Forest?" someone asked. "Why isn't he here?"

"Forest McCready," Emma whispered. "The lawyer."

"As most of you know," Matthew continued, "our purpose here is the preservation of a prehistoric Indian—"

"Speak for yourself," a man interjected. "Some of us are just nosy."

Phillip's better half rose, hands on her ample hips. "Is the drowned boy Roger Gilbert's youngest?"

"Hearsay only," the minister replied. "No positive identification of the deceased has—"

"It's the Gilbert boy," Emma told the woman.

Murmurs rippled through the church, and Abbie was certain she heard the gray-haired woman behind her say something about a curse.

Matthew tried again to regain control of his audience. "Mere speculation. We need to focus on the purpose of this gathering. As most of you already know, Thomas Sherwood, a life-long resident of Tawes, died without a will, and a great nephew, Robert Mellmore of Baltimore is his next of kin. This Mr. Mellmore has accepted an option on the property by the Onicox Realty Group, which wants to build a marina and condos on our island."

"Mainlanders!"

"Please, please. We'd like to keep this short tonight. Nothing is definite yet. There's a question about whether or not Thomas Sherwood owned the land."

"You just said a sale is pending," Phillip reminded him.

Emma got to her feet. "Forest McCready got a judge to hold everything until the title is straightened out. He thinks Sherwood's father was just a tenant farmer."

"For sixty years?"

Laughter erupted from the back of the church.

"Who paid the taxes on the land?"

Heads turned. The soft question brought the gathering to silence. The speaker, lean and graying, with rough features that could have been chiseled of red oak, stood as straight as a Roman column. Not much Indian blood in him, if any, Abbie thought, but he carried himself with the innate dignity of most of the tribal elders she'd known.

"Will Tawes, the famous artist," her mother whispered. "Bailey's great-uncle."

"Good question, Will," Matthew said. "I don't know, but I'm sure Forest McCready could tell us. They may have been paid from the island trust."

Abbie glanced at her watch. She knew she should have passed on the town meeting. If it dragged on, she'd just get up and leave. Her mother could deal with the locals.

Emma interrupted the minister. "Excuse me, Matthew, but I promised our experts that they wouldn't get bogged down in island politics. We don't want to drive them off before they do what they came here to do. It was bad enough that Dr. Knight had to find young Gilbert's body, but we can't help that."

"He's gone to a better place," Phillip's wife intoned.

"Mary Love, will you take your own good advice and hold your tongue long enough for Matthew to say his piece so we can all get home tonight?" Emma remarked.

Snickers erupted into genuine mirth. A waterman near the door shouted, "The boy shouldn't have dug in that marsh in the first place."

Mary Love glared at Emma. "And who on this island's got a bigger mouth than you?"

Emma laughed. "Not many, I expect." She waited until the titters had settled and then continued. "So, as I see it, this realty company may or may not have bought a good-sized chunk of Tawes. Tom Sherwood should have sold the property to one of us, or left a proper will. Shame on him. And if any of you are in the same fix, shame on you." She glanced at Abbie and her mother. "For a few hundred years, no property on Tawes has passed to a mainlander."

"Except for Bailey," a freckle-faced woman called.

"Is she an outsider?" Emma said loudly. "She's a Tawes."

" 'Nuff said," Phillip agreed.

"All right. That's been our custom—law, if you want to put name to it—for three hundred years. Ours to ours. But Tom broke that code and left the island open to attack by these mainland pirates. If we don't stop them, we'll look like the western shore of the bay, all high-rise apartments, highways, and shopping centers. Now this Onicox Realty is a real threat to our way of life."

"Shoot 'em!" an octogenarian shouted. "It's what my granddaddy did to the Yankees!"

"None of that talk," Emma scolded. "There'll be

no shooting of anybody—unless I'm forced to set some of you back a few pegs." She paused for effect. "Matthew?"

"Absolutely," the minister agreed. "We on Tawes are law-abiding people, and we don't condone violence."

A woman chuckled. "Not much."

"Not unless we're pushed," a man added.

"All right," Emma continued. "Now bite your tongues if you want to get out of here before midnight." The crowd quieted. "Like I've been saying all week, Matthew and Bailey Tawes called in Dr. Knight, who is a genuine archaeologist and an expert in American Indian stuff, to see if the Indian burial ground should be protected. If it is a genuine historic site, maybe the State of Maryland will forbid the sale, and things can stay the way they are."

"Thank you, Emma. Well put. That's about it. Dr. Knight has agreed to help us. We're glad to see so many of you here in support of protecting Tawes, and I'll call another meeting as soon as we have more information. Good night and God bless. Thank you all for coming, and I hope to see this many at Sunday-morning service."

Abbie attempted to escape by a side door, but Emma blocked her exit.

"Don't rush off yet. Matthew's got something in the office he wants you to see. Something . . ." She shook her head. "It won't take long." She motioned to Matthew and lowered her voice. "Cut the jabbering short and show Karen and Abbie what your father gave you."

"Yes, yes. I did want to do that. Give me five minutes to see my congregation out." Matthew flashed his minister's smile.

Slowly the assemblage began to file out.

"Emma!" A thin, childish voice came from the rear

of the church. A tiny woman in a yellow striped dress and a white Mother Hubbard apron waved her cane.

"That's my mother," Emma said. "Maude Ellen Mc-Cready Parks. Everyone but me calls her Aunt Birdy."

"Hold your horses, girl," Mrs. Parks called to Emma. "I want to meet Bailey's friends."

Abbie watched as Mrs. Parks felt her way to the aisle and then used her cane to walk to the front of the church. As she drew closer, Abbie saw that the elderly woman's eyes were cloudy with thick cataracts. "Pleased to meet you." Mrs. Parks extended a tiny hand.

Abbie clasped it, surprised to find how strong the thin little woman's grip was. "Mrs. Parks, I'm Abbie Night Horse."

"Of course you are, child." Aunt Birdy tilted her head as if listening to something no one else heard. "You're one of the first people, aren't you?" she asked in her sweet, reedy voice. Slipping her cane over the edge of the pew back, she patted Abbie's wrist. "Can I touch your face, honey?"

Abbie's favorite grandmother had been blind, so she understood that it was the old woman's way of seeing. Abbie cradled the bony hand and lifted it to her cheek.

"Eyes and hair black as a crow's wing," Emma murmured. "She favors her mother. Beautiful, too."

"Don't need you to tell me that, girl," Mrs. Parks retorted.

Her fingertips were warm and light as thistle down.

"I'm Karen Knight, Abbie's mother," Karen said. "I'm pleased to meet you. And thank you for allowing Abbie to put her helicopter in your pasture."

"Pshaw, cows don't care. I wouldn't mind havin' a ride in the contraption, though. Never did get any higher than the attic of my farmhouse."

Abbie smiled and stepped back. Aunt Birdy turned toward Karen and then stopped and gripped Abbie's hand again. "There's something dark hoverin' over you, dear. You take care, you hear?" She shook her head. "Emma?"

"Yes, Mama?"

"Didn't you warn these ladies about that marsh? It's a bad place, always was. Spirits walk there, not good ones neither. The ghost of an Injun medicine man. Evil pagan he was, and evil he still is. The old-time people say his own kind were scared of him. Wicked, godless creature." She tilted her head as though she was peering up into Abbie's face. "Some folks don't believe in haunts, but you do."

Abbie's mouth went dry. "No, I—"

"No need to feel shame, child. Old-time folks believed, and the first people believe. There's lots of things in this world that some don't see, but they're real just the same."

"Now, Mama, don't go scaring these ladies with your ghost talk."

The old woman turned on Emma and shook her cane. "Listen at you. How many times have I heard you talk about that swamp? It's a bad place," she repeated.

"Dr. Knight, Miss Horse." Matthew hurried toward them. "If you'll excuse us, Aunt Birdy. We have some business in the office. Ladies, if you'd follow me."

"Don't forget," the old woman warned. "There's danger in the marsh. And something evil in that burial ground."

Uneasiness prickled Abbie's skin as she followed Matthew Catlin out of the sanctuary. Superstitious nonsense. It was foolish to let an old woman's fancies make her uneasy.

"I'm anxious to see what you mentioned earlier in your correspondence," her mother said. "And it's Abbie Night Horse, not Abbie Horse."

It was clear to Abbie that her mother was amused by

the minister's mistake. Mom might have changed her name to Knight with a K after she and Dad had split and before receiving her doctorate—she'd believed her modified name would help her blend more easily with mainstream academe—but Ànati was still Indian, blood and bone. And, despite the adversarial relationship between her parents, Abbie suspected they still loved each other.

A door off the sanctuary led to a hall and small office. Matthew switched on a light, beckoned them in, and closed and locked the door. "My father came to believe that the Irish reached North America a thousand years before the Viking voyages to the New World, and I'm convinced he was right. He was positive that he had proof there was contact with the Chesapeake natives, and that at least one early Irishman was buried on Tawes."

Abbie smiled. She'd heard the theory, but it was nothing more than speculation, like tales of the lost Atlantis and Welsh expeditions to the Great Lakes country.

"Father was certain that the things I'm about to show you were Irish Bronze Age," Matthew said. "I don't know whether they are or not, but I know they are genuine and very old." He unlocked a desk drawer, removed a worn leather case, and opened it. "See for yourself, Dr. Knight."

Abbie stared.

Two objects nestled against a stained green lining: a decorative bronze pin, more than six inches long and as thick as her middle finger, and a collar of bright, twisted metal. Too surprised to speak, Abbie looked into the minister's smiling face.

"You're positive they were dug at the site?" Her mother's eyes sparked with excitement. "You dug them yourself?"

Matthew frowned. "No. My father purchased them more than forty years ago from a Paul Millington. He had a farm near the burial ground. He was hunting a lost muskrat trap, and he found the pieces in the marsh after a storm washed out one side of the hill.

"They are Irish Bronze Age, aren't they?"

Abbie couldn't hold back a sigh of disappointment at Matthew's account of how the items were found. If her mother had excavated the pit or made the discovery herself . . . if the soil around the pieces had been below the plow line and undisturbed, then there was a possibility that such an unlikely theory as to their origin might be fact. She reached out to touch the torque, but her mother caught her hand and shook her head.

Feeling her cheeks grow hot, Abbie averted her eyes. She knew better than to touch, but temptation had overridden years of education in the proper handling of artifacts.

"Do you have gloves?" her mother asked Matthew.

He produced a pair of thin plastic gloves packaged for medical use. "I may be a country cleric," he said, "but I'm not totally ignorant of how artifacts should be handled."

"I never supposed you were." Karen pulled on the gloves and carefully picked up the pin, inspecting the intricate pattern of geometric swirls. Abbie was certain her mother could guess the weight of the object within grams.

Matthew peered over the rims of his glasses. "They are genuine?"

Excitement made her mother speak with unnaturally precise diction. "I'd need to have it authenticated, but this pin does appear Bronze Age to me." She nibbled at her lower lip. "Actually, Reverend Catlin, the question isn't *what they are,* but *how they got here.*"

His face fell. "I can assure you that if my father said he purchased the torque and the cloak pin from—"

"You misunderstand," Abbie interjected. "My mother's credentials are impeccable, but if she were to present these pieces as proof of early Irish contact, she'd be the laughingstock of her university."

"Not that I wouldn't try to make a case for it if I had more proof," Karen said. "But what's to say that the jewelry wasn't carried here by some settler three hundred years ago?"

"I don't understand." Matthew removed his glasses and scratched his head. "My father's reputation—"

"Scientifically," Karen said, "the discovery of something so far-fetched has to be documented by an expert."

"But I assumed you were—"

"My mother is an expert on Native American prehistory, not Irish Bronze Age," Abbie said.

"Celtic," he said.

"Not necessarily Celtic," Karen corrected. "Actually, many of the finest Bronze Age discoveries predate the Celtic migration."

Matthew grew animated. "That doesn't mean there couldn't be other artifacts as fine as these, perhaps even more wondrous."

"And I'm willing to sink test pits to see what we can find," Karen replied. "But I can make no guarantees. This is worse than hunting for the proverbial needle in a haystack. It's searching for Irish mist in a Chesapeake fog."

Matthew replaced his glasses. "My father kept a journal. We might find an entry that confirmed the purchase."

"That would be valuable," Abbie said, "but not scientific proof." She stared again at the torque and pin.

"Father was right about the origin of the items," Matthew insisted. "They are Irish, early Bronze Age, aren't they?"

Her mother replaced the pin and lifted the heavy collar with both hands. Her eyes met her daughter's, and Abbie felt a thrill. She knew her first impression had been right.

"The pin is bronze," Karen said. "But I believe your father was mistaken about the torque. This is crafted from a single bar of gold."

CHAPTER THREE

"You've heard the stories just like I have." Abbie heard Emma's emphatic voice coming from a group standing under the trees outside the church. "Abbie! I want you to meet somebody. This is George Williams. He's the one who helped your mother and Bailey when they found Sean Gilbert's body."

"Ma'am." George tugged at the brim of his ball cap. "Weren't much. My place just happens to be the closest. Pleased to make your acquaintance."

"Mr. Williams, yes, thank you. Mom told me about you. It must have been awful. I appreciate your assistance." George was a short, stocky man with skin as shiny black as obsidian and sleepy eyes nearly hidden in an accordion of wrinkles. His soft voice was heavily accented by the unique flavor of the Chesapeake Bay country. On first impression, the middle-aged waterman seemed more accustomed to laughter than tragedy. One cheek was puffed out, and from the stain on his lower lip, Abbie suspected George chewed plug tobacco.

"Anybody would have been glad to help out," the black man replied. "Terrible thing for your mother and Bailey Tawes, finding that poor boy with the crabs gnawin' him."

"Shame it was too late for anybody to help him," a second man said. "Even if the boy was up to no good out there."

"Abbie, this is Phillip Love," Emma explained. "He and his wife Mary run Dori's Market."

"I'm the manager. Mary places orders and waits on customers." Phillip was tall and lean, a little older than George, with heavy eyelids, an auburn mustache, and a strident tone.

"Pleased to meet you. You and Mrs. Love were sitting near us."

"We were just talkin' about the curse on that marsh." George shifted a plug of tobacco from one cheek to the other and indicated Phillip and Emma with a thrust of his chin. "Bad place—real bad. Haunted, a lot of folks claim."

"And I was saying, drownings happen on Tawes. Nothing strange about that." Emma kicked absently at the grass, and Abbie noticed that she was wearing heavy rubber boots. "There's always been stories about the curse, but—"

"Always give me the creeps, that marsh." Phillip's match flared as he lit his pipe. "You wouldn't catch me digging up those graves. Course, some of them people are probably my kin, so they might not bother me. My granny was Nanticoke. Great Granddad Love and two of his brothers married three sisters, all of them bonnyfied Injuns. Pop used to claim his granddaddy was blood brother to them. Hunted ducks together every winter; pack'm in ice and haul them up to market in Balt'mer."

"I never did hold with disturbin' the dead," George

said, "That boy was diggin' in them graves sure. Fresh holes near his boat. Broken pieces of Injun pottery. Chips. He was huntin' stuff to sell."

"Granddaddy kept tame ducks to use as decoys," Phillip continued. "Shot ducks and geese by the hundreds every winter. We're old stock, us Loves. Makes me sort of a blood brother to them what's buried out there too."

George shifted his tobacco from one side of his mouth to the other and wiped the corner of his mouth with a clean handkerchief. "Blood brother or not, I'll bet you ten dollars you wouldn't spend the night out there in that marsh. Dogs won't go there, I'll tell you that. Can't make'm. And that's always a sign that a place is haunted. Dogs can tell."

"Might be just tall tales," Emma admitted. "But there's something creepy about the place. Got to admit it raises the hair on your neck after dark."

"You wouldn't think it was just talk if you'd ever been out in that swamp on a foggy night," George said. "Howls from no animal I ever heard. Moanin'. My granddaddy claimed he heard Injun drums."

Emma snickered. "Bad moonshine, most likely. Your granddaddy liked the drink. Come to think of it, George, so did you."

"I ain't had a drink in twenty years." George shook a stubby finger. "Not since I got saved at that tent revival on Deal. Matthew Catlin can swear to it."

"Have you ever heard them drums?" Phillip demanded.

"Didn't say I did, didn't say I didn't," George replied. "But if I did, weren't whiskey made me hear'm."

Searching for a quick escape, Abbie glanced toward the street. The area around the church remained crowded, and she didn't want to get caught up in further island introductions.

Emma tapped her arm. "Just follow this walk. It leads to an iron gate that opens on the next street over."

"Thanks. Nice to meet you." Glad to get off so easily, Abbie hurried away. As Emma had promised, the worn brick path led around the back of the church and then turned to run between the old tombstones. A hazy mist was settling over the churchyard, but Abbie wasn't daunted by shadows or old cemeteries. The air was humid, but it didn't feel like rain, and she hadn't heard any thunder.

Ghostly fireflies flickered between the monuments, and Abbie wondered if the island children liked to collect the insects in glass jars as she had when she'd been small. She'd loved to keep the jar by her bed and watch the tiny blue-white flashes of light until she fell asleep.

Unable to tear herself away from the Irish treasure trove, her mother had remained in the church office with Matthew. Abbie chuckled. Once Ànati locked onto an exciting find, she was tenacious. No child surrounded by brightly wrapped packages on Christmas morning was ever as excited as Karen was with the possibility of a new discovery. That had always been one of her mother's most endearing traits.

Common sense told Abbie that anything too good to be true was just that. How many startling archaeological finds in the last century had turned out to be deliberately planted or clever forgeries? Abbie knew better than to start building castles in the air, and yet . . .

She exhaled softly into the gathering dusk. She smiled, wondering if all archaeologists were Indiana Joneses at heart. So much for scientific detachment. What would such a discovery mean to her mother's career . . . or to her own? And what would it mean to this sleepy island in the Chesapeake?

Matthew clearly expected his magnificent artifacts to save Tawes from exploitation, but he was sadly mistaken. If Mt. Everest—at the ends of the world—had become crassly commercialized, what would happen to this tiny bit of paradise within a stone's throw of the nation's capital? She could only imagine the invasion of scholars, politicians, and student excursions. In five years, Tawes would be concrete and neon lights from shore to shore, and venders would be selling plastic leprechauns in sailor hats.

If she and her mother wanted to help the citizens who'd come to tonight's meeting retain their Brigadoon, they would laugh off Reverend Catlin's Bronze Age finds, climb into her Beta II at daybreak, and never look back. But the chances of that were somewhat less than her being killed by a meteor while walking back to Emma's farmhouse.

Abbie wished now that she'd remained with Matthew and her mother—insisted on inspecting the torque more closely. The thought of holding a collar that had graced the throat of a two-thousand-year-old Irishman thrilled her as she imagined the weight of the old gold between her fingers.

"Taxi, lady?"

Startled out of her reverie, Abbie looked up to find the village Mountie grinning down at her from the back of a large, silver-gray horse. No saddle; Buck was riding bareback.

"It's after eight," he drawled in that lazy, teasing baritone. "We waited at Emma's for a while, and then figured that Matthew's meeting had gone on longer than you expected."

"Yes, well, something like that." For some unfathomable reason, Buck Davis not only fascinated her—

he scrambled her wits. She found herself, a woman who'd never been at a loss for words, stumbling over responses to his simplest statements.

"You did say you ride?"

She laughed, grasped his outstretched hand, and scrambled up behind him. She half expected the horse to shy at the added weight, but the gray stood as if his muscular legs were rooted to the earth. "Does your friend have a name?" she asked as she encircled Buck's waist with her arms.

"Toby." Buck gave a soft click, and the horse moved off in a flat walk, surprisingly easy to sit, even without a saddle. "He's a Tennessee Walker. I bought him last year at an auction."

"In Tennessee, I suppose."

"Florida." He patted the animal's neck. "Toby was seized in a drug raid on a big estate south of Tallahassee along with a private jet, a string of sports cars, and an armored truck for transporting cash."

"I take it the last owner dealt in illegal merchandise."

"Yep. By the time he gets out of federal prison, Leon will be one hundred and sixty years old, give or take a few decades. Toby would be long gone, so he's better off with me, even though his current stable is a few steps down from what he was used to."

"And how do you get a horse to Tawes?"

"We swam from Crisfield." Before she could react, laughter rumbled in his throat. "A friend brought him out on his skipjack."

"On a crab boat?" She was dubious. The commercial vessels she'd seen were small, without the deck space necessary to safely carry a horse.

"Toby's very well behaved. He minds a lot better than my nephew Johnny." He pointed. "Down that way is the Tawes school."

Buck smelled of gun oil, Irish Spring soap, and af-

tershave. His hair was still damp; he'd obviously showered since he left Emma's. Abbie relaxed her grip on
his waist, maintaining her balance with her knees and
thighs.

"You're not new to riding, Ms. Night Horse."

"Did you think I would be?"

"No, ma'am. You strike me as a woman good at anything she sets her mind to."

"My father bought me my first pony when I was two.
And it's Abbie. You've about exhausted your charm on
my last name."

"No insult intended . . . Abbie."

"None taken from a grown man who calls himself
Buck."

"You mean for a man with all his front teeth who
doesn't chew tobacco?"

"You don't strike me as a redneck."

"My neck is pretty red. Maybe you just don't know
me well enough."

"What makes you think I'd want to?"

He groaned and kneed Toby into a faster gait.

Abbie grabbed Buck's shoulders and kept her seat.
"Nice try."

"I thought so." He glanced back to look into her
face. "Wouldn't want you to take a tumble."

Sweet Zeus! There was definitely an attraction between them. "No fear of that," she managed.

"We can go slower."

"Not necessary. I'm into speed."

"A lady after my own heart." He reined Toby to the
right and continued on down a narrow alley until they
reached the dock. It was high tide, and the sound and
odors of the rushing water filled her head. Coming
night softened the outlines of the anchored boats and
the shabby pilings. "Smell that?"

Abbie could pick out a dozen different scents. Crabs. Wet feathers. Tar. Seaweed. Fish heads and oyster shells, to name a few. It reminded her of the small Greek fishing villages clustered along the Aegean. Coming from Oklahoma, she'd always loved the sea and found it a never-ending novelty. "What in particular?"

"The bay. Tawes." He threw his right leg over Toby's neck and slid down, then raised his arms. She followed, and he caught her effortlessly. "I used to rent a house in Bowers Beach," he said as he wrapped the horse's reins around an upright reinforcing rod that stuck out of a chunk of cement. "That's a little fishing town on Delaware Bay. It was a lot like this, but it wasn't the Chesapeake.

"When they offered me a chance to come home to Tawes as Chief of Police, I walked away from the state police, my vacation time, and my pension and never looked back."

They walked out to end of the dock. He sat down and let his legs dangle over the edge. The only sign of life was a golden retriever on a patch of sand pawing at a crab shell. "Pretty quiet for only"—she glanced at her watch—"quarter to nine."

He grinned. "It is, isn't it."

"I like it."

"My father is John."

She looked up at him. "Excuse me?"

"Buck. You wanted to know how I got the name. My grandfather's still living. He's John, too."

"So your father is John Jr.?"

"They call him Little John."

"And I suppose you're John, as well." She was beginning to feel like the straight half of a comedy team.

"Yep."

"So you had to be—"

He grinned. "Anything but John. My younger brother Nate used to climb on my back, kick me in the ribs, and yell, "Buck! Buck!"

She chuckled. "In a perverse way, it suits you."

They sat there in companionable silence until twilight settled over the harbor. Across the narrow inlet, lights winked on in the houses. Boats rocked rhythmically on their mooring ropes, and the gulls' raucous cries faded. A single star glowed faintly over the bay.

"Do you swim as well as you ride?" he asked.

"Try me."

He nodded. "I'd like to." Standing, he kicked off his shoes, unzipped his jeans, and stepped out of them. Buck had a horseman's legs, lean and hard-muscled, and his belly was flat. "Last one in . . ." Without finishing, he dove off the dock into the river.

Her top and shorts landed close to his jeans. She hit the water only seconds after he did. She'd remembered to unbuckle her watch, but hadn't taken the time to remove her Victoria's Secret thong.

It was deeper than she'd expected, the current strong, but she somersaulted a dozen feet down and came up within arm's reach of Buck. The water was surprisingly warm. It felt like liquid velvet on her skin.

"Glad I didn't bet money against your taking that plunge," he said.

She kicked hard, but the tide pushed her steadily away from the mouth of the inlet and the dock. When he gathered her in his arms and kissed her, she wrapped her legs around his waist.

He kissed as good as he smelled. Not greedy, but slow and tantalizing.

"I think I like you, Abbie Night Horse."

"I'll reserve judgment." He tasted of peppermint.

He kissed her again, but made no attempt to grope her naked breasts or run an exploring hand between her thighs. She hadn't decided yet how far she'd let him go, but his self-control surprised her. She hadn't expected him to hesitate.

Something alive in the water brushed her bare foot, and she gasped.

"Shark?" he joked.

"Crab, probably."

"Don't know," he teased. "Some great whites have been caught off this pier."

"Right." She splashed water in his face. "Tell it to the tourists, cowboy."

He laughed and splashed her back.

"Race you to the other side!" She twisted free and began to swim.

Buck beat her to the far dock by six feet. Still laughing, he heaved himself out of the water and stretched out on his stomach. She found a ladder, climbed out, and wrung the water from her hair.

"I like your mother's long braid," he said. "It would suit you."

"Too much work." She ran her fingers through her chin-length bob. "Lots of archaeological sites are in dry country."

"Most men like long hair on women."

"And you, Chief Davis?"

"I like variety."

"In women or hair styles?"

"Both."

She dropped onto the weathered walkway beside him and propped her chin up with her fists. The boards were still warm from the late afternoon sun and smelled of salt and seaweed. "You never said if you were married," she reminded him.

"Nope."

"Not married, or not saying?"

He caught her hand, turned it over, and traced slow

circles on her palm with a callused thumb. Shivers of pleasure bubbled in Abbie's belly. Buck Davis, she decided, was no country yokel. He was smooth, funny, and very sexy.

"Miss Emma would have thrown a net over me at dinner if my affections were otherwise engaged. She's a force to be reckoned with on Tawes."

"Funny, she doesn't strike me as a particularly righteous woman, but she is odd."

His voice grew serious. "Emma's different, that's for certain."

"In more than one way?"

"She's one tough lady, and we respect individuality on Tawes. We've always protected our own. Some things haven't changed in two hundred years."

"How conservative can the island be if the sole officer of the law is skinny-dipping in the heart of town?"

"Conservative, but practical. You and I are consenting adults. We're alone, and I'd say I'm properly dressed for the sport in which I'm engaged."

"Swimming."

"Exactly."

She smiled. Part of her wanted more, and part of her was enjoying the novelty of a different kind of man. She was no prude, but she was particular. It had been two months since she'd spent that long weekend on Santorini with Arri. It had been fun, but Arri had proved a better dancer than a lover. Like a lot of men, he put his own pleasure first, and was too quick to sprint to the finish line.

"If you're serious about giving me a tour of the island, I could take you up in the Robinson tomorrow."

"I'd like that. We could fly over the dig site. You could judge if there's any landing place closer than Bailey's farm."

"What time?"

"I'm expecting an important call around ten. How about we go up as soon as it gets light? That will give me time to get back to the office for my call."

She nodded. She had the feeling that they weren't going to score tonight. She wasn't sure why, and she didn't know whether she was pleased or slightly piqued. He'd seemed interested enough. She wondered why he'd backed off.

"You and your mother are not like any archaeologists I've ever known."

Abbie gave a sound of amusement. "Do you know many?"

"No. One was a tall, skinny man with knobby knees, and the other a dignified female scholar of mature years."

"I've got another year and a half of work before I get my doctorate—if it doesn't take longer."

"Your mother's anything but stuffy."

"She's neat, isn't she? And she's smart. She knows her stuff."

"See?" he remarked. "You are different. A mother and daughter who respect one another."

"It's more than that," Abbie replied. "It may be an old cliché, but Mom is my best friend."

"Is your father living?"

"He lives in Oklahoma. They separated when I was two. Mom always made certain I spent part of the year with him. They alternated holidays. She didn't want me to lose touch with my tribal roots. We're Delaware—Lenape. Dad's big into the Indian thing."

"And you?"

"It's good. It's where I came from, but it's my past, not my future." She shrugged. "I'm a hopeless romantic. I can't think of anything I'd rather do than spend a summer in hundred-and-ten degree heat, sifting through four-thousand-year-old ruins."

"Did you go to school in Oklahoma?"

"Home-schooled, mostly. Or you might say, site-schooled. Wherever Mom was working a dig. Formal school? Let's see. I think I spent four months at a Navaho kindergarten, part of third grade on a Montana res. Mom was recording some rock paintings there. Seventh grade, a Catholic girls' school in New Mexico. Freshman undergraduate—London. Loved the city, hated the climate."

"And the rest?"

"Finished undergraduate and my master's at Penn. And you?"

"I started in West Virginia, Morgantown, then transferred to the University of Delaware."

"You always wanted to be in law enforcement?"

"I didn't know what I wanted. Started out as a biology major, switched to psychology, and finally to physics. It took me nearly six years to get my bachelor's degree."

"But you like this? What you're doing now?"

"So far." He grinned. "I like it a lot tonight. Not so much yesterday when I had to call that boy's folks and ask them to identify the body."

"Somebody has to do it."

"That's what I keep telling myself." He stood up. "You up for the swim back? I don't want to leave Toby there too long. He's liable to get ideas about slipping his bridle off and going home without me."

"He's done that before?"

"Twice."

They dove in side by side. The current wasn't nearly as swift as it had been, and the swim was easy. Buck scooped up his clothing, turned his back, and dressed. The golden retriever materialized out of the darkness and sniffed at Abbie as she tied her shoes.

"Hey, there, Bess." Buck produced a dog biscuit

from his jeans pocket. "Bess is usually down here nosing around the docks."

They mounted Toby and rode back through the quiet streets of town to Emma's house. Buck walked Abbie to the porch. "I had fun," she said. "Thanks."

"Me too. See you at ten."

She waited for him to kiss her, but he didn't. Buck got back on the horse and rode off into the foggy night, leaving her with more questions than answers.

CHAPTER FOUR

"They're a bunch of fools," Will Tawes said. "And Matthew Catlin is the worst of the lot."

"I have to agree with you." Forest McCready poured a measure of Wild Turkey into a pewter stirrup cup and passed it to Will. The two were seated on the stern of *Gone Fishing*, the attorney's 32-foot Grady White, moored to Will's private dock. It was half past midnight and so dark and cloudy that Forest couldn't make out a single star. Far off, from the western shore of the bay, thunder rumbled and an occasional lightning bolt illuminated the sky. "That's why I skipped tonight's meeting."

"I wanted to, but Bailey was bound and determined for me to go. Daniel weaseled out of it. Something about repairing a loose towel bar in Bailey's fancy new bathroom. I should have told her it was a two-man job."

"That niece of yours winds you around her little finger. Just like Beth always did."

Will snorted. "Don't I know it? Wanting me to mix more with folks. Act civil to that yellow skunk of a preacher. It sticks in my craw to shake Matthew's hand, I'll tell you that."

"At least you're not shooting at him." Forest sipped at the whiskey. Bailey had drawn Will farther back into the community than Forest had ever expected, but his friend's temper hadn't mellowed much with age. There was bad blood between the Catlin and the Tawes families, a stain so deep that no amount of scrubbing could ever wash it clean. Will was capable of violence, and he had good reason for disliking Matthew. So long as he didn't drag the minister into the Chesapeake and drown him, Forest guessed they were making ground.

He offered the bottle, but Will declined. "We need Matthew as a figurehead," Forest said. "Being a member of the clergy carries respectability with the public. We have to convince the media and politicians that the majority of the islanders are against development. Give the dispute a David-and-Goliath slant."

"Since the first settlers came to Tawes in the early sixteen hundreds, we've been invaded by hostile Indians, redcoats, and deserters from one army or another. Now it's these damned mainland pirates."

"What worked in the past won't fly now," Forest cautioned. "You can't start taking potshots at tourists."

"Don't see why not," Will grumbled. "A few well-placed bullets might dampen their enthusiasm."

"Now that we have this archaeologist here, I can continue to delay the sale." Forest set his cup on the table. "Believe me, Will, I don't want development any more than you do. I need time to prove that Tom Sherwood's grandfather never owned that farm. I believe he was always a tenant, and I'm tracing old records and property transfers to prove it."

"Who paid the taxes?"

"The island fund. Sherwood's taxes never amounted

to much, and no one wanted trouble from outsiders. He didn't pay a cent out of pocket."

"I've heard that before—that old T.J., Tom's grand-dad, was just a squatter. And you have to be careful about bringing up the fund in court. That money's not something we want the law to know about."

Forest shook his head. "You don't have to worry about that. As far as the tax offices are concerned, the property taxes were paid from a trust." The men in Forest's family had always studied the law, and they had instilled in him the knowledge that with position and personal wealth came responsibility.

The emergency fund had been created by the is-landers before there was a welfare system or Social Se-curity, even before Tawes men marched off to fight in the French and Indian War. The McCreadys might not have been smugglers or moonshiners, but for two and a half centuries they'd collected, invested, and admin-istered tithes on all illegal activity. Fortunately, there'd been a lot of it.

If a man fell ill and couldn't bring in his crop, neighbors stepped in to fill the gap. If the fishing was bad, or the rains didn't come, the fund paid the taxes on farms and the payments on boats. No child went hungry on Tawes, and no widow had to do without medicine or a warm coat. And because the islanders had contributed the money, no one felt the shame of taking charity. By the same token, since Forest knew the strengths and weaknesses of each man and woman, sloth, drink, laziness, or stupidity were no ex-cuse to profit from the labor of others.

What troubled Forest was that he'd never married and had no son to continue the tradition. Soon, he'd have to find someone to take over his role. Will would have been a candidate—not in his wild youth, but now, if he hadn't been too old. No, the duty had to pass to someone younger . . . someone smart and honest . . . perhaps somebody like Daniel Catlin.

"The fund has worked for us for a long time," Will said. "Kept my kin from hard times during the Great Depression. But once outsiders move onto Tawes, the system would fall by the wayside."

"True enough."

"Some folks start thinking about what they want, instead of what they need."

"You're right. It's one of the things that makes me want to stop Onicox Realty from getting a foothold on the island."

"I could go into court," Will suggested, "swear to what I was told about Tom Sherwood's granddad being a tenant farmer, but I've got a criminal record. Who would pay heed to what I said?"

"You won't have that record for long. I expect a full pardon from the governor for you in another few months."

Will scowled. "If I was as pure as Adam's well water, what my granddad and uncles told me forty years ago is nothing but hearsay. It won't hold dirt in a courtroom."

"Let me see what I can manage before you do anything crazy."

"All right. Try it your way." Will propped his feet up on a tackle box and settled back into the deck chair.

"I need you to keep a rein on the hotheads. People respect you."

"They're scared of me, you mean." Will swirled the whiskey in his cup and stared off over the bay." " 'Spect we'll get that rain."

"I need your word that you'll be patient."

"I'll hold off as long as I can. But if you can't keep these pirates off our land, there's some will fall back on island justice."

*   *   *

Waves of fog seeped up from earth and water after the storm, drifting over the wetland and woods, filtering through the rain-soaked mass of leaves, vines, and intertwined marsh grass. From somewhere inland, a screech owl shrieked, the eerie cry drifting over the misty swamp, adding to the cacophony of night birds' calls, a rabbit's high-pitched death scream, the flutter of wings, and the ceaseless croaking of frogs.

Its ears raised and nostrils flared to catch the scent of danger, a doe stepped out of the phragmites. Behind her trailed twin fawns, young enough to bear spots still. The deer snatched a mouthful of grass and took a half-dozen steps, then froze as she caught a glimpse of movement in the trees. Her pupils expanded as a formless shadow emerged from the gloom and glided down the slope toward her. With a frantic bleat, the doe reared on hind legs and plunged into the rippling salt grass. The fawns darted after her, leaving swaying fronds in their wake.

Oblivious of the deer's flight, the shadowy figure moved among the trees, bow and arrow gripped tightly in his hands. On nights like this, he roamed this marsh, guarding the old graves, listening for the drums and the whispers of those long dead, feeling the damp mist on his face and the wet ground soaking through the soles of his deerskin moccasins.

Rage churned in his bowels, and hot, salt tears blurred his vision and streaked his weathered cheeks as he found the spot and dropped to his knees on the sand. The bow and arrow fell from his clenched fingers, and he hugged himself, rocking back and forth in mute agony until he could bear it no longer. With head thrown back, an inhuman wail of grief issued from his distended throat and echoed through the night.

* * *

Sunrise exploded over the silver-gray surface of the bay in fluorescent shades of orange, orchid, gold, and vermilion, and Buck Davis had a front-row seat through the windshield of Abbie's aircraft. "Sort of takes your breath away, doesn't it?" he said.

Abbie manipulated the cyclic stick and brought the Beta II around to hover over Bailey's narrow strip of beach. The helicopter was high enough to avoid the treetops, but still low enough to give them a bird's-eye view of the eighteenth-century house and outbuildings. "Nice," she replied. "Very nice."

"Never the same. The sunrise."

"Breathtaking." She glanced down at her control panel before guiding the aircraft out over the edge of the bay. Below, the water sparkled and she could see crab pots bobbing on the waves. "Have you seen the sun come up over the Grand Canyon?" She wasn't wearing a helmet, and both headsets were voice-activated so that carrying on a normal conversation was easy.

"Nope. Never been to the Southwest. Always thought I'd like to."

"The mesa country—around the Four Corners, where Utah, Colorado, Arizona, and New Mexico meet. Different from this, but still magnificent." She circled over the dock and river and rotated away from the farmstead.

Buck pointed. "Over there is a big field where you can land, if you've a mind to. It was recently mowed. Bailey uses it for pasture, but the horses are grazing in the south meadow for the summer."

Abbie surveyed the open area. "Looks good. I'm anxious to take a look at the dig site. From the air."

"Hang a left. Not far as the crow flies."

"So much green. Reminds me of the British Isles."

"What made you decide to fly one of these?" Buck

glanced around the interior of the aircraft. "Pretty fancy."

Abbie chuckled. "Dad saw the Beta II at an air show. Had to have one. It's reliable and convenient. Cruises at one-hundred-and-ten mph. And quiet—as helicopters go."

"What's the range?"

"Three hundred miles. Dad has a lot of ranch to oversee."

"I've been up in the Delaware State Police helicopters, but I'm no pilot. How much weight can you carry?"

"About four hundred pounds with a full tank of fuel."

"You're used to traveling light?"

She nodded. "A backpack. Books. And my camera."

"There." He peered out through the left door window and indicated the wetlands that flowed into marshland, interspersed with pools and meandering waterways that spilled into the edges of the bay. "There's some high ground with old hardwood forest. But the hill places are being nibbled away by rising water."

Below, a deer started up out of the carpet of tall grass and leaped away. Abbie saw flocks of ducks and shore birds and a pair of Canada geese. "Looks almost primeval."

"Mainlanders assume there's nothing there, but the marsh is full of life. Turtles, fish, frogs, snakes. Birds of every kind. Deer, fox."

"Is that what I am? A mainlander?"

He laughed. "I barely escaped being one myself even though I was born on this island. My folks have lived here since the 1700s. Philadelphia's Main Line has nothing over Tawes when it comes to exclusivity." He pointed again. "Down there. Just beyond those cedars. That's where Sean Gilbert was digging in the

Indian burial ground. See that rise? With the oak grove? Swing around to get a look at the far side. Closest to the beach. That's where Matthew's Irish stuff came from."

"You know about that?"

Buck grinned. "This is Tawes. Not many secrets here. You'd have to be blind and deaf not to be privy to Matthew's hoard of Irish treasure. I must have been about seven the first time I got a good look at it."

Abbie stared at the wooded slope. With the heavy ground cover of vines, bushes, and saplings, there wasn't much to see. But the scenario fit. If a bronze-age Irishman had been buried here thousands of years ago, flooding could have exposed the grave. If . . . She cautioned herself against building theories on *if*. All that mattered in archaeology was scientific proof.

Sunlight glinted on something farther back in the marsh, and she leaned forward to get a better view. Two figures were making their way along a narrow path through the reeds. "Unless I miss my guess, there's my mother now. And Reverend Catlin."

"Ambitious lady. They must have started before first light."

"Once my mother gets the scent of a new find, she's worse than a bloodhound. Chances of discovering a bronze-age grave site are slim. About six million to one. She didn't get to bed last night until after two. She and Emma were out on the porch for hours. Emma says the site is haunted by the ghost of an Indian medicine man."

"Lots of stories about this marsh. They say a Yankee patrol went in there searching for a deserter. He never came out, and neither did the soldiers chasing him. Never found hide nor hair of them. I suppose they could have stumbled into quicksand. Easy to get turned around in that swamp, and there are low spots with quick sand. Even hunters and trappers tend to stay clear."

"Apparently not Matthew and his amateur archaeologists."

"Lots of folks think Matthew's fey."

"Fey?"

He tapped his forehead. "Touched. Not entirely sound of mind."

"What you're telling me is that we've come to track down the tall tale of a man who's mentally challenged?"

"No, not exactly crazy, just a tad off plumb."

"And you? Do you believe in things that go bump in the night?"

"When I settle on an answer, I'll let you know."

Karen and Matthew waved up at the helicopter, and Abbie waved back. "If you don't mind, I'll cut our tour short. Take you back to town and come back out here. Ànati's expecting me to bring some of her equipment for the preliminary test pits."

"Fair enough. Drop me in Aunt Birdy's field and land at Bailey's, if you want. The walk's shorter from there. Bailey can show you the way." He smiled at her. "Thanks for the ride."

"My pleasure."

"I could show you more of the island after supper, if you've a mind."

"Will I need a swimsuit this time?"

"Can't say," Buck replied. "Depends on what strikes your fancy."

"Entertainmentwise?"

"Exactly. I aim to please."

"Good," she said. "And I hope for your sake, you're not promising more than you can deliver."

"Emma tells me that the locals are afraid of this place." Karen gave the wooden peg a final blow and laid her hammer on the grass beside her backpack. She removed a roll of string and proceeded to stake out a six-by-eight-foot rectangle. "Some tale about a vengeful shaman?"

"Superstitious nonsense." Matthew squatted down on a dry section of sand and handed her a much-folded and creased hand-drawn map. "You can see here the areas that we've dug. Over there"— he indicated a low spot about ten yards from the shoreline—"there was a lot of shell on top. We excavated that pit two summers ago. We found hearth features, a nice hand ax, a Jacks Reef Corner notched point, and several flint triangular arrowheads—all late Woodland era."

"Mmm." Karen shook out a canvas drop cloth and spread it on the ground. Next she removed a small folding stand and topped it with a framed mesh screen. "According to your map, you've never dug here?"

"Correct. Most of our excavation was several hundred yards in that direction. That's where I have reason to believe the graves were concentrated. One was indicative of a flexed burial. We didn't find bone, but there was a nearly intact pot with a lovely pressed corncob design, and a steatite amulet. The cord was long gone, of course, but the hole for stringing the amulet was perfectly drilled and polished."

"You documented the artifacts?"

"Absolutely. One of our volunteers actually dug up the ax, and he kept it, but the amulet is at the church. I'd be happy to show it to you."

"I take it you don't believe in ghosts or in long-dead medicine men?"

"I'm a man of God," Matthew answered stiffly. "Many of our parishioners are backward people, superstitious, but you wouldn't expect me to accept or condone such claptrap."

"I don't expect anything. I've excavated hallowed

places all over North America, and I try not to make
assumptions about finds or people."

"Naturally. I didn't mean that in a condescending
manner."

"Naturally." She unfastened a small folding spade
from her pack and began to remove four-inch squares
of grass and sod from the enclosed spot.

"As an educated man—"

"And a cleric," she supplied. "You doubt the existence of . . . of forces we can't readily see or feel."

"Yes, that's correct."

"I find that interesting." She glanced at him. "Hold
the frame steady. I want to sift all of this surface material.
I would doubt that any of this ground has been tilled in
several hundred years, but we can't discount early European influence. There may be buttons or coins, clay
pipes, perhaps even metal objects or pottery."

"Never found any here," Matthew said. "White men
would never have farmed this marsh."

"The original inhabitants may have raised crops
here. And white settlers tended to plant their crops
where the first people raised their corn and beans.
Saved clearing the fields." She carefully shook a section of grass over the screen and combed through the
roots with her fingers. "All those stories about forests
stretching from the Atlantic to the Mississippi is just so
much folklore. There were plenty of trees, but the
original peoples along the East Coast farmed extensively."

"I know that you and your daughter are Indian, but
with your education, surely you—"

"Lenape," she corrected. "Or Delaware, as some
prefer to call us. Abbie's father is Delaware, Shawnee,
and Cherokee. And I do believe in what I can't see, Mr.
Catlin. Some of the sites I've worked have definitely
been haunted."

"Yes, well . . ." Matthew cleared his throat. "I'm sure you believe—"

"You are a Christian, aren't you?" Karen rubbed her hand over the pile of dirt accumulating on top of the screen and carefully discarded bits of organic material.

"Naturally!"

"Then your work is built on faith and spirituality."

"Yes, well . . ." His face reddened. "That doesn't mean superstition."

"One man's superstition is another man's gospel. Can you define faith? Can you weigh it or measure it in any scientific manner?"

"No, of course not."

"But it is real. It does exist."

"Yes, but . . ." He pursed thin lips. "I don't see how such word games—"

"So everything that's real isn't necessarily visible to the naked eye? And insight and intelligence aren't limited to persons with degrees or a certain skin pigment. Much can be learned from other cultures and from the wisdom of those who lived before us."

Gradually, as she worked, the thick tufts of grass gave way to raw earth, black with damp, decaying vegetable matter. When the entire rectangle was stripped of grass, Karen pulled a trowel from her belt and began to scrape away a thin layer of dirt.

Matthew, clearly miffed, continued to sift through the excavated material. "I'm surprised you don't want to start with the hillside," he said, breaking the silence that had stretched between them for more than a quarter of an hour. "I can show you exactly where Paul Millington discovered the artifacts. I came here and measured off the area so that there'd be no doubt when—"

"How long ago?"

"Years. I marked off exactly where Father's source acquired the torque and the cloak pin."

"Yet, you never dug in that spot."

"No, the trees . . ." He appeared uncomfortable. "The roots would have made excavating on the hillside difficult. I assumed the grave no longer existed."

She leaned back, as comfortable kneeling as she imagined he must be standing at his pulpit in front of his congregation. "I need a wider picture of the site," she explained. "We need to prove without a doubt that the area was inhabited during the Archaic era and not just during the Woodland time period."

"You must realize that time is of the utmost importance," Matthew said. "The Onicox Realty Group promises that they will not intrude on the Indian burial grounds, but if the sale materializes, the extent of the marina and the accompanying condominiums—"

"Time is always a vital factor in archaeology. But if you want my opinion, Reverend, you must let me do this my way." She smiled at him. "I do know my stuff. I've been at this for years; I imagine as long as you've been writing sermons."

"Of course. I didn't mean to imply that you were incompetent."

"Good." Karen removed her hat and wiped the sweat off her forehead as Matthew rambled on. The day was going to be a hot one, and she was certain that her ears would weary of his endless chatter long before he would tire of talking. She had no doubt that he was sincere, or that he was filled with a sense of his own importance. A big fish in a small pond, she concluded.

She continued to expand the scraped area, patiently gathering each handful of dirt to be sifted for bits of charcoal, shell, or bone. She didn't expect to come across native material until she was below the plow zone, but you never could tell. The good thing about archaeology was that it continually surprised you. She hoped Abbie would arrive soon. Her daughter was an excellent field technician. And she knew the value of silence.

". . . A section of a dugout canoe," Matthew droned on. "Cypress, I believe. The wood was in terrible condition, as though it had been burned. Unfortunately . . ."

Karen concentrated on the soft earth beneath her trowel. She'd worked her way from one side of the pit to another, careful to keep the sides intact, so that she was now kneeling with her back to Matthew's precious wooded rise. He had given up sifting and had assumed a sitting position on the far side of the test pit, facing her. By the angle of the sun, she guessed that she'd been working the better part of two hours. Surely Abbie would be here any minute to divert some of Matthew's enthusiasm.

". . . Pardon me," Matthew said. "Call of nature . . . bladder. Not the man I once was." He got awkwardly to his feet and meandered down the beach to disappear behind a grove of cedar trees, leaving Karen blessedly alone.

She sighed in contentment. Not that the peaceful quietude was really silent. The salty breeze played a haunting melody through the reeds; she could hear the harsh rasp of a Virginia rail in the marsh to her left. From overhead, came a shrill cry. When she looked up and shielded her eyes from the sun, she saw a black-and-white osprey, a bit of nesting material clamped in his beak.

Oddly, the sight, which should have given her pleasure, was marred by a ripple of unexplained uneasiness. "*Kenahkihi, xansa,*" she murmured in the Algonquian tongue. *Watch over me, brother.*

She watched the osprey until he became a tiny speck against the blue sky and finally vanished altogether, but her sense of something wrong didn't dissipate. Cold sweat trickled down the nape of her neck, and she shivered, despite the July heat of the morning.

She rose to her feet and turned to stare at the oak trees on the low hillock. What was it? Prickles rose on her arms, and she glanced at her backpack, reassuring herself that she had protection if she needed it. For more than twenty-five years, she'd carried a handgun when she was working on isolated sites, and she knew how to use it. She'd just taken a few steps toward the hill when Matthew shouted.

"Hey! Dr. Knight! Your daughter's coming."

Karen turned toward him. Whatever had caused her apprehension had vanished at the sound of his voice. She felt a little foolish. All this talk of ghosts and spirits was getting to her. She took a deep breath and hurried to meet Abbie. Her apprehension was nonsense, simply the result of too little sleep and the excitement of a new project.

"Ànati!" Abbie called. "Sorry I'm late. But Emma insisted on sending lunch." She held up a wicker picnic basket. "Wait until you see what's in here. It smells delicious."

"Good," Karen replied. "I'm starving." She glanced over her shoulder. Nothing there that shouldn't be. No ghosts, no angry Indian shamans, and no predators. Maybe Matthew was right; maybe she was giving too much credibility to superstition.

Maybe, the quiet voice in her head whispered, *but maybe not.*

CHAPTER FIVE

Bailey looked at the clock. It was 7:38, and she'd told Daniel that she'd have dinner on the table at 6:30 sharp. It wasn't like him to be late, not for a meal. With a final glance at her shriveled baked potatoes, she slid the cooling plate of crab cakes into the refrigerator beside the salad and poured herself another glass of iced tea. Puzzle, her corgi pup, cocked her head and watched every move.

"If you're hoping for a treat, you're out of luck. You'll be fat as . . . fat as me." Bailey made a face.

Despite her own queasy stomach, she'd wanted to show off her newfound cooking abilities. Whenever Daniel arrived, she could heat the crab cakes in the microwave and serve them as a sandwich. But the baking potatoes she'd picked out so carefully at Dori's were destined for the compost pile.

Wondering if maybe the phone service was out, a common occurrence on Tawes, she picked up her house phone. Hearing a reassuring dial tone, she checked her cell. It seemed to be working, and she had no missed messages. Daniel had told her that he'd be finishing trim on the cabin all afternoon, so there was no logical reason why he should be late. Growing more frustrated by the moment, she punched in his number on her cell.

"Hey. This is me. I'm not picking up, so you're out of luck. Leave a number, and I might call back."

"Funny. Very funny." Scooping up her glass of tea, Bailey went out onto the screened back porch. Emma was right. It was time to tell Daniel about the coming baby. Twice, she'd started to, but each time something had occurred to make her reluctant to share her secret. She knew that he would insist on setting a date for the wedding.

The trouble was, she didn't know if she was ready to be married again. Her first marriage to Elliott had proved a disaster, both emotionally and financially. And since she'd come to Tawes, little more than a year ago, her entire life had changed. She was happy about the baby . . . about having Daniel's baby . . . at least she thought she was. It was the commitment part that had her scared.

She and Daniel both brought considerable baggage to their relationship. She loved him, but she just wasn't sure she could trust her own judgment. Hadn't she thought she loved Elliott when they'd eloped to Las Vegas? And hadn't she known him a lot longer than she'd known Daniel? It wasn't as if she couldn't provide for her child. She had a home, money in the bank, a job she was crazy about. For the first time in her life, she felt whole.

Complete.

Puzzle whined and ran to the screen door, her round corgi rump bouncing. Bailey set her tea on the antique sewing-machine cabinet she used for an end table and followed the now barking dog onto the porch step. "What is it, girl? Is Daniel here? Is it Daniel?"

But, she saw with a sigh of disappointment, the tall, lean figure that rounded the house wasn't Daniel. It was Will. "Come in." She forced a welcoming smile. "You're just in time for dinner. Supper." It would take forever for her to remember that the islanders called any meal served between 4:00 P.M. and breakfast supper.

"No need for that, darlin'." Will stooped to pet Puzzle's head. A silent command sent the three dogs trailing after him down on their bellies on the grass. Puzzle spun and hopped with excitement, apparently torn between Will and the presence of Blue, Raven, and Honey.

"Bring the dogs inside," Bailey said. "They're better behaved than Daniel."

"No need. We came by the bay path, and they're all wet and muddy. The three of them will do fine outside."

Bailey raised herself on tiptoe and kissed his weathered cheek. "I've made your favorite. Crab cakes."

"I didn't come to eat."

She tugged at his arm. "I insist. If I know you, you've been working on that otter carving since breakfast and skipped lunch." Will was an artist, and the demand for his wildlife carvings was so great that there was a three-year waiting list for one of his pieces.

He removed his baseball cap and smoothed back his graying hair. " 'Spect I could eat a bite, just to be neighborly."

She laughed as she led the way into the kitchen. "Wait until you taste my crab cakes. I caught the crabs myself, off my dock."

"Wouldn't have any blueberry pie, would you?"

"For you, I might." Will could have the slice she'd set aside for Daniel.

Later, as Will finished his supper and she toyed with hers, Bailey asked, "Have you seen Daniel today?"

Will wiped his mouth with a napkin, took a sip of tea, and nodded. "Matter of fact, he went by my place just before noon. In the skiff."

"He was in his boat?" Daniel hadn't said anything to her about going fishing or to Tawes. "I expected him two hours ago, and he hasn't called."

"Hmm." Will tossed a morsel of crab to Puzzle under the table. "Not like Daniel to break his word. Something must have come up.

Bailey pushed back an uneasy twinge. Last summer, when she'd first come to Tawes, the *something* that had come up had nearly cost them their lives. Daniel had recently retired from the C.I.A. and a stint in the Far East, and there were people who hadn't wanted him to quit.

"Nothin' to worry yourself over."

He covered her hand with his, and Bailey noticed how similar in shape their hands were. For a moment, her apprehension over Daniel's unexplained absence was overwhelmed by her affection for Will.

"I love you," she whispered, gazing into eyes that were almost identical to her own.

Will blinked, gave her hand a quick squeeze, and cleared his throat brusquely. "You stop worryin'. Daniel's not going to get himself into any more trouble. All that is past and done with."

"I hope so."

"He gave me his word when he said he wanted to marry you."

"We had words over the marina project," she admitted. "After I got back from the meeting. Daniel believes that development will ruin Tawes. He's violently opposed to it."

Will didn't answer, and she knew that he agreed with Daniel. "Things can't remain the same forever,"

She said. "New people would mean jobs, more children in our schools, more tax revenue for the island."

"No use us chewing over the same old bone. You don't know what's at stake here, what can be lost forever."

"Daniel thinks that if I'd grown up on Tawes, I'd look at development differently. I think he's being pigheaded."

"He's a good man—in spite of being born a Catlin—but he won't be easy to live with. Keep that in mind, girl. Daniel's always going to have secrets he can't share with you. The places he's been, the things he's had to do . . ." Will's stare grew hard. "You think about it, darlin'. What you're takin' on if you decide to be his wife."

"I love him."

"I loved your grandmother, but she knew better than to marry me."

"Daniel's a good man. We just don't see eye to eye on this issue. If we can't increase enrollment, we could lose the elementary school. And if it closes, some of the younger families will move off the island. Cathy agrees with me. She said that she and Jim haven't spoken a civil word to each other for a week."

"This island is a little like an egg warm from the nest. It's sound, maybe smudged some, but solid. Once there's a crack in the shell, it will go bad in no time. A lot of people have shed blood for Tawes. It's not so easy to see it handed over to strangers."

"If Onicox Realty buys Mr. Sherwood's land, they have a right to develop their property."

Will's countenance darkened. "Thanks for the meal. It was fine." He stood.

"Wait, don't go—you haven't had your blueberry pie."

Will took his hat off the back of the chair. "Best you remember you were born a Tawes. You don't want to take sides against your own."

"I have a right to my own opinion."

"You do. But you're carryin' a baby and there may be trouble. If it comes, lay low and stay out of the line of fire."

"Don't talk like that. You scare me." She put her arm on his shoulder.

He brushed her off and walked to the door before glancing back. "I mean what I say, Bailey. There'll be no condominiums and no marina built on my island. Not so long as I draw breath. And you can put that in your pipe and smoke it."

Matthew Catlin couldn't sleep. He'd taken his nightly glass of sherry, all of his medicines, and the blue sleeping pill that he found in a container at the back of the medicine cupboard . . . one prescribed for Grace by a doctor two years ago. Still, he lay awake, eyes wide, thoughts churning in his head, staring up at a cobweb on the ceiling.

He really should go downstairs, get the broom, and sweep away the spider and the struggling fly trapped in the web. Grace would have insisted, if she'd seen it. She couldn't abide spiders or other vermin in her house. But getting up, putting on glasses and slippers, finding his robe, and going all the way downstairs to the pantry seemed overwhelming. Then, after he disposed of the spider web, he would have to reverse the whole process. Two trips downstairs—and it was after ten o'clock. Instead, Matthew stared idly at the spider and worried if Grace would approve of his sharing his father's Irish treasures with Dr. Knight and her daughter.

"It seemed the right thing to do, Grace," he murmured. "Father always said that the Irish came here long before the Vikings. Some of the Indians had gray eyes. Did you know that? I know I've told you that before. Father believed that the Irish might have established a colony here on the Chesapeake. And if we can prove it, no one can come here and make Tawes into another Kent Island. Don't you agree?"

Grace didn't reply, but she rarely did. It wasn't that she was ignoring him; it was simply difficult for her to bridge the gap that stretched between them.

"They seem very nice, the archaeologists. They're Indians, I understand, but they don't wear feathers or beads. They look just like everyone else—perhaps their skin is a little darker, reddish really. I suppose that's why they call them *redmen.*" Matthew chuckled at his own joke. "I don't know why they don't say *redwomen?* The daughter's name is Abigail Night Horse. Isn't that an odd name? Horse?"

Nothing.

"Are you put out with me, dear?"

No answer.

Precious whined and hopped up on the bed.

"No, no. In your basket," Matthew said firmly. "You know how Mother feels about you on the bed." The terrier nipped at him with needle-sharp teeth as he caught it and lowered it gently to the floor. "No bitey! Naughty! Naughty, Precious." A drop of blood welled up from the teeth marks on his finger, and Matthew sucked it away. "That's it. Go night-night. There's a good Precious."

The sunflower-shaped night-light cast a yellow glow over a section of one wall. Matthew never went to bed without his night-light. If he needed to use the toilet, he didn't want to fumble for the lamp, and it wasn't safe to wander about the house in the dark. Besides, the small light comforted him. He didn't like sleeping alone. Precious was company, but not the same as having his dear wife share his bed.

Sometimes, Matthew got through the nights imagining Grace standing in the shower soaping her long white legs and standing wet and dripping on the bathroom rug, toweling herself off, and powdering her underarms, her breasts, and bare bottom. Sinful, he supposed, thinking about his wife that way . . . thinking about her dusting powder in the pink hollows between her toes.

From the first night of their marriage, Matthew had discovered what a modest woman Grace was. Naturally, he'd respected her wishes. Not once had they shared marital privileges in the daylight or undressed in front of each other. The night-light was the only daring deviation Grace permitted. She always came to their bed decently covered in a long flannel nightgown, summer or winter. Her shyness, he supposed, came of being raised so strictly.

So, his imagining Grace naked in her bath, picturing in his mind's eye her tight little upright nipples slippery with soap, her shell-like belly button, and her long, creamy-white feet covered in silky baby powder were naughty indulgences, but they helped, keeping him from other sins. Abuse. Self-stimulation. Dirty magazines. And other unclean practices best not mentioned aloud in a parsonage.

Abbie and Buck had ridden on horseback to an isolated sand beach surrounded by old-growth woodland. Now that the sun had gone down, the temperature had dropped into the seventies—heavenly after the heat of the dig site at the marsh.

"I'm flying Mom to Philly early tomorrow," Abbie said as she dismounted. Bailey Tawes had loaned her a sweet-gaited black horse to use as long as she remained on the island. "Ànati has a friend at Penn who's an expert on Irish Bronze Age. She's going to examine Matthew's artifacts."

Buck caught her around the waist before her feet

touched the ground. His hands were strong, and the feel of his fingers on her bare midriff made her breath catch in her throat.

He lowered her to the grass and turned her around to face him. The black horse nosed against her back and she glanced down, surprised to find the reins still clutched in her hands. She felt her cheeks grow warm as she gazed into Buck's amused eyes.

Abbie had enjoyed a long shower and washed her hair before Emma's evening meal, but the cool tingle of her skin had been supplanted by a growing heat.

It really had been too long since she'd made love to a man.

A slow grin creased his features. Damn, but he was good at seducing a woman . . . and he knew it. She waited, expecting him to make the first move, but he kept devouring her with those intense blue eyes . . . eyes that invited her to lose herself in them.

"No great discoveries today?" He broke the spell teasingly. They'd left Emma's sometime after eight and ridden for at least three-quarters of an hour. She supposed it must be close to nine, because deep shadows from the trees laid dark patterns over the mirrored surface of the water.

Wild mint grew where the path left the woods and entered the clearing. The horses' hooves had crushed it, and the heady scent mingled with the smell of salt and leather. She noticed a tiny nick on Buck's cheek where he must have cut himself shaving. Just below it on his right jawline ran a thin white scar.

"You're a beautiful woman, Abbie Night Horse." He took the reins from her hand. "He'll stand. They both will."

Funny how Buck's deep voice struck a chord in the pit of her stomach, making her feel as though she'd been downing glasses of champagne instead of sweet tea over ice. "Mom started one pit, but the earth had been disturbed well below the level of the plow line. I staked out a second pit a few yards away." Her own words sounded breathy, her speech stilted. "We're hoping to find hearth material, pottery . . . some indication that this was more than a hunting camp."

He pulled his T-shirt off over his head. "Ready if you are. There's a nice bottom here."

Abbie glanced toward the water and then back at him. He had great shoulders, sinewy and hard without being artificially built up by steroids. His broad chest was freckled and bore a light dusting of fair hair that darkened to a tawny gold below his belt line. Swallowing the knot in her throat, she unsnapped her denim shorts. This time she hadn't bothered with underwear.

"Don't be afraid," he murmured. "The water's fine." He slowly traced her lower lip with two fingers before trailing them down to brush the rise of her breasts at the vee of her bra. "All my life, folks referred to the Indian site as a burial ground. You have reason to believe it's not?"

"No, I—"

He leaned close and kissed the hollow of her throat. She sighed with pleasure as the tip of his velvet tongue flicked against her skin.

"I don't have any opinion yet," she managed. She unzipped the zipper on his shorts and slipped her hand inside. He hadn't bothered with underwear either. "Give me time."

He inhaled sharply. "All the time you need, darlin'."

She stroked the length of his erection, pleased by the raggedness of his breathing. "Construction companies may go in with backhoes, but my favorite tool is a trowel I picked up at a yard sale."

He groaned and kissed her mouth. "Maybe I can change that," he said when they broke for breath.

"If you don't have a—" she began.

"Don't worry. I do."

She heard the rip of a foil packet and caught the distinctive odor of a condom being opened. "Let me help you with that."

"I thought you'd never ask."

She laughed with him as they took the necessary precaution. It wasn't the first time she'd done this, but it felt like it. Buck was a big man, and her heart raced like a hormone-driven teenager's. He was no stranger to kissing, and as their caresses intensified, she parted her lips and drew him in to savor the taste and texture of his tongue. Other than the lap of waves against the beach, the rasp of his breath, and the thudding of her heart, the cove was absolutely quiet.

"The horses?"

"They'll be fine." His arms tightened around her, and one hand caressed her buttocks.

She must have taken a step backward, because suddenly she became aware of the heat and solid bulk of the horse behind her. Buck's hands were all over her, gentle and teasing, driving her crazy with need. She stroked him harder. He was more than ready, and she could feel the tension knotting in the pit of her belly.

"Are you wet, darlin'?"

She was. All she could think of was having him inside her.

"Let's see?" He slipped a finger into her vagina and she moaned with pleasure, clenching around him, wanting more. He lowered his head, nuzzling aside her bra and drawing a nipple between his lips to suckle it.

The first tide of sweet pleasure surged through her. "Please," she begged him. "I . . ."

He dropped back onto the sand, pulling her with him. She yanked her bra off and arched against him, offering her breasts to be kissed and laved and sucked. He wiggled out of his shorts, seized her hips, and lowered her down on top of him. He slid into her sheath, deep and then deeper.

Buck groaned and clutched her against him. Slowly she withdrew and then with an abandoned cry, slid down over his swollen length. After what seemed an eternity, they found a mutual rhythm. Quickly, she climaxed, shaken by multiple tremors of pure physical joy. Still, they hurtled on, caught in a maelstrom of hot, sweaty passion, until finally Buck gave a great shudder and she came again. This time, the peal was even brighter and more intense than before.

They lay together on the sand, breathless and sated until the buzz of mosquitoes drove them into the water. The water was as warm and the bottom as clean as Buck had promised. They swam and splashed and played like kids until desire brought them together again. This time, their lovemaking was slower and more deliberate, but no less fulfilling.

They dressed, and Buck took insect spray and two bottles of beer from his saddlebag. "The beers were cold when I put them in there."

Abbie chuckled as he produced apples for the horses. "Nice touch."

"They've been patient. They deserve a reward."

He washed the apple bits and juice from his hands in the bay and then returned to sit beside her on the beach. The moon had come up over the water and it cast a ribbon of silver over the waves.

"Do you do this for all your hot dates?" she asked.

"Nope. Consider yourself special. I don't usually pick up young ladies on Tawes."

"No?"

He chuckled. "It's a small island, and it could get uncomfortable—"

"If you love'em and leave'em?"

"Something like that."

"The island has its own rules; it's not really part of the twenty-first century." He scuffed the damp sand with a bare foot. "Somehow I don't believe it ever will be."

"You can't stop change."

"It won't come easy here."

"It didn't come easy in Oklahoma either. Not with the tribal people. But you can't live in the past."

"That sounds funny, coming from a woman who makes her living by studying the past." He caught her hand in his and held it.

Another small bubble of happiness rose in her chest. She liked Buck. She really did, but she had to keep reminding herself that they both knew the rules. This was fun, nothing more. "You've never been tempted to find an island girl, build your own little hideaway, and continue the tradition?"

"Me? No, not yet. The Davis men don't settle down until they have to. Nate married at thirty, and he broke the record." He unfolded her hand and massaged her fingers, one after another. It felt wonderful. "You have nice hands," he said. "Strong hands for a woman."

"I think that's a compliment."

"It is." He took a sip of beer. "I want you to be careful out there at the site."

"Why? I can swim. If the mosquitoes don't eat me alive, what's—"

"Can't say, really. Just . . ." He shook his head. "Something about that Gilbert boy's drowning doesn't sit right. He's a Deal Island kid; he could swim like an eel before he could walk."

She looked up into Buck's face. His features seemed more rugged in the moonlight, almost Indian. "He might have gotten a cramp."

Buck nodded. "True enough."

"You don't sound convinced." She got to her feet and brushed the sand off the back of her shorts.

He got up and collected the horses. "I'd best get you back to Emma's. If you mean to fly up to the city in the morning, you'll need your beauty rest." He led the black horse over and held the stirrup for her. "Just be careful. Keep an eye out."

"I always do."

"I mean it. There's something about that marsh that worries me. I don't want anyone else getting hurt, especially not you."

"I'm not helpless," she said. "My father insisted that I study self-defense when I was a teenager. I stayed with it until I reached the level of black belt, and I've got a wall-ful of trophies that I won in statewide competitions."

"That's good, but don't let it make you cocky. Don't take unnecessary chances. I've found it's always better to avoid trouble than to get out of it."

"I'd agree with that," she replied, "but I've traveled extensively since I was fourteen—Athens, Lima, Delhi, Marrakech, even Ankara. So far, I've never found myself in a situation that I couldn't handle."

"There's always a first time, Abbie. Remember that. Nothing in this world is as certain as coming up against somebody or something tougher than you."

CHAPTER SIX

"I'm hoping to see Irene this afternoon." Karen pushed the briefcase containing the Irish artifacts farther under the table with the toe of her sneaker and glanced at the menu. She and Abbie were seated in Vin's, a popular pub at the Philadelphia airport that served authentic Delhi dishes as well as South Philly favorites.

The flight up from Tawes had been uneventful. Karen was planning on taking the train into the city and stopping in Mt. Airy long enough to shower and change before her meeting with Irene at her office. Maintaining a base within commuting distance to Penn was important, even when the house was empty for months at a time. Besides, now that Abbie was working on her doctorate at the university, she had a real home.

"Ànati?"

Abbie's reminder that the waitress was standing by their table jerked Karen out of her reverie. "Cheese steak and whatever she's drinking," Karen said hastily. "Be patient, dear. I was having a senior moment."

"Water with lemon." Abbie chuckled. "And you know you don't like lemon in your water." She rolled her eyes. "Why take so long reading the menu if you're always going to order the cheese steak?"

Karen shrugged. "I like to have the choice. You never know, something else might strike my fancy." She returned the menu to the holder against the simulated old oak paneling. "I want you to continue work on the test pit I started before—"

"You've told me, Mom. Twice." Abbie smiled. "I think I can handle it. But I'd rather go with you. I can't wait to see what Dr. Goldstein thinks of the pieces."

"I'm dying to see what she has to say."

"There has to be a logical explanation. Either the good pastor bought them on the black market thirty years ago or some settler carried them from Cork and threw them out the window of his log cabin back in the 1700s."

"They seem genuine to me."

The waitress returned with the water and asked Abbie if she wanted the dressing for her Cobb Salad on the side. Karen waited until the girl was gone before picking up her train of thought. "I'll call you when I'm ready to come back. Provided the phones are working on the island." She raised one eyebrow. "And if you're carrying your cell."

Abbie grimaced. "Guilty as charged. I didn't take it last night. I didn't think I'd need it, not when I was out with the entire Tawes police force."

"Just don't get any ideas about that one. He's an islander born and bred. Emma said that Buck—"

"Mom, please." Abbie raised her hands, palms up. "Stay out of my love life. Mind your own business."

"Your father and I went together for two years before I let him talk me into getting married. And he got none of the perks until I had a ring on my finger."

Abbie smiled. "When in Rome, Ànati. The times they are a-changin'. Besides, Grandpop would have staked him on an anthill if he'd taken advantage of his daughter. All that honor stuff."

"Just be careful. I don't want you getting hurt. And I don't want *him* getting hurt. He seems like a nice young man." She flashed a mischievous smile. "But I can't say as I blame you. If I were twenty years younger, I might be taking evening rides on his pony too."

"I'm not even going to dignify that with an answer."

The waitress brought their order, and Karen settled down to enjoy the cheese steak. There was enough fat in it for entire week, but when it came to eating, there were some things that she simply wasn't willing to give up. Life, after all, was for living to the fullest.

"So you have no idea how long this will take? Two days? Three?"

"You know Irene. I want a definite answer on this before I come back."

"Are you leaving the torque and cloak pin with her?"

Karen shook her head. "No. Can't. Matthew Catlin was absolutely inflexible about that. He said his wife wouldn't want them off the island any longer than necessary. They were not to be out of my sight, and when I return to Tawes, I have to deliver them into his hands personally.

"Mmm," Karen licked her fingers. "This is really good. Sure you don't want some?"

"No, thanks." Abbie added a little more dressing to her salad. "This is plenty."

"Give your dad a call before you fly back. He misses you."

"For a divorced couple, you two worry a lot about each other."

Karen wiped her mouth with a napkin. "We were friends before we got hot and bothered, and we remained friends after the fire died. A part of me will always love him for giving me you, and the rest of me wakes up every morning and shouts, 'Thank you, God,' for setting me free."

Abbie laughed. "Crazy people. I have crazy people for parents."

"If I'm crazy, remember that it's inherited. Mothers get it from their kids."

"Ouch." Abbie leaned over and kissed her cheek. "Have fun, and remember poor me, slaving away in that mosquito-infested marsh."

"Bailey assured me that you're more than welcome to use her horses; that will save you a long walk. Don't forget insect spray for you and the animal, and don't forget to carry your knives." Karen rose to her feet and hugged Abbie tightly. "Fly safe. Anything you need on Tawes, ask Bailey or Emma. And don't trust Matthew around the pits. He doesn't know half as much as he thinks he knows about archaeology."

"That's what you say about most people."

"Only because it's true. Oh, and don't swim out there alone."

"Yes, Mother, I hear and obey."

"Right. It will be the first time."

Abbie chuckled, left two twenties on the table, and strode away without looking back. Karen watched her until she turned the corner. "*Nuxati*, watch over her," she murmured. Glancing at her watch, she saw that she had time to catch the next train if she hurried. She slung her bag over her shoulder, picked up the briefcase, and left the restaurant.

Bailey threw another forkful of manure into the trailer and looked at her watch. Three o'clock. In three more hours, Daniel would be twenty-four hours late for the meal he'd promised to share with her. She was worried and angry. She hadn't called the Coast Guard or the mainland hospitals yet, but she'd wanted to. This wasn't like Daniel, she told herself.

But she knew it was.

Twice before, he'd done this. Someone had called him, and he'd vanished without telling her where he was going or when he'd be back. The first time had been Christmas Eve, and then again in March. She suspected that his old employers at the agency were at fault, but Daniel refused to give her any information. Dozens of explanations had come to mind, but she'd rejected all except one. Daniel wasn't a compulsive gambler and he wasn't addicted to drugs or alcohol. He wasn't running heroine, illegal aliens, or stolen property. There was only one possibility left. The agency. Despite his promises that he'd broken off all ties with them, his disappearances had to have something to do with the C.I.A.

The possibility frightened her, and it made her angry. If he couldn't trust her, then how could he expect her to become his wife? And how could she expect him to be the father her coming baby deserved? How did she know he wasn't sprawled in some South American barrio with his throat cut, or floating face down in the Mediterranean? She shuddered. Maybe—at this moment—he was lying on a rooftop with a high-powered rifle, waiting to assassinate an enemy of the American government. The thought made her sick.

There was also Daniel's financial status. He refused to discuss his monetary situation, saying simply that he'd bought good stock years ago. He didn't spend money foolishly, but he'd surprised her with tickets to Florence on her birthday—first class. They'd spent a glorious ten days exploring Tuscany, Rome, and

Venice. It had all seemed a fairy tale, until reality had set in and she'd begun to wonder how a country carpenter could afford such an expenditure.

Everything she knew about Daniel's life in the last decade had been what he'd told her. What if he hadn't been completely honest? Elliott had fooled her. Was she one of those stupid women who couldn't see past a sexy body and a sweet line? Did she want someone so badly that she would rush into a second marriage that was doomed from the start? Or were her hormones so out of whack from pregnancy that she was overreacting to normal male imperfections?

Her cell rang. She dropped the pitchfork, wiped her hands on her jeans, and answered it. "Daniel?" She realized as she spoke his name that it couldn't be Daniel. His ring tone was a Jimmy Buffet oldie.

"Sorry, just me." Cathy's cheery voice didn't sound the least bit sorry. "What are you doing?"

"Cleaning horsesh—." Bailey clamped her lips shut on that crude answer, took a breath, and started again. ". . . Stable. I'm cleaning the stalls." The sound of a baby fussing came through the connection. "Sounds as though somebody's ready for a nap."

"Had his nap. Part of a nap. Two cats were fighting under the house. He's cutting a tooth, so it doesn't take much to wake him. I was wondering if you and Daniel would like to come for dinner tonight."

"I'd be glad to," Bailey replied, "but Daniel is a sore spot. He—"

Bailey heard something behind her, turned, and gave a start. "Daniel! Damn it. You scared me half to death, sneaking up on me."

"Bailey?" Cathy called. "Is Daniel there?"

She raised the phone. "I'll get back to you. Promise." She ended the call and glared at Daniel. "Where the hell have you been?"

A flush tinted his tan. "Sorry about last night, hon."

"Sorry? You're sorry?" She jammed her phone into the back pocket of her jeans. "I made dinner for you last night. Then I lay awake half the night wondering what happened to you." He took a few steps toward her, but she raised a hand in warning.

"Please. Just hear me out," he said.

"What? So you can tell me again that I have to trust you? That you can't explain why you stood me up for the third time?" She shook her head. "I don't know. I'm not even sure how I feel about us anymore."

"Honey, you know I'd tell you if I could. It's just not safe for you—"

"Does this have anything to do with *Lucas*?"

His lower lip twitched, and even his poker face couldn't conceal that she'd made a direct hit. "What do you know about him?"

She swore. "I've heard you say his name enough in your sleep. You have nightmares. You refuse to admit it, but you do. Whatever's haunting you, you need to share it with me or seek professional help." She fumbled with her engagement ring, pulled it off, and threw it at him.

He caught the ring and tightened his fist around it. "You can't mean that."

"We need time to straighten this out. And if we can't, I won't marry you. Ever." She tried to rush past him, but he caught her and pulled her into his arms.

"I love you, darlin'. I love you more than—"

She stiffened. "Not this time. That won't work anymore. You need to be honest with me." She pulled free of his embrace.

He looked into her eyes. "How can you accuse me, when you haven't been honest either? Why didn't you tell me about the baby?"

She could feel hot tears well up in her eyes, and she blinked them back. "Who told you? Was it Emma?"

"Hell, no, it wasn't Emma. You forget where you're at. There are no secrets on Tawes. Word gets around fast."

"Who, then?"

"Phillip and Mary's daughter-in-law Polly saw you buying one of those pregnancy test kits in a pharmacy in Crisfield."

"What do you have? Spies?"

"It's just Tawes. You'll get used to it." His Adam's apple bobbed with emotion. "You should have told me. I'm the father."

"I was going to. Last night. But when you didn't show up, I . . ." Her fingers knotted into tight balls. "Where were you?"

He shook his head. "I can't tell you."

"Then consider this engagement on hold."

His eyes clouded, shutting her out. "Keep the ring. I want you to marry me. I want to raise our child together."

"We need to settle this first."

He brushed a stray curl off her face. "Tell me you don't love me."

Her stomach clenched. "I do love you. That's my problem, I do. But I'm not going to screw up again. I'm not going into another marriage with my eyes full of stars. You talk about trust? It's all up to you." And this time, when she walked away, he didn't stop her.

She was proud of herself. She didn't shed a tear until she reached the house, undressed, and stepped into the shower.

The weather was nice when Karen left the cottage that evening, but she still put on her nylon windbreaker and tucked the pistol inside one of the zippered pockets. She wasn't afraid of the city, and she'd never felt unsafe traveling back and forth to Penn. Still, she wasn't oblivious to the possibility of a woman being accosted on the street. And tonight, she was carrying a fortune in antiquities. She hated to think what the torque would be worth for the weight of the gold alone.

She'd hoped to meet Irene late this afternoon, but when she got to the house, she'd found a message on the answering machine. Irene's lecture at Princeton was running late, and she couldn't get back to town until after eight. She'd asked Karen to come to her office at the museum, where they could inspect the artifacts.

Karen had started out the door, then went in again to ring Abbie to make certain that she'd arrived safely back on Tawes. She knew that helicopters were a necessity, and Abbie was a competent pilot, but Karen was a typical mother. She worried. When she got no answer on Abbie's cell, she tried Emma's house.

Nothing.

She keyed in Bailey's number and her friend picked up on the second ring. "Hi," Karen said. "You haven't seen anything of Abbie, have you?"

"As a matter of fact, I did. I saw the helicopter over the house about five. Is there a problem?"

"No, no problem. I'm on my way to see Irene."

"I'm anxious to hear what she thinks," Bailey said.

"Me too." They exchanged pleasantries and ended the conversation. Karen started for the door when the phone rang. Thinking it might be Irene, she reached for the handset, but when *blocked* appeared on the Caller ID, she let the machine pick up.

"Abbie? Karen? Aren't either one of you there? Damn. I was hoping to . . ." Despite the years since they'd split and the distance between them, Vernon's voice tugged at her heartstrings. Reluctantly, she let herself out the side door as Abbie's dad continued talking. He was a good man, a wonderful father. But he hadn't been the right husband for her. Maybe no one would have been. Maybe she was a woman who was better off without any man in her life.

Except for the sex. Vernon had been incredible in bed. It had been the one place they'd always been in tune. And good sex with a man she cared about was the one thing she missed about her marriage.

She followed the curving walk through the cedars toward the street. The home she had purchased more than twenty years ago had once been a carriage house for the grand Victorian mansion that shared the same block. She'd loved the place the first time she'd laid eyes on it, and she still loved it. Surrounded by boxwood and evergreens and set well off the street, the cottage had been her oasis in the city.

She was halfway down the walk when abruptly something flew up out of the cedar branches in front of her. She jerked back, heart racing as she recognized the compact body and powerful wings of a great horned owl. One moment he was there, so close she could almost touch him, and the next he was gone.

Karen swore. An owl! Old superstitions crept in, raising gooseflesh on her arms. Owls were night predators. Seeing an owl in the daytime was the worst sort of luck. Among many of the traditional people, they were considered a messenger of death.

"Just a damn owl," Karen muttered. It was ridiculous to be afraid of a bird. What next? Fleeing from black cats and ladders? She tried to laugh at her own foolishness, but brittle unease settled in the corners of her mind and made her watchful.

She got off at Thirtieth and walked toward the museum. Dusk was gathering over the Schuylkill; she could hear the faint rush of water whenever there was a lull in traffic. A young couple with multiple chains, piercings, and fluorescent Mohawks strolled past hand in hand, followed by several boys on bicycles. A man with a white cane and dark glasses and guided by a seeing-eye dog walked toward her. An ice cream truck passed, speakers blaring a scratchy tune. Three crows flew overhead, returning to their colony for the night. There weren't many tractor trailers or delivery trucks at this time of the evening, but Karen was aware of how noisy the city was after the quiet of Tawes.

Half a block from the museum, she quickened her step, trying not to think about the owl her late father claimed to have seen outside his door the morning he crashed his truck. She tried to shake off her nervousness. Hadn't she spent hundreds of nights camping alone at Mesa Verde and dozens of other isolated sites? Hadn't she fought off a knife-wielding rapist in Idaho and helped send him to prison? She was no pushover. She could damn well take care of herself.

Footsteps sounded behind her. Stopping short, she whirled around. A man hurried toward her, a tall man with hunched shoulders and face averted. He was about ten yards away, dressed all in dark clothing and wearing a wide-brimmed, black hat. Her fingers tightened on the grip of her pistol as she waited for him to come closer.

She moved to the edge of the sidewalk. A motorcycle sped by, followed by a car crowded with youths. The windows were down, the radio blaring reggae music. The driver blew his horn and yelled at her.

Karen stared at the approaching man in black. He held something in his hands, but she couldn't tell what it was.

Suddenly he noticed her, lifted his head, and smiled. "*Gut evening.*"

It was all she could do not to laugh out loud at her own foolishness. Her would-be mugger was an Old Order Amishman, and the weapon in his hand was a child's wooden toy. "Good evening," she managed, letting go of the gun and raising her hand in greeting. So much for owls.

With the briefcase containing her precious artifacts clutched tightly in her left hand, Karen turned back toward the museum. She had nearly reached the entrance and had stopped once more to scan the street when she heard someone call her name. She twisted to see a figure partially obscured by the shadows.

Her eyes widened in confusion. "What are you—"

Too late, she reached for the pistol. She had it halfway out of her pocket when her world shattered in an explosion of splintering bone and pain. She gasped as her knees slammed into the sidewalk. Another blow rocked her. Crimson shards whipped to a whirlpool of color, and as the vortex swallowed her, she was aware of nothing but the fluttering wings of a great horned owl.

CHAPTER SEVEN

Abbie pushed aside the mosquito netting and crawled out of the two-man dome tent just as dawn was breaking over the treetops. She'd hiked in to the site the evening before and set up her camp near the water, well out of the area where her mother had staked out the first test pits. Despite Emma's warnings of wandering spirits and strange noises, no ghosts had disturbed Abbie's sleep. She had awakened rested and eager to begin her day's excavations.

Breakfast was a warm can of pineapple juice and two granola bars. By eleven o'clock, she'd dug her mother's first pit down another six inches and was certain that this wasn't virgin soil. Either the spot had once been tilled by early settlers or Indians, or it had been dug up for some other reason. She'd found no hint of burials at this level, but she had uncovered the bowl of a clay trade pipe, a broken arrow point, some bits of charcoal, and a handful of stone chips.

Extracting each artifact from the damp earth took

time. The larger items had to be photographed in place, sketched on the plot map before she put them into plastic bags, and marked with identifying codes. She'd discovered nothing unusual, but her mother was tough. This was a Karen Knight dig. Each step had to be followed meticulously, and any assistant— daughter included—who didn't follow procedure to the letter was tossed off the site. It was a lesson Abbie had learned by the time she was ten.

An early-afternoon thunderstorm sent her dashing for the shelter of her tent, where she devoured another granola bar, a bag of raisins, and a pack of peanut butter crackers. The downpour lasted more than half an hour, and once it passed, she returned to her work in the test pit. She was lying on her stomach, brushing muddy soil away from another clump of charcoal with a toothbrush, when she heard the faint sound of a boat motor.

Perhaps five minutes passed before the bow of the boat appeared. Abbie got up and rubbed the worst of the mud off her clothing. By the time she'd walked to the water's edge, Buck had slowly maneuvered the flat-bottomed craft through the tangle of reeds and into the partially enclosed pond. "Hey!" she called. "What brings you here, Chief?"

He raised his hand in acknowledgment, but didn't smile, making her wonder why he was so solemn this afternoon. Buck cut the motor a few yards from shore, dropped anchor, and lowered himself over the side. The water rose to his hips as he waded in.

"What's the matter? Too lazy to hike in?" He had his cop face on, which was way too serious, and a chill slid down her spine. "Buck?" He stopped on the wet sand. She noticed that he was barefooted.

"I have bad news." Avoiding her gaze, he pulled off

his ball cap and slapped it against his dripping shorts.
"It's your mother—"

"Ànati? Has there been an accident?" A sick feeling
rose enveloped her. "What—"

"Abbie . . ."

A metallic taste filled her mouth.

"There's no easy way to say this."

"How bad is she hurt?" His eyes told her that it was
worse than that, but she refused to accept the truth. So
long as he didn't say the words, her suspicion couldn't
be true.

He took her hand and clasped it between his larger
ones. She felt calluses on his palms and caught the
scent of his soap. "They couldn't save her. She's dead."

"No!" She jerked away from him. "No!"

"It happened last night. I just got the call. Apparently, there was some confusion about where your
mother was staying on Tawes."

"No," she repeated. "You've been misinformed."

"I'm so sorry, Abbie. There's no mistake. A member
of the Penn faculty made a positive identification. A
Dr. Irene Goldstein."

"No!" Abbie insisted. She began to run. He came after her, caught her in his arms, and pulled her against
him. She smacked his chest with the palms of her
hands. "No . . . no . . ."

She started to tremble. She clamped her teeth together to keep them from chattering and breathed
deeply through her nose. Tears scalded the insides of
her eyelids but she blinked them back.

"Abbie."

"Give me a minute. Just a minute." The sun seemed
too bright. She walked to the shade of a tree and sat
down on the grass as Buck's soft words echoed in her
head. *No mistake . . . Positive identification . . .*

Abbie lowered her head. She felt dizzy. Disoriented. As though she'd been struck by lightning. She forced herself up on her feet. Why did her voice sound so tinny? Distorted. "What happened? Was she hit by a car?"

Buck's weather-bronzed face was pasty gray. "God . . . Abbie. I hate to be the one to tell you. I'm so sorry. I know how close the two of you—"

"No." She shook her head. "You don't know. You can't possibly imagine." A muscle twitched along his cheek. He must have shaved this morning. She could hardly see any trace of beard.

"I can't, can I? You're right. I'm sorry."

"Stop saying you're sorry. You didn't do anything wrong. You're a police officer. You must have had to tell people that their loved ones were dead dozens of times." She took another deep breath. "I'm being irrational, aren't I? This isn't your fault."

He swore. "I didn't know your mother . . . Dr. Knight . . . well. But what I saw, I admired. She was smart . . . and funny." He laid a rough palm on her cheek.

"She is, isn't she?" Abbie sank onto the damp sand. A pair of Canada geese flew over. A dragonfly lit on a piece of driftwood. A tiny fish jumped. The day was no different from what it had been earlier . . . but it had irrevocably changed. Ànati was gone. Not gone completely, but farther away than she'd ever been since Abbie had first drawn breath. And she felt the separation in ways she'd never suspected she could.

She scooped up a handful of white sand and let it trickle through her fingers. "Tell me."

He squatted so that they were on the same level. "It happened last night between eight-forty and nine p.m. outside an entrance to the Penn Museum of Anthropology and Archaeology. The sergeant who called me, a Sergeant Malone, had only sketchy details. From what I can gather, the detectives believe that your mother was the victim of random street crime."

"She was meeting Irene—Dr. Goldstein—at her office at the museum. They were colleagues. Irene was going to examine the torque and the cloak pin."

"Apparently, your mother was attacked on her way there. It's my understanding that Dr. Goldstein mentioned those two items to the detectives. Since they weren't found at the scene, the suspect or suspects must have stolen them after the attack."

"Why would Mom be going to Irene's office so late? They were supposed to meet in the afternoon."

"I don't know. Dr. Goldstein discovered your mother's body and made the call to the emergency dispatcher. They responded within five minutes, but it was already too late. It was Dr. Goldstein's belief that Dr. Knight was already dead when she reached her."

Abbie spread her fingers and stared down at them. Her hands were like her mother's, but unlike Ànati, she'd never worn rings. She wondered if the mugger had taken her mother's turquoise ring, the one Dad had given her when they were young. "Was she shot?"

He shook his head. "Cause of death appears to be blunt force trauma. The autopsy will—"

"Tell me. Everything."

"Sergeant Malone believed the weapon was a stone ax . . . an Indian ax. One was found at the scene."

"With her blood on it?"

He nodded. "The assailant may have taken it from her during the robbery. If there was a struggle, he probably—"

"She didn't have an ax with her. She had the bronze

cloak pin and the gold torque in her case. Why would she have an ax?"

"Maybe she found it here at the site and carried it to—"

"And didn't record it? Didn't mention it to me? Impossible." Abbie got to her feet. "She'd never remove an object from a site without proper identification. And she always had her pistol with her. Why didn't she protect herself?"

Buck stood and pulled her to her feet. "We don't know all the details yet. The detectives—"

"You're telling me that someone killed my mother with an Indian ax and they believe she carried it there from Tawes? That's absurd." She turned abruptly and waded out through the water toward the boat. "Take me back to town. Now! I'm going to fly up there. Talk to them."

"It's better if you wait until after the autopsy."

She stopped and looked back at him. "I'm going now. If you want to help, you'll find someone to watch over the site while I'm away. My mother would have wanted the area to remain pristine while—"

"You're in no condition to pilot an aircraft. If you insist on going today, I'll take you to Crisfield, pick up my SUV, and drive you myself."

She heaved herself up over the side of the boat. "Flying is faster. I can be at the airport in—"

"Like hell. Philadelphia detectives may not know or care where Tawes is, but they'll still give me professional courtesy. My badge will make the process smoother. Maybe get you quicker answers." He scrambled aboard.

"It wasn't a random mugging," she said. "Someone went there to kill her. Someone from Tawes."

"Don't torture yourself with conspiracy theories," he cautioned.

"You have to protect the site, Buck. There's something here that the murderer doesn't want us to find."

"That's jumping to conclusions, Abbie. It's a common reaction by next of kin, but not realistic. Street crime happens every day, especially in a city as large as Philadelphia."

Abbie glared at him. "Bull! She knew how to take care of herself. My mother died because someone didn't want her to excavate this site. What's this marina project worth? Millions? People die all the time for ten dollars, let alone ten million."

"Exactly. Your mother was simply at the wrong place at the wrong time." He pulled the starter.

"You're the one who said that something about this site worried you," she reminded him.

"This site, not Philadelphia. Your mother's death has nothing to do with this dig."

"We'll see, won't we?" Images of her mother's face rose behind her burning eyelids. How could Ànati be lying still and cold on a steel table in a medical examiner's lab?

Abbie swallowed, trying to breathe normally, trying to ignore the pain in her chest. Buck might be a good cop, but he was wrong if he believed this was just a crazed druggie out to make a quick hit. Her mother had died because of this project—because of what someone was afraid she'd discover. Abbie was as certain of it as she was that none of the authorities would listen to anything she said.

If the murderer had killed her mother with an Indian ax, he'd done it deliberately to make a statement, and he'd been the one to carry the weapon to the scene. . . . Which meant he'd intended to commit murder. The place to start the investigation wasn't in the city where her mother had died. It was right here on Tawes.

* * *

Nine days later, in a nineteenth-century frame church in Sweet Water, Oklahoma, Abbie spread a blue and red Hudson Bay trade blanket over her mother's simple wooden casket. Her father, standing beside her, laid a single eagle feather on the blanket and then wafted the smoke from a smoldering bundle of cedar bark through the air.

Father Joseph stepped forward, and Abbie—wearing her mother's turquoise ring—took her seat in a pew between her dad and his sister, Aunt Kate. Cousins, uncles, friends, and neighbors filled the small church. The familiar scents of incense and oil mingled with the cedar smoke as the priest's words blended with the echo of traditional drums from the churchyard. She tried to concentrate on the service, but her thoughts kept returning to her frustration in the days following her mother's murder.

The detectives had been sympathetic and professional. The case was still open, but no witnesses had appeared, and the torque had not surfaced at any city pawn shop. If robbery had been the motive for the attack on her mother, the killer had made good his escape and was lying low, or had taken the antiquities out of state for disposal.

Buck had kept his promise, taken her to Philadelphia, and helped her through the ordeal. He'd remained three days in the city before returning to his duties on Tawes, and he'd promised to keep her informed of any evidence or suspects. In due time, the proper procedures had been carried out, and she'd been permitted to bring her mother's remains home for burial. But Abbie knew the funeral wouldn't end her nightmare. There could be no closure until the murderer paid full measure for the crime.

Her dad nudged her elbow, and Abbie accompanied him to the front of the church. Six men, including her father, carried the casket out the door to the churchyard. As was the custom, she walked behind them, chanting old words in Algonquian, half-forgotten phrases from her childhood.

The interment and gathering that followed passed in a blur. Dr. Goldstein and her mother's colleagues and non-Native American friends paid their condolences and departed. Minutes stretched into hours as relatives and friends told Abbie how sorry they were and how much they would miss her mother.

Her father's home was large and modern, and guests filled the downstairs and spilled out on the porches and into the yard. Kitchen and dining-room tables groaned under platters of beef and pork, trays of relishes, huge bowls of salads, vegetables, and fruit. Cakes, cookies, pies, and other sweets covered every inch of countertops and sideboards, claiming space between pitchers of lemonade, tea, and liter bottles of soda pop.

Someone put a plate and fork in her hand, and Abbie pretended to eat. She distinctly remembered complimenting her Aunt Nettie on her fry bread. Babies cried, old women gossiped, men talked, and children dashed in and out of the crowded room. Teenaged girls in bright lipstick and blue eye shadow wobbled in heels too high and whispered to each other amid bursts of subdued giggles. Sullen-faced youths tugged at their too-tight ties and pretended not to notice the girls. The house smelled of ham and apple pie and pumpkin bread. It smelled of mourning.

Abbie's dad woke her the following morning with a mug of black coffee and a slab of peach pie. "Eat something," he urged. "You didn't have a bite yesterday. Karen wouldn't like it."

She sat up in bed, groaned, and rubbed her eyes. "Mom's not here. I don't have to eat if I don't want to."

"OK. Suit yourself." He set the coffee on a stone-topped table beside her bed. "But you need to be ready in half an hour. Your Aunt Kate and two of your cousins will be here at nine to pick you up. Grand-mother Willow is having a sweat in your mother's honor."

"I'm not going. I'm not into this Indian stuff." Willow wasn't really her grandmother. She was a tradi-tional woman much respected in the community. She'd been old as long as Abbie could remember. "I've seen enough relatives, and I'm not going to any sweat."

"Aunt Kate was pretty set on having you there. It's women only, and I think there must be ten or so com-ing from your mother's side. If you're late, it will make Kate look bad."

"I am not stripping off my clothes and sitting half the day in the middle of a bunch of my mother's sisters and cousins. This is the twenty-first century."

"It may help."

She climbed out of bed and hugged him. He seemed smaller than she'd remembered. His hair, which he'd always worn long and pulled back into a single braid, was more silver than salt-and-pepper, and there were shadows under his eyes. "Maybe you should be the one going to a sweat, Dad. It's your thing. Not mine."

"I did. Two days after . . ." His thin lips firmed. "You have so much of your mother in you. You fit in out there, more than I ever could. But don't forget who you are. Don't forget what people you come from."

"Republicans?"

He frowned, squelching her pitiful attempt at hu-mor.

"Dad. I can't be what you want."

He glanced at his watch. "Make that twenty-three minutes."

It had been longer than half a day; it had been hours and hours. Abbie didn't know what time it was. She didn't have a stitch on. And there were more Lenape women packed inside the log sweat lodge on Grandmother Willow's back forty acres than she could have thought possible. Abbie had had nothing to eat since the bite of pie she'd snatched before jumping in the shower and nothing to drink but warm spring water.

She felt empty, light, as though the natural laws of gravity had temporarily ceased to exist. She hung suspended, somewhere between grief and acceptance.

Someone threw water on the heated rocks and steam swirled up, filling the lodge, making it harder to breathe. Chanting filled Abbie's head. Her Aunt Nettie began to play her flute; high, haunting, primeval notes seeped into her blood and bones. Drums and rattles joined in—rattles made from the shells of turtles, painted gourd rattles, and rattles fashioned from deer hooves. Naked bodies pressed close around her. Once, Abbie was certain she felt the brush of wings against her bare skin and heard an owl hoot.

Her Aunt Kate knew only a few words of the old language, but she had a voice as sweet and pure as wild honey. The singing embraced Abbie and lifted her to another place, dulling the knife-edge of raw aching, filling her with strength and resolution. And when Grandmother Willow took her hand and led her outside into the starlit night, Abbie made no protest.

The elderly woman's words were barely whispers as

she touched Abbie from the crown of her head to her naked feet with a bundle of herbs and painted her face with ocher made from crushed rock. Younger hands turned her round and round, and two of her cousins linked hands with hers and they waded together into a swift-running creek.

"You have to duck under," Diana urged.

Hannah, younger, shivered. "It's really cold."

The water felt freezing to Abbie, and she had to remind herself that it was July, not November. She felt the cold more due to the sudden change in temperature from the heated interior of the sweat lodge.

"All the way," Diana said.

Abbie plunged in. The next thing she realized, she was standing on the bank again. She must have waded out of the creek, but she didn't remember it. Someone tucked a wool blanket around her shoulders. It was warm and scratchy and felt like a grandmother's hug. The drums and voices faded, and she was alone, sitting on the grass watching the stars. Had they ever been so close before? So bright?

A calf bawled in the distance. She heard the rustle of the wind through the branches of the trees. She heard the rush of the water. And suddenly she felt the presence of her mother. For the first time, tears welled in her eyes and spilled down her cheeks.

"Ànati?"

No answer. No sound but a cricket's piercing chirp.

Emotion filled her. She reached out. "Ànati? Are you there?"

And then, as quickly as she had come, she was gone.

"You cannot follow her," Grandmother Willow said.

Abbie wondered where the old woman had come from.

"Some day, but not now. It is not your time."

"It isn't fair!" Abbie cried. "She was young. She never hurt anybody."

"What is fair?" Grandmother Willow gasped, began to tremble, and her eyes rolled back in her head. "Blood." Her voice deepened to that of a young man's, sending an icy chill down Abbie's spine. "The earth . . . is soaked with blood."

"The street where my mother was murdered?"

"*Ku.*"

No. The Algonquian word rang into the night. "Grandmother . . ."

The old woman moaned, began to rock back and forth. "I feel a twisted spirit . . . powerful . . . evil. He hunts the night."

Abbie's eyes widened. In the dark, Grandmother Willow's features seemed distorted—harsher, younger, almost masculine.

"The marsh where we've been digging? Is that what you see? They say it's cursed."

"Evil," willow repeated. "His bones are dust . . . yet he walks . . . seeking strength from the living. Take care."

"Stop it!" Abbie cried. "Stop." She gripped Grandmother Willow's bony arm.

"I hear weeping. Three. Three more . . ." The strength seemed to go out of her and she went limp, collapsing like a puppet with cut strings.

"Grandmother!" Abbie caught her frail body and lowered her to the ground. Her eyes were wide open—shell eyes, white and glazed in the moonlight. "Grandmother!"

Her wrinkled lips moved, and Abbie leaned close to hear her whisper, no longer that of a strong man but that of an old, old woman. "Three more will die."

"Who? Who will die?"

"Take . . ." She was shivering now, her skin cold to the touch. "Take . . . care . . ."

As she lifted Grandmother Willow's head into her lap and wrapped the blanket around her, Abbie remembered Buck saying exactly those words. "Don't die," she begged her. "Please don't die." She sat, holding her for what seemed an eternity, and just when Abbie thought she would have to leave her and run for help, the elderly woman stirred in her arms and sat up.

"*Kesa tamwe,*" she muttered.

"What? I don't understand."

"Nothing." She spat. "A bad taste in my mouth." She wriggled out of Abbie's grasp. "Just don't sit there. Help me up."

"Are you all right? I thought—"

Grandmother Willow shook her head. "I saw . . . Yes, I saw a place of water. No houses. No roads. Water, trees. A river?"

"You talked about a night hunter."

"In the voice?"

"It didn't sound like you," Abbie admitted.

"I am sorry, child. I did not mean to frighten you. Paah!" She spat again. "I have a bad taste in my mouth." She shook her head. "Evil. I smell evil."

"Can you walk as far as your house? Do you want me to get help?"

Grandmother Willow snorted. "I'm not senile. I have visions. Since I was a girl. And I'm not crazy."

"I didn't say you were."

"But you were frightened."

"Yes."

She sighed and took Abbie's arm. "It is a burden to be blessed with visions."

"You said something I didn't understand . . . in the old language. *Kesa . . . kesa tam—*"

The old woman chirped amusement. "That you

should know. *Kesa tamwe!*" She shrugged. "In English . . . maybe . . ." She chuckled. "Holy shit!"

"Uh-huh, OK." Abbie hesitated. "Do you remember—what you told me?"

"No. The visions come and they go. Sometimes the seeing comes to pass and sometimes it doesn't." She squeezed Abbie's hand. "But I take them as a warning of what could be. You must be careful, child, that you do not go to an early grave."

"Maybe that wouldn't be so bad. I couldn't help wondering, why my mother, why her instead of me?"

Grandmother Willow's gnarled fingers were soft and warm as she touched Abbie's cheek. "Each must walk her own path."

"And mine? What's my path? What am I supposed to do?"

"Who killed your mother, Abigail Chingwe Night Horse?"

"I don't know." She drew in a ragged breath. "I don't know, but I'll find out." Where had that come from?

"And then what? What will you do, child?"

The words rose up unbidden. "I'll give her justice."

"I think there is more you must do. I think you must put to rest this evil that haunts you."

"That makes no sense."

Grandmother Willow made a sound that might have been agreement . . . or might have been doubt. "Maybe I am a foolish old woman whose time has passed."

"I think you're a very wise person."

"Do you?" She sighed again. "Wise or foolish, I see great danger for you, and for another you care about. I cannot see his face, but I see a pale horse."

Abbie shivered. Buck's horse? But she couldn't think of him now, couldn't let herself be distracted from what was important. "I will avenge my mother's death."

"Easy to make an oath. Not so easy to fulfill."

"I will. I swear it." Her voice came out a croak.

"The white world may not understand. If you do this, there may be a terrible price to pay."

"Then I'll pay it. Whatever it costs, I'll pay it."

CHAPTER EIGHT

"Sounds to me as though you're in deep, Daniel. A wonder she didn't pitch your ring in the bay and send you home with buckshot in your ass." Brush in hand, Will stepped away from his worktable and studied the figure of the yellow-crowned night heron that he'd been painting.

"I didn't—"

"Quiet!" Will scowled. "Can't you see I'm thinkin'?"

Daniel bit back a terse retort and forced himself to hold his temper. Bailey's great-uncle was the closest thing he had to a real father. Daniel had always supposed that he'd come along too late in the marriage for either of his parents to be thrilled with his arrival, and his childhood would have been a lonely one if it weren't for Will Tawes. He owed Will more than he could ever repay. A little patience wasn't too much to ask.

Artist, woodsman, and extreme individualist, Will Tawes was one of the old breed of Chesapeake Bay watermen who lived by the code of earlier times. Will had seen his share of trouble, and if anyone could help Daniel out of this mess, he would be the man.

Will cleaned the brush, laid it aside, and reached for another. His mouth tightened into a hard line as he completed the feathering on the bird's crest with a few deft strokes.

"It looks real enough to fly," Daniel observed.

"If it don't, I've no business charging as much as I do for it. Serve me right if I was arrested for highway robbery."

Will's wildlife carvings were sought after by collectors as far away as Japan and New Zealand. Bailey had told him that one of her uncle's waterbirds had recently sold at auction for over thirty thousand dollars. Not bad for a self-educated Tawes islander who'd once served hard time in the Maryland state penitentiary for a crime he didn't commit.

Daniel took a sip of the tea Will had brewed earlier. "This is good tea."

"Thought you'd like it. A Yunnan." The older man picked up his own John Deere mug and led the way out of his studio onto the porch that overlooked the dock and bay. Hundred-year-old pin oaks shaded the two cane rockers. Will took one seat and waved Daniel to the other. Will's three dogs, a pair of big Chesapeake Bay retrievers and a tricolored mongrel, settled around them. "So, Lucas claims he'll sell the boy for three hundred thousand dollars. How far can you trust him?"

"About as far as you'd trust a mainland lawyer. Lucas is a bottom-feeding lowlife . . . but deadly."

"A hired killer."

"The worst kind. One that enjoys his work."

Will's eyes narrowed thoughtfully.

"Or you might call him a patriot." Daniel added.

"Same as you."

Daniel shook his head. "Lucas and I were both with the agency, but I didn't do wet work. I was nothing more than a pencil pusher. I gathered information."

"Yeah." Will folded his arms over his chest. "And I'm an Eagle Scout."

"You warned me not to sign up with them." Disillusioned by corruption in the American government and rocked by personal tragedy, he'd walked away from his career with the C.I.A. and returned to the island over two years ago. Unfortunately, resigning from the agency was more complicated than joining. He knew too much, and that knowledge was dangerous to people in high places.

"You gave Bailey your word that you were through with all that."

He had quit the agency before he'd met her, but his past had complicated their relationship and made it hard for him to trust anyone. Will, Bailey, and Emma were exceptions to the rule. Them, he would trust with his life . . . and had. His only brother, Matthew, hadn't made the cut. "So far, I've been able to keep my promise."

Will reached down to stroke the big Chesapeake that nudged up against his legs. The dog, *Raven*, closed his eyes in bliss. "You think maybe Lucas's talk about a child is a smoke screen—that it's the agency trying to suck you back into their net?"

"There's always that possibility. I trust them about as far as I trust Lucas. Christmas Eve they called me in for questioning. I was told that Lucas had dropped out of sight in the middle of an operation and they wanted to know if I'd been in contact with him. I told them I hadn't heard from him since last summer."

"You ought to be the last person who'd know where he is," Will observed.

"They suspected that I'd killed him."

Will folded his arms over his chest and listened.

"On my way out of the compound, someone stopped me in the parking lot and suggested meeting later in a bar." He'd worked with Sue some time before, but Will didn't need to know her name. It was dangerous to reveal as much as he had, but he needed Will's perspective. He was an old fox that had survived more than one attempt on his life.

"I reckon it wasn't just to talk over old times." Raven nosed against Will's shirt pocket, and Will dug out a biscuit, broke it in pieces, and dispersed it to the three dogs.

"I went to the bar, waited, but no one showed. When I went back to my car, I found a matchbook on my seat."

"And you don't smoke."

Daniel nodded. "Inside was a phone number. I drove to a pay phone and called it." Actually, the first time he'd tried the number, he'd gotten a stranger in the Baltimore-Washington Airport. He'd waited twenty minutes before making a second attempt. That time Sue answered. "The message was that the agency had severely reprimanded Lucas late August. My name was prominent in his file."

Will waited.

"Lucas blamed me. Made threats."

"You always did have more nerve than common sense." Will scratched absently at the graying stubble on his chin. "You tangle your anchor line with a killer, and then you come here wanting advice after you've taken advantage of my girl."

Daniel stared out over the water. "Sounds bad when you put it that way."

"Damn right, boy. Sounds bad because it is. Lucky for you, I've mellowed in my old age. Time was, I'd have filled you full of buckshot, tied a weight to your feet, and dropped your body in the deepest hole in the marsh."

Daniel grimaced. "It's not me holding up the wedding. Besides, if you put a bullet in me, you'll orphan your great-great-nephew before he sees the light of day."

"Better for you if you'd told Bailey the truth from the start."

"I promised her she didn't have to worry about Lucas stalking either one of us."

"Maybe you promised more than you could deliver."

"That's what I'm afraid of. She said she wanted to be a carpenter's wife, not a secret agent's."

"But you think this polecat might have murdered Bailey's friend?"

Daniel swallowed. "I don't know. It sounds far-fetched that Lucas would come back here to kill Karen Knight."

"Unless he had unfinished business on Tawes."

"Exactly. He only worked for the agency because they paid more than the opposition. I was hoping maybe he might be dead—until he contacted me the day before Dr. Knight's murder."

"Takes one kind of man to shoot someone in the back, another to beat a woman's face in with a tomahawk."

"Lucas could do either one and not break a sweat."

"Real coincidence," Will said. "Lucas showing up in the middle of this fuss over the marina. Nobody hates Onicox more than I do, but that don't mean they'd hire scum like Lucas to do their dirty work."

Daniel leaned forward in his rocking chair. "It's hard to know what's real and what's conjecture. But what if Lucas approached Onicox? He wouldn't list *assassin* on his résumé. Maybe they weren't too particular what he did if he could make certain that the sale would go through."

"Seems as though paying off a few politicians would be easier."

"Not if Dr. Knight had turned up something of historical importance in the marsh."

A skiff motored past, and the sole occupant waved. Will returned the greeting. "Looks like George Williams," he said. "Must be on his way to Tawes to do his dealing. Wrong tide for fishing."

Daniel's gut knotted.

"You don't care much for old George, do you?" Will said.

"It's Lucas I'm concerned about. Not George Williams."

"And you say this Lucas contacted you about a baby he claimed was your son—when exactly?" Will asked.

"The day before Karen Knight was killed."

"And that's the first inkling you had that the boy existed?"

Daniel exhaled softly. "Yes."

"It all could be a lie. A trick on Lucas's part."

Daniel nodded. "He says if I don't want the boy, he'll recoup his expenses somewhere else. He claims the child is light-skinned. There's always a market in third-world countries for pretty boys."

"That kind of evil has been with us since time began. Too much of it in this country as well."

"True. But children aren't Lucas's weakness. This scheme of his is just business. Or spite."

"Sick bastard, ain't he? Might make good crab bait."

"Sometimes, Will, I wonder if the old island ways of dealing with vermin weren't best."

Will scratched the soft hair under Raven's chin. "It might not have been according to Hoyle, but it worked." Will's blue eyes were hard as they met Daniel's. "Did you agree to pay him what he asked?"

"Lucas? No, I said I wanted more proof than a photograph." His hands knotted into fists so tight that half-healed scabs on his knuckles cracked and trickles of blood oozed down his hand. "It's not the money."

"Didn't suppose it was." Will was quiet for several minutes, then said, "Pay once, you'll keep paying."

"Thought you'd want to know what was happening."

"What's this Lucas look like? In case I should stumble over him."

"Nothing to make him stand out. Forty, maybe. Olive-skinned. Not too tall. His eyes are what give him away. Flat. Small eyes. No emotion. Like the glass ones you set in your carvings."

"I'll ask around. You mentioned this to Emma?"

"No."

"I'll take care of it."

"I don't want Emma involved. Not in—"

"Don't take me for an old fool, Daniel. I may have lost some of my speed, but not my bite. I can handle Emma. Not much happens on this island she don't know about. Nosy as a blue jay. Always was."

"I'm concerned about Bailey," Daniel admitted. "Lucas would have no reason to threaten her, but . . ."

"Other than to get even with you."

"Watch over her for me."

"No need to ask. No harm will come to her if I can help it. Or to that babe she's carrying." Will climbed to his feet. "I'll be seeing Emma in an hour or so. Meeting—about the marina project."

"I hadn't heard anything about—"

Will smiled. "There's meetings and there's meetings. You're welcome to come along if you want."

"No, I'm going to walk over to Bailey's. See if she'll talk to me."

"Be best to come clean. Tell her everything . . . my way of thinking." He folded lean arms over his chest again. Will might be in his sixties, but he was in better shape than most forty-year-olds Daniel knew. "'Course, you couldn't pick a worse one to ask about dealing with women. God knows I've made my share of mistakes."

"Haven't we all?" Daniel stepped down off the porch and turned toward the path that led along the shoreline from Will's to Bailey's farmhouse.

"Keep your powder dry," Will called after him. "And if you have to shoot the son of a bitch, don't go soft. Shoot to kill."

Will watched until Daniel disappeared though the trees before reentering his studio. He shot the bolt on the door and rolled back a rug near the fireplace on the far wall. The floorboards here looked no different from the others, but Will knew where to ease his fingers under one plank and raise the hidden trap-door.

A crude ladder led down into a low, brick-walled room. Light streamed through the hatch illuminating an area near the entrance, but the corners of the space were in shadow. Will retrieved a flashlight from the space behind the steps and used it to locate a wooden chest bound with leather straps. An oversized key turned the lock. The chest had been in his family a long time, close to two hundred years, but what lay inside was even older. Carefully Will lifted the lid and shone the light inside.

Tiny hairs prickled on Will's arms as he gazed down at the fourteen-inch-long bronze horn etched with a random spiral pattern. No one could rightly say how long it had lain in the earth, untouched by sun or rain, unseen by men. It was Will's guess that whoever had buried the horn wanted it to remain there, but nothing lasts forever—not even the peace of a grave.

Matthew believed that the other pieces, the ones he'd given to Karen Knight to take to the university would help to save Tawes, but Will knew better. Any whiff of buried treasure would bring the outlanders here as thick as fleas on a dog's back.

He couldn't let that happen. His own years were numbered, but there was Bailey's child to think of. It might be up to him to see that there was still a Tawes here for that babe to grow up on.

The trail that led between the two properties was heavily wooded so that it made a leafy green tunnel around him. To Daniel's left lay the bay; to his right, thick forest. It wasn't likely that Lucas or anyone else would come through here to reach Bailey. Will and his dogs roamed every inch of this ground at all hours of the day and night.

Daniel tried to think of what he'd say to Bailey, how much to say. Finding out that she was carrying his child had blown him away. He loved Bailey—wanted to make her his wife—but the pregnancy couldn't have come at a worse time. Karen Knight's death . . . Lucas's attempts at blackmail . . . How could he tell Bailey what he'd been hiding from her? She might be new to the island, but she was pure Tawes when it came to stubbornness. She wouldn't hesitate to raise their child alone if she felt she could no longer trust him.

He'd hoped that Will would come up with a solution, but mostly, the older man had just listened. That was what he'd always done. Will was sparse with words and long on wisdom. He thought that it was best to level with Bailey. Yet it might never be the same between them if he did. And there were things in his past that he couldn't share even with Will—let alone the woman he wanted to make his wife. Bad memories haunted his dreams . . . nightmares he'd take to his grave.

If there was any possibility that Lucas was telling the truth, he had to do something. He couldn't abandon his own child. Lucas had promised him that the boy was healthy, that he could produce him in three days, once Daniel withdrew the cash from his offshore account. If Daniel didn't want him, Lucas had another eager buyer. All Daniel had to do was wait for his phone call and say yes or no.

A viselike pain settled into the back of his head as he reached the edge of Bailey's property line and her brick farmhouse loomed up ahead. What would he do if she slammed the door in his face? Refused to talk to him? Bailey was the best thing that had ever happened to him. At least, he thought she was. He'd never been lucky with women.

Now, here on the island where he'd been born and grown up, his years of intrigue with the C.I.A. in the Mid-East seemed far away, almost another lifetime. Even the face of the beautiful Afghani resistance fighter with whom he'd shared a brief but heated passion had faded. After Mallalai had betrayed him and died so tragically, he'd thought there would never be a woman he could love and trust.

He'd been wrong.

Daniel didn't see Bailey at the dock or working in her flower beds, so he went to the back porch and let himself into the house. "Bailey?" When she didn't answer, he passed through the large kitchen and into the dining room. She'd polished the Queen Anne table and chairs until they gleamed. An arrangement of black-eyed Susans filled an antique pitcher on the Irish hunt sideboard, and he pulled a flower out and held it behind his back. "Bailey?"

"Daniel?" she called from the head of the staircase.

He stopped at the bottom and grinned up at her. "Don't shoot. I come bearing gifts."

She didn't smile—a bad sign.

He held out the daisy.

Ignoring the flower, she descended the steps, the expression in her Tawes blue eyes as stubborn as Will's. "I'm nauseous and not in the mood to be charmed. If you have an explanation for what's been going on, I'll listen. Otherwise, we have nothing to say to each other."

"Bailey . . ."

She folded her arms over her apple-green shirt. Her face was a little pale, but she didn't look sick to him. God, how he ached to hold her in his arms.

"All right. There is something. I didn't want you to worry."

Her eyes narrowed. "I'm waiting."

"Marry me, Bailey. Now. As soon as we can get the license." He rested his hand on the banister. "Honey, I love you. I want to take care of you and our baby."

"What exactly is the *something*?"

His throat constricted, and he knew how her students must feel when they were caught doing something they shouldn't. She might be a little bit of a woman, but she was tough.

"You remember when I was in Afghanistan with the agency?"

Her lips pursed.

"I told you about Mallalai."

"Yes, Daniel, I remember Mallalai."

He drew in a deep breath. Why was this so damned hard to say? "There may be a problem."

Her eyes widened. "What do you mean? What problem? She's not dead? You already have a wife?"

"No! Hell, no. You know better than that. And we were never married. That was the—"

"Tell me." She came down another two steps. Her eyes were huge and she looked as if she were about to burst into tears.

"There might be a child. My child."

"What? How . . . What do you mean?"

"That's all I know. You asked why I hadn't shown up on time—for dinner that night."

"And you didn't know about this before? How could you be a father and not know—"

"Damn it, Bailey, you wanted to know what was wrong. You wanted me to level with you, so I have."

"How old? Boy or girl?"

"A boy. About two and a half years old. It's all the information I have. All I can tell you."

Moonlight played over the narrow strip of beach, turning the grass to silver, casting long shadows into the open pits. The solitary figure moved from the trees down toward the sand. There were no deer tonight, no human intruders. He liked it when he heard nothing but the marsh sounds: the crickets, the frogs, the rasping bark of a Virginia rail, the rustle of the wind through the reeds.

He crouched in the tall grass and rubbed a small piece of weathered bone between his thumb and forefinger. The familiar sensation calmed his soul and helped him to draw strength from the blood that had soaked into this ground long ago. He closed his eyes and sucked in the raw scent of anguish. He could sense the spirits around him . . . taste their presence . . . feel the throb of drums echoing through his flesh. The uneasy ghosts accepted him and knew he was watching over them.

They understood him and knew he was guarding the old ways. They never judged him. And he had kept the old ways, honoring them by hunting as they did, never wasting game, and living close to the land. If anybody was blood brother to these ghosts, it was him. He was never lonely or afraid when he was here with them.

He'd protected these graves for so many years, and

he was good at what he did. Anyone fool enough to dig here would pay the price, and he would extract it, drop by drop. If enough blood flowed, maybe they'd learn that the curse was all too real.

CHAPTER NINE

Abbie had flown from Oklahoma to Philadelphia and spent two days in the city attempting to extricate information from the detectives assigned to her mother's case. She'd hoped that they would have made progress in the time she was away, but basically, they had nothing new to share with her. Disappointed, she'd hired a helicopter to bring her back to Tawes early this morning. The trip was uneventful, and the pilot touched down in Birdy Parks's cow pasture where she'd left her little Robinson.

Abbie hadn't talked to Buck since before the funeral, but she'd gone over and over in her head what she could possibly say to convince him that she was right—that the excavation on Tawes was the cause of her mother's murder.

Emma was up and rattling pans and dishes in the kitchen when Abbie entered the B&B, and Emma met her at the door with a hug. "Well, aren't you a sight for sore eyes, girl? You're just in time for breakfast. Biscuits will be out of the oven in ten minutes."

Abbie had smelled the baking bread, the frying bacon, and the coffee when she'd pushed open the gate, but she wasn't in the mood for eating. What she wanted most was to talk to Buck, without Emma's interference—however well-meaning. She made appropriate responses to the older woman's condolences and accepted the steaming cup of coffee that Emma pushed into her hands.

"Is Buck up?"

"I heard the shower running earlier. He should be down those stairs any minute. One thing you can say about the Davis boys, they're never late for a meal."

Abbie set the cup on the table. "I don't mean to be rude, but there's something I need to discuss with him. Privately."

"You go right ahead. Won't hurt my feelings." Emma sniffed. "Lord a'mighty, something's burning." She rushed back into the kitchen just as Abbie heard Buck's footsteps on the steps.

"Abbie!" he called as he caught sight of her. "When did you get back?"

"Just now." She hurried to meet him, put both hands on his chest, and literally shoved him onto the side porch. "We need to talk, Buck. What are you going to do about finding my mother's killer?"

"Whoa, whoa," he said. "Babe. Peace." He raised both hands. "Take it easy. I'm not the enemy here."

"I never said you were." She forced herself to speak slowly, calmly. "But the police don't understand. The detectives insist on treating this as a simple robbery. Assault and murder by some teenage thugs or druggies. That isn't what happened."

"And you know that for certain?"

She knew it. What she couldn't explain to him was how she knew. It was more than a hunch—it was a certainty. "It's the only thing that makes sense. Ànati had her gun with her, and she was a crack shot. The thief didn't even take her pistol. He didn't take her turquoise ring. It was still on her finger."

"The detective told me about the gun."

"You talked to them again—since the day you took me to Philly?"

"Last Tuesday. While you were in Oklahoma."

"And?" Why was it that whenever she came face to face with him, his hair was always damp and curling around his face? A tiny dot of dried shaving cream clung to his throat. She found that oddly endearing. Was he living in the last century? Did men still shave with a straight razor on this island? "The cops didn't think it strange that this crazed junkie wouldn't steal a pistol after he'd just bludgeoned her to death? Or a valuable ring?"

Buck's features tightened. She didn't budge an inch. If he thought he could intimidate her with his stony cop face, he'd better think again. Her ancestors had invented the inscrutable stare.

"Sit down, Abbie. You asked me a question. Now listen." He pointed to the porch swing. "I'll tell you everything I've been able to find out about the investigation, which isn't much more than you already know."

"I don't want to sit down. I want to—"

"Sit!"

She did.

When she started to get up again, he put a firm hand on her shoulder. "Calm." His expression softened. "First, let me tell you how sorry—"

"No, you've already said that. I know you're sorry." She wanted to slap away his hand, but he wasn't to blame. Whoever had turned her wonderful, wise Ànati into that wax mannequin in the pine box was the enemy, not Buck. "Everyone's sorry," she managed, "but that doesn't find her murderer."

"The pistol was still in your mother's jacket pocket—apparently tangled in the torn lining. She never got it out."

"My mother would never have let a stranger get that close. She might have come out of the Oklahoma hills, but she was streetwise."

His expression hardened. "So are the detectives working the case. I talked to them. I questioned the medical examiner. I went to the crime scene. They could be right. The simplest answer is that some hopped-up punk or junkie in need of a fix tried to rob her, and it went bad."

"Bludgeoning is messy."

"You're right. Usually, it's more a crime of passion than an impersonal assault."

"Exactly. Why would some punk—" Abbie broke off as Emma pushed open the screen door.

"Eggs are ready. Why don't you two come in, sit down and eat, and argue afterwards?"

"We aren't arguing." Abbie noticed that Emma's usually tidy bun had come partially undone this morning. Short, stiff spikes of graying hair stood out at the back of her head, and she looked as though she hadn't slept well.

Emma sniffed. "Sounds like arguing to me."

"Breakfast. Good idea," Buck agreed. "I'm ready to run up the white flag. Why don't we eat first and then fight?"

"I'm not hungry." Maybe she wasn't that far away from her warrior ancestors. If it took her the rest of her life, she'd find her mother's murderer and see that he paid in full measure for his crime. She'd strangle the bastard with her own two hands if she got the opportunity.

"You may not be hungry, but I'm starving," Buck said with false heartiness. "And since our Miss Emma has gone to all the trouble to cook breakfast, I think we should do it justice."

"At least have some more coffee," Emma urged. She opened the screen door wider. "Lord knows your mother liked my coffee."

Outnumbered, Abbie followed the two of them inside. Buck held out a chair and she sat down at the table. Emma refilled her coffee cup. The serving platter of bacon, sausage, and scrapple looked large enough to feed half the island, but it smelled heavenly. Abbie's stomach growled. She couldn't remember when she'd eaten last.

"Have some scrambled eggs," Emma said. "They're fresh. I got them out of the henhouse an hour ago."

"No, thank you," Abbie protested. She couldn't be hungry. Her mother hadn't been buried a week. How could she possibly be hungry? It was disloyal. Didn't she have enough on her conscience? If she hadn't been in such a hurry to get back to the dig, if she'd stayed in Philly with her mother, she might still be alive. What were the chances the killer would have attacked if Ànati hadn't been alone on the street?"

Emma slid a portion of fluffy eggs onto Abbie's plate. "A few bites of egg. A biscuit and jam. Peach. Made yesterday. You need to keep up your strength. Especially if you're going back out to that burial ground."

"Are you certain you're up to it?" Buck offered her the plate of breakfast meats.

"I tried to talk her out of it originally," Emma said, "but she's as stubborn as Will Tawes. The burial ground is cursed. I told her it was too dangerous for her to be alone out there."

"Do you think I won't finish what my mother started? I don't know what's buried there, but I'm going to keep looking. And you don't need to worry about me. My mother didn't insist on piano lessons when I was eight like my friends' moms—she sent me for instructions in Lenape knife throwing."

"Did you learn enough to hit anything?" Buck asked.

"I've been proficient enough to give demonstrations at powwows since I was ten." She flushed and averted her gaze. Grandmother Willow would have scolded her for bragging, but he'd asked. And she was good with a knife and proud of her skill.

"Still, it's a lonely place," Emma said. "You shouldn't go alone."

"I won't be. Matthew Catlin and Bailey have offered to help."

"And if you don't find anything?" Emma lifted the lid of a crystal bowl of glistening jam. "Try some of this." She looked at Buck. "Talk some sense into her. There's something evil out there. It's not right, disturbing the dead. Matthew's always had the brains of an onion, but Bailey should know better. And her expecting."

Her mother's friend was expecting? Abbie hadn't guessed that. She wondered if her mother had known. "I'm an archaeologist. It's what I do. It's what you and half the people on this island asked us to do."

Abbie took a biscuit. It was so light, it almost floated out of her hand. Emma Parks was one of the least attractive women she'd ever met, but certainly one of the best cooks. Abbie's stomach rumbled loudly again.

"And you said you weren't hungry," Emma chided. "Lord knows you've got reason to shed a bucket of tears, child. But if your mother could talk to us, she'd tell you to take care—to stay strong. She'd want you to go on living every day the best you could. She'd want you to be happy."

"I've got to go back. Either I find something of archaeological significance that will make the State of Maryland stop the project, or I prove there isn't anything there to be found."

"I figured that was the way you'd feel," Buck said. "My younger brothers, Harry and Bowman, have been taking turns watching the site for you every day. Nothing has been disturbed."

Surprised, she looked at him. "Your brothers?"

He shrugged. "Keeps them off the street. Harry should be there this morning."

"Why ask them to guard the site if there's nothing to worry about?"

Buck gave her a rueful look. "I told you that there's something about that marsh I don't like. Besides, I've learned never to discount a woman's intuition."

"I've never met any of your brothers. What does Harry look like?"

"A lot like me." Buck grinned. "Younger. Not as handsome."

"Right." Emma helped herself to another biscuit. "Nothing modest about you Davis boys, is there?"

"Thank you for taking my concerns seriously." Abbie nibbled at her upper lip. "I didn't think—"

"Harry and Bowman owe me plenty of favors. I just wanted you to know they were around, in case you go armed."

She was in no mood for his backwoods humor. "I don't carry a handgun, but I have my own methods of self-protection."

"You might think about a gun," Emma put in. "Guns are great equalizers."

"I told you, my father taught me some useful things about self-defense, and I know karate, too."

Emma screwed up her mouth. "Karate? Give me a twelve-gauge any day."

"I don't like guns."

"So you said," Emma retorted. "But sometimes they come in handy. You might be too educated to believe in curses, but if you live as long as I have, you'll know there's things that can't be explained." She glanced at Buck. "You see that piece on TV last night about that waterman from Deal who George Williams found dead in the marsh twenty-odd years ago?"

"Here on Tawes?" Abbie asked.

"Yeah, but not just on Tawes—in the marsh near the burial ground."

Buck shook his head. "Didn't see it."

"You've seen that reporter Tess Quinn on the evening news, haven't you? "Well, she's investigating the death. Calls it a genuine mystery."

Buck arched an eyebrow skeptically.

"The dead man was Fleming Caulk. I remember when it happened, but it's been so long ago, I clean forgot. Caulks are good people, been on Deal Island almost as long as Parkses have been on Tawes."

"I know the surname, but I don't remember his death," Buck said.

Emma nodded. "You must remember. Everybody talked about it. Fleming Caulk? Middle-aged. Crabber? George Williams found Fleming stone dead on his boat."

"What was the cause of death?" Abbie paused in spreading peach jam on her biscuit.

"Head injuries," Emma said. "Authorities said it was an accident. Mainland authorities, state police, or a medical examiner from the county. We didn't have any law on Tawes back then."

"But if it was an accident—" Abbie began.

Emma raised a hand dramatically. "Found Indian arrowheads and a bloody stone mortar next to the body." She sniffed. Accident? Bull pizzles! Fleming Caulk sure didn't trip over his own feet, fall, and crack his skull on that corn grinder. What he did was dig up that Indian stuff in the burial ground to sell at the auction in Church Hill. Whoever or whatever killed him, it was no accident."

Daniel threw back the sheet, got out of bed, and opened the Roman shades so that a flood of sunlight illuminated Bailey's bed. She groaned, rolled onto her stomach, and buried her head under a pillow. "Let me sleep," she mumbled.

"Have I told you what a nice ass you have?"

"Mmm. Go away."

He returned to the bed, sat on her side, and patted her bare buttocks. "Nice and smooth," he teased. "Perfect. Really a perfect little ass."

"It's the middle of the night."

"It's eight forty-five. Time to milk the cows."

She moaned and burrowed deeper. "No cows."

"Then we should get some." He caressed the curves of her bottom with the palm of his hand before running his fingers up to massage the small of her back.

"Mmm. Higher. Scratch. My back itches."

"Your wish is my command, darlin'."

"Not quite. You didn't fix the towel bar."

"I told you. I have to buy longer screws next time I'm in Crisfield. Dori's Market is out of them." He scratched her back before massaging her shoulders and the nape of her neck.

"Don't stop. It feels heavenly."

"You have freckles," he pronounced, kissing one after another. "If I had a Magic Marker, I could connect the dots." He began to tickle her ribs, and Bailey squealed, rolled over, and threw her pillow at him.

Daniel arched over her, careful to brace his weight on his knees and elbows. "Got you!"

Bailey laughed. "Cheater." She wrapped her arms around his neck and pulled his head down until their lips met.

Her kiss was slow and sweet. He could taste minty toothpaste. Sometime before dawn, when she'd made the second or third trip to the bathroom, she must have brushed her teeth before returning to bed. Their kiss deepened, and he moaned in contentment as waves of pleasure swept through him.

Tingles of desire became a rush. He could feel himself growing harder. She felt so good. He wanted to bury himself in her and stay there forever . . . never leaving this room . . . never being hassled by the agency or dealing with Lucas's threats and blackmail. Never having to think of a small boy who might be in danger.

She made a small sound in her throat, and his breathing quickened. She was so small, so vulnerable. The thought that she was carrying his child made her all the more precious to him. He wondered if he could ask her to mother a stranger's child, born half a world away.

"Love you," she whispered in his ear.

"Me too." He nuzzled her neck, thinking she was the best thing that ever happened to him. "You smell good."

"Don't think this lets you off the hook." She wound a lock of his hair around her finger and tugged at it.

"Ouch! What's that for?"

"To remind you that you aren't forgiven." She nibbled at his shoulder and goose bumps rose on his skin.

"Not even a little?" He pushed his fears to the far corners of his mind and grazed the hollow of her throat with the tip of his tongue. She made a small sound as he slid a hand down to explore her inner thigh. "Mmm, nice."

"Daniel . . . We don't have time. I promised Abbie—"

She gasped as he lowered his head and drew her nipple between his lips. He suckled gently, savoring the exquisite sensation of her warm body beneath his. "Woman—do you have any idea what you do to me?"

"I mean it, Daniel. Oh . . . "

He kissed her other breast, circling the pink aureole with his tongue until her nipple grew taut and erect. "I should have noticed. They're growing, aren't they?" he asked.

"I'll be huge."

He laughed and trailed kisses between her breasts. "Fine by me." God, but the scent of her made him crazy. They'd made love twice the night before, but he wanted her as much as he had the first time he'd taken her to his bed.

She pulled his hair again. "My belly . . . not my breasts. I'll look like a walrus."

"Then you'll be a beautiful walrus." Daniel pressed his cheek against her stomach. "Doesn't feel any fatter. Are you sure there's a little Catlin in there?"

Bailey rubbed against him and sighed. "I'm sure. So will you be in another month or two."

"Are you in there, Angus?"

She giggled. "We are not naming our daughter Angus."

"Son. That's a son. Aren't you, boy?" He raised his

head and peered up at her. "He's says he's got a willie and that makes him a boy. All the Catlin males in our family had willies."

"Get off." She twisted out from under him.

"Why? It was just getting interesting." He moistened her belly button with his tongue. "Maybe a little farther south . . ."

"Nope." Bailey sat up and curled her legs under her. "You're sweet, and it feels good, but it's just not happening for me this morning." Her dark red hair tumbled in damp tangles over her pink cheeks. "We really don't have time to play. It's late. I have to meet Abbie."

Disappointed, he rolled over onto his back. "You know how to take the wind out of a man's sails."

"You're oversexed. It's all you think about."

"Not my fault," he countered. "It's yours, darlin'. You are one hot babe."

"With my new boobs."

"Those too." He grinned. "And I didn't get any complaints until—"

"Until I got preggers and started throwing up?"

"I'm sorry, hon."

"Sorry you've lost your playmate, or sorry that we're going to be parents?"

"You know better than that, Bailey. I love you, and I think you're more beautiful than ever. Even if you are bitchy in the morning."

"I know I am. Cathy says it's my hormones." She grimaced. "I hope you aren't sorry five months from now when I look like a whale."

"I thought it was a walrus." He leaned close and kissed her. "Why don't I make you some breakfast? Bring you some hot tea, a few scrambled eggs. Sausage. We could—"

"No eggs. And no sausage. Yuck. Toast. Tea. And I need to shower before I ride out to the site."

He leaned over and kissed her bare shoulder. "We could shower together. I'll scrub your back."

"How about a rain check?"

"One-time offer. Going fast."

She covered her ears. "No. No. No. You make tea. I'll shower. Alone." She rose and padded barefoot toward the adjoining bathroom.

Bailey had inherited the old farmhouse a year ago, and when she'd decided to live in it instead of selling, the first change she'd made was to turn a bedroom into a custom bath and dressing room. Daniel loved the rain shower.

"You play dirty."

"Do I?" She paused in the doorway and looked back at him. "No more secrets, Daniel. I mean it. I don't understand how you and Mallalai could have had a child without—"

"We weren't together that often. Sometimes I didn't see her for months on end. You wanted to know what was wrong, and I told you. What else do you want from me?" He hadn't told her about Lucas or the blackmail, and he had no intention of doing it. Not unless the situation became more volatile. Explaining why Lucas had contacted him would mean telling Bailey about the money in the Caymans. He wasn't prepared to open that can of worms.

"And this boy is the right age? He could be yours?"

"He would have had to be born . . ." He thought back, trying to remember. "It was crazy over there, Bailey. Mallalai was killed almost two and a half years ago. I suppose the boy—if he is mine—would have to be a little older than that, but not three yet."

"And that's it? That's all you know?"

"I said so, didn't I?" He pulled on his shorts. "Sure I couldn't interest you in blueberry pancakes?"

"Just toast and tea."

"Coming right up." He pulled his shirt over his head. "Are you certain you're up to working on the site?"

"I'm pregnant, not an invalid. At least I won't be, once I get over the morning nausea."

"I could take you there in the boat."

"No. I'd rather ride horseback. And George's house isn't that far away if I'm not feeling well."

Daniel shook his head. "Don't mess with him. He's not—"

"I thought he was nice. When Karen and I found the body, he couldn't do enough for us."

"Take my word for it, hon. I've known George all my life. Stay away from him."

"That's what you told me about Uncle Will when I first came to Tawes," she reminded him.

"For the love of God, Bailey. Do you have to make a drama out of everything I say? George is an old drunk."

"If I didn't know you better, I'd think maybe you were a closet racist." She disappeared into the bathroom.

"Fine. Suit yourself," he called after her. "You always do."

She ducked her head back into the doorway. "On second thought, Daniel, forget breakfast. Go home and yell at your cat. Just lock the door behind you on your way out."

"I don't want to argue with you this morning."

"Good. Neither do I. So don't be an ass, and we won't have any reason to argue."

"I'm sorry, I didn't mean—"

"Just go, Daniel. Go before we really get into it."

"Are you still coming to supper tonight? I promised Will soft crabs."

"Tonight," she agreed. "But you'd better be on your best behavior."

Right, he thought. He wondered if he was working himself out of a bad situation or just getting in deeper.

CHAPTER TEN

Heart hammering in his chest, he opened the barn door and crossed the dusty floor to the ladder. He was cautious, watching to make certain that no one saw him leave the house or followed him to the stable. He hadn't been here in a long time. No one had.

Spiderwebs hung from the rafters along with rope, crab floats, and a trap in need of repair. His mouth was dry, and he felt blood pounding in his veins. He could still taste the coffee he'd had with his morning eggs, and he knew he should have made a new pot instead of drinking what has been sitting on the stove all night. Leftover coffee never tasted as good, even if he sweetened it with four spoons of sugar. He liked sugar, always had. When he was a boy, he'd buy candy whenever he got the chance. His mother told him that his teeth would turn black and fall out, but that never happened. He wondered what it was about mothers that made them take pleasure in stopping boys from doing what they loved most.

Outside, it was bright and sunny, not a cloud in the

sky. It was dark in here. No light filtered through the dirty windows. He supposed they hadn't been washed in . . . He laughed, and his voice echoed through the sagging building. He didn't think the windows had ever been washed.

No animals lived in the barn now except a stray chicken or two, those the foxes and weasels hadn't caught. He remembered when the barn had sheltered cows and horses. No more. It didn't pay to keep a cow. It was easier to buy canned milk from the store.

He looked down at the tracks his mocassins made on the dusty floor and then back at the ladder. He hoped the ladder would hold him. The third rung was missing a nail and had dried chicken poop on it. The fifth rung was rotten. He'd have to take care.

He reached into his pocket, removed the small section of bone, and rubbed it between his fingers. He'd found it in the burial ground years ago, and he carried it with him always. He didn't know what he'd do if he lost it. It felt warm to his touch. He wasn't certain what it was. He thought it might be a section of a child's rib bone, but the salt water had softened the edges so that it crumbled if he squeezed too hard.

He knew he was stalling. He hoped he wasn't making a mistake, but sometimes his need was so bad that there was nothing for it but to take the chance and come to the barn. He should have gotten rid of what was in the box a long time ago, but he couldn't do it. It was such a comfort, knowing his box was safe . . . waiting for him . . . knowing he could go to the barn and open it whenever he wanted to.

Sometimes he had to leave the island, go to Easton or Crisfield . . . even as far as Baltimore. It was easier to find what he needed in the city. It wasn't cheap, but easy. Still, it wasn't the same. Not as good. Like the difference between fishing in another man's boat or owning your own. Not the same at all.

He pushed the bone back into his pocket and wiggled the loose ladder rung. The smartest thing to do would be to cut a new crossbar and nail it up solid. It wouldn't do for him to fall and hurt himself, not this morning when everything was going so well for him. If he fell and broke a leg, he might lie here for days before anyone came looking for him. It was better if he fixed the bad rung on the ladder before it was too late. This was his place . . . all his own. He had lots of memories here, mostly good ones but some not so good.

He liked things to be the same. He didn't like surprises, and he'd had one this morning, a big one. He'd gone to the burial ground before first light and found signs posted on the marsh path and the shoreline. *NO TRESPASSING!* They were large and yellow with black lettering, official looking. At the bottom, the signs read, *Peter Elderson, Esq., Onicox Realty Group.* He hadn't realized they could do such a thing, but now that the grave-robbing Dr. Knight was dead, maybe everything was different. Maybe they could put up signs. He wondered if the signs would keep people away. It was hard to tell about people. Some listened to reason, and others had to be brought to common sense the hard way.

He gripped the worm-eaten ladder and tested it. The wood creaked, but it felt strong enough to hold him. He needed to get up there in the loft today. He hadn't opened his tin box for a long time—too long. Some nights his need was so bad, it made him sick. He woke up in his bed sweating. Even the palms of his hands sweated.

He wondered about that . . . wondered if the sweating was a sign that he'd been healed . . . if God had heard his prayers and forgiven him. If maybe . . . after so long, it was all right for him to remember. With the sweating came an aching in his gut. He wanted to open his box and hold his pictures, see the faces, but he was so scared. He knew that it would be safer to forget them, but that was something he'd never been able to do. They meant too much to him.

He knew he was different. He'd always known that. He never could understand why, and it troubled him. He'd pondered on it, tried to think on why God created him like He had. His mother had told him that everything he needed to know about living was in the Good Book. He'd read her Bible from cover to cover so many times that the pages were coming loose. He couldn't say that he was a faithful churchgoer, but he didn't believe that would matter to God in the end. He'd never known a man or woman who didn't have something to hide. Sometimes the worst people were those sitting in the amen corner.

Anybody could make mistakes. According to what he'd read of God's word, what mattered most was to see your mistakes, repent, and ask forgiveness. The Bible said that God was a loving father. God understood that men and women were weak. They might stumble on the road of righteousness; that had been the way since the creation of the world.

It said plain in the Bible that even Adam and Eve disobeyed God in the Garden of Eden. They disobeyed God, but He still forgave them. If He forgave them, He'll forgive me my weaknesses and my stumbles. After all, shouldn't He take some of the responsibility? He made me, didn't He?

And the boy had to share some of that blame. He hadn't meant for it to happen. It was an accident, but the boy had brought it on himself. He was clumsy and stupid. The others were smarter. He should have had more sense. He'd been warned, but that's the way it is with some boys. They need to be taught a good lesson.

He caught his breath as he climbed, but the ladder held and he stepped safely onto the loft floor. Not that these old boards were any too solid either, but at least it was easier to see up here. The hinges had broken off the door at the far end where the hay lift was. The opening let in plenty of light. It let in rain and other stuff too. The loft smelled of musty hay and dead pigeons.

He wondered how many outbuildings there were like this on the island. Not many farmers left; lots of barns and sheds going to ruin. It came of all this dealing with outsiders. He'd never think of living anyplace else but Tawes. If a Garden of Eden existed on this mortal earth, it was here.

He rubbed his hands on his pant legs. His palms were sweating, and he couldn't risk ruining what meant so much to him. The tin box was where he'd left it, buried safe in the hay in a plastic box with an airtight lid to keep out rain and damp. He knew better than to be careless with his pictures. They were all he had left of his little friends.

He pulled his T-shirt over his head, turned it inside out, and dropped it on the moldy hay. Trickles of sweat rolled down his face, but he paid it no mind. He was breathing hard, not from the climb, but from the anticipation of seeing their faces again. And then, when he could wait no more, he opened the tin box.

Buck's cell phone vibrated and he took the call. "Abbie? Is that you? Is everything all right out there?"

"No. It isn't." She sounded upset. "Onicox Realty has put up *no trespassing* signs all over the property. We were asked to come here. I thought the prospective buyers had agreed to the excavation. How could Onicox change their minds without giving me the courtesy of a phone call?"

"You think they put them up in the night?"

"Your brother Harry says that they were up when he arrived at six o'clock this morning."

"Is he there? Let me speak to him."

"Hey!" Harry's husky voice came over the line. His little brother was nineteen and topping six feet, but it was difficult for Buck to think of him as a man even if he was starting college in September. "Just like she said. It was posted when I got here."

"How'd you come? Boat?"

"Yeah. Bowman stayed until dark. Bastards must have snuck in during the night. You hear anything about why they did it?"

"No, I haven't."

"I've a mind to light a bonfire with these signs."

"Don't do that, Harry. I don't want to arrest my baby brother for destruction of private property."

"You would, too."

"Wouldn't want to. But I can't play favorites. You break the law, I have to come down hard on you."

"Not if you didn't know who burned the signs."

"Forget it. There's a legal way, and we'll find it. Put Abbie back on."

"They stole my tent—my tools," she said. "The stakes have all been pulled up. Pit walls kicked in."

The signal wasn't great, and it was hard to hear her clearly, but he got the gist of it. Harry and Bowman had been taking turns watching over things for him while Abbie was in Oklahoma. Until today, nothing had been disturbed.

"Now do you believe me? Somebody's gone to a lot of trouble to keep me from finishing the site evaluation."

"Why don't you let Harry bring you back in the boat?"

"What? It's difficult to hear you."

"Come back to town with Harry. Let me see what I can find out."

"This is not going to stop me, Buck. I swear to you—"

"We'll straighten this out. I promise."

His first call after ending the conversation with Abbie was to Emma. She didn't answer. His second was to the parsonage. Apparently, Matthew wasn't home either. His third call connected with Forest McCready on the fifth ring.

"We were told that the archaeological excavations would not be disturbed," Forest said once Buck informed him of the situation. "Let me see what I can do about this. What time is it? A little after eleven? I might be able to catch a friend for lunch."

"Abbie Night Horse will want to know something definite. It was all I could do to keep Harry from tearing down those signs. She claims that her tent and equipment were stolen."

"I'll get back to you in a few hours. Keep the lid on everything there until I do."

It was half past two when Forest rose from the corner table at the King James Tavern and shook his lunch companion's hand. "I appreciate the favor, Miles. With your Eastern Shore roots, you're in a unique position to understand what we're up against with Onicox."

"Glad to help. If there's anything else I can do, don't hesitate to call. And when the rocks start biting, don't forget me."

"Have I ever?"

The judge smiled. "My Livia isn't particularly fond of seafood, but she makes an exception for rockfish, especially the way our cook broils it with lemon."

"Give her my best."

"I'll do that."

Forest finished the pleasantries, left a generous cash tip for the waitress, and picked up his briefcase. He took time to greet associates, friends, and politicians as he made his way slowly out of the crowded dockside restaurant. The King James was a favorite watering hole for lawmakers in Annapolis, and he often thought more disputes were settled and alliances formed there than in the statehouse a few blocks away.

Once outside, he strolled down the waterfront past tourists and locals admiring the sailboats and feeding the seagulls until he reached the *Gone Fishing*. He stepped off the dock onto the deck, walked up to the bridge, and punched in the number of the Tawes police department. "I have what we need," he said when Buck picked up. "Signed by Judge Carver."

"Don't know him."

"Sure you do. Miles Carver. Tall black man. Distinguished. Wears glasses and walks with a limp. You went tuna fishing with me and Miles three, maybe four years ago, out of Ocean City."

"Oh, yeah. Good fisherman. Wasn't he in Desert Storm?"

"Yes, that was where he lost his left leg from the knee down. Good man. I called him right after I spoke to Pete Elderson. Pete's Onicox's chief attorney. Not a bad sort, but he moved here from Chicago. High-powered city lawyer. It will take him a while to figure out how we do things in Maryland."

"Did he give any reason for posting property they haven't taken possession of?"

"Some nonsense about the Gilbert boy's drowning and Dr. Knight's death. They were afraid that they might be liable for any accidents out there. You know how sue-happy people are today. I told him that I doubted Onicox could be held responsible, but he wasn't particularly open to my opinion."

"Did you ask about Abbie's tent and tools?"

"Elderson denied that his people removed anything from the site. He said that if vandals had stolen or destroyed property, that was all the more reason it should be off limits to the public."

"And that was when you reached out to Judge Carver?"

"I thought it was time to stop Onicox before they started putting up barbed wire and sentry boxes. Miles didn't take kindly to the loss of Miss Night Horse's property."

"Neither do I. There hasn't been anything stolen on Tawes since I've been here. At least, no one has come forward to complain of theft."

Forest chuckled. "Not likely. Not on our island. We wouldn't tolerate a thief among us."

Buck waited, knowing that Forest liked to spin out a tale as well as the next man, but eventually he would get to the point.

"Told Miles what I needed. We had lunch together, and I got the paperwork." Forest glanced at his briefcase. "I imagine that Elderson will cry foul, but we've pretty much tied the corporation's hands for three months. That will give me time to follow up on a lead."

"That Sherwood's claim to the land wasn't valid?"

"Exactly. And that might be easier to do than finding out who the next of kin really is. You know how the family trees are intertwined on Tawes. McCreadys and Parkses are related to everybody else. The ones who aren't cousins would have been if their parents had been married."

"You can say the same about the Davis clan. The only folks I know I'm not related to are the Williamses and the Washingtons."

Forest chuckled. "Not certain you can say that either. Our black families have been here longer than the McCreadys, the Tilghmans, or the Loves. And they've always been freemen."

"I know that the island was antislavery."

"Probably because so many of the early settlers married Nanticoke Indian women. Especially Tawes men."

"All right, Forest, let me get this point clear. If Abbie Night Horse and anyone accompanying her go onto the Indian site, they're not breaking any laws."

"Not only that, son. In layman's terms, what I have here states that Sherwood's relative, one Robert Mellmore, has no clear claim on the land. Thus, he has no legal right to sell to Onicox or anyone else until the matter is settled. The option is on hold, and Onicox may not break ground or exercise any control over the property until the matter is settled in a court of law."

"Sounds good."

"Excuse me!" An attractive brunette in her mid-forties was calling to Forest from the dock. Behind her stood a young man with a large camera balanced on one shoulder. "Mr. McCready?"

"I've got uninvited company," Forest said to Buck. "The press. I'll show you the papers when I get back to Tawes."

"Roger that," Buck answered.

Forest descended the bridge to offer his hand. "Miss Quinn, I believe. I'm flattered. What can I do for you?"

"I wonder if you could answer a few questions."

Forest flashed his professional smile and waved her to a chair. "Certainly. If I can." He noticed that the camera appeared to be running.

"This is Ron Link." She indicated the cameraman. "You don't mind, do you?"

"What would you like to know?" He'd seen her

piece on the island curse earlier in the week. Tess Quinn was all charm and sweetness on air, but he'd heard she was a shark when tracking down a story.

"As I understand, you're a longtime resident of Tawes?"

Forest nodded. "My family settled on the island in the eighteenth century."

Tess smiled into the camera. "Tawes has remained isolated, an island with one foot in the past and the other in the future." She turned to McCready. "Is it true that no outsiders have purchased land on Tawes for over two hundred years?"

"That may be," he conceded. "Certainly not in my lifetime."

"And that no motor vehicles are permitted on the island?"

He shook his head. "Tractors, motorbikes, gators, even a go-cart or two, but no cars or trucks." He smiled. "Our roads are not the best."

"And most of the inhabitants still make their living from the bay?"

He nodded. "Most do."

"Yet . . ." She consulted her notes. "You have a substantial law practice in Annapolis as well as on Tawes."

Forest chuckled. "I don't know if you could call it substantial, Miss Quinn, but I do practice law."

"And you are one of the driving forces attempting to keep development, specifically Onicox Reality, from building a marina and housing complex on Tawes?"

"I wouldn't say that."

"Come now, Mr. McCready. Haven't you brought legal action against Onicox Reality, to prevent them from building on land they recently purchased?"

"No comment."

"But you are against the construction of a marina?"

"Have you tried to drive around Kent Island on a weekend? There are so many tourists, it's a nightmare."

"Are you the one responsible for bringing in a noted archaeologist—Dr. Karen Knight—to investigate the possibility of a significant Indian burial ground on the property?" Tess thrust a handheld microphone closer to his face. "A respected scholar who was murdered two weeks ago in Philadelphia?" She looked back at the camera. "It has been alleged that the murder weapon was a two-thousand-year-old Indian hatchet."

"Yes," Forest admitted. "I've heard that a stone ax was found at the crime scene and it may have been the murder weapon."

"Our sources confirm that blood found on the hatchet was that of Dr. Knight," Tess said, looking at him for a reaction.

"I'm sure your sources are more accurate than mine."

"And the Native American burial ground on the marina site has long been regarded by the islanders as cursed. Is that true, Mr. McCready?"

He smiled. "Some may believe that." *Damnable female*, he thought. *I'm bound to end up looking foolish if this piece airs.* "I can't say that I believe in ghosts."

"Dr. Karen Knight, herself a member of the Delaware Indian tribe, isn't the first person connected to the burial ground to fall victim to foul play," Tess declared. "Earlier this month, a midshipman, Sean Gilbert, met a tragic death under unexplained circumstances. And several decades ago, a Deal Island waterman, Fleming Caulk, was found dead aboard his fishing vessel in that same marsh. Both Mr. Gilbert and Mr. Caulk had been digging in the burial ground shortly before their deaths."

Forest leaned back in his chair. "It's my understanding that Mr. Caulk's demise was ruled accidental, and young Mr. Gilbert's cause of death is still being determined."

"Three unexplained deaths," Tess said dramatically, turning to face the camera. "An ancient Indian burial ground, a curse, and the deaths of three people who dared to dig in hallowed ground. Could it be that there are more things between heaven and earth than can be rationally explained?"

CHAPTER ELEVEN

Bailey lifted her shirt and stared at herself in the full-length mirror in her dressing room. Her belly looked a little pudgy, and her jeans were getting tight. The baby couldn't be any bigger than a walnut. How could she be getting fat already? She'd barely had an appetite for weeks. Emma had warned her that all that would change soon enough, but if she was gaining weight now—what would happen when she started eating for two?

She'd been walking out the door when she'd gotten the call from Abbie telling her that Onicox Realty had posted the property. She was both surprised and disappointed. Karen's tragic death had robbed Abbie of a loving mother and her of a good friend. Knowing how close Abbie had been to her mother had made Bailey all the more willing to do whatever she could to ease Abbie's pain.

Bailey was certain Abbie would need her help to complete the site evaluation. She didn't doubt that the young woman was a competent archaeologist. Karen had praised her highly, and she was a hard taskmaster when it came to a dig. But this was Tawes. What worked on the mainland didn't always fly here. The islanders were superstitious and set in their ways and didn't trust anyone whose great-great-grandparents hadn't been born here. They could find a hundred ways to delay or impede the project if they wanted to. Bailey might be a newcomer to Tawes, but she was one of them—blood kin. And that meant everything here.

Bailey couldn't imagine why the realty company would want to cause trouble by suppressing the excavations they'd already agreed in writing to permit. Denying access to the Indian burial ground would set Tawes in a spin. By evening, half the couples on the island wouldn't be speaking to each other. And she was afraid that some of those who'd been in favor of progress would change their minds.

She and Daniel had taken opposite sides on the marina project. The morning had started out so great, she'd hoped she could convince him to see her side. She'd only taught one year in the Tawes school, but the future of these children—of her own child— meant the world to her. She'd prepared some good arguments, but after they'd exchanged words, she hadn't even wanted to be in the same room with him until they both had time to cool down. She couldn't help wondering if falling for Daniel so quickly had been another huge mistake.

Not the pregnancy, however. Unplanned or not, now that she'd gotten over the shock, she wanted to be a mother desperately. She couldn't imagine a better father for her child than Daniel. He'd be terrific. Her concern was with her own judgment in choosing him as a second husband.

Sure, sex between them was fantastic—the stuff of romance novels. She was mad for him, and she knew he loved her. At least, she hoped he did. But nothing on Tawes was ever simple, and Daniel held true to the mold. He was the most secretive, endearing, and exasperating man she'd ever met. And if they didn't have trust as a foundation, how could they build a lasting marriage?

She dropped her shirt and made a face at herself in the mirror. What was it Emma was fond of saying? "You can't make an omelet without breaking eggs." She had certainly broken a few eggs this morning when she'd practically thrown Daniel out of the house. But he deserved it. He was so . . . so damned male. She didn't believe that he'd told her everything he knew about his possible son. How could he be so thickheaded that he couldn't understand her need to discuss such an important problem?

If Daniel did have a son in Afghanistan, where did that leave her and their coming baby? Would he want to fight for custody of Mallalai's child? If the little boy was being cared for by loving grandparents or other relatives, would it be fair to intervene? Was she being selfish? She'd never thought of herself as a jealous person, but she had zero experience with babies and small children. Was she capable of caring for a toddler and a newborn? In all likelihood, the boy wouldn't understand English. How would she communicate with him?

A small bubble of regret surfaced . . . an ache that another woman might have given birth to Daniel's first child and that the boy would always be a living reminder of his mother.

Shame that she could worry more about her own insecurities than about a motherless child enveloped her. If Daniel had a son, that little boy deserved to know his father. She loved Daniel Catlin, and she'd have to have a hard heart if she could deny a motherless child a place in her life.

Starting married life with two small children would be difficult, but when had anything ever been easy for her? She had friends on Tawes; she had Will and Emma. If she could just convince Daniel to share his secrets and concerns with her, they could be happy together, couldn't they?

She slipped her feet into flip-flops and made her way downstairs to the kitchen where she'd used a kiddy gate to lock Puzzle in the kitchen. The coating Daniel had applied to the old wide boards in this room made it impervious to puppy errors, and there wasn't anything for the dog to chew here but her toys. At eight months, Puzzle was theoretically housebroken, but she did commit an occasional transgression. Bailey didn't want to risk her Aunt Elizabeth's beautiful rugs or the small Oriental one that Daniel had given her for her birthday.

She petted Puzzle and went to the refrigerator for something cold to drink. She'd taken the mandatory prenatal vitamins earlier with a rice cake, but her stomach still hadn't settled enough for orange juice. She decided to weed the flower beds so the day wouldn't be a total loss. One way or another, she was determined to get her hands in dirt this morning. Maybe she could work out her frustrations by yanking wire grass and deadheading her marigolds.

An hour later, she rose from her knees, dusted off her hands, and admired the progress she'd made. If it didn't rain this afternoon, she'd have to run a hose down here and give the flower bed a good watering. Her back ached, but her black funk had lifted and she felt much better.

Puzzle was happily pouncing on unwary grasshoppers in her fenced-in yard. The little dog had gone into a frenzy earlier, barking and running back and forth, without apparent reason. Corgis, Bailey had discovered, were nothing if not drama queens, but the pup seemed content now. Bailey decided to leave her outside and went back into the house alone. She hoped she could find feta cheese. She was suddenly ravenous for a Greek salad with olives, onions, and fresh tomatoes.

Bailey had washed her hands and was rummaging in the back of her refrigerator when she heard a baby crying. "What in the world . . ." Had she left the television on in her bedroom? The crying sounded as though it were coming from upstairs, but she couldn't remember watching TV this morning. She put the jar of black olives on the table and hurried through the dining room to the stair hall.

The crying came again . . . this time fainter. Could the electricity have fluctuated and the television come on by itself? Stranger things had happened in this house, and that could have been what had set Puzzle barking earlier. Hadn't she read that a dog's hearing was many times greater than a human's?

Bailey started up the stairs and stopped at the hall landing. She couldn't hear anything now. Had she been imagining she'd heard a baby? All her worry might have—No. There it was again.

She had taken two steps toward her bedroom suite when she heard a loud smack followed by a shriek. She ran the rest of the way, threw open the bedroom door, and rushed in. There was no sound but the loud tick of her mantel clock. The room was empty. A rush of adrenaline made her shiver.

"Who's there? Is anyone there? Daniel, if this is your idea of a joke . . ." She crossed to the dressing room and pushed open the door.

A child's sobs filled the room. Bailey's eyes widened as she spied a silver tape recorder lying on her makeup table.

"Bailey Elliott, I presume?"

She whirled to face a man standing in the doorway and couldn't hold back a gasp of fright.

He was holding a knife.

"All taken care of," Buck announced as Abbie entered his office, followed by his brother Harry. "I've just gotten off the phone with Forest McCready and he worked his magic with a friendly judge. You can dig to your heart's content."

"For sure?" Harry opened the small refrigerator and took out a soda. "You thirsty, Abbie?" he asked. "I see green tea, bottled water, diet iced tea, root beer, grape, and orange." He popped the top of his can and took a drink. "Hot as he—"

Buck's scowl cut him off in mid-word.

"Hot as fried eggs, out in that marsh." Harry reddened. "Sorry, ma'am. You should have seen the sheep fly I swatted. Big as a yearling calf."

Abbie smiled. "I don't think it was quite that big. I'll have green tea, please." She glanced at Buck. "Unless we're about to consume public property, Officer."

He grinned. "Tawes pays my salary and for my uniform. The fridge and contents are all mine. Help yourself. There's lunchmeat and cheese in there if you're hungry."

"Sounds tasty." Harry dug out a loaf of bread and a jar of pickles. "I could eat something. How about you, Abbie?"

"No, thanks." She sat on the edge of Buck's desk.

"Do you want to go back out to the site?"

"No, it's too late. I'll go out first thing in the morning. I need to order a new tent and some tools to replace the ones that were stolen. Trowels, a roll of twine, notebooks. Luckily, I didn't leave my camera or Mom's notes in the tent."

"You can probably get some of the stuff at Dori's."
Harry paused in the construction of his sandwich.
"Got any tomatoes?"

"No tomatoes. Sorry." Buck met Abbie's gaze.
"There are some great sporting-goods stores in Salisbury. We could take the boat over to Crisfield and
drive up—"

"No, thanks," Abbie said. "It's probably just as fast to
order what I need on the Internet. The company I
deal with offers overnight shipping."

"This is Tawes, babe. You'll be lucky if they can find
the island, let alone deliver in less than a week. If you
want to replenish your stock, I'd suggest you take me
up on the offer."

She adjusted her sunglasses and peered at him.
"And you can just walk away from the office? Aren't
you on duty?"

He grinned. "It's the nice thing about being chief.
The good citizens of Tawes aren't likely to complain,
so long as I put in a full week's work."

"He—heck," Harry corrected. "It's not like we're
having a crime wave here." He realized his mistake
and blushed again. "I mean here on Tawes. Haven't
had a fight at the local pool hall since I was fifteen."

"The communal billiards played on this island are
mostly in Emma's barn. Not many people want to risk
getting on her bad side. She can crack some heads."
Buck gestured toward the door. "I know some good
restaurants in Salisbury just down the highway from
the sporting-goods store."

Abbie looked uncomfortable. "I need the supplies,
but I'm not really in the mood for—"

"Supper?" He shrugged. "You can't work without
your equipment, and if we're in Salisbury, you still
have to eat."

"It . . ." She hesitated. "My mother is—"

"Abbie, she wouldn't expect you to go hungry. If you want to start excavating first thing—"

She nodded. "All right. Supper. But . . . nothing else."

Buck glanced at his brother. "Let the answering system pick up any messages. If there's an emergency, you can reach me on my cell. And lock up when you leave."

The cell phone rang and rang. After the eighth or ninth ring, a computer voice declared that the number was temporarily out of service "Damn." Bailey must be already out at the dig site. Daniel snapped his cell shut and wondered if the wisest thing was to join her there or to simply contact his former superiors at the agency and tell them that Lucas had attempted to blackmail him.

After he'd left Bailey's, he'd been too frazzled to work on the cabinets he was replacing for Emma. Instead, he'd gone into the Tawes market and bought honey for his tea and a few other necessities, such as toilet paper and a newspaper. While he was there, he checked his post office box in the back room of Dori's Market. His bank statement was several days overdue, but still hadn't arrived, typical for mail delivery on the island. His only mail was an envelope marked with the logo of a company that printed checks, business cards, and labels. He nearly tossed it in the trash, but at the last minute he had a hunch and decided to open it. He ripped the end of the envelope just as Phillip Love strolled into the room.

"Need any stamps today, Daniel?"

"No, thanks," he replied. "I've still got that book of twenty you sold me last week. It's not as though I have a lot of pen pals."

"I suppose not," Phillip said. "Would you tell Bailey

I ordered some of that fancy cheese she's been asking for? Emma and Miss Maude said they would buy it too. Guess it would be worth my while. I'm not runnin' a supermarket. Just plain staples. Crab nets. Bait. Canned soup. Stuff folks can't live without."

The bell on the front door tinkled. As Phillip hurried out into the main store, Daniel exited by the side post office entrance and walked to the back of the building near the dock where he'd moored his skiff. There, sheltered from curious passersby, he examined what was inside the envelope. Plain tan cardboard cut from a carton was folded and taped around two 5 x 7 black-and-white photographs.

His stomach knotted.

The first picture revealed a small dark-haired boy sitting on a bed. The child wore nothing but a diaper. Bruises showed on the crying toddler's arms and legs.

The second 5 x 7, smeared with a black, sticky substance, had been torn into four pieces. When Daniel laid the ragged sections together on the grass, he saw that it was a photo of Bailey leading a horse out of her stable. Scribbled across the picture in block letters were the words LOOSE ENDS, followed by a question mark.

Daniel stared in disbelief at his finger. Not black, but red.

Blood.

He ran for his boat.

"You have a nice place here," the man said.

His speech was precise, without accent or inflexion, the speech of one whose native language was not English. Bailey guessed who he was—who he had to be. "Lucas."

Her knees felt as though they were made of water. She wasn't certain she could stand, let alone run, but she couldn't let him know how frightened she was.

"Smart lady."

She swallowed. If he took a step closer with that knife, she'd vomit all over him.

"So he's told you about my little proposition. About his bastard."

She nodded.

"It wasn't easy, you know. Smuggling the boy out of Afghanistan. I expected Daniel to leap at the chance to get to know his son."

She didn't answer. She clamped her teeth together and tried to keep her balance. Lucas stood between her and the door. She'd have to get past him to have any chance of escaping, and she was so light-headed she could hardly stand.

"Wouldn't you think a man's son would be worth a few hundred thousand dollars?" His thin lips curved into a semblance of a smile. The smile didn't reach his eyes.

Bloodsucker, she thought. Waves of nausea caused a buzzing in her ears. She couldn't keep her gaze off the knife. The six-inch blade was blue-black and thin. "What do you want with me?"

"I thought we could get to know each other better. Since Daniel and I are such good friends. Comrades-in-arms, really. If you know who I am, you must know what Daniel did for a living before he retired to"—he motioned with his free hand—"this backwater."

"If you touch me, Daniel will hunt you down and skin you alive," she said, trying to hide her terror behind bravado.

"Tut, tut, such talk from a beautiful woman like you." He frowned. "And foolish. I don't imagine you've ever seen a man skinned alive, have you?"

"Get out of my house."

"I don't mean you harm. I'm a reasonable man. Do you think I run around invading people's homes for pleasure? I'm a professional, Bailey."

"Professional what? Assassin?"

"Harsh words."

Pins and needles numbed her hands. He was going to kill her. She had to do something or he'd cut her throat and leave her to bleed to death on the floor. And if she died, her baby would die with her. She knew there would be no chance to get past him, but if she could run into the bathroom . . . He couldn't know there was a second door leading out into the hall.

Abruptly she lunged to the right as though attempting to dodge past him. Lucas slashed at her with the knife, but she'd already turned and dashed into the adjoining bathroom.

She threw her weight against the door in an attempt to close and lock it against him, but he was too fast for her. He was strong. Inch by inch, he shoved her backwards. Knowing she couldn't hold him, she ducked aside. The door swung inward, and Lucas came with it. The force of his rush carried him past her and over the rim of the raised tub.

"You son of a bitch!" Seizing the loose towel rack, she ripped it out of the bracket and slammed it against Lucas's head. He screamed, fell, and tried to claw his way out of the tub.

Bailey smashed the heavy metal bar against his head a second time. Lucas tumbled back, blood streaming from his forehead where the loose screws had cut into his face. Bailey brought the bar down again. He slumped down in the Jacuzzi, arms flung wide, legs sprawled over the edge of the tub.

Bailey fled out of the bathroom into the hall and down the front staircase. She ran out of the house. Puzzle barked from her dog run, and Bailey glanced back over her shoulder. If Lucas wasn't critically injured, he would come after her. The gate was at the far end of the fenced yard. As much as she cared for the little dog, she couldn't stop. She ran for the boat and reached the dock just as a bloody Lucas staggered out the front door.

Puzzle saw him, skidded to a stop, and turned to face him, snarling.

Lucas looked at her, then glanced at the dog run.

Bailey flung herself onto the boat and climbed into the captain's chair. When she looked back, she saw that Lucas had opened the gate to the dog run.

"Nice doggy," Lucas said. "Come. Come here."

The pup's hackles rose, and she growled as she crouched down.

Lucas walked toward the dog.

"Puzzle! No!" Bailey shouted. "Leave her alone, you bastard! You bastard," she wept. The key was in the ignition as always. With shaking fingers, Bailey turned it and the engine roared.

Lucas moved closer to the corgi. "Good boy."

Puzzle wiggled uncertainly.

"Come here, doggy."

Sunlight gleamed off the blade of Lucas's knife.

CHAPTER TWELVE

Lucas lunged for Puzzle, but the corgi was too fast for him. The little dog darted away, staying just out of reach. Lucas looked at Bailey and wiped the blood out of his eyes. From the deck of the boat, she could see that he was bleeding profusely. She cast off the mooring lines but kept the motor in idle, ready to pull away from the dock if Lucas came toward her.

The rumble of a boat motor caught her attention, and Bailey glanced toward the bay. Daniel's skiff appeared around the wooded point. He was moving fast. He steered into the shallower water near her sand beach and cut the engine. "Bailey?"

"I'm all right!" she shouted, gesturing toward the house. "There!" Lucas was gone. He'd obviously heard the approaching boat motor and fled around the far corner of the house. Puzzle had darted out of the fenced yard but had run toward the dock instead of chasing Lucas.

Daniel waved to Bailey, and she eased the throttle into reverse, backed away from the dock, and then moved forward toward the mouth of the creek that opened into the bay. Daniel brought his boat up alongside hers. "Are you hurt?"

"That bastard! That sneaking son of a bitch!" she yelled. "It was Lucas! He was in my house! And he had a knife!"

"Did he touch you? What did he say?"

Puzzle yipped and ran toward the path that led to Will's place. Will's dogs burst out of the wooded lane. Seconds later, Will appeared, striding hard, shotgun cradled in one arm.

"I asked Will to watch over you," Daniel said. "I never thought Lucas would come here." He glanced toward the house and orchard. "I'll kill him."

"No! We need to talk." She put the motor in gear and turned the boat in a wide circle, returning to the dock. By the time she reached it, Will was there to secure the lines. Puzzle was in her glory, circling Will's dog Blue and the big Chesapeake retrievers.

"I thought you were going to look after her, Will," Daniel shouted as he approached Bailey and Will on the lawn.

"And I thought you were still here with her." Will scowled. "You spent the night. How was I supposed to know that you left her alone?"

"Leave Lucas to Buck Davis. He's the police on Tawes." Bailey's fear had turned to anger. "Lucas came in my house—threatened me with a knife. I'll press charges against him. I don't care who he works for." Daniel reached to embrace her but she stepped away. "I want the truth—all of it," she demanded.

"He didn't come here to harm you. He came to scare me into paying him three hundred thousand dollars for my son. I've been stalling because I don't know if it's a ruse. I've got no proof the child exists, let alone that Lucas has him."

"Let me set the dogs on his trail. Nothing like a shotgun blast to the knee to set a fellow to talking." Will's thin lips tightened. "On Tawes, we take a dim view of mainlanders threatening our women."

"No, let him go," Daniel said. "Even if he has the boy and we do catch up with him, he'll never tell us where the child is."

"He'll talk for me. I guarantee that," Will said.

"I doubt it. A few years back, Lucas was captured in Somalia. They tortured him for thirteen days. Starved him, staked him in the desert. He never told them a thing." He met Will's gaze. "On the fourteenth day, Lucas escaped, killed five men, and crawled for two days to the pickup site. When they airlifted him to a hospital in Pretoria, he had a broken femur, a shattered jaw, and a dislocated shoulder."

"Maybe he isn't as tough as you think," Bailey flung back. "I beat the sh— . . . Well, let's say I bent that loose bathroom towel bar over his head and messed up his face. He'll be lucky if I didn't blind him."

Amusement danced in Will's blue eyes. "Did you, girl? Now, that's something. More of your mother in you than I suspected."

"You'll contact the agency, won't you?" she urged Daniel. "They can't condone this sort of—"

"Lucas isn't with the agency anymore. He vanished months ago. Last December, when they called me in to the office, they were asking about him. Same in the spring."

"All the more reason you should tell them," Bailey said.

"Maybe. Maybe not."

Bailey sighed in frustration. "When exactly did you learn about the baby?"

"Just before Karen's murder."

Her voice dropped to a near whisper. "Do you think

it's a coincidence that Lucas reappears on Tawes and then she's the victim of a random street crime?"

"Maybe Bailey's got something. Maybe this hired killer had a hand in the murder," Will suggested.

"It's possible, but I doubt it. It's not his style. He's usually not that messy."

"No? It seems I recall another death that wasn't so clean," Bailey reminded him.

"That was different. What happened last summer was quick, and it could be passed off as hit and run. Karen's murder was different. She was bludgeoned to death. There would have been blood spatter—evidence. If Lucas were the killer, he would have gone to her house when she was asleep and garroted her. Or shot her."

"I was certain he meant to kill me," Bailey said.

He shook his head. "If he had, you'd be dead. No, it was a message to me that he's serious."

"We have to tell the police," she insisted.

"I doubt that Lucas is a danger to anyone but me," Daniel said. "He isn't a madman. And he's not irrational. But I'm not taking any more chances with you. I'm not letting you out of my sight until this is finished."

"Finished how?" she asked. "Can't we just go to the police? Or the C.I.A.?"

"It's too risky. If I called in the agency, they might catch him or they might not. But Lucas would take it as a professional insult. He wouldn't rest until he'd gotten satisfaction."

"Satisfaction?"

"Killing both of you," Will supplied.

The fear Bailey had thought gone crept back. Her arms prickled with gooseflesh as she saw the two men she loved most in the world exchange meaningful glances. "You promised me, Daniel. You promised me all this was over."

Will knelt and scratched Puzzle behind the ears.
"How do you want to handle this?"

"I'll wait, keep Bailey safe. Lucas will get in touch
with me. He won't give up the possibility of all that
cash so easily."

"You're not going to pay him?" Bailey's eyes widened
in surprise. "Blackmail? And where would you get that
much money?"

"Trust me, hon. I'll handle this."

"Sure you will. I can see what a wonderful job you've
done so far."

Buck's SUV was parked in a secured area at one of the
smaller Crisfield marinas. Within two hours of dock-
ing the boat, they'd driven north to Salisbury and
completed the shopping. "We can pick up anything
else you think of after we eat," Buck said as he loaded
Abbie's new tent and camping gear into the back.
"What are you in the mood for?"

He'd been right. She was hungry. They decided on
Mexican, and ten minutes later, they were sitting at a
table in a crowded restaurant and perusing the menu.
"What do you suggest?"

A lazy smile transformed him from attractive to
sexy. "I like it all. Surprise me."

The waitress took their drink orders—beer for him,
iced tea for her—and brought spicy salsa and chips.
Diego's was noisy, but their booth gave them enough
privacy to talk without shouting.

Abbie touched his hand. "Thanks. You made it all
easy. What would I have done without you?"

He beamed. "You'd have managed. I doubt that you
let anything stand in your way once you decide to do
something."

"You make me sound formidable."

"Aren't you?"

"I like you, Chief Davis." She smiled. "Even if your name is Buck."

"And I like you, even if you are a hostile."

The waitress brought their drinks and wrote down Abbie's requests. "I hope you're hungry," she said. "I'm not much of a drinker—that Indian thing—but I'll wager I can eat you under the table."

"Haven't seen much of this appetite at Miss Emma's."

She folded her arms and rested her elbows on the colorful tablecloth. "Have you heard anything more from the detectives? Anything new?"

He shook his head.

"And you won't. Not if they're looking in Philadelphia."

Buck removed the section of lime from the lip of his beer bottle and took a sip.

"You don't like lime?"

"In iced tea. Not in my beer."

She took a sip of her iced tea and added sweetener. Near the kitchen, a server placed a candlelit confection in the center of a crowded table while a procession of waitresses in red and green dresses clapped and sang "Happy Birthday" to a white-haired Hispanic woman in a wheelchair.

Buck waited until the cheers and laughter of well-wishers had subsided before saying, "There were two hundred and fifty murders in the city last year. A lot of them will never be solved."

"It's not just my mother. There's Sean Gilbert."

"I'm still waiting for the boy's autopsy report. But drownings happen all too often on the bay."

She laid her hand on top of his. He had large hands, nicely shaped, not clumsy as some big men's hands were. Her mother had always said you could tell a lot about a man by his hands. Buck's were spotlessly clean

with a fine dusting of red-gold hair on the back and
nails filed straight across.

"It's hard," she said. "I keep forgetting that she
isn't . . ." Her vision blurred and she blinked back
gathering tears. "Sorry." She wiped her eyes with a tis-
sue from her purse. "I thought I was past that."

"Same way with my dad. It comes back when you
least expect it."

She nodded. "I think of something I want to tell her,
and then I realize I can't. I'll never be able to."

"Missing them—it never goes away. Maybe it's not
supposed to."

"It's not fair."

"Nope."

"When did you lose your father?"

"I was a sophomore in college."

"Illness?"

"Car accident. Dad was a reservist. Coast Guard. On
his way to a weekend training exercise. Drunk ran a
light and hit him broadside."

"I'm sorry."

"The driver had just gotten out of jail for another
DUI. Hadn't even gotten his license back."

"Does it get better? Do you ever stop missing them
so bad you want to die yourself?"

He turned his hand over and squeezed hers. "It gets
better. It doesn't go away, but it gets better."

"The difference is, *you* knew who to blame."

"Don't waste your life hating a shadow."

"What would it take to make you believe me—to
make you see that Ânati's death wasn't a random
killing?"

"Facts. Solid, indisputable facts."

"That's fair. And if I can produce facts, you'll help
me find her killer?"

"Deal."

She leaned over and brushed his cheek with a kiss.

Buck caught her arm. "I think we can do better than that." He kissed her mouth.

Abbie closed her eyes and savored the taste of his lips, mingled with the flavor of the salsa, salt, and Mexican beer. "I don't suppose you know of a nice motel near here . . ."

"Thought you'd never ask."

They left a trail of clothing from the door to the bed.

Buck barely got the door closed before she stepped out of her shorts and yanked her tee over her head. She was wearing a bra today, but it wasn't much more than a handful of lace. Her thong panties left little to the imagination.

He was as hot for her as she was for him. He groaned as she nibbled her way down his chest and dropped to her knees. He was full and ready and breathing in deep gasps, but she stroked and kissed him past the point of no return.

There was nothing tender in their lovemaking tonight. Her need was raw and his was driving. When he pressed her back against the heaped pillows, she was wet and sobbing with wanting him. But Buck had other ideas. He spread her legs wide and buried his head between her thighs. She gasped when she felt the touch of his warm tongue. He knew all the right places. As he was so fond of saying, he aimed to please.

She wasn't disappointed.

They had sex again and shared laughter in the shower. Buck Davis had a great sense of humor, and he was no slouch when it came to stamina or knowing what a woman liked best.

Later, he held her, stroked her hair, and listened as she talked about small things she and her mother had done together—burnt dinners, flat tires, fishing trips when no one had remembered to bring hooks. He was as good a listener as he was a lover. When they finally fell asleep sometime in the wee hours, she slept, really slept, and had no bad dreams to haunt her in the morning.

Forest found Emma's mother in her henhouse gathering eggs. Her sheepdog barked a greeting, and he waited for Aunt Birdy to realize she had company.

"Morning," she called. "Who is it?"

"Just me. Forest. You're out and about early." He stepped aside as she made her way out of the chicken house with a wicker egg basket over one arm. "Skip." The dog came obediently to her side. The elderly woman was so short that she could easily grasp a handful of shaggy hair. "Come on into the house. Have you had breakfast yet?"

"I did," he said. "But don't tell me that's peach pie I smell. Have you been baking already?"

She chuckled and—guided by the dog—led the way up the porch steps and into the big kitchen. Three pies stood cooling on a sideboard, and the table was set for two with cups, saucers, forks, and spoons. A bouquet of wildflowers spilled over a white crockery pitcher in the center of the tablecloth. "Sit down, sit down. I'll pour you some coffee."

Forest sat in one of the high-backed oak chairs. "You look awfully pretty this morning, Aunt Birdy."

She twittered. "Hush that slick lawyer's tongue, Forest McCready. You lie like a rug. You think just because I'm old, you can get around me with honey talk? Why do folks always talk to old people like they're half-witted?"

He laughed. "I think I can talk you out a slice of that peach pie to go with my coffee."

She brought the coffeepot to the table. "Who do

you think I bake these pies for, son? Emma will be by directly. I always have company when I bake pies." She chuckled. "You want cream? It's in the refrigerator."

"Yes, ma'am." He retrieved the cream, and they talked about the weather and the price of soybeans this year. In true island fashion, Forest knew better than to bring up the reason for his visit without enjoying a little hospitable conversation first.

"A terrible shame about that nice lady being murdered in the city, wasn't it?" Aunt Birdy said. "Emma thinks it was the curse killed her. Old-time people knew better than to disturb the dead, even if they were Indians."

Forest stirred sugar into his coffee. "What do you think? Do you believe in curses?"

Aunt Birdy pursed her mouth and closed her sightless eyes. "Depends on whether it's day or night. Sometimes, in the dark of night, I could swear I hear Emma's father padding barefoot down the hall. He always used to check that front door to make certain it was locked. Wasn't that foolish? Nobody on Tawes ever locked a door in the old days, but he wanted that front door bolted. Not the kitchen door, just the front. And once he took off his shoes, he'd go around in stocking feet, winter or summer. When I hear those footsteps, I think maybe there's ghosts. But curses? I never did believe in curses."

She rose, took a knife from a drawer, and returned to cut a generous piece of pie. It was still warm, and the scent filled the kitchen.

"Nobody makes pies like you do."

"Not too many make pies at all. Emma tells me that foolish Mary Love has store-bought pies for sale in Dori's. You know they've got to be stale. Pie is like sweet corn. Best eaten the same day it's cooked."

"I was wondering about something, and I thought

you might be the one to help me," Forest said. "I need to know about the old families on Tawes. The Tilghmans, the Catlins, the Parkses."

"Tawes. They was here first," she reminded him as she served the pie. "Why on earth would you want to know that? And why not go to Matthew? He fancies himself a historian—least, that's what Emma says."

"You know I don't want this land sale going through any more than Emma does."

"Or me. I sure as hellfire don't want mainlanders here, racing up and down in their little sports cars and dirtying up our water." Aunt Birdy took a dainty forkful of pie and lifted it to her mouth. "Needed more cinnamon. I was worried about that."

"The pie is wonderful," Forest said. "Perfect."

"Would be if it had more cinnamon."

"Thomas Sherwood never paid the taxes on that farm. Neither did his grandfather. The taxes were always paid out of the fund."

She nodded solemnly. "And the fund came from folks all over the island putting in part of their whiskey-making money, and before that, smuggling. To keep the pirates in Annapolis from seizing island land and auctioning it off at sheriff's sale."

"Exactly."

"You're not telling me anything I didn't know." She sipped her coffee. "Old man Sherwood never owned the place outright. He was a tenant farmer. Rented the ground off of Sam Tilghman. 'Course, old Sam died in the trouble between the states. On one of them ironclad boats, I think Mama said. Sam never married. No kids."

"I've heard that before—that Sherwood never owned the property. But I need proof. I'm examining the deeds in the county courthouse and in Annapolis. The records are not good before the Civil War. Sherwood's farm seems to be one of the missing. There's a later bequest to Thomas from his father, mentioning the farm. But if the grandfather never held title to the property . . ." He took another forkful of peach pie. "The best you've ever made."

"Maybe. Peaches were good this year." She nibbled at the crust. "That land was originally part of a grant from Lord Balt'mer hisself. Should be papers going all the way back."

"Should be." Forrest chuckled. "What's that saying? Shoulda, woulda, coulda?"

"I believe I heard that a Tawes girl married a Parks sometime after the British come up the Chesapeake and burned Washington. They built the brick house on that land."

"The War of 1812?"

"Yeah, that was it. But that farm traded hands again maybe ten years later when Peregrine McCready bought it off John Parks's widow. It went to Peregrine's oldest boy when he passed. Seems to me that Mama said Sam Tilghman bought it in the fifties, 1850s that was. Let me think on it. My memory's not what it used to be, but it will come to me."

Forest wiped his mouth with a napkin. "If Robert Mellmore's attorneys can't produce a clear land title, I want to prove who should have inherited and who it belongs to now."

"Handshake was the way old-time people did business. Old Sam and Sherwood might not have writ up papers on the deal." She sighed and threw up her hands. "Long time ago."

"We have to find proof if we want to stop the sale."

"Church records would be the best."

"I'd hoped you might have a family Bible. Old letters. Something that mentioned the families who lived on that land."

"You know I have my great-granddaddy's Bible. I showed it to you once. It has marriages, births, and deaths listed in it. I know a few other folks who have their old Bibles. I've got Parks, McCready, Tilghman, a Davis or two. Lots of old letters too, but none with what you're lookin' for."

"I'd appreciate it if you'd look, ask around for me."

"For hard proof, your best bet would be the old Methodist journals," she said. "Every baptism, every death, and every marriage should be in there."

"A lot of records to hunt through. Like looking for a lost crab pot in Queen's Sound."

"Good luck, boy. I'll say a prayer for you. Methodist ministers are good for short sermons and womanizing, not so good on keeping records. But it's a place to start. We sure don't want to be overrun by those mainlanders." She cut him a second slice of pie and slid it onto his plate. "Indeed, we do not."

Looking at the pictures had been a mistake. He'd given in too easily, allowed himself to take pleasure in holding them too soon. It should have made him feel better . . . given him a measure of peace. It didn't. It brought back nightmares.

He had awakened in the night with the boy's screams echoing in his ears. He could feel the cloth in his hands, feel it tear, feel it rip through his fingers. The finality of the *thud* had brought him upright in his bed, wet with sweat, tears streaming down his face.

That was all behind him. He shouldn't have to suffer it again. What was done was done. Anything that came after wasn't his fault. The boy had probably been too stupid to live. Some boys were.

He promised himself that he'd be more careful, discipline himself, remember that it was his wits that had kept him safe this long. No one would understand . . .

no one ever had, except his special friends. He'd loved them, and he missed them so badly.

". . . Ben . . . Isaac . . . Daniel . . . Jonah . . . Le'ron . . . Kwasi . . ."

Just speaking their names aloud made his hands shake and longing fill his heart. It wasn't fair. He needed to remember that he had special work to do. Whatever it took before they realized that the dead were not to be disturbed. His conscience was clear. He was keeping faith with his blood brothers, and most of all with the guardian who'd watched over the graves before he was born.

CHAPTER THIRTEEN

By noon the following day, Abbie had the island dig site organized and all her volunteers at work. George Williams had arrived early and offered to set up Abbie's sleeping tent and a second larger one for storing equipment, food, and any artifacts they might discover—well away from the high-tide waterline. He'd also dug a fire pit, collected dead branches and driftwood for fuel, and set up a crude worktable on sawhorses he'd brought from his farm. Abbie liked George. He saw what needed to be done, consulted with her to find out what she wanted, and completed the task without chitchat or further instruction.

Since so much time had been lost, Abbie had decided to remain here on the dig site until she completed the evaluation. The only thing she lacked was a source of fresh water for cooking and drinking, and George had promised to ferry in containers every day from his well. She'd considered keeping Bailey's horse to get back and forth from town, but decided that tending the animal would be more trouble than hiking in. She doubted that she'd need to go to Tawes often.

Matthew Catlin, Maria Turner, and Phillip Love were excavating one pit, with Mildred Bullin, a seventy-four-year-old retired archaeologist and island native, firmly in command of a second. Abbie, Buck's brother Harry, and Bailey made up the third team. They were staking a rectangle that extended from the base of the hillside up into the trees, the area where Matthew insisted the Irish artifacts had been found.

"We can't sink a proper pit, not without destroying trees," Abbie explained. "What we can do is dig core spots to ascertain the undisturbed layers of soil."

"What if we find traces of a burial?" Bailey asked.

"Then we send Harry for a chainsaw and do serious excavation."

Will Tawes and his three dogs had accompanied Bailey this morning, although he'd hadn't come to assist with the dig. Instead, he'd found a spot on the knoll where Bailey said he could sketch the rare fox squirrels that lived on this part of the island. Will, Abbie noted, had brought a double-barreled shotgun with him. Since it wasn't hunting season, she wondered who or what he meant to shoot at, but she hadn't asked. Bailey's great-uncle was a taciturn man, not someone with whom Abbie would choose to exchange light conversation.

She looped a roll of string around a sapling and stretched the cord tight before moving on to hammer in a third marker. Despite her lack of sleep the night before, she was eager to continue with the work. Buck had brought the tents and supplies to the site early this morning. Not that she wasn't perfectly capable of carrying them in by horseback or hiking in with them, but it pleased her that he was willing to help.

There were a lot of things about Buck that pleased

her. Last night . . . She reminded herself that it was better not to mix work and pleasure. If she started thinking about him and the passionate night they'd shared, she'd be way too distracted. Buck was a complicated man, and she didn't need complications in her life. Not now . . . especially not now. What was important was finishing her mother's dig and finding out who'd killed her and why. She thought she knew why, but she had to have proof—proof powerful enough to convince a judge and jury. Anati's murderer couldn't walk away. She wouldn't allow it, not even if she had to step outside the law.

"I found something!" Harry waved a trowel heaped with black dirt. Sticking out of the organic matter was a thin shard of stone. "I think it's flint."

"Let me see." Abbie, followed by Bailey, Harry, and Matthew, carried the stone down to the beach and washed it. "It's flint, all right," she said, passing the postage-stamp-sized object back to Harry. "Probably from an early flintlock rifle."

Bailey peered at the creamy-gray stone. "A settler's rifle?"

Abbie shrugged. "No way to tell. It's probably not more than two hundred years old, but it would be impossible to tell whether it belonged to a European settler or an Indian. By the eighteenth century, the long rifle was used by both."

"Well, it's something valuable," Harry insisted. "And I found it."

"You did," Abbie agreed. "And now we have to measure the depth of the hole you found it in and properly record the artifact."

"Just because a white hunter passed through here doesn't mean that it wasn't an Indian settlement," Matthew said. "Other than sections of clay trade pipes,

I've never discovered anything of European origin. Not counting the Irish grave goods, of course."

Abbie didn't comment. The missing items were the last things she wanted to discuss. Matthew had taken the loss of the objects hard and repeatedly bemoaned having lent them to her mother and allowing her to remove them from the island.

"I blame myself," he whined. "All those years I kept them safe, and now they're lost . . . to us—to history. What proof, other than my photos, do we have that they existed? Not to speak ill of the dead, but Dr. Knight should have known better than to carry such irreplaceable artifacts on the street at night. I never dreamed she'd be so irresponsible."

Matthew was still talking when Abbie walked away and returned to the wooded slope. For a minister of the gospel, Matthew Catlin showed little humanity or compassion, and it was all she could do not to tell him so. No one would have regretted the losses more than her mother, but it wasn't carelessness that had lost them, and Abbie refused to allow Matthew to disturb her any more than she would Buck Davis.

Daniel's cell phone rang. He'd been expecting the call, but he was surprised that it had come so soon. He would have thought that Lucas would have wanted him to sweat before making contact.

"I pity you." Lucas sounded tired.

"Why so?" Daniel asked.

"She's a royal bitch."

"She can be."

"I wouldn't have hurt her, you know."

Daniel fought for control. Anger would only cloud his judgment, and he needed every advantage to deal with Lucas. "Do I?"

"Danny, Danny, Danny. You know this is strictly business. I like pretty women. They have their place. I take no pleasure in mistreating them."

"She didn't know that."

"She wasn't reasonable. She hurt me."

"Am I supposed to say I'm sorry?" The thought came to Daniel that Lucas might still be on the island—might be just outside the cabin. He peered through the curtainless kitchen window.

"It was a mistake on her part," Lucas insisted.

In the background, Daniel could hear voices, the clink of metal on metal, and a siren. City noises. Lucas wasn't on Tawes. "Are you at a hospital, Lucas?"

"Are you listening? I had to have stitches."

Daniel leaned against the sink. "Remind me to send flowers."

"I assume you collected your mail."

"I did."

"And . . . ?"

"Why have you been spying on Bailey?"

"You know me. If we've never been friends, you must at least have respect for my work. Yet you seem to believe that I'm not serious. Do you want the boy or not?"

"You sent me the photo of a child. How do I know it's my son?"

"Do you think I'm playing games?"

"Bailey is no part of this. Stay away from her."

"What she did was stupid. She was hysterical."

"If I'd been there, I would have killed you."

"You weren't. You never are, are you? Not when you should be."

"Are we talking about the bombing?" Daniel had always wondered if Lucas had had a part in Mallalai's death. He'd never know.

"That's over and done with." Lucas paused. "I may need plastic surgery. It's expensive."

"Is this your clever way of telling me that your price has gone up?"

"Exactly."

"How do I know this isn't a scam, Lucas?"

"No names. Keep that in mind, unless you'd prefer we break contact."

"I need proof that the boy is my son."

"Would DNA suit? I could send you his toothbrush. Or something more substantial. An ear, perhaps?"

"No body parts. What if I didn't go through with the exchange? Mutilating your merchandise would lower his market worth. A toothbrush or a hairbrush would be sufficient to get DNA."

"The problem I see is time. National security being what it is, I find it troublesome to use the commercial airports. And your little island is much too close to Washington for my taste."

Daniel heard the squeal of the fax machine from his second-floor home office. "You've come up with a better solution than DNA," he guessed.

"I will call you one more time. The choice is yours, and the price is now five hundred thousand dollars, wired to my Swiss account. Think it over. I don't like loose ends."

The connection ended, and Daniel raced upstairs to his office. A single sheet lay on the hardwood floor in front of the fax. He snatched it up and carried it to the window.

The black-and-white photo image was slightly out of focus, but Daniel recognized one of the two men in Afghani garb standing in the snow outside a nondescript mud-brick house. Mallalai's brother Zahir carried a Russian Kalashnikov and wore a sheepskin hat and coat, crisscrossed with ammunition belts. The street looked like that of a typical rural village, but what Lucas had wanted him to see was the round-faced toddler with dark ringlets clinging to Zahir's leg . . . a child with Mallalai's eyes.

The tall trees cast late-afternoon shadows across the ruins of Creed Somers's house. Already wild rose and honeysuckle had crept over the blackened timbers and blurred Daniel's memory of what he'd found in the ashes last summer. A man had to concentrate to catch the odor of charred wood, and the salt bay wind had swept the place clean of the stench of death.

Daniel waited in the shelter of the trees until he heard hoofbeats on the grown-over dirt lane before he cupped his hands over his mouth and mimicked a crow's call. Another crow, a bit raspy, cawed back.

"Buck."

His cousin acknowledged his greeting, reined in his horse, and swung down out of the saddle. Daniel steadied the revolver tucked in his belt and strode down the embankment to meet him. "What kind of a sick crow was that?"

"Maybe one dying of West Nile Virus?" Buck said. They both laughed and shook hands before he dug in his saddlebag for two bottles of green tea and offered one to Daniel.

"Thanks for coming out here."

Buck unscrewed the cap and took a swallow of tea. "I take it this isn't police business."

"Strictly off the clock."

Buck dropped the Tennessee walker's reins on the ground and followed Daniel back into the shade, where they found a mossy log to sit on. "Trouble?"

"More than I can handle alone."

"What are cousins for?"

Daniel explained Lucas's attempted blackmail and his invasion and threats to Bailey. Buck listened without comment.

"That's pretty much it," Daniel said.

"You don't feel comfortable taking this back to your former employers?"

"Would you?"

Buck drained the last drops of tea from his bottle and stood it upright in the sand beside his left boot. "Are you going to pay the money?"

Daniel nodded. "I can't see any other way to go."

"You think this is your son?"

"Maybe. Maybe not. How the hell do I know? It's possible. It's also possible that Lucas has some other poor kid up for auction."

"You're willing to take that chance? To pay half a million for an Afghani child that might not be yours?"

"Hell, yeah. Wouldn't you?"

"Sure." Buck laughed. "But you were the bright one of the bunch. I thought you had better sense."

"Will wonders if Lucas may have been in on Karen Knight's murder."

"You think that?"

"You know how Will is—suspicious as hell," Daniel said. "He sees shadows behind every tree."

"Will's a handful, but he's no fool. Funny, Lucas tries to blackmail you, and Abbie's mother is murdered and robbed in the same week. Could be just the luck of the cards . . . or something else. And you say this Lucas is an assassin?"

"No, I can't see it. Beating someone to death with a rock isn't indicative of murder-for-hire."

"My feelings exactly," Buck agreed. "Anytime a victim suffers multiple blows, you have to look at someone close to them."

"I've done some research into Onicox. Regardless of the amount of money to be made in the marina project, nothing tells me that they would be involved in murder."

"It's a wonder we didn't lock horns on the Internet." Buck grinned. "I've spent a few hours trailing that hound myself. I came to the same conclusion." He rested a fist on his hip. "Drugs can make for a bloody crime scene as well. And we could be dealing with a crazy."

"Emma showed me an article about that waterman from Deal who died on his boat a couple of decades ago. If you take him, add Sean Gilbert, and Karen Knight, you have to start wondering if there isn't something to the curse."

"Or something there that nobody wants dug up?" Buck spun the bottle idly in the sand. "I'd hate to think that this poison was rooted on Tawes."

"Will?"

"Will's capable of killing for the right reasons. Killing a man." Buck shook his head. "I don't know if he could murder a woman. I doubt it."

"Emma wouldn't hesitate if she thought it was needed."

"I thought of that. Wish I hadn't, but I did. Some of these islanders would do anything to stop development on Tawes."

"So it's possible that this isn't as complicated as it looks? If Karen Knight dies before she can complete her investigation, people on Tawes might start to wonder if there is something in that burial ground Onicox Realty doesn't want found. People are quick to think the worst about big companies. It wouldn't take much to fire up public sentiment. Enough bad press, and Onicox might rethink buying the property."

"I look at it like a chessboard." Buck used a stick to wipe an area clean of leaves and twigs. "We've got a swamp that folks believe is cursed and a section of prime waterfront property attached. Common sense tells me that there's more money tied to bayside land than marsh."

"Good goose hunting there, though," Daniel observed. "And deer."

"Thick as fleas on a dog's back. Ducks. George Williams claims to have found wildcat tracks out there."

"He's nothing but a drunk. And a liar. You can't believe a word that comes out of his mouth," Daniel insisted. "There hasn't been a bobcat seen on Tawes in ninety years."

"But it's possible. There's enough cover and food to support a pair or two. Could be the source of those screams Emma says she heard."

"Emma's too superstitious for her own good. And she's been known to spin a few tall tales when she's in her cups."

"We've got two deaths—three if you count that old one, twenty years ago. The waterman. And every victim had been digging out there just before they died."

"Lucas can't be a suspect if you go back as far as the man on the boat."

"No, he couldn't be, but he might have killed Sean and Karen Knight to scare people away from the property."

"In which case, Onicox or whoever's behind the murders knows that there's something out there to be found."

Buck used a stick to mark indentations in the sandy soil. "It's a crowded chessboard. I still can't see a way to connect the dots."

"I can count on you to back me up with Lucas? It's a lot to ask. If something goes wrong, it could cost you your career."

"Yeah, it could, but you risked more than a job when

I fell through the ice that time we were skating on Aunt Birdy's pond in March. You were the only one who had nerve enough to crawl out on the ice to throw me your coat."

"I guess I was too stupid to know better."

"Not stupid, Daniel. You could have run like the other kids, but you didn't."

"I knew if I left you there to drown, I could never face Will."

"Blood ties, cuz. They still matter on Tawes."

"A few other places too, I imagine."

"This Lucas—does he work alone?"

"Always. He wouldn't trust the risen Christ to back him up." Daniel frowned. "But he's good, Buck. Really good. You take care, do you hear?"

"I hear you." Buck rose and kicked the sketch until there was no trace left of his musing. "You hear anything from this bozo, you give me a call. I'll come running, and maybe we'll show him what's what."

As Buck rode his horse past her house on his way back to the office, Emma came out on the porch and waved him down. She was wearing her rubber knee boots, coveralls, and a flowery Mother Hubbard apron. "Hey, everybody in town's been looking for you."

"What's up?"

"You had a call from your cousin Tiffany Jackson, John J.'s oldest girl—the one who's a secretary in the state medical examiner's office in Balt'mer. Nate stopped by the police station to check your answering machine. Just in case you had anything important come in. And that's how he found Tiffany's message. She wants you to call her back right after work. She left a number for her cell phone and said call that, not her office number. Sounds important."

"Nice of Nate to do my job for me. Maybe I should deputize him."

"Don't get yourself in a tizzy, boy. Tiffany's his cousin too."

"She wasn't calling Nate, was she? And he's not a deputy yet."

"See what she wants. Funny she called the station instead of your cell. And odd she wanted to talk to you right away, but didn't want you to call her office."

Buck tucked his thumbs into his belt. "Have you thought about starting a town paper? There might be somebody on this island who doesn't know my business before I do. I could buy you a laptop, install a second fax machine in your kitchen, and—"

"Get out of here," Emma fussed. "But don't be late for supper. I've made a pork roast with new red potatoes, homemade applesauce, and beaten biscuits."

"Sounds good for starters. What's the second course?"

She waved her apron at him. "Enough of your nonsense. I've got bread pudding in the oven. Like as not it's burning while I'm standing here jabbering with you."

At the station, Buck checked his mail and finished some paperwork while he waited to return Tiffany's call. At 4:40, when he was certain she'd be on her way home, he punched in her cell number.

"Buck?"

"Hey, how are you? Have you and Dale set a date yet?"

"Are you kidding? That man wrote the book on noncommitment."

"How's your mom and dad?"

For a few minutes they exchanged the necessary family gossip before she finally got to the point of the conversation. "They did the autopsy on Sean Gilbert yesterday."

"And? Any surprises?"

"Do you know how long it will take for them to get the official report to you?"

"I've got a pretty good idea."

"Right, and I guess you know what a state that body was in?"

"Yeah, pretty bad."

"Crabs. They ate—" She broke off. Buck heard Tiffany's old mustang accelerate and the muffled sound of a car horn. "Read between the lines, jerk!"

"Not me, I hope."

She snickered. "No, not you. The Phillies fan in the purple minibus with spray-painted windows."

If he knew Tiffany, she was probably applying eyeliner, drinking a Coke, and munching fries while she maneuvered through rush-hour traffic. He wondered what hand was free to share hand signals with rival drivers.

"Well, wait until you hear this, Buck! Your drowned middy didn't drown. Somebody murdered him."

"Could you repeat that?"

"You can't say a word to anybody. It could cost me my job."

"I know that, hon. Just give me the facts."

She did.

It took him ten minutes to get what he needed and another five to give his airhead cousin enough attention to make certain he'd get a similar *heads up* if he ever had need of it again. "Appreciate the favor."

"Any time," she promised. "You know I'd do anything for you. But remember, mum's the word."

"Absolutely."

"Give Nate and Faith my love."

"Will do."

"And we want a bushel of Number One Jimmy's for Dale's birthday in September."

"Done."

He sat there for a long moment after Tiffany ended the call before uttering a single word. "Shit."

Sean had not died from drowning as everyone had supposed. According to Tiffany, the condition of the boy's lungs proved that he had been dead before he'd gone into the water. Cause of death: blunt force trauma, a blow or blows to the back of the neck inches below the base of his skull, resulting in crushed vertebras and a severed spinal cord.

Sean Gilbert's death hadn't been accidental. He'd been murdered, and the manner of death had an uncanny similarity to those of the waterman and Karen Knight.

CHAPTER FOURTEEN

By six o'clock, everyone had left the dig site but Abbie. Matthew had been the last to depart, trailing Bailey and her uncle Will; he was still complaining about the loss of his Irish artifacts. Although nothing unusual had come to light this afternoon, Abbie was well pleased with the day's work. She'd stripped off her grubby clothes, gone for a swim, and washed her hair, rinsing out the ecologically safe shampoo she always used in the field with well water George had brought in the morning.

It was oddly quiet as she pulled on clean jeans shorts and a cotton tee. There was no sound but the whoosh of the incoming tide lapping on the shore; and the frogs and crickets; she might have been a thousand miles from civilization. No aircraft flew overhead, and she couldn't hear a single boat motor. Even the wind had died. The leaves and marsh grass hung becalmed and motionless. The redolence of crushed grass, newly turned earth, and primeval saltwater marsh filled her head with every breath, but it was the silence that disturbed her. Not a single birdsong resonated from the marsh or wooded grove.

Usually, Abbie enjoyed solitude. Matthew Catlin and Phillip Love talked enough to give anyone a migraine, but now she missed Bailey and the endless chatter of her eager volunteers. The hush over the clearing gave her a hollow feeling, making her question her stubborn insistence on camping on site instead of returning to her comfortable bed at Emma's.

Maybe the marsh did harbor uneasy spirits, Abbie mused. Grandmother Willow had thought so, and so did Aunt Birdy, here on the island. Many people believed that old women and men were demented when they spoke of the supernatural, but she'd always found wisdom in their words. Well, if there were ghosts here, they'd just have to adjust to company. Abbie wasn't easily frightened, and she doubted if nights alone in a Tawes swamp could be anywhere near as spooky as camping in a lonely canyon in Mesa Verde Park or on a two-thousand-year-old Greek battleground.

She wasn't stupid, and she didn't believe that she was invincible. She was certain that Ànati's death had been connected to this dig, but she wasn't a detective or a superheroine. She didn't know of any way to discover her mother's killer other than to find what that person or persons didn't want found. If she did, when she did, the evidence would lead to the guilty party. And if her mother's murderer wanted to come after her to prevent her from making the discovery, she was ready. Sheathed at her belt were two bone-handled throwing knives. She could hit a two-inch circle nine times out of ten at thirty feet.

A rustle from the phragmites drew Abbie's attention. She left the tent, walked to the edge of the marsh, and peered into the tall grass, wondering what had caused the sound when there was no breeze. When she saw nothing to alarm her, she decided she must have heard a muskrat, a snake, or a marsh hen.

Shaking off her apprehension, Abbie finished preparations for the next day's dig. Once her tools were in their proper places, artifacts photographed and bagged, and final notes recorded, Abbie opened her laptop and pulled out a volume on Aegean grave sites that she was using as a reference for her dissertation.

In late August, her work at Penn would begin in earnest. She'd be expected to assist Dr. Maynard, to teach some classes, and to edit an article that Dr. Maynard was preparing for publication. She also had a speaking engagement scheduled for mid-October. She'd be giving a talk and a PowerPoint presentation on her work at Phaistos on Crete two summers ago. September would be so crazy that she'd wanted to get her CDs and notes together now.

Of all the excuses for not being prepared, she didn't want to have to say, "I'm not prepared. I lost the entire summer because my mother was murdered in July."

Realization of the finality of her mother's death brought a lump to Abbie's throat. Shared evenings on a dig site had always been special for the two of them. They'd talked and laughed over the day's triumphs or disappointments, and argued over whose turn it was to prepare the evening meal or who had screwed up dinner the night before. Her mother hated gas grills, preferred cooking over an open fire, and loved her food highly seasoned and heavy on the carbs. Abbie enjoyed her food spicy, but never to the extent Ànati did.

Her mother had been known to add hot chilies and Thai pepper sauce to everything from scrambled eggs to mashed potatoes.

Abbie chuckled as she remembered the spicy Navaho chili, Indian fry bread, succotash, and German chocolate cake with habanero icing that her mother had served to her twelfth-birthday-party guests. Abbie would never forget her best friend Rachel's eyes when she took a large forkful of that fiery cake.

The doctorate and education that had been Abbie's goal for so many years no longer seemed as important. Maybe after she found who'd killed her mother, and after that person was facing a lifetime behind bars, she could find excitement in archaeology again.

She forced herself to concentrate on the article she'd been composing. Her mind felt as sluggish as wet concrete, and her creativity level was at empty. Her piece seemed boring, the writing trite and wooden. When she reread the last paragraph, it made no sense. With a sigh of frustration, Abbie backspaced, deleting most of the screen, then stood and stretched.

A red-winged blackbird flew up out of the reeds, landed on a branch, and delivered an angry tirade. Abbie glanced around the clearing and rubbed her bare arms. The temperature was perfect, in the seventies, and there was no breeze. Still, she shivered. She was definitely losing it. "Back to work," she told herself as she returned to her folding chair and her article. She promised herself she wouldn't stop for dinner until she'd completed four solid pages.

A mosquito buzzed around his head, but he ignored it. He'd worked too hard to reach this spot without being seen, and he wasn't about to give himself away. He wished it were dark, but dusk wouldn't fall over the marsh for hours. The waiting was the worst.

Why hadn't she given up and gone away after her mother got what was coming to her? Why hadn't she learned? He would have let her live. Not now. Now, she had to die like the others. Some people had to pay the price for being stupid.

He'd watched her while she took off her clothes and went into the water as bare as an egg. Splashing, swimming. She had no respect for the dead, showing off her naked body like a whore of Babylon.

He closed his eyes and felt for the section of bone in his pants pocket. He rubbed it, rolling it between thumb and fingers. It felt warm and solid. Holding the small piece of bone comforted him and eased his mind. He would take care of the whore tonight while she was asleep. He didn't know how, but it would come to him as it always did.

He took a deep breath and listened. He was alone now. Sometimes, when he came here to this place at night, he could feel them all around him. All those haunts, and one stronger, more powerful, than the others. He'd never seen their ghosts, not really seen them, but he could make out their shadows in the trees . . . hear them whispering to him. And he knew what they wanted him to do.

Tonight had to be done right. He was sorry he'd thrown the ax down on the sidewalk outside the museum when he'd had to run. It was the doctor's fault. If she hadn't fought so hard and screamed, he wouldn't have gotten frightened and left it behind. It was the finest celt he'd ever seen, perfect, and he'd put great store by it.

He and Daniel had found the ax right here on the beach years ago. He wished he could think of some way to get it back. He wanted his ax, and it wasn't fair for the police to keep his property. But he was too afraid. Better not say anything . . . not give anybody reason to ask questions.

It would have been fitting to kill Abbie Night Horse with the same stone celt he'd used on her mother and the Gilbert boy. Way back in olden times, the celt had been carried here from off somewhere in the mountains to the north. One of the people who was buried here, maybe even the medicine man, had carved it out of rock and used it, maybe even killed his enemies with it.

Now that his ax was gone and he couldn't think of a way to get it back, he had to decide upon a way to do for the girl. He had to make people know it was the curse that killed her for disturbing the dead. Putting a bullet through her head would be quick and easy, but it wouldn't make the ghosts happy. That wasn't their way. They would want him to finish her in the old way. They trusted him, and he couldn't disappoint them. He had to do it right so that people would stay away from the burial ground once and for all.

Abbie heard someone call her name, looked up, and saw Buck striding toward her from the marsh trail. Her mouth gaped. Trotting gaily beside him was a black bear. Not a bear, she realized with a start, but one of the biggest dogs she'd ever seen. This one had to be either a Newfoundland or a Bernese Mountain Dog. Buck carried a knapsack and a bedroll, and the animal wore a harness and carried saddlebags strapped to his back.

She laughed. "What now, Chief? First a white horse and now a bear. They'd love you on the Vegas strip."

"Hey, pretty lady." He grinned at her as she knelt to pat the dog's head.

"What a handsome fellow," she crooned. The dog's

eyes were huge, intelligent, and deep brown. "You have beautiful eyes," she said to the dog. "Yes, you do." She glanced up at Buck. "Does he have a name?"

"Archimedes. Actually, it's Seafarer's Archimedes, but he answers to Archie. He's a Newfoundland."

"I wondered. Are they usually this big?"

"He's oversized for showing. Just a growing boy."

The dog's paws were the size of luncheon plates. He was crow-black with a long thick coat and a single white patch on his chest. "Is he yours?" She patted Archie's head, and a thin trail of drool dripped from the corner of his grizzly-bear mouth.

"My brother Bowman's. Not exactly Bowman's. He was keeping Archie temporarily for his buddy Chuck because the guy is in the military and he couldn't have Archie in the barracks, but then Chuck got shipped overseas. Archie is sort of between homes at the moment. Bowman's fiancée is allergic to dogs and I thought—"

"No." She stood up. "Absolutely, positively not."

Archie offered her his right front paw. She shook it, and he offered the left.

"See that? He likes you."

"Thank you, but I don't need a dog."

"Every woman needs a good man in her life. And Archie's the perfect housemate. He never hogs the TV remote or the bathroom. And he doesn't insist on turning on football when you want to watch ice skating."

"I like football."

"Yeah? Who do you like? Some—"

"Baltimore Ravens."

"No kidding." He laughed. "Hope for you after all, Ms. Night Horse."

"But I'm not taking the dog."

Buck looked down at the Newf. "Did you hear that?

Cover your ears, Archie. I don't remember my offering this wonderful dog to you. I probably wouldn't allow you to take possession of him if you begged me."

"Lucky for me, then."

Buck scowled. "How do I know how you'd treat him? I've never met any Oklahoma hostiles before. Maybe you'd like to serve the dog roasted along with turkey for Thanksgiving dinner."

"Funny. Very funny."

"*I* thought so." He dropped his heavy pack on the ground. "Want company?"

"Not especially," she lied. She was glad to see him, wanted him to stay here with her, wanted his presence to keep away the loneliness.

"Too bad. I'm the law on Tawes, and I'm here whether you like it or not." He unrolled his pack, revealing a small patched and faded tent.

"That's what you brought? You expect to sleep in that?"

"Perfectly good tent. Used it all the time when Harry and I went camping."

"When? 1960?" She could see holes in the moldy fabric that she could poke a finger through. "It looks as though goats have been chewing on that thing. And it smells musty."

"Trouble with you is, you're a pessimist." He looked at the sky. "It's going to be a clear night. So long as it doesn't rain, I'll be as dry as toast."

Rafi curled into a ball and hugged the bun-nee. It was already getting dark and soon there would be no light in the window. Rafi didn't like the dark. He was hungry and the good drink in the cup the Big Papa Man called *kok* was gone. Rafi could still smell the paper that had had the good food in it, the food the Big

Papa Man had called a *hot dog* and *flies*. Rafi couldn't remember eating dog or flies at his uncle's house, but he'd been so hungry he hadn't fussed. He'd liked it, too. It was good and he wanted more hot-dog.

Don't fuss. Don't cry. That was what the Big Papa Man said.

The Big Papa Man was mean, meaner than Uncle, meaner than Frogh who was Wali and Seema's mama and said *Never never call me Mama!* and hit him on the head with a spoon. The Big Papa Man talked funny and locked him in the dark place. If he fussed, the Big Papa Man twisted his arm. Hard!

Rafi wanted to go home. He wanted to see Frogh's cat and Uncle's brown goat. Bun-nee was soft and nice, but it wasn't real. Rafi was big enough to know *real*. The Big Papa Man called it a *toi-rabbit*, but it did not look like a rabbit. Rafi had fed Seema's rabbit and it was a real animal with soft ears and teeth. Bun-nee was a funny rabbit. No teeth. Not a dead rabbit. Not a real rabbit. But nice.

Rafi missed the brown goat and he missed his bed. He missed the good smell of nan and cheese. His belly hurt and he had to make water again. His pants smelled funny, so he knew he'd been bad.

Fat tears rolled down his cheeks. He wiped them away. He did not like it here. He didn't like the Big Papa Man, and he didn't like the dark place. He'd never been all alone before. Always in his uncle's house there had been smells from the kitchen, people, dogs barking, sheep and goats baaing. This place was bad. There were no goats, no warm milk, and no good nan.

Rafi began to rock and sing to himself. He couldn't remember the words, so he just sang "Moon . . . moon . . . moon . . ." over and over. He wished Uncle would come or even Wali. Wali was big, but not as big as Seema or Frogh. Wali might pinch him, but Wali would know the way home.

Rafi did not know how to find his uncle's house. When he had followed Seema and Wali to the well, Wali remembered the way home. Wali was big. He laughed at Rafi and called him two fingers. Little. Rafi knew it was bad to cry. When he cried, the Big Papa Man hurt him.

Rafi cried anyway.

Bailey stepped out of Daniel's shower and he handed her a terrycloth robe. She wrapped her wet hair in a towel and pulled the robe on. "That feels heavenly." She'd come home from the dig dirtier than she'd been in a long time.

Puzzle wound around her ankles, wagging her non-existent tail.

"Will said he was going into Tawes. He'll pick up your mail."

"He's not staying for spaghetti?" She could smell Daniel's sauce bubbling on the kitchen stove.

"Said he had some things to do."

She slipped her feet into her sandals and padded into the kitchen. She was tired and her back ached. She wanted nothing so much as to curl up with a book, but she and Daniel had a lot to talk about. He refused to allow her to go home unless he accompanied her. She understood his protectiveness, but it didn't make the situation any easier. Thoughts of Lucas and his threats were enough to send her screaming off the island.

But she was a Tawes woman now, and Tawes women didn't run. This was her home, and she'd be damned if she'd let some psycho ruin her life.

Daniel handed her a glass of iced tea as she came into the kitchen. "Decaf. Lots of lemon."

"I could get used to this."

"I hope so."

She took a seat at the round oak pedestal table. "I do love you, you know."

He moved to stand behind her. His hands were warm as he massaged the back of her neck and her shoulders.

"You're supposed to say, 'I love you too,'" she prompted.

"I love you three."

She twisted to smile up at him. How could she care so much for him and yet be so confused about their future together? "What are we going to do?"

He leaned closer and brushed her mouth with his. She reached up to cup his cheek. When he began to kiss her again, she turned her head away.

"It's that way, is it?"

She nodded. Catching his hand, she laced her fingers with his. "Talk first, kiss later."

"If there is a later."

She pointed to the chair across from her.

"The water's boiling. The pasta—"

"The pasta can wait." She looked into his beautiful eyes and felt a rush of emotion. After Elliott, she'd never expected to find love again. But Daniel was more than she'd ever dared dream of. And now that she'd found him, he was everything to her. How could she face life without him? "As Will would say, we need to find a way out of this brier patch."

"Bailey—"

"No. No sweet talk. No *honey*. Let's start with the basics. Three questions. And I want straight answers or . . ."

"Or what?"

"Or I'm out the door. For good, Daniel."

"Fair enough."

She pulled the robe tighter around her. "Number one. Why would Lucas think you could raise that much money? You didn't earn a fortune working for the government."

"No, I didn't." He squeezed her hand. "I'm not rich, but I'm not a starving carpenter either. I've made some good investments in the stock market."

"OK . . ." Something told her that he was telling the truth—just not all the truth. And maybe he never would. "Can you swear to me that you didn't break any laws to acquire that money?"

"That's two." He smiled at her, the killer smile that always tugged at her heartstrings and made her crazy-mad for him. "Hell, no, I didn't rob any banks or smuggle any drugs. I don't have a still under the back porch, and I don't even cheat on my income taxes. Whatever I do or have done, my life is an open book to the agency. And what they know, Lucas has access to."

"Three."

"The magic number."

She took a deep breath, trying not to burst into tears. "Do you still love her?"

"Mallalai?"

"I've answered that one before," he reminded her.

She gripped the edge of the table. "Humor me. I need to hear it again."

"No, babe. I don't love her. I love you. Maybe I never did love Mallalai. How the hell would I know? I was in a foreign country. People were trying to kill me. Everything I thought I knew was coming apart, and I found someone to fill the lonely nights. Infatuation? Who knows? Maybe I was just too long without a woman. But she betrayed me, murdered a good friend of mine, and tried to blow me to hell. Do you think I'm crazy enough to still be in love with her?"

"But you could love her son?"

He didn't protest that that was number four. He just squeezed her hand and answered with a question of his own. "Could you?"

"I hope so . . . I could try . . . would try."

"So we're in this together?"

"I want to be."

He bent and kissed her. "Trust me, Bailey."

"I'm trying."

Later, she curled up in a big leather chair in front of the hearth while he went to shower. She had a book, but she found herself reading the same page over and over with no idea of what she'd read. Marking her page with an advertising card out of a magazine, she tossed the book onto the floor and stared into the cold hearth.

July was too warm for a fire, but she vividly remembered a blustery night in late March when she and Daniel had spread a blanket on the floor and shared a picnic of apples, cheese, bread, and wine. After they'd stuffed themselves and finished a bottle of Merlot, they'd made love. It was on that night they'd decided to go to Princess Anne and get the marriage license . . . and the night they'd made a child together, she thought.

The kitchen wall phone rang, pulling Bailey out of her reverie. She got up and answered it. "Hello?"

"Bailey? I thought you might be there."

She gasped, and the handset nearly slipped out of her hand. "Lucas?"

"Are you alone?"

"Daniel's in the other room."

"Good. I have a proposition for you."

She sank down into the nearest kitchen chair. "I have nothing to say to you."

"Don't you?"

"What do you want?"

"I thought it was fair to give you a chance to make a counteroffer," Lucas said. "How much is it worth to you to keep Daniel from ever laying eyes on the kid?"

CHAPTER FIFTEEN

Abbie and Buck lay wrapped in each others' arms listening to the fat raindrops spattering on the tent walls. "What made you come out here tonight?" she asked sleepily. They'd just completed a very satisfying session of slow, delicious lovemaking, and vibrations of honeyed pleasure still echoed and drifted through Abbie's body.

He kissed her lips tenderly. "You can ask that after inviting me into your sleeping bag and attacking my body?"

She chuckled. "Is that what you call it? Seems to me I was taken advantage of. Seduced by a fast-talking cop." She was trying to keep things light between them, but it was getting more difficult by the moment.

She liked Buck. A lot. Maybe too much. She didn't have time in her life for a significant other. She had her life planned out. Once she found her mother's killer and saw that he got what was coming to him, and after she completed work on her doctorate, she'd spend summers in Greece and Turkey and winters teaching at an American university. At least, she hoped she would. It had been her goal for so long.

Buck nibbled the lobe of her left ear. "Mmm. Nice."

His breath was warm on her throat, and she sighed and arched against him. The man was a devil for knowing how to push her buttons. "Isn't there a law against police torture?"

"Not on Tawes." He stroked the curve of her back and rolled over, pulling her on top of him. "No jury would convict me."

She nestled her head against his shoulder. "Seriously, why did you come out here? It wasn't just for a few tricks in the sack."

"You'd be surprised how far I'd come to be with you." He pulled her head down and kissed her again.

She shivered. Sweet Zeus, but he was habit forming. "Seriously."

"No," he admitted, "it wasn't."

From outside the tent, Archie whined and thrust his big, wet nose into the open door-flap. "No!" Abbie protested. "There's no room for you in here."

"He's wet. Maybe we could squeeze over a little."

"And have my sleeping bag smell like wet dog for a month? I don't think so." She zipped the door closed. "He can go in your tent if he wants."

"It leaks."

"I told you that."

He threaded his fingers through her short hair. "I don't remember."

"I did. I distinctly told you that your tent was worthless, that it had holes in it. Just before you told me it wasn't going to rain."

"I take the Fifth."

She straddled him and sat up. "It won't work, you know. Changing the subject. What's up, Buck?"

He laughed.

"Besides the obvious." She dug her knees into his ribs. "I said to be serious."

"I'm trying, but you make it hard."

She smacked his bare chest.

"Ouch!"

"Enough of your crude humor. I warn you, we traditional people are masters at the art of torture. Next I start yanking chest hairs."

"OK, OK. I have reason to believe that you could be in danger, and I plan on making it my business to see that no one harms a hair on your head."

"You think I was right—about my mother's death?"

"It's starting to look that way." He shifted his arms, lacing his fingers behind his head. "I got a heads up on Sean Gilbert's autopsy from a friend. There's good reason to believe that his death wasn't an accident."

"What? And you didn't tell me?"

"I'm telling you now, aren't I?"

"How did he die?"

"I shouldn't be sharing anything with you. I don't have the complete autopsy report, but it looks as though the boy might have died of a blunt-force injury. One or more blows to the back of his neck. I've contacted the lead investigator working on your mother's case and asked him to call the chief medical examiner's office in Baltimore."

"I don't understand."

"They need to compare Sean Gilbert's blood with DNA samples taken from the murder weapon."

"The stone ax?"

"Yeah. It's a long shot, but just maybe if he was murdered by the same person who attacked your mother, he or she may have used the same weapon."

"So traces of his blood might be on the ax? Wouldn't the killer have washed it off?"

"Not so easy as you might think. Forensics are a lot

better than they were even five years ago. If Sean was murdered with that ax, there's a good chance the evidence is still there."

Matthew kicked the sheet off and rolled onto his side. He'd been listening to the rain on the bedroom windows for what seemed like hours. He should have been asleep long ago, should have been exhausted from the physical work he'd done at the burial ground. He'd told himself that tonight he would sleep; he wouldn't be bothered by bad dreams or the restlessness that had troubled him in the last year.

"It's wrong, Grace. I tell you they aren't giving me the respect I deserve on that dig."

Matters were not proceeding as he would have hoped, and they seemed to be getting worse. Now that Dr. Knight was gone, he'd hoped her daughter would be willing to heed his advice, to take advantage of his experience. He might not have a degree in archaeology, but he wasn't ignorant of the science.

They had to find something of worth, objects that would prove the value of the site. He'd had them, and he'd let them slip through his hands, or rather Dr. Knight had. He wondered if he should contact Tess Quinn, that television personality who'd written the article about the curse. If he told her that Irish Bronze Age treasures had been found on the island, it might bring other scholars and archaeologists, people who would believe him. She might even be willing to publish the photos. He still had those, at least.

"Do you think I should, Grace? She seems like such a nice young woman, that Miss Quinn."

But what if she didn't believe him? What if Miss Quinn laughed at him? He didn't think he could stand any more insults.

"Martha was short with me today, dear. She told me

that I was scraping the sides of the pit wrong. She said it right in front of Phillip Love, and he agreed with her. Can you believe it?"

Without his diligence, there would be no excavation, and doubtless backhoes and bulldozers would already be destroying the ancient gravesites. It would serve them all right if he didn't go back to assist tomorrow morning. No one appreciated him, so why should he waste his valuable time? He hadn't completed Sunday's sermon yet. He sighed heavily. It seemed as though they were harder and harder to write.

How he missed his dear, dear Grace! He glanced at the wall where her large oil portrait hung. He'd had it done from a photograph last fall, and it had been worth every penny he'd spent on it. It comforted him, having her here where he could see her lovely face before he closed his eyes at night and the first thing when he opened them in the morning.

"You're not forgotten, darling. No, indeed."

The year since she'd passed seemed an eternity. Even continuing his work as a pastor had been more difficult without her beside him. Grace had always contributed to his sermons, told him when he was straying from his subject or growing too wordy. Losing her, when she was still so young, so vibrant, made him question God's purposes. If only Grace were here. She could advise him on how to deal with this rash young archaeologist and with Martha. Grace never failed to know the right thing to do.

Sometimes he wondered if he could go on living here without her. But this was his home, the only home he'd ever known, except for the years when he'd attended seminary on the mainland. He couldn't imagine living anywhere else; yet he couldn't deny how lonely he was.

The parsonage was too large for one person. When he'd been a child, there had been his mother and father, his maiden Aunt Dorothy, and his father's brother, *Poor Chester*, who'd been kicked by a mule and never talked—or left the house except to go to church—and hated having his hair cut or his beard shaved. Poor Uncle Chester didn't like children or cats, and he would pinch you hard enough to leave a blood blister if you got too close, but even Poor Uncle Chester's presence had helped to fill the big rooms and long hallways of the house.

By the time Poor Uncle Chester and Aunt Dorothy had passed on to their heavenly reward, Matthew's younger brother Daniel had been born. Daniel had always been a disappointment as a brother—a rascal, not the proper sort for a pastor's son. Their mother had complained that he was a trial and said that Daniel must be a changeling, left on their doorstep by forest brownies.

Mother had been a staunch Methodist, but she'd been born a Swift in Dames Quarter on the Eastern Shore and had had a superstitious streak. When Matthew was small, he'd seen her set a bowl of milk for the brownies on the back porch every evening. She said that if you forgot the brownies, they would cause mischief—sour the milk, let flies get into the butter, or snap the clothesline so that a week's washing fell onto the ground and had to be done over again. Every morning, Matthew remembered running to check and finding that the milk bowl had been licked clean.

Father had shouted, "Don't be ridiculous! Stray cats drink the milk!" He called Mother wasteful and said she set a bad example for the congregation. Father had spent hours building elaborate traps to catch the cats, but he never succeeded. Mother never argued, smiled her secret smile, bought a new hat whenever he scolded her, and continued to leave milk out for brownies as long as she lived.

Matthew had often wondered why, if Mother had been so diligent in catering to them, the brownies had left Daniel anyway. The house had been more orderly without a noisy, dirty baby who grew into a rowdy boy. He and Daniel had never been close, and Daniel didn't visit much anymore. Obviously, Daniel didn't appreciate him either.

"Grace . . . Grace." He tried to imagine the shower running, imagine seeing her shadowy figure behind the curtain, but tonight, even his little mind games failed him. How he missed her! At times, his life seemed empty, and nothing, not even saving Tawes, seemed worthwhile.

So many regrets gnawed at him, keeping him from sleep. Old memories . . . old sorrows . . . but losing Grace was his deepest wound. She'd been sick for a long time. If they'd gotten the right help for her sooner, things might have turned out different. But that was all water under the bridge, as the cynics said.

Matthew wondered if perhaps he should consider remarrying. Finding someone to replace his Grace wouldn't be easy. She had been the perfect pastor's wife, always willing to shoulder a share of his responsibilities, always beyond reproach . . . except for the lapses in judgment that her terrible illness had caused in her last year. He'd even considered Martha, despite the fact that she was no spring chicken, but that was before she revealed her true nature. If she couldn't give him the proper respect due a pastor, she was obviously not the woman for him.

Matthew climbed out of bed and found his glasses. After sliding his feet into his slippers, he went to the dresser. Grace's dresser. Snapshots of her were grouped on the top—Grace in her wedding gown,

Grace outside the Lincoln Memorial in Washington, and various photos of her through the years. His mother's antique Victorian mirror reflected the glitter of the heavy silver frames. It comforted him to see Grace's sweet face, but it saddened him as well.

Nothing had been changed in the house since her passing. Grace had known where the old furniture and the decorative pieces were best displayed, and he wouldn't attempt to question her good judgment. Regardless of her illness, he'd chosen well when he'd picked Grace to be his wife.

"I wish you could tell me what to do," he said. "I can't let this go on, can I? Something drastic has to be done. They have to realize who they're dealing with."

Maybe his idea of contacting Tess Quinn was a good one. Maybe that's what Grace would have wanted him to do. He took off his pajamas, dressed in khakis, a plaid shirt, and his athletic shoes and made his way downstairs. He could hardly go out in his nightclothes. As Grace would have said, he had his position as a member of the clergy to uphold. He'd just dash over to the church and see if he could find those photos. He knew where they should be—in the album on the shelf over the boxes of arrowheads, pottery shards, and other pieces he and the archaeology society had discovered over the years.

When he opened the front door, he found it was still raining, so he exchanged his shoes for boots and took the large umbrella. The rain was warm, but there was no sense in taking chances with his health. He'd always been sensitive to getting wet, and *Better safe than sorry* as his dear, departed Grace would have said.

Water dripped off the trees and beat against his face as Matthew hurried through the cemetery to the back of the church. Any other time, he would have stopped at his wife's gravesite to pay his respects, but not tonight. He'd bring flowers tomorrow when the weather cleared, he promised himself. He'd been neglectful lately about the flowers, and that set a bad example. Too many people didn't give the departed proper respect.

The steps leading down to the office door were slippery with leaves and water. Matthew braced himself against the brick wall as he fumbled with the doorknob. The church office was never locked. Neither was the sanctuary. In the years since Reverend Thomas had established the first log chapel here, no one had ever given the pastor reason to lock out the parishioners. Not like the mainland. No, sir. All the more reason to stop the invasion by realtors. No telling what kind of people might be attracted by new development.

Matthew found the light switch just inside the door and turned on the light. He held his umbrella out, shaking off the excess water, and closing it before he brought it into the office. Superstition said that open umbrellas indoors were bad luck. Not that Matthew was superstitious, but it just made sense. Why chance putting someone's eye out?

He crossed the room and went to the wall that housed his collection of Indian artifacts. Large volumes filled the shelf over the bins and boxes. Matthew scanned the notebooks for his photo album with the 8 x 10 shots of the gold torque and bronze cloak pin.

Where was it? The album always stood here, between the book containing pictures of church picnics and the one with photos of the congregation. Matthew stiffened. "It can't be. Where . . ." Frantically he began to pull down the binders. "Red . . . red . . ." he mumbled. The album cover with the Irish treasures was the only red one. "No!" he protested.

His precious album, his only proof of the finds, was gone.

* * *

"Hold it right there." Will leveled the barrel of his shotgun on the small of the stranger's back. "Move one muscle and I'll send you to hell."

The man froze.

"Drop the rifle." The phragmites rustled as the weapon slid into the muddy foliage. "Good. Now get your hands up where I can see them and turn around, slow like."

"If it's money you want, I've got a wallet in my back pocket."

"What do you think this is? A robbery? I'm no thief." In the rain and black of night, Will couldn't get a look at the man, but the way he'd crashed through the marsh, it hadn't been hard for the dogs to track him from Bailey's farm to the edge of the Indian burial ground. "State your business."

"Who are you?"

The man had an accent Will hadn't heard before. He steadied the butt of the shotgun on his hip, unsnapped a small flashlight from his belt, and shone it into the intruder's face.

The man blinked and threw a hand in front of his eyes. He was small, with graying hair pulled back at the nape of his neck. His eyes had an almost Oriental tilt to them, and his olive complexion was acne-scarred. He wore expensive boots, but no slicker. The rain had soaked clear through to his skin. What mattered most was that he fit the description Daniel had given him of the CIA's hired killer, Lucas.

"I said, *don't move*," Will reminded him. "I'll shoot you dead. I swear to God I will. I'll bury you so deep in this swamp, the buzzards won't even find you."

"Who are you?"

Nervy for a man with a twelve-gauge burning a hole in his belly, Will thought, but he respected that.

Daniel had said Lucas was someone to be reckoned with. "You first. You're trespassing on my island."

Blue growled, and Raven's hackles went up. Honey, the female retriever, didn't stir a hair and didn't take her eyes off the mainlander.

"Who's there?" a familiar voice shouted.

"Buck? That you?" Will answered. "I'm maybe thirty feet off the trail, and I've got company. Caught a stranger sneaking up on your camp."

"I'm here to protect—" the man began, but Will cut him off.

"Shut up." He quieted the dogs with a hiss. "I wouldn't try anything crazy if I were you. The big Chesapeake is mean, but the bitch will rip your throat out before you go three feet."

"Will!"

"I'm all right. Want me to bring him out or are you coming in?" Will heard Buck say something that he couldn't make out, and then the phragmites snapped and rustled.

"Stay there! I'm coming in."

The male Chesapeake growled. "Easy, Raven," Will soothed.

"I don't know who you think I am, but—"

"Shh," Will said. "You'll get your chance." Rain trickled down the back of his cap and dripped under his collar. Damn, but he was getting too old to play games in the marsh at night. He was glad it was summer.

The man stood waiting, eyes squinting against the light.

Blue shifted uneasily and whined. Will didn't look down at the dogs, but he knew Raven was baring his teeth and his muscles were tensed to leap if he gave the command. "Easy, boys, it's just Buck."

The phragmites parted, and Buck, pistol in hand, appeared at Raven's side. "I'll take it from here, Will."

Blue gave a short bark and peered anxiously into the grass. When the dog started to move, Will hissed at him again. "Down!" Then to Buck, Will said, "Careful, he had a rifle. It's lying in the grass right over there." He thrust his chin to the left. "I think this might be the hired killer who broke into Bailey's house and threatened her."

"You've got the wrong man. I haven't done anything wrong."

Buck glanced at him. "Just take it easy. I'm a police officer. You're not in any danger unless you bring it on yourself. Are you carrying any weapons or drug paraphernalia?"

"I don't use drugs," the man replied. "And I've got a knife in my waist sheath."

"Check his boots," Will suggested. He carried a little knife in his own boot, a habit he'd gotten from his daddy and his before him.

"Nothing else but the hunting knife."

Buck scoffed. "I hope you're not going to tell me you're deer hunting."

The man didn't answer.

"Your name wouldn't be Lucas, would it?" Will asked as Buck frisked the intruder. Raven whined again, and Will signaled him to lie still.

"No, it's not. It's Vernon."

"Good," Buck said. "I hope for your sake that you're telling the truth." He stepped back with the knife, picked up the rifle, and unloaded it. Waving toward the path he'd just forged through the phragmites, he said, "I want you to walk out to the road, easy like."

"Am I under arrest?"

"Not yet, you're not. Do you have any ID on you?"

"Yes, I do. A driver's license, credit cards."

Will kept the shotgun on him. "Do as he says. Remember, these dogs are quicker than you are." Fol-

lowed closely by Blue and the two anxious Chesapeakes, the three men moved out through the reeds.
Suddenly Will heard a deep baying from the trail that
could only be a fourth dog.

"Buck?" Abbie called. "What's happening?"

"Stand back out of the way," he called.

"Abbie?" the stranger shouted. "It's me!"

Flashlight bobbing, she plunged into the tall reeds,
followed by something big and black that looked like
a bear.

"I told you—" Buck began.

Will's dogs began to bark furiously.

Buck's warning was cut off by Abbie's surprised cry.
"Daddy? What are you doing here?"

CHAPTER SIXTEEN

"Bailey?" Lucas's precise, emotionless voice came softly over the phone. "Are you there?"

"Yes, I hear you." Her mouth was dry; black specks blurred her vision. "Go on."

"This is a private conversation. I'd hate to think you'd share it with Daniel."

"Why wouldn't I?"

"Let me say that it would be"—he paused—"unwise. Dangerous for all concerned."

She sank into a chair, gripping the handset so hard that her fingertips felt numb. "You're threatening me. Don't. I'm not afraid of you."

"A lie. You disappoint me, Bailey."

"Why would you think I'd betray Daniel?"

"Self-interest is hardly betrayal. We're wasting time. Time that neither of us has. Either you're interested in my proposition or not."

"Why should I believe you?"

"You don't understand me at all, do you?"

Biting her lip, she glanced toward the hall. She could hear the shower running. "What do you want?"

"You aren't a stupid woman."

"Money."

"Affirmative."

She shivered. "Why should I trust you? You've already said that I'm not stupid."

"Tut-tut. Do I detect a note of righteous anger?"

"You don't know me if you think I'd be party to injuring an innocent child!"

"I told you that I'm not a monster. I don't, as a rule, murder civilians."

"But you'd kill Daniel's son?"

"The boy is attractive. I have other options."

"How much?"

"Two hundred thousand."

"You asked Daniel for five. Why would you settle for two from me?"

Lucas chuckled, and his dry sound of amusement was somehow more frightening than his threats. "Because I intend to collect the five hundred thousand from him as well. Our arrangement would be a separate business proposition."

"What would keep you from taking my money and giving the boy to Daniel anyway?"

"Bailey!" Daniel called from the bathroom. "Could you get me another bottle of shampoo from the pantry?"

"He's coming," she said to Lucas. "I can't talk any more."

"Are you interested or not?"

"Let me think about it. I'd need time to raise that much cash."

"Very well. Keep in mind that we have only a few days."

"How can I contact you?"

He laughed again. "Don't try to be too clever. I'll call you."

"I have to go," she said.

"Remember, not a word to Daniel."

"I *said* I'd think about it," she repeated sharply. "But you have to swear that the boy won't be harmed."

"Word of honor."

Bile rose in her throat. "I'm serious, Lucas. Don't hurt him or you'll never see a cent."

"I'll be in touch." He broke the connection.

Bailey clapped a hand over her mouth. She wanted to scream, to call Lucas every foul name she'd ever heard. Instead, she picked up the glass of iced tea Daniel had made for her and flung it against the stone fireplace. The glass shattered, and bright shards showered the hardwood floor. Tea splattered across the hearth and braided rug, and the section of lemon spun and bounced, finally coming to rest under the kitchen table.

"Bailey!" Daniel came down the hall, a bath towel knotted around his midsection. "You're bleeding!"

She looked down at her ankle. A thin sliver of glass was sticking out of her leg. Oddly, she didn't even feel it.

Daniel pulled the splinter out and stanched the bleeding with a corner of his towel. "Did you fall? Are you cut anywhere else?"

"No." She shook her head. "No, I'm not." Trembling, she rose and threw herself into his arms. "Hold me—just hold me."

"What's wrong?"

"We have to talk." Tears stung her eyes. "Lucas . . . He called me while you were in the shower."

"Not on my cell. I had that—"

"On the house phone. It was me he wanted."

"What did he say? Did he threaten you?"

"Daniel," she murmured against his chest. "He is a monster. He thought I would pay him to murder a helpless little boy."

"This is your father?" Buck lowered his weapon.

The dogs whined and barked and circled each other, sniffing and wagging their tails. The Newfoundland's tongue lolled as he wiggled all over with excitement.

"Vernon Night Horse."

Abbie threw her arms around him and he embraced her. "Daddy, what are you doing here?" she repeated.

"Strange damn way to come visiting, I say," Will grumbled.

"Damn strange way to welcome visitors," Vernon snapped back.

"Come in out of the rain." Abbie tugged on her father's hand. "You too, Buck, Will." The rain was coming down in sheets and she had to raise her voice to be heard.

"Tight quarters, that little tent," Will said.

"It's dry." She glanced at her father. "Dad, this is Buck Davis, the police chief. And this is Bailey's uncle, Will Tawes."

Will's gaze flicked from Abbie to Vernon. "Guess you two must be kin all right. You look enough alike to be. But it doesn't answer why he'd be sneaking through the marsh on a night like this."

"I was worried about her safety." Her father moved closer and put his arm around her. "I've hired a private investigator to look into my wife's death, and he believes that I have reason to be concerned."

"Can we please get in out of the rain?" Abbie said.

"I'll just mosey on home with the dogs," Will said. "A hot cup of tea would do me a world of good. You can fill me in later, Buck," He looked at Abbie's father and held out his hand. "Sorry about this. No hard feelings?"

Her dad shook Will's hand. Buck and Will spoke too low for her to make out the words, and the older man strode off into the night with his dogs. Buck, Abbie, and her father made a dash for the campsite and ducked into her tent. The beam of Abbie's flashlight had passed over Buck's sagging shelter, and it was all she could do to keep a straight face when her father asked how many of her staff were staying on site.

"They're all volunteers," she explained as she handed each man a dry blanket and stowed their wet shirts at the back of the tent. "Buck's here for the same reason you are. He was worried about me too, so he came out to make certain I was all right."

"I'd appreciate it if you'd tell us what your investigator found that alarmed you," Buck said. He'd found the thermos of hot coffee and poured each of them a cup.

"Ray Zerillo," Vernon said. "Twenty-five years with the Philadelphia police force. My attorneys in Oklahoma City arranged the contact. He comes highly recommended. Do you know him?"

"No, sir, afraid I don't."

"Seems a good man. I've only spoken to him three or four times, but he must be legitimate; his fees are high enough." The Newfoundland whined, and Vernon lifted the door flap so the dog could get his head in. "Nice dog. Yours?" he asked Buck.

"Abbie's. His name's Archie."

"He is not mine!" she protested.

"Been telling her she should get a dog," her father said. "A woman needs a dog."

"Just what I told her, sir."

Abbie elbowed him. "It's not my dog." Archie wiggled his shoulders inside, and her father squeezed over. The smell of wet dog enveloped the small space. "Dad!" she protested.

Her father drained the thermos cup and handed the empty container back to Buck. "Ray Zerillo knows people still on the force. It's odd that neither Karen's ring nor her pistol were stolen during the attack. If it was some punk out for a quick score, why didn't he take them?"

"Isn't that just what I've been saying?" Abbie interjected. "And Buck's just learned that the young man Ànati and Bailey found on the beach died under suspicious circumstances."

Buck scowled at her. She knew that he hadn't wanted her to share that information, but she didn't care. Her father had a right to know what was going on.

"It doesn't explain why you're here in the middle of the night," Buck said.

"I've been worried about Abbie I called, but I couldn't get through. Don't you have phone service on this island?"

"We do, but the signal isn't great," she said. "How did you even get here?"

"The usual way. By plane. Jerry flew me into Salisbury airport. I rented a car and drove to . . . Crisfield, is it?"

"Yes, sir."

"Got some fisherman to bring me out to the island." Buck glanced at his watch. "At this time of night?"

"Well, it wasn't this time when he dropped me off. Karen had told me the location of the site. The fisherman dropped me off at some private dock and drew a map that showed how to get here. It's not like this spot is a secret. The captain knew just where I wanted to go."

"And you came without a raincoat or a flashlight?" Abbie asked.

"I thought I'd be here long before dark. And I didn't know it was going to rain."

"Me either," Buck admitted.

"Anyway," her father continued, "I got turned around back there in the swamp. Then those devil dogs got on my trail, and Daniel Boone came after me with a long rifle."

"I believe it was a shotgun." She tried not to smile. "And he could have killed you. Will Tawes isn't anyone to take lightly."

"Would you mind clearing something up for me, sir?"

"What's that? And my name's Vernon."

"I understood that you and Dr. Knight were divorced."

Abbie rolled her eyes. "It's confusing. Everything about their relationship is confusing."

Her father's impassive features softened. "Karen always told people that. She lived her life as though she was single. Truthfully, Karen filed for divorce when Abbie was small. I didn't want it, so I never signed the papers. She never pushed. We simply avoided the subject. My wife and I had our differences, but . . ."

"They loved each other. Daddy would have done anything for her." She handed her father a towel, and he dried his face and wrapped the towel around his braid to soak up the water dripping down his back.

"But legally you were still man and wife?" Buck pressed.

Surprised, she said, "Why does it matter? You're not suggesting that Daddy—"

"I'm not suggesting anything, Abbie. I just need the facts for my files."

"I didn't have her killed, if that's what you're thinking. We may not have shared a bed in years, but we shared a lot more. And the oil wells are mine. I had nothing to gain and everything to lose by Karen's death."

"I didn't mean the question as an insult."

"I hope not," Abbie said, attempting to hide her annoyance. What was Buck thinking? She couldn't blame her father if he took offense.

"I'm just doing my job. I have to—" Buck's cell phone rang. "Excuse me." He turned to answer it.

Her father passed back the damp towel. "How can he get a signal out here and you can't?"

"I told you, it comes and goes." She poured him the remainder of the coffee, hoping he wouldn't notice that the tent contained two sleeping bags. She'd passed the age of consent a long time ago, but Vernon Night Horse wouldn't see it that way. Her father could be very old-fashioned where her honor was concerned, and she didn't want to involve Buck in what could become an embarrassing situation.

"All right. I'll look into it first thing in the morning." Buck tucked the phone into his pocket and glanced at her. "That was Matthew. He claims the church has been robbed."

"The church? Was anything of value taken?"

"Matthew says his photo album is missing. The binder containing the only pictures of the missing Irish artifacts."

Emma carried a pot of coffee from the kitchen. Forest, Buck, his brothers Harry and Bowman, Abbie, and Vernon were seated at the dining-room table for Sunday breakfast. "I can't go to church," Abbie said. "I don't have a dress. I don't even have a pair of decent slacks."

"I think you look beautiful." Buck passed her a stack of blueberry pancakes.

"Yep, me too," Harry agreed.

Forest smiled. "I'll second that."

"Buck has to be there," Bowman put it. "Bailey wants you and your dad to come. She told us she'd kill us if you didn't show."

"To your church?" Abbie looked at her father. "Dad, I—"

"Thank you." Vernon paused in buttering a biscuit. "I'd like that. Bailey was your mother's friend. It would be rude to ignore her invitation." His dark eyes flashed with amusement. "Plus, a little religion wouldn't hurt you."

"Why do you have to be there?" Abbie asked Buck.

"Can't tell you," Harry put in.

"It's a surprise," Emma said.

"Will you all let me tell her?" Buck leaned forward. "Please?"

Bowman gestured with his cup. "Floor's all yours, brother."

"Bailey sent something over," Buck explained. "Your mother had bought it for you. It was hanging in the closet at Bailey's house."

"Upstairs on your bed," Emma said. "Daniel brought it by before you got here."

Abbie looked from one to another. "Something my mother left for me? I don't understand."

"It was for your birthday." Emma's eyes glistened with moisture. "I don't know when it is, but—"

"August fourteenth," Vernon supplied.

"Excuse me." Abbie slid her chair back. "I'll just—"

Emma blocked her escape. "Nope. Breakfast first.

Lots of excitement today. If your mother was here, she'd say 'Eat your pancakes, drink your juice, and have another cup of coffee.'" She glanced at Buck for support. "Right?"

"Yes, ma'am." He grinned at Abbie. "May as well do as she says. Miss Emma can be awfully stubborn."

Minutes later, stuffed with more eggs, bran muffins, and pancakes than she would have thought she could hold, Abbie hurried up the front stairs to her room. She opened the door, switched on the light, and stopped short. Spread out on the bed was a gorgeous leafy-green silk dress. A shoebox held Italian leather sandals.

"Ànati . . . thank you." Abbie picked up the shoes, cradled them against her breast, sat down on the rag run in the middle of the floor, and cried.

An hour later, Buck, wearing a gray pinstripe suit and tie, escorted Abbie and her father to a pew near the back of the crowded church. "I'll sit with you as long as I can," he whispered.

"Why—" Abbie began.

He put a finger to his lips. "You'll see soon enough."

Matthew took his place and led the congregation through the shortest service Abbie had ever witnessed. Two songs, a five-minute sermon, and the christening of a Parks infant took less than half an hour. Two youths, hair slicked back, faces shining, passed antique wooden offering plates down the rows of worshipers, and the choir stood to sing a hymn of praise as the children returned to the pulpit with the collection.

Then Matthew spread his hands and smiled. "May the Lord bless each and every one of you," he said. "Today could have been a day of sorrow, but it's not.

Instead, this is a day of rejoicing. It is my pleasure to ask all of you to witness the vows of two people near and dear to this island."

Waves of whispers flowed through the pews. Heads turned, children bobbed up and down, and an old man demanded, "What? What did he say about a deer?"

"Sit tight," Buck said to Abbie. "That's my cue." She stared after him in confusion as he rose and made his way along a side aisle to the front and exited the church near the choir pews.

Warm laughter flowed through the church. Matthew cleared his throat. When the murmurs continued, he waved to the choir director, who signaled a stout woman in a large-brimmed hat to drown out the chattering with a spirited organ rendition of "Let Us Gather at the River."

When the last note died away, Matthew raised his voice. "It is my great privilege to join Bailey Tawes and my brother Daniel Catlin in holy wedlock. They came to me this morning and asked that the ceremony take place during service. I hope you are as delighted as I am—as I know my dear departed wife would be—to share in their happiness."

Heads turned again as the organist began to play the bridal march. Abbie looked toward the door and saw a tiny giggling girl—no older than five—enter the church carrying a basket of wildflowers. As poised as any crown princess, the freckle-faced sprite in a pink organdy tutu and white patent Mary Janes danced up the center aisle pursued by a three-year-old boy in red cowboy boots and a Raven's ball cap.

"Aww, isn't Johnny adorable?" a woman in the next pew whispered.

"Wait, Sammy," the boy shouted. "Wait for me!" Halfway to the front of the church, Johnny dropped his pillow and the ring rolled into the nearest pew. George Williams retrieved the ring from the floor, smiled, and handed it back to him.

The pillow forgotten, the three-year-old dashed on with the ring clutched in one tiny fist. "Sammy! You're 'sposed to wait for me! Mommy said!"

Sammy didn't look back, and she didn't miss a step. Ignoring the pleas of her small escort, she spun and twirled her way through the admiring congregation toward Buck and the waiting bridegroom. Black-eyed Susans and Queen Anne's lace tumbled out of her wicker basket and left a trail of crushed blossoms in her wake.

Behind the dynamic duo came a nervous and solemn-faced Emma, wearing a navy blue dress with a white lace collar, and finally, Will Tawes and Bailey, trailed by Will's three dogs and Archie. The enormous Newfoundland had distinctly muddy paws.

The bride wore an azure suit, simple pearl earrings, and silver heels. White rosebuds trailed over the Bible in Bailey's hands, and a small cluster of rosebuds was tucked in her auburn hair. Will walked stiffly beside her, his arm in hers, his eyes straight ahead, seemingly oblivious to the animals.

As they passed her pew, Bailey met her gaze and smiled. "Isn't she beautiful?" Abbie whispered to her father.

"Yes, she is."

Daniel and Buck stepped from the choir door and waited for the bride. Daniel had eyes only for Bailey, but Buck glanced toward the back of the church before the ceremony began.

Nervously Emma took Bailey's Bible.

"Who gives this woman in marriage?" Matthew asked.

Will's voice rang out through the sanctuary. "I do."

"Dearly beloved, we are gathered together . . ." Matthew began.

Abbie reached for her father's hand and squeezed it, wondering if he remembered another marriage ceremony . . . and wondering if there would ever be a day like this for her.

CHAPTER SEVENTEEN

Every pair of eyes in the church were focused on the bridal couple, every pair but one. Cautiously he glanced around the sanctuary through narrowed eyes, finding first one guilty person and then another. With each passing moment his anger grew. How dare they come here and make a show of their religion, Bailey with her growing belly and Daniel equally guilty of sin?

Daniel Catlin had been born and raised on Tawes, and he should have known better. Hadn't he been one of those who invited Dr. Knight and her daughter to the island, who welcomed them here? And if he'd allowed them to disturb the burial ground, wasn't he as much at fault? Bailey hadn't listened to reason either. Everyone had told her to stay away from that marsh, but she'd dug into the sacred ground, and she would keep on doing it until something happened to make her stop.

Something bad.

He couldn't kill them all. He knew that. He wasn't

all-powerful, and he wasn't an evil person. He'd never wanted anyone to die. The boy's death had been an accident. He'd loved him, almost as much as he'd loved Daniel. If the boy hadn't run . . . hadn't fallen . . . hadn't screamed and screamed until he had to make him stop, things would have been different. And the woman should have stayed away. He never would have hurt her if she hadn't butted in where she wasn't wanted. So in a way, her dying wasn't his fault. It was the stupid boy's. If he hadn't made such a fuss, they could have gone on being special friends.

He didn't like to think about the father's death. That had been bad. He'd been sick afterwards. It had troubled him for a long time, that killing. It had been bloody, and he'd never liked blood. But a man had a right to protect himself, and sometimes it came to kill or be killed. Even the Lord could understand that. Was it too much to ask that people stay away and leave him alone . . . that they let the dead rest in peace?

It would have been all over for Dr. Knight's daughter if Buck hadn't come to the burial ground last night. He would have gone to the tent and finished her. It would have been easy—no one to hear her screams, no need to be in a hurry to get away. But Buck and the dog had come, and it was too dangerous to try to kill them all.

If they'd come in the morning and found the girl dead, it would have been the end of the digging. Nobody would've dared venture there to trespass on the marsh again. Nobody would have disturbed the old graves. Things would have returned to the way as they had been for years. And he would have gone on protecting the sacred site.

It wasn't as easy for him now as it had been. He

wasn't getting any younger. The wet and cold bothered his arthritis and made his joints ache. But if he died out there, he'd never be alone. He'd be with his blood brothers. They knew that he was one of them, and they never judged him. They understood why he'd had to do the things he'd done . . . why he had to do the really bad thing.

And soon.

The impromptu wedding reception at Emma's B&B spilled out onto the dock and over the back yard. The bride and groom danced on the grass to music played by men with violins and women with flutes, drums, and guitars, a boy with an Irish tin whistle, and a gray-haired old lady with a small handheld harp. An eighty-year-old man strummed the strings of a handmade banjo, while piano notes drifted through the open windows. Children chased one another in and out of the house, danced together or with their parents and grandparents, and played with the babies.

Steamed clams, oysters, and shrimp appeared as if by magic. Neighbors produced platters of fried chicken, baked ham, chilled watermelons, sliced peaches, fresh tomatoes, and huge bowls of potato salad and coleslaw. Nate Davis came with a keg of pickles under one arm and a heavy aluminum roaster with a cooked turkey in it under the other. Forest brought Aunt Birdy in a yellow-wheeled pony cart filled with pies and rolls. Phillip and Mary Love carried in tubs of sodas, pretzels, and chips.

Teenaged boys set up tables and carried folding chairs and benches from Emma's shed, and girls tended babies and laid out silverware, glasses, and dishes. Older people shared memories and jokes with their friends and relatives and remembered other weddings and loved ones from times gone by.

Bailey, the thin gold ring on her finger gleaming, clung to Daniel's hand in a happy daze. She laughed and murmured responses to well-wishers, but never really heard a word. "I love you," she whispered when he tugged her behind the big silver poplar tree for a private embrace. "Love you, love you, love you."

"And you've made me the happiest man in the world."

"Will you still be happy when you're a father twice over?"

"If I have you, I can do anything."

She sighed and raised her hand to admire her wedding ring. "How did you have time to find a ring? I never thought of it when I proposed to you last night."

He laughed. "When we proposed to each other, you mean. The ring was my grandmother's. Matthew found it for me in my mother's jewelry box. If you'd like, we can go to Annapolis and pick out a nicer one."

"This one feels right on my hand, and it's a perfect fit. Just try to get it back."

"Do you know how much you mean to me?"

"I hope so." She snuggled against him. "Hold me."

For seconds or moments, he did, until Daniel's cousins Jim and Buck found them. "None of that now," Jim said. "You have to wait until after it gets dark." Jim had his sleeping ten-month-old in a blue and yellow baby-carrier on his back, and Buck's arm was linked with Abbie's. She appeared happier than Bailey had seen her since her mother's death.

"You have to come and see the cake," Buck said. "Cathy's found you a proper Deal Island wedding cake."

"How did she manage that?" Bailey looked from

Jim to Daniel in amazement. "We didn't know we were getting married ourselves until last night. And we didn't say a word to Matthew until six o'clock this morning."

"Simple," Buck explained. "Somewhere between breakfast and the morning service, Matt told Mary Love, who told Forest, who called Cathy. Her cousin Billy was supposed to get married a week ago over in Princess Anne, but his fiancée changed her mind when she decided to stay at William and Mary for her master's in something. Anyway, Billy's aunt lives in Crisfield. She had the cake in the freezer, and—"

"Whoa, whoa. Stop." Daniel laughed. "We get the picture."

"Cathy's Uncle Chuck said he'd bring the cake over in his Bayliner," Jim explained, "if he was invited to the wedding. Cathy would have caved and said yes, but I held out for a case of champagne, too."

"You didn't," Bailey protested.

"He did." Buck grinned. "Jim gave him his credit-card number. Consider it your wedding present from him and Cathy."

"Of course, Chuck brought his girlfriend Shelly," Jim added. "And her mother. They're the three over there by the crab cakes with the matching skull-and-chain T-shirts and studded boots. Cousin Chuck has the blond ponytail and the can of Bud."

Bailey tried not to laugh. "I thought there was no alcohol at Tawes parties."

"Not a drop." Buck grinned even wider. "Unless you count those two crocks of cherry cordial that Aunt Birdy hid under the seat of her pony cart."

"And the champagne," Jim reminded them. "The kind with real corks, none of that cheap stuff. Can I get a glass for the bride?"

"Just a half glass for me," Bailey said. "Baby on board."

Jim shrugged. "Your days of sleeping late are over, Daniel. But you did well for yourself. Bailey's a keeper." He leaned and kissed her lightly on the lips. "Be happy, darling. You deserve it."

"I hope I can make Daniel happy."

"Cathy's calling me. I think I promised to dance with her." Jim groaned. "I hate dancing. I've got two left feet. Can you dance with a baby-carrier?"

"I'm sure you can," Bailey answered. "Although I can't imagine how little Jamie can sleep though all this noise."

"He's recharging his battery," Jim said. "Wait until he wakes up. You'll wish he was still asleep."

"Jim Tilghman! Get over here!" Emma shouted. "Your wife wants to dance."

He groaned and glanced at Daniel. "And you gave up single life for this?"

"Afraid so, cuz."

When Jim hurried away, Bailey turned back to Abbie. "The dress looks fantastic on you."

"Ànati always could shop for me."

Abbie looked near tears, and Bailey reached out to hug her. "She outdid herself this time."

"Thank you, and thanks for thinking of the dress," Abbie said. "I would have had to come in shorts otherwise." She elbowed Buck. "This one gave me zero notice."

"Didn't know it myself," Buck said in self-defense.

"But I have to admit, he cleans up good," Abbie teased.

Buck tilted his head and inspected her. "You're not so bad yourself."

Abbie laughed. "Down, boy."

"I understand your father is here," Bailey said. "I hope I get to meet him."

"I'll make certain of it," Abbie promised. "And don't let his stern expression scare you off. He's a pussycat under the stoic Indian countenance."

"I'll keep that in mind. It must be difficult for him, not knowing anyone. I hope he enjoys himself."

Abbie pointed toward the house. "Do you hear the piano? And the singing? Off key? That's my dad. I'd say he's having a good time." She glanced around. "This is nice, really nice, Bailey. These are special people."

"I think so," Bailey said. "I was a long time coming home."

Buck slipped his arm around Abbie's waist. "I promised to feed you." He rolled his eyes for Daniel's benefit. "She eats like a horse, this one. I can see where she got her name."

"Buck!" Abbie protested.

Bailey laughed. "Pay him no mind. He's probably been into Aunt Birdy's cordial."

"I wanted to get back to the site today," Abbie said, "but my police escort has other ideas."

"Woman does not live by work alone," Buck said. "Come on, Ms. Night Horse. There are raw oysters over there calling your name."

Once they were alone, Daniel drew Bailey into the grape arbor and kissed her again. "Are you sorry yet that you came to this island?"

She shook her head. "No."

"Sorry you met me?"

"Never."

His eyes clouded with worry. "Not even after last night?"

"Lucas can threaten us," she said, "but whatever he

does, whatever comes of it, we'll have a better chance of beating him together."

"You know it could go bad."

Her lower lip quivered and she swallowed. "I know it. I don't want to think like that, but I know it."

"And you're still not sorry you said 'I do'?"

"Never. I'll never be sorry. Not for one minute."

Daniel kissed the tip of her nose. "You are one special woman, Bailey Tawes Catlin. Your Mama would be proud."

"You think so?"

"I know so."

Matthew finished a plate of fried chicken, potato salad, and crab cake, ate a slice of peach pie and a square of gingerbread, and left his dirty dish by the back step. He was eager to be away, but he didn't want anyone to notice his departure.

It had given him satisfaction to perform the marriage ceremony for his brother, and he wouldn't have dreamed of missing Sunday service or the celebration at Emma's house. But he'd stayed long enough to circulate among his parishioners, to speak to the faithful in his congregation and remind those not so dutiful about church attendance that the door was always open.

He'd admired numerous babies, chatted with Mary Love, and listened to Aunt Birdy's long tale about the haunted marsh, and how the curse began with a massacre in the late 1600s. As the gruesome account went, a group of friendly Nanticoke Indians who lived on nearby islands had gathered on Tawes to celebrate the wedding of the beautiful daughter of one tribal chief to her beloved, the greatest hunter and archer of another clan. In the middle of the joyous ceremony, tragedy struck. A drunken company of British soldiers attacked the wedding party and slaughtered the bride and groom and all of the wedding guests.

Matthew had listened patiently to Aunt Birdy, even though he'd heard the tale a hundred times. He knew it so well, he'd been tempted to recite the traditional ending of the story with her, but good manners had prevented him from doing so. The words echoed in his head, and he murmured them aloud now. "One hundred and nineteen peaceful Indians, young and old, babies and grayhairs, scalped and mutilated, and left naked for the wolves and the carrion birds in that godless massacre."

Most of the dead, according to the saga, had been buried by the white settlers of Tawes, who'd come to see what had drawn so many buzzards. And when they had laid the broken bodies to rest in the ancient Indian burial ground, grown men had wept.

Every member of the two Nanticoke clans had died that day, all but one man. A powerful wizard, a shaman or medicine man as some called him, remained alive. This shaman had not been invited to the wedding because he had desired the bride for his own wife and she had refused his hand in marriage. Out of anger and jealousy, he'd gone deep into the swamp and bitterly cast an evil spell on the young lovers. But when he returned and found all of his kinsmen murdered, his grief and regret drove him to madness. Howling like an animal, he'd stood at the open graves and uttered a terrible curse on any who would disturb their bones. And, so the legend claimed, he'd guarded the marsh for more years than any mortal man could draw breath.

Matthew thought it a pagan myth, one not fit for children's ears, or appropriate to be told at a wedding feast. The massacre had probably never happened, at least not as Aunt Birdy told it, but the people on Tawes believed every word.

Superstitious nonsense. Good for nothing but frightening drunks and children, but it still gave Matthew the creeps and he wished Aunt Birdy hadn't dragged the story up again. Well, he reminded himself, Aunt Birdy wasn't long for this world. She'd be gone soon enough, and when she was, he hoped the massacre tale would pass on with her.

The loss of his precious photographs had wounded him deeply. Buck Davis had written a police report, but Matthew doubted that the chief believed him. People thought he was fey, that he was a tad off plumb because he still talked to Grace as though she were alive. It didn't prove he was crazy. If talking to his dear wife gave him comfort, what business was it of anyone else? Doubtless Buck and even Daniel believed that he'd mislaid the album, that it would turn up in time, but Matthew knew better. Someone had deliberately taken the only remaining proof of the Irish artifacts, and that someone, he was certain, was also guilty of Dr. Knight's murder.

Perhaps the Irish pieces were more valuable than anyone suspected. In any case, no one would believe him unless he found something else left by the early Irish Bronze Age voyagers. And today, while the site was deserted, was his opportunity to dig. There had to be something more still buried in that ground, and it was his destiny to be the one to discover it. He felt it in his heart, and he knew it was his duty to his father, to Grace, and to Tawes to muster on and find indisputable proof.

"Come on." Buck kissed the nape of Abbie's neck. "I dare you."

"Dare me to do what?"

He caught her hand. "Come with me. Upstairs." They were standing at the foot of the staircase leading to Emma's second floor. The parlor and hallway were crowded with laughing, talking people. Children darted in and out of the screen door, and a pack of giggling preteen girls was moving down the steps. Abbie's father, his back to them, was still at the piano, belting out old country-and-western tunes, while the attorney Forest McCready and Buck's cousin Jim sang backup.

"You're out of your mind," Abbie whispered. "The upstairs bathroom is ladies' central, and I know for a fact that Jim's wife is in my room nursing her baby."

"Ye of little faith." Buck started up the steps, and she followed. Outside the bathroom door a line had formed. Buck walked past to the end of the hall and opened a narrow board-and-batten door. He glanced back at her. "Coming?"

Abbie laughed. "A closet? You want me to go into a closet with you? If we were on a plane, I suppose you'd suggest I join you in the public toilet."

"Shhh." Buck held a finger to his lips.

"Lead on, fearless leader."

Buck switched on a light and led the way up a narrow staircase. Apparently, this wasn't a closet as she'd supposed, but an entrance to the attic.

"What's up here?" she demanded. "Ghosties and things that go bump in the night?"

"Nope. Better."

As she reached the top of the steps, she saw that the attic was divided into several large rooms. Furniture lined the walls, and the floor was bare but surprisingly free of dust, with nary a cobweb in sight.

"This way," Buck said.

They passed from one room into another until they reached the end chamber lit by a single window. "What are you—" she began.

"Front-row seats to the best show in town."

The window was open; voices and laughter drifted up from the party below. Spread out in front of the window were a pile of blankets, several pillows, a plate of oysters on the half shell nestled in a bed of ice, an open bottle of champagne, and two champagne glasses. "Madame."

"You've didn't do this alone," she accused.

"It helps to have brothers who owe you money."

"What, exactly, did you have in mind?"

He grinned. "Privacy."

"For?"

"Honey, if you don't know, I've got the wrong woman up here."

Laughing, she turned around. "Unzip me, supercop."

"I thought you'd never ask."

"Did you bring—"

"Honey, I was a Boy Scout. I always come prepared."

She felt his warm breath on her spine as he eased the zipper down, inch by inch, kissing each uncovered spot. Anticipation made her giddy. "Hurry up," she urged him.

"No need to hurry, darling. We've got all night." He slipped the dress off one shoulder and nibbled her bare skin. Bright shivers surged to the soles of her feet.

Abbie turned back and caught his tie. "I don't know whether I should loosen this or tighten it," she said breathlessly.

He stopped kissing her long enough to shrug out of his coat and toss it aside. As it fell to the floor, Abbie heard a clink of metal against metal.

"What's that?"

He grinned. "Handcuffs?"

"Handcuffs? Were you planning on making an arrest?"

"You never know. You might like it so well up here that you'd decide to chain me to the wall and hold me prisoner."

"Braggart."

Buck's eyes sparkled with mischief, and his lazy laugh made goose bumps rise on her arms. "We'll have to see about that, won't we?"

CHAPTER EIGHTEEN

Matthew was out of breath as he trudged along the marsh path, swatting at mosquitoes and greenhead flies and wiping the sweat off his face. Occasionally the muddy track—interspersed with deer trails—would run uphill and thread through a tangle of trees, mostly swamp willow, pine, and cedar, before plunging into another low spot.

The marsh teemed with insects, birds, waterfowl, and snakes. Matthew was grateful for last night's rain. The water made the trail slippery and soaked his shoes, but it was simple to stay on the path. In dry weather, a hiker could easily wander off into the swamp and fall into a deep, stagnant pool or a patch of quicksand. Jim Tilghman swore that there wasn't any such thing as quicksand on Tawes, but Matthew knew better. Too many hunters and dogs had been lost over the years, and once, one of George's cows had bogged down and sank in the gooey slime before anyone could save her. Matthew had no intention of drowning in a bottomless pit. When his time came, he wanted to be buried decently beside Grace and his parents and grandparents in the churchyard.

It would have been far easier to reach the burial ground by boat, but Matthew had never been at ease on the water and was unfamiliar with the maze of muddy channels that threaded through the swamp to the site. Every year the bay devoured more of the island, and it was easy to become lost in the morass of overgrown creeks, mud flats, and expanses of reeds.

If dear Grace were alive, or even Creed Somers, either of them could have navigated the marsh. Grace had always been handy with boats and motors, and she'd known every inch of Tawes, forest and mash. He'd never set foot on their Boston whaler since she'd died, and he wasn't certain that the boat would even start. Besides, it would have been impossible to pass Emma's dock without any of the wedding guests seeing him and wondering where he was going. And traveling the other way around the island took too long.

Matthew had ridden Grace's old bike on the dirt road out of town and left it in the weeds at the edge of Elizabeth's farm. It was a long walk from there to the beach, several miles at least, because the path twisted and turned. Matthew had been forced to climb over logs, wiggle through wild rose patches, slog through puddles, and duck under wild grapevines. He hoped he wouldn't be exhausted by the time he reached the site.

Once he'd set his mind on a task, it was his way to finish it. His father had always praised him for that quality. "You're not a particularly bright boy, Matthew," he'd say, "and there's nothing remarkable about you, but you are dependable. I always know what to expect of you." He'd had no such good words for Daniel. It seemed Father and Daniel had been at odds since Daniel had been old enough to talk and question his parents' orders. Their father had been sparse with compliments, so any Matthew got, he cherished and remembered, word for word.

He knew his father would approve of his leaving the wedding party to search for proof that his theory about the Bronze Age Irish in America was correct. Matthew would have liked to remain long enough to share supper with them. Doubtless the celebration would go on until after midnight, and he knew there'd be kettles of clam chowder and oyster stew served later in the evening.

He regretted not sampling Aunt Birdy's cherry cordial. Not that he was a drinking man, but one glass of spirits to toast the bride and groom could hardly be considered a major sin. Aunt Birdy's cordials were always a temptation, even for a man of God.

Thinking of Aunt Birdy made him remember the story she'd told. Tidewater summer days were long, and dusk wouldn't descend over the marsh for hours, but shadows lay heavily across the narrow pathway, and the tall reeds rustled ominously in the wind.

Matthew didn't like to think of the massacred Indians or the bodies lying on the blood-soaked beach with crows picking out their eyes and chewing at their exposed sexual parts. He could picture the bare-breasted women, long dark hair stained red with gore, and tender nipples and privates torn and desecrated by the teeth of foxes and the cruel talons and sharp beaks of stinking buzzards.

Not even the women's lovely high-arched feet would have been spared by the scavengers. Images of slender, honey-colored feet and tender, plump toes gnawed to the bone by rats and weasels filled Matthew's head and made him nauseous. Surely some of the Indians had fled into the marsh, to be hunted down and shot or clubbed to death. Their bloated bodies must have washed up on the shores of Tawes for weeks afterwards.

Matthew shuddered. He didn't want such thoughts in his head, but they returned over and over. The marsh was a lonely place with far too many spooky tales told about it. He didn't like to think of the drowned midshipman or the waterman found on his boat with his skull crushed in . . . the poor man who'd come to this spot to dig and never reached his home alive. It was all too easy for Matthew to imagine he could hear the long-dead shaman shaking his turtle-shell rattle just off the trail to the right, or see his ominous shadow elongated and distorted by the waving phragmites.

With audible relief, Matthew finally reached the clearing where Abbie Night Horse's tent stood. He saw, to his surprise, that a second tent had been erected since he'd left the afternoon before. It was obvious that no was here, so he felt free to remove his jacket, tie, and long-sleeved shirt. Underneath, he wore a white tee, the type that Grace jokingly had always referred to as a *wife-beater*. It was cooler here in the open, out of the thick marsh grass, and the breeze felt wonderful on his bare arms. Spraying himself liberally with insect repellent, he approached the slope where Abbie had been working.

He hoped last night's heavy rains might have washed away enough of the hard-packed soil to reveal a treasure. He inspected the muddy tree roots and scraped at the cut in the earth with the side of his trowel, turning up a few chips and a broken arrowhead, but nothing of greater interest.

The ground here was still black, filled with vegetable matter, not as promising as he'd expected. But he was positive he'd been drawn here today by divine providence, and he had no intention of leaving without finding what he'd come for.

Minutes became hours. Glancing at his watch, he wiped away the mud, and saw that it was nearly five. He didn't need to leave yet, but he wanted to allow himself plenty of time to hike out of the swamp to his bike. Overhead, a crow cawed to a companion, and off to the west, he saw a flock of seagulls heading for the bay.

Sunlight gleamed through the leafy canopy, painting the thick foliage in Lincoln and apple green, turning fallen leaves to autumn gold and rust, and revealing tiny insects scurrying through the grass. Matthew paused, took a sip of warm water from his canteen, and used a handkerchief to wipe his forehead. His back ached, and several mosquito bites on the backs of his knees itched mercilessly. He removed his sunglasses, rubbed them clean on a corner of his shirt, and put them on again.

His eye caught a gleam of gold through the trees, a metallic glitter that seemed too bright to be a leaf. Like a plucked guitar string, excitement thrummed through him. His eyes widened. This was no illusion! He scrambled over the rim and clawed his way through the greenbriers. "Grace! Grace," he cried. "Whatever is—"

One moment he was plunging—heart in his throat—through the weeds and undergrowth toward the golden torque, and the next instant something snagged his ankle. Matthew screamed as he was jerked upside down into the air. His glasses fell off. He screamed as his head slammed against a tree and he spun helplessly, his missing torque whirling in front of his eyes. His cries became a gagging croak as he finally stopped moving and hung suspended over his missing torque. The precious treasure lay on a bed of green moss only a few feet from his grasp, but impossible to reach.

"Help! Help me!"

Matthew tried to think what had happened, how this could be. Without warning, he was suddenly ill. Vomit spewed from his throat, spraying the precious artifact. He clamped a hand over his mouth, but he threw up and threw up until nothing came out but a thin stream of acrid bile.

He moaned. "Help me, somebody. Please . . . help me."

Twigs snapped.

"Hello! Is someone there? I'm trapped."

Brush rustled.

Matthew twisted, trying to make out the figure clad in fringed buckskin and carrying what looked like a bow and arrow. The movement sent him twirling again, so that he could catch only distorted glimpses of the war-painted savage that approached. Without his glasses, it was impossible to see well enough to . . .

His mind seized on a thought, then rejected it. An Indian on Tawes? No! It was bizarre. Impossible. The painted face was vaguely familiar, but he couldn't focus on it.

"Please . . ."

Matthew heard the whoosh of the feathered arrow as it left the bow, and he screamed again and again and again.

Rafi's head hurt. He held Bun-nee tight and sucked his thumb. He curled into a ball. He felt hot all over. He didn't think about nan and cheese anymore. He didn't even think about the hot dog or the sweet kok the Big Papa Man had given him. He tried to keep his eyes open, because when he closed them he saw bad pictures that frightened him.

He thought the Big Papa Man had come back when it was dark. He wasn't sure if that was real or if it was the pictures behind his eyes. Rafi thought he remembered the man opening the door and making sounds he didn't understand. He hadn't brought hot dog or kok in the dark. He had something in his hand, something Rafi had never seen before. It was pretty. Colors and colors.

Rafi was big enough to know his colors. He knew brown like the goat and blue like the sky. He knew red. He liked red. Not when he cut his knee. That was bad red. But he liked the red color on the papa chicken's head. Clouds were white. White like curds. Curds were good to eat. So he knew all the colors, brown, blue, red, and white. He knew his numbers too. One, two, four.

He tried to sing but his throat hurt. He sounded funny. No "Moon, moon, moon." Just "Maa, maa, maa," like the goat. He rubbed his eyes with his fists. His eyes hurt. He didn't cry. No more tears. No more fuss.

"Wake up!"

Rafi moaned.

"I said *wake up!*"

Rafi opened his eyes.

"Here. I brought you something to eat."

Rafi shook his head. His belly hurt. He tried to say "no," but the word wouldn't come. He squeaked like a mouse.

"Are you sick? Don't go getting sick on me. I don't have time for it."

It was the Big Papa Man. Rafi thought he should be afraid. Maybe the man would shake him. But he was tired. He closed his eyes again.

"Here. I brought you some juice. You like grape juice?"

Rafi nodded, but when the Big Papa Man held the bottle to his mouth, he choked and some ran down his chin.

"Drink it," the man said.

He said more, but Rafi couldn't understand the sounds he made. Like on the big plane. Everybody made sounds on the plane he didn't know. It had made him afraid.

"I brought you a banana. Kids like bananas." The Big Papa Man held something to Rafi's lips.

Banna. What was banna? Rafi didn't know, but he was too sleepy to care. He hugged Bun-nee and turned his head away.

"Eat it, damn it. Eat the banana."

The Big Papa Man put his hand on Rafi's head.

"You're burning up."

Rafi tried to tell him that he wasn't. He had not gone near the fire. It was bad to go near the fire. The fire bit you. But he didn't have the words. He was so sleepy.

The man held the juice to his mouth again. Some ran down Rafi's throat and choked him. Some ran out his nose and choked him. The Big Papa Man hit him on the back. Rafi fussed. He knew it was bad to fuss, but he didn't want the juice. He was so tired. The man picked him up and carried him outside. Rafi knew it was outside because the sun shone in his eyes and hurt him.

He closed his eyes. The dark came.

Daniel dropped anchor in a sheltered cove on the far side of Tawes. The breeze was off the water, and the crescent moon rose, brilliant against a velvet sky studded with stars. He and Bailey had accepted the loan of Forest's Grady White for their honeymoon hideaway. Several hundred yards away, Buck anchored his brother Nate's less elegant but roomy 23-foot skiff.

"I can't believe we did it," Bailey pronounced as she hugged Daniel.

"Me either." Daniel tilted her head up to kiss her lips.

"Sorry?"

"Hell, no, you know better than that."

Something was wrong. She felt it. It was more than Lucas and the blackmail and Daniel's fears for the little boy.

She stepped back and gripped his hands. "Whatever's troubling you, it's my problem too. You're my husband now. You have to share."

"Nothing's wrong. Everything's right—at least between us."

"Liar." She touched his bottom lip with two fingers. His muscles were tense, the ridges of his face hard in the moonlight. "Is it Mallalai? Are you sorry it wasn't her there at the altar with you this morning?"

"God, no, Bailey. Get that out of your head, once and for all. That's over and done with. Mallalai's gone, and she's never coming back—not unless you keep dragging her up and throwing her in my face."

Hurt flashed through her. When she answered him, her tone was thick, close to tears. "I need you to be honest with me. You promised—no more secrets. If it's your child, I told you that I—"

Daniel rubbed his eyes. "You're making mountains out of molehills. Nothing's wrong. I'm tired, that's all."

"Everything's peachy between us?"

"Everything."

She glanced over at the lights on the other boat. "When we have to have an armed escort? When we need to have a chief of police guarding us on our honeymoon?"

"It was Buck's idea, not mine. He said we should be able to forget Lucas for one night, that once this night was over, we couldn't get it back, no matter how much we might want to."

"He's right," she agreed. "And I don't mind Buck. Not really."

"And he's not suffering. Abbie's with him. He tried to leave her at Emma's, but she threatened to take Emma's boat and follow him. So I doubt he really expects Lucas to come after us. Remember, I offered to take you to a nice hotel in Annapolis."

Bailey shook her head. "No. Elliott and I spent our wedding night in Vegas. A very nice hotel. I'd rather be here, on this boat with you, close to home."

"Good. Buck's going to back me when I make the exchange with Lucas."

"Will you have to give him cash?"

"Hell, no." He laughed. "You've been watching too many TV shows. It's all done painlessly by Internet." He shrugged. "I doubt there is any real money these days. Banks just pass on electronic data, round and round."

"You have it? That much money?"

"Don't worry about it. We won't starve, even with our enlarged family."

"I didn't think we would. Aunt Elizabeth left me so much, and there's my teaching pay. I'd like to take off at least a year after this one comes." She patted her slightly rounded belly. "Especially with the two little ones. Not that I'm worried. After all, if I can manage a classroom of fourth graders . . ."

"I'll be here for you," he promised. "I swear I will. For all of you. I'll be a better father than mine was if it kills me."

It was Bailey's turn to chuckle. "Fatherhood isn't supposed to kill you. Some men even enjoy it."

"My father didn't." He hesitated, and the silence stretched between them before he stroked her cheek. "He was really a shadow father," he said. "Pastor first, scholar second."

"And husband to your mother?"

"I hope I can do a better job at that too. They were

distant cousins, and Mother was well past the age of first bloom for those days. There was always an air of mystery about my mother. She was a self-contained person, and everyone thought her standoffish. My brother was born eight months to the day of their marriage."

"A preemie."

Daniel smiled. "A large and hearty preemie, according to Aunt Birdy. Her favorite expression is that second babies take nine months—the first can come any time."

Bailey laughed. "Apt, considering my condition. You'll have more than tinsel under the Christmas tree."

"But you, my dear, are not the pastor's wife." He kissed her tenderly. "And a good thing, because it's a rough life. Like Caesar's wife, she must be beyond reproach."

"So what you're telling me is that your parents couldn't have been too distant before the nuptials?"

"No." He kissed her forehead. "That isn't the scandal. The scandal is that some on Tawes suggested Father wasn't the father at all. Her parents were well off and provided a handsome dowry, so I'm told. Of course, that was long before my time."

"So Matthew might be your half-brother?"

"Could explain why we have so little in common, but I doubt it. Mother and Father barely tolerated each other, and I don't believe either was ever cut out to be a parent. By the time I was born, both had lost all interest in anything but Father's calling. I always felt like a nuisance, not quite as welcome as my mother's cat."

"And you're afraid I might make this little boy feel the same in our home?"

"No. I know you better than that."

"How do you think Lucas got him? Kidnapping? Are we doing something illegal by taking the child?"

Daniel gripped her hand and stared at the black water just beyond the gunwale. "I wouldn't put that past him, but he is just as likely to have bought him from a relative."

"Bought him? A child? That's got to be illegal—even in Afghanistan."

"Of course it is. Afghanistan—the Muslim world has strict rules protecting children, but Mallalai's son, if this is her son, may have fallen outside the boundaries of law. Giving birth to an illegitimate child is a sin, sometimes punishable by death. Her family would be shamed, so much so that they might not even acknowledge the boy's existence."

"They'd blame him for his birth?"

"It depends on the family, the village mullahs, and how strict they are in the observance of the law. Slavery is officially outlawed, but an illegitimate child in a rural village would be little better than a slave. The chances are that he'd never be given an education or an opportunity for advancement. He might even be hidden from others in the community."

"Did you know her family?"

"I knew Mallalai and her brother Zahir. He was brave and smart. A decent man. I'll never know whether Zahir was my enemy, but he must have been. I never saw him again after her death."

"Do you think this is your son?"

"Lucas offered me the boy's ear for DNA testing."

She clapped a hand over her mouth. "That's horrible."

"Just what I thought. He could be bluffing, but I don't think he is. I believe this is my child, but if he wasn't, I'd want him anyway. Can you understand that? I saw so many kids over there, dirty, ragged, hungry. Kids with nothing, no hope for the future. Maybe taking one, giving him a mother and a father, might make up for some of the wrong that was done to those people."

"You think it's wrong—what our country has done over there?"

"I don't know. It's not easy. Men have been fighting over Afghanistan since before the time of Alexander the Great. Maybe we've helped, and maybe we've hindered the Afghans. I don't know. I just know I met a lot of good people, and I felt helpless to do anything to make things better for them."

"We'll do our best to get him, this little boy. And to keep him," she promised, "if we can find a way to do it legally. But there's nothing more to do tonight. Can't tonight be just for us?"

He swept her up into his arms. "I take that as an invitation, Mrs. Catlin."

"Daniel, put me down." She squealed. "Stop. Put me down."

"In my bed, woman." He carried her down into the cabin, where Emma had made up the double bed with fresh sheets and sprinkled them with rose blossoms. "You'd better not be allergic to roses," he teased, "or we're both in trouble."

She was right. Buck would keep watch over the boat, and there was nothing they could do until tomorrow about Lucas. This night belonged to Bailey. Daniel knew he hadn't answered the question she'd asked, knew he couldn't. Not now, not ever. There were things in his past that he'd have to bury . . . memories that he couldn't share, because if she knew . . .

But she never would. No one would. He wasn't a boy anymore, and whatever had or hadn't happened wasn't his fault. He couldn't go on blaming himself.

He laid her down on the bed and flopped onto his back beside her. "Ravish me, darling. I'm in your hands, and too weak to put up a fight."

She laughed and kissed him, and the scent of her perfume and the soft feel of her skin drove everything else away. "I love you, Bailey Tawes Catlin," he murmured. "And I always will."

CHAPTER NINETEEN

The gentle rocking of the waves stirred Abbie awake. She pushed back the blanket, yawned, and took a few seconds to remember why she was on a boat this morning rather than crawling out of a tent at the dig site. She lay on her back and tugged on her shorts before finding her T-shirt on the floor. She pulled that over her head, ran her fingers through her hair, and stepped up onto the deck.

"Morning, sleepyhead."

Abbie shielded her eyes against the bright light and wondered where she'd left her sunglasses. Squinting, she glanced around and saw that the Grady White was still anchored in the cove far enough away to give the honeymooners privacy.

When she looked back at Buck, she saw that he was clad in the same shorts and Hawaiian shirt he'd changed into after the reception. He'd obviously been swimming this morning, because his hair was wet. He'd taken the trouble to comb it, but he hadn't shaved. She found the golden stubble on his cheeks and throat endearing. "You wouldn't have any fresh coffee in your back pocket, would you?"

A lazy smile spread across his face. "Wish I did. Once I see life over there, we'll chug over and have some of theirs. I can smell it brewing. Forest McCready is nothing if not prepared. He's probably got a fancy coffeemaker, a grinder, and premium, shade-grown Colombian beans stashed in his galley."

"Coffee and bagels wouldn't be bad."

Buck shook his head sadly. "What am I going to do with you, Ms. Night Horse? I thought you'd be happy with a few mussels, some dried pemmican—"

"Enough with the Indian jokes. I've heard them all, and they aren't funny."

"Ouch!"

"Exactly." She couldn't see his eyes behind his polarized sunglasses, but she'd bet they were bloodshot from lack of sleep. Otherwise, he showed no signs of having been up all night—or of the partying they'd done at the wedding reception. Other than the few minutes they'd stolen for a quickie, Buck had remained on deck, keeping watch over Daniel and Bailey.

"Seriously." His deep voice grew husky. "What am I going to do with you?"

She swallowed. "What do you mean?" She tried to keep her tone light, but he wasn't fooled.

"Now who's playing word games?" He pulled her onto his lap and kissed her. "You like me. Admit it. A lot. I'm better than a ten. I'm a twelve, at least."

"On what scale?"

"Seriously, darlin'."

"Seriously, I've just lost my mother," she protested. "You can't expect me to make any decisions . . ."

"Excuses, excuses. If she heard you, she'd laugh. I didn't look for this either, Abbie, but it found us. Maybe we have to grab happiness by the throat while we can."

"I had a plan for my life." She sighed. "I do like you, but there's no way—"

"Philly's not far for a lady with a helicopter."

"Buck . . ." She removed his sunglasses and looked into his eyes. They were bloodshot, but they were more than that. She wished she hadn't taken the glasses off. She wished her stomach wasn't doing flip-flops, and she wished she didn't feel guilty making love to him when she was supposed to be mourning the loss of the most important person in her life. "It could never work."

"Have I asked you to marry me and bear my strapping sons and beautiful daughters?"

"No, but . . ." What was it about this man? She got near him and broke out in goose bumps. Maybe she was allergic to him.

"There you have it. You're jumping the gun, woman. Call me a redneck, but in this neck of the woods, you're supposed to let the gentleman do the proposing."

"I wasn't proposing to you! I wasn't even insinuating—"

"No? What would you call it?"

He kissed her again, and she put her arms around his neck to keep from sliding off his lap. Was it her fault that she hadn't had caffeine this morning, and she'd spent the night on a boat, and she was too lightheaded to deliver a resounding and convincing denial of affection?

"Marry me, wench. You know you want to."

"No!"

"Marry me, or I'll throw you to the jellyfish."

"You're out of your mind, Buck Davis. I'm not going to marry anyone—ever."

"Yes, you will."

"Well, I can't marry you. We're too different. We come from different backgrounds. If you had any idea what crazy things I do when I'm with my friends and relations . . . the food . . . the superstitions . . . the customs. I'm not the same person when . . . when I'm . . . Indian. Or when I'm part of the academic world. With my kind of people."

He laughed. "I'm your kind of people. Only you don't know it yet. Let's just agree that some things between us are best left unshared. You paint your face and run around in the dark beating drums and talking about how the white man ruined your culture. And I'll get roaring drunk once in a while on homemade whiskey, rub potatoes on warts, and play hide-and-seek with the game warden."

"You're making a joke of this. But our differences are real, Buck. There isn't a chance in hell that we could make it work."

He arched one eyebrow. "Maybe one or two. I agree the odds aren't the best, but being head-over-heels for you should count for something."

"It's sex. Nothing more. Trying to make it more would be crazy."

"It's more than sex."

"No, it isn't." She threw up her hands. "And I won't marry you, so you may as well stop talking about it."

"In that case . . ." He seized her around the waist, lifted her above his shoulders, and flung her over the side of the boat.

She hit the water ass first. Shrieking, she went under, swallowed a mouthful of bay, and came up sputtering. Buck nearly landed on top of her. "You idiot!" she cried as she struck at him with the flat of her hand.

He caught her by the waist and they both sank. Water closed over their heads. She stopped fighting him and they surfaced together. "I warned you." He was laughing and she was laughing.

"You're crazy," she said.

"As a loon," he agreed. "Then again, I'm not the one who threatened to follow me out of town in a dory, swim over, and assault my body in a sexual manner."

"I had champagne. I told you, Indians can't drink. And I'm definitely not marrying you."

He treaded water. "I'll find a bigger cove. I'll take you out of sight of land and throw you in."

"You'd drown me?" She was giggling as water trickled out of her nose. "You're certifiable!"

"Nope." He pushed her toward the ladder at the back of the skiff. "Just passed my Maryland State Police psych test with flying colors."

"You're a Davis," she reminded him. "You don't believe in early marriage. You stay bachelors until you're forty. You told me so yourself."

"Who said anything about getting married?"

"You didn't just propose to me?" she demanded as he climbed the ladder onto the stern of the boat and turned back to offer her his hand.

"Did I?" He pulled her out of the water onto the deck, kissed her again, and lifted her in the air.

She laughed. "You've lost your mind. You live and work on this island. I'm going to be a classical archaeologist. I'll spend four or five months a year in Greece. I cannot live on Tawes."

"That's a minor problem." He put her down. "Is there a towel around here anywhere?"

"Minor?" She retrieved one from a chair. It was damp, and she guessed that he'd used it when he'd gone swimming before she got up. In any case, it was a towel. She wrapped it around her shoulders.

"Your career. It's not a big difference between us. Not like religion or politics. And who said anything about us getting married?" He tugged at the towel playfully, but she wouldn't give it up. Buck contented himself with drying his face on one corner.

"You did," she reminded him. "You proposed marriage to me not two minutes ago. Do you intend to quit your job and follow me around the world?"

"No. I like it here. You do, too." He glanced at his watch. "And it was more like four minutes ago." He shook his wrist. "Good thing this watch is waterproof."

"So you do remember? And now you're trying to back out of your proposal?"

He set her feet on the deck. "Are you telling me you hate kids?"

"No, I didn't say anything about children, but—"

He interrupted her. "Did I throw my sunglasses in?"

"I hope you did. And I do like kids. I just don't know how they fit into my life plan."

"Oh, that's right. You have a serious life plan."

"You're trying to evade the question." She spied the glasses out of the corner of her eye, lying on the deck, partially hidden behind the chair. "I think you did dive in with your sunglasses on."

Buck peered over the side. "Hmm. I'd always thought I'd want two or three. Kids, that is." He grinned at her. "Guess I'll have to go in after the glasses."

She smiled with wicked satisfaction as he dove in and spent the next ten minutes searching the bottom for the glasses that she'd now propped on his deck chair. She was about to confess when Buck's cell rang.

"Answer that, will you?"

"What?"

"Answer the damn phone."

She retrieved the cell from where it lay on top of a tackle box. "Good morning," she said sweetly. "Tawes Police Station. Abbie speaking. May I help you? Oh, hi."

Buck was climbing out of the water.

"Just a moment, Mr. McCready. Chief Davis is on another line, but he'll be right with you."

Dripping, Buck motioned toward the cell. "Give me the phone."

She held it behind her. "What's the magic word?"

"Please give me the phone," he said between clenched teeth as he unbuttoned his wet shirt and shrugged out of it.

Abbie laughed and handed it to him. She went into the cabin, looked around for a dry towel, but couldn't find one. She wrapped a blanket around herself and came back out onto the deck. He was still on the phone, so she busied herself by spreading her soaking tee and his brightly patterned shirt on top of the cabin to dry.

Sometime during the conversation, Buck found his glasses, grimaced at her, and put them on. When he ended the call, his mood had changed from teasing to thoughtful.

"Bad news?"

"Weird." He motioned her toward the deck chair and took the captain's seat at the wheel. "Forest said he had a call from Peter Elderson first thing this morning. Elderson is one of the attorneys for Onicox—the realty company that wanted to build the marina."

"How is that weird?"

"Mr. Elderson wanted to share some information about Robert Mellmore. He's the supposed heir to the land, and the man who initiated the sale of the property to the realty people."

She waited, knowing Buck would finish what he'd started once he found the right words.

"It seems Mr. Elderson advised Onicox not to go through with the deal. He felt that there was too much bad publicity and that the inhabitants of Tawes would cause more delays and legal expenses than the project was worth. He's suggested another property on the western shore of the bay that's just come on the market—an area ripe for development and closer to Washington."

"That's good, isn't it? Fantastic, if you don't want the marina."

"True. It is. A lot of people will sleep easier tonight."

"But?" Something about Buck's expression told her that there was a large *but*.

"Robert Mellmore."

"The heir. You're afraid he'll sell it to some other buyer?"

Buck shook his head. "Not likely."

"Why?" Her eyes widened. "Don't tell me he's dead, too?"

"Hardly. The man doesn't exist."

She stared at him in disbelief. "What do you mean, he doesn't exist? How can he not exist?"

"Elderson tried to reach him last week to arrange a meeting. When something about Mellmore's excuses for not coming to the office didn't ring true, Elderson sent a courier to his home address. It turned out to be an abandoned filling station. His place of business was equally false. And the phone calls were routed through an answering service."

"This sounds like something out of a spy movie."

"Doesn't it?" Buck took a bottle of spring water from a cooler on the deck, opened it, and handed it to her. "Elderson and his aide spent the better part of four days chasing down Robert Mellmore's references."

She took a drink. The water was cool and refreshing. "Go on," she urged him. "I'm fascinated."

"To make a long story short, Mellmore appears to be a solid citizen on paper. College, detailed employment records, Social Security number, passport, credit cards, and bank accounts. But they're all imaginary.

Fakes. The real Robert Mellmore was born at Johns Hopkins on July 14, 1951 and died nineteen days later without ever leaving the hospital."

"That makes no sense." She finger-combed her damp hair. "Why would anybody—"

"It appears to be an elaborate hoax, an entire fictitious identity constructed for the purpose of—"

"Inheriting Thomas Sherwood's farm," Abbie supplied. "Whoever is behind this scheme would have sold that property to Onicox Realty for a fortune."

"Exactly." Buck folded his arms over his chest. "And it would have worked if Sherwood had legally inherited it from his grandfather, and if Forest McCready hadn't put up such a legal battle to block the deal."

"But who's behind it? Not Elderson."

"Hardly. Elderson got suspicious and discovered the truth. And it isn't anyone at Onicox. Forest says he doesn't have a clue."

"How is that possible? To create a fictitious identity? You'd have to break into public records and do away with Robert Mellmore's death certificate. How would you acquire a passport? Just getting a driver's license in a new state is a hassle."

"Not really," he said. "Not if you are or know a topnotch computer wizard."

"I suppose anything's possible," she admitted.

"If the military can't keep their records intact, who can?"

"It's unbelievable."

He nodded. "But it apparently happened."

"So, if there's no Robert Mellmore, he can't inherit the land. Who is the heir? And if there isn't one, does the property go to the State of Maryland?"

"Forest believes he can find a lawful heir, preferably one who lives on Tawes and is part of the community.

And he's certain a judge will appoint him executor of the estate, now that Mellmore has vanished in a puff of smoke."

Abbie nibbled at her lower lip. "Does this mean my mother died for nothing? Or did whoever conjured up this scenario engineer her death to keep her from finding something on that site?"

Buck removed his glasses. "I wish I could tell you that, hon."

"Will Forest let me keep digging? He has to. I can't stop now."

"I don't see why not. Wait until I tell Daniel about this." He reached for the phone.

She put her hand on his wrist. "Could this have something to do with whatever hush-hush thing is going on with Daniel and Bailey? Why you felt you had to stand guard over them last night?" After the reception, when Buck had said he was following the newlyweds, he hadn't told her why, only that it was a necessary precaution. She hadn't pressed him for an explanation, probably due to her three glasses of champagne. Or was it four?

Her father would definitely be unhappy. She'd left him in Emma's capable hands, true, but Dad was conservative. She'd rather he didn't inquire into her sex life; and when he did, she usually skirted the issue. It wouldn't be so easy to placate him this morning. "How long did you intend to stay—" The sound of Daniel's boat motor interrupted her.

"Bailey's pulling anchor," Buck said. "I guess we'll get that coffee."

Abbie waved. "I hope there are bagels. With cream cheese."

"You eat more than any woman I know. Even more than Emma, and that's saying a mouthful."

"Bad pun."

He grinned. "I thought so." He touched her shoulder. "No need to announce our engagement just yet. Don't want to steal their thunder."

"What are you talking about? What engagement? I did not agree to marry you."

"Hmm." He tilted his head. "I thought you agreed to consider it."

"I did not." She dropped the blanket, went to the cabin, and retrieved her wet T-shirt, which she pulled on.

"You don't need to cover up for my sake. I like the scenery."

"So you're such a pervert that you don't care if I shock Bailey and Daniel?"

"Daniel's a good ole boy. He's not as easy to shock as you think. But you can't change the subject. We were discussing how many kids you wanted. That means you intend to marry me. It's just a question of when."

"No, we weren't. And you're wrong. It wouldn't work. You're a nice guy, but—"

"But what?"

"You're white."

"I am?" He looked down at his tanned and freckled arm. Buck didn't have a lot of body hair, but a sprinkling of golden hairs caught the sunlight. "You think that's white? It looks more pink to me, maybe toast brown."

"You know what I mean. My dad expects me to marry a Native American."

"Ha! So you admit that he expects you to get married." He folded his arms over his chest and peered down at her. "It isn't your father. The trouble is, you don't know if you have the stamina for such great sex every night."

"No, that's not it."

"It wasn't great? I thought it was. Unless you were faking it. Were you? When you pulled that feather out of the pillow and—"

"That was you with the feather."

"Was it?"

"Buck, enough! Stop."

"Yes, ma'am. I'll consider that a definite maybe. How do you feel about emeralds? I was never partial to diamond rings."

"No ring. No kids. I will not marry you."

"A long engagement, then. That's the best. See if you're fertile."

"You son of a bitch." She smacked his bare chest. "Can't you be serious for one minute?"

"Now, now, Abbie, those are fighting words on Tawes. My mother was—still is—an honorable lady."

"I don't know your mother. I don't want to know your mother. I can't marry you."

"But you want to. You're considering it. Admit it." He winked. "And you'll love my mother. She's one of a kind." He looked at his arm again. "Maybe I need to consider wearing a summer uniform. I wouldn't want to get too pale. Then you could call me a—"

She clamped a hand over his mouth. "Stop. Please."

"Will you think about it? Even a lady Indiana Jones needs a home base."

"All right. I'll think about it. But the answer will still be no."

He blew her a kiss. "Time will tell, lady. I'm irresistible when I put my mind to it."

Daniel brought the Grady White alongside the skiff and tossed a line. Buck caught it and handed it to Abbie. Daniel cut the engine, and Buck used a gaff to keep the two boats from colliding. Buck held it steady as Bailey came out of the cabin holding a cup of coffee.

"Breakfast anyone?" Daniel offered.

"I'd love some," Buck answered. "But Abbie's not hungry."

She climbed up on the gunwale and stepped across

to the Grady White. "Push off and leave him," she said to Daniel. "He doesn't deserve coffee or breakfast."

Bailey laughed.

Abbie could smell sausage and cinnamon rolls. "What have you got in there?" she demanded. "A bakery?"

"They're just those frozen things, but they look good." Bailey handed Abbie the cup. "Careful. It's hot. Come below. I've got juice and scrambled eggs too."

After the two women entered the galley, Buck motioned to Daniel. "Any word from your contact?" he asked in a low voice.

Daniel shook his head. "If I know Lucas, he'll wait a few days. Try to make me sweat."

"Let me know if you hear anything."

"I will."

Buck beckoned him with a finger. Daniel stepped over onto the smaller boat, and the two men walked back to the stern.

"What's up?" Daniel asked.

"I just had a call from Forest. You'll never believe this."

Buck told him what McCready had said. Daniel didn't interrupt. Buck finished by saying, "So the question is *who* and *why?*"

"The why's got to be money, but it took a lot of nerve to try something like this. Obviously, it's someone who knows his way around the Internet."

"Just what I thought," Buck said. "Did you get to talk to Abbie's father last night?"

Daniel shrugged. "A little. Nothing beyond polite conversation. Why? Do you suspect him?"

"Should I?"

"I'll admit it was odd, his showing up at the site last night. What do you know about Vernon Night Horse?"

"Not a lot," Buck admitted. "I gather he's rich. Oil wells. And I found out that he and Karen Knight weren't divorced."

Daniel's mouth tightened.

"And he claims to have hired a private detective to investigate his wife's murder."

"That doesn't make him guilty of anything."

"No, it doesn't. And Abbie would take it hard if she knew I was even wondering about him."

"He could be just what he said, a man worried about his daughter's safety."

"True enough," Buck admitted, "or he could be a wealthy man who believes a dead wife is a lot less expensive than a divorced one."

CHAPTER TWENTY

Will crouched in the bushes, resting his weight on one knee, and looked at Matthew Catlin. The minister's body hung suspended by one ankle from a rope tied to a tree limb and swung slightly to and fro in the stiff breeze.

Matthew was dead. There could be no doubt. Matthew's staring eyes were fixed and dilated; his mouth gaped wide in a silent scream of pain and horror, and his shirt and face were soaked deep scarlet with his own blood. Three feathered shafts protruded from the center of his chest. The pastor's left hand clutched one of the arrows in a death grip, as though seeking the strength to pull it loose. His right hand stretched, frozen fingers extended, as though clawing the air above the mossy ground. His free leg dangled at a grotesque angle.

The sight would have been comical if a man had a sick sense of humor, Will thought. Or it might have been funny if Matthew hadn't voided his bowels and bladder in the agony of his death throes so that the grove stank worse than the midden heap outside a crab-picking house. Other creatures had been there ahead of Will, but not the crows. Matthew's eyes hadn't made a meal for the birds. That much the man had been spared. His body, such as it was, would go relatively whole into his casket.

Will listened, and when he heard a fox squirrel chattering to its mate and the indignant scolding of a Carolina wren, he knew that there were no other humans nearby. Will stood and moved cautiously away. He whistled to the dogs, and his own three came bounding to his side, but the Newfoundland didn't return. Will retreated down the far side of the rise and circled the outcrop of old oaks and cedars. He saw the big dog on the beach side of the grove, pawing at something on the slope where Dr. Knight's daughter had been digging on Saturday.

Will whistled again, and the Newf raised its head, and then turned back to the hole he was digging. Will listened, looked around, and approached the dog. "Come on, boy." He glanced into the hole to see what had attracted the dog and noticed something gleaming in the loose soil. He pushed the dog aside and reached down to tug a twisted circle of metal from the earth.

Dirt clung to the band, but beneath the grime, Will recognized the rich color of gold. Tucking the bracelet into his pants pocket, he used a stick to probe the hole. Several stone beads rolled out of the hollow, but Will could find nothing else, so he snapped a leash onto the Newfoundland and led the dog across the camp area to the marsh path. Blue and the pair of Chesapeakes followed hard on his heels.

No more than a hundred yards down the narrow track, he turned and backed off onto a nearly invisible game trail, overgrown with reeds and briers. It was an old Indian trick he'd learned from his grandfather. If anyone passed that way, they'd think he had come out of the marsh, not gone into it. Fifty feet from the main path, where water closed over his boots, Will turned again, and hurried on. Within two minutes, the swamp grass closed in behind him, leaving no trace that he and the dogs had passed that way.

The message was waiting on Daniel's fax when he and Bailey reached his cabin. It was simple.

```
   Send your lady to the center court
at the Annapolis Mall to collect the
boy. Tonight. Six p.m. You go to the
Maritime Museum in St. Michaels. Take
your wireless laptop and come unarmed.
Wait at the public phone outside the
visitors' center at 5:45 for my in-
structions. You can pick up a Wi-Fi
signal there without a password. If
you contact the police or the agency
again, if you deviate from my instruc-
tions, both the boy and Bailey Tawes
become troublesome loose ends.
```

Daniel scanned the fax sheet. "I won't do it."

Bailey took it from his hands and read it. "We have to. We may not get another chance to save the boy."

Daniel shook his head. "It's not worth it. You shouldn't be a part of this."

"But I am." She gripped the paper so tightly that it crumpled in her hand. "We're a partnership, remember? That's what Matthew said in church."

"I don't care what Matthew said. I won't risk your life . . . our baby's."

"Lucas isn't going to hurt me. He wants the money. If he wanted to harm me, he could have done it a long time ago."

"I'll call the agency. Get them to form a—"

"You didn't do it before," she reminded him. "Why not? Why didn't you contact them before this?"

"Because I thought it was too dangerous. Dangerous for us, for the boy—"

"Then it still is. How do you know they'd even believe you? And if you go to them, ask for their help, they'd want something in return. They'd force you to come back, Daniel. You know they would."

He embraced her, holding her so tightly that he could feel the beating of her heart. She was trembling. He was overwhelmed by the need to protect her . . . to protect her unborn child. His child that she carried under her heart. But part of him yearned for that other child . . . the one Lucas held prisoner. He didn't think Lucas would kill him. Hadn't he said that the boy was much too valuable? He'd sell him to the highest bidder, and Daniel wondered if the child would be better off dead than used as a sexual slave for some twisted pervert.

Bitter memories seeped up to chip away at the core of his sanity. He forced them back. Not that. He wouldn't think of that. Not ever again. But he wouldn't risk this unknown boy's future either. If he got the child, he'd never do the DNA testing. He'd accept him as Mallalai's gift, and in saving him, maybe he'd save a part of himself too.

He wanted to speak to Lucas, to argue with him. There was no reason for him to be so far away from Bailey. They could easily make the trade from the mall parking lot. But Lucas hadn't wanted further conversation. Daniel decided he'd have to content himself with sending Buck to watch over her while he went to take Lucas's call in St. Michaels.

"Just give him the money, Daniel. Give him the money, and he'll go away and leave us alone."

"I guess that makes sense," he allowed. He'd bested Lucas before. He hoped he could do it again. He needed to think clearly, and to do that, he had to be certain Buck was protecting Bailey. If luck was with them, maybe the nightmare would end. Lucas would have what he wanted. The man could disappear in some far corner of the world, and he and Bailey could concentrate on finding happiness here on Tawes.

If luck was with them . . .

Daniel was in St. Michaels by 4:33. He moored his skiff at a public dock and set out on foot. The town wasn't very big, but the amount of traffic surprised him. Flocks of tourists wandered in and out of the shops and up the shaded streets. He hoped Tawes would never be discovered. He had no quarrel with people who made their living selling knickknacks, antiques, reproduction pewter mugs, and endless paintings of ducks and snowy egrets, but he preferred the Eastern Shore communities the way they'd been when he was young.

He hadn't eaten since breakfast, but he wasn't hungry. He didn't know when he'd be hungry again. He found a restaurant and drank three cups of Earl Grey with honey at a table outside. He wanted to call Buck, to make certain Bailey was safe, but he thought it best not to use his cell in case Lucas tried to reach him on it.

Lucas had no reason to come to St. Michaels. It would be the last place Daniel would expect him to show up. The town lay on a narrow strip of land between the broad waters of the Miles and Choptank rivers. There was only one road out of St. Michaels leading to the Eastern Shore and Route 50. If Daniel had called in the agency, Lucas could easily be trapped with no escape route. No, Lucas wouldn't come here. He'd be in Annapolis—or Havana or Buenos Aires, or even Bangkok. A man with half a million dollars could do worse than to change his identity and live out his life in Thailand or Burma.

At 5:15, Daniel walked the few blocks to the Chesapeake Bay Maritime Museum, paid his entrance fee,
and went in. For the next twenty minutes, he strolled
through the waterfowl exhibits and the collection of
old sailboats. He was surprised at how many families
were here on a Monday and at how many more new
displays there were since he'd visited last. Maybe he
could bring Bailey and the kids here some day. The
kids . . . funny how he was thinking plural, as though
Lucas was telling the truth . . . as though he really
meant to hand Mallalai's child over.

He looked at his watch for the third time in the last
twenty minutes and wondered if he dared call Bailey.
She and Buck must be outside the Annapolis Mall by
now, waiting as he was waiting.

His cell vibrated and he snatched it out of his
pocket. "Yes."

"Daniel?"

Not Lucas—Will. Sweat beaded on Daniel's forehead. His heart hammered against his ribs. "I can't
talk now," he said.

"Where are you?"

"I'll get back to you, Will."

"Something's happened. Something bad."

"Bailey?" He felt as though he'd plunged through
the ice into a pond in the dead of winter. "What's happened to Bailey?" He hadn't left Tawes until he'd seen
her and Abbie take off in the helicopter for Annapolis.
She shouldn't even be on the island. Unless they'd
crashed. "Will—"

"Not Bailey. Bailey's fine, so far as I know. She's not
here."

"No," Daniel said. "She wouldn't be. Not now.
What—"

"It's your brother Matthew. He's dead."

"Matt?" The ice that had gripped his limbs solidified in his chest. "Matthew's dead?"

"Out at the burial ground. He must have gone out there alone yesterday to dig."

"Yesterday."

"Yep. Been dead fifteen, maybe twenty hours by my way of thinking. He was alive yesterday afternoon at your reception."

Matthew. His only brother. Daniel took a deep breath. "Who found him?"

"Me. I went out there to have a look around before Bailey and Karen Knight's girl went back there."

Daniel waited for the blow to hit, but he felt oddly empty, almost as if he were hollow. Sweat trickled down his neck, but he felt chilled. Matthew was dead, but Bailey was safe. He wondered if it was some weird kind of trade.

"You all right?" Will asked.

"Yeah." Realizing that he'd been holding his breath, Daniel exhaled and drew in another gulp of air.

It didn't seem possible. Matthew was always whining about his health, but Daniel hadn't seen any difference in his appearance. "Was it his heart?"

"Nope. Afraid not. I thought you'd best hear it from me. He was murdered in cold blood. Somebody caught him in a deer snare and used him for target practice."

"What? Repeat that." Daniel leaned back against a display case. "Murdered?"

"Killed with a bow and arrows. I found moccasin tracks, but I doubt if we're looking for an Indian ghost. Like Abbie Night Horse has been saying, there's something out there that the murderer doesn't want found."

Daniel swore softly. Matthew killed. It didn't seem

possible. He wondered for a minute if it had been Lucas's idea of a joke. But a bow and arrow? He didn't think so.

"Daniel? You there? What do you want me to do? I called Buck, but there was no answer at the office or on that confounded cell phone of his."

"He's not on the island. Neither of us is."

"Where the hell are you? And where's Bailey?"

"Abbie took her to Annapolis."

"The longer we wait, the fainter those tracks are going to get."

"Do whatever you have to, Will. I'll be back as soon as I can."

"You're not going to tell me where you're at, are you?"

"St. Michaels. I'm waiting for Lucas to contact me. We're making the trade today."

"For the boy?"

"Yes."

"You're on a fool's errand, Daniel. That son of a bitch won't give him to you. There may not even be a kid."

"I have to chance it, Will. Don't do anything until Buck and I get there."

"Don't know if I can wait. Matthew had his faults, but he was one of us."

"He was my brother."

"A weak vessel, all the same. But blood kin. I think I'd best round up Emma and a few good ole boys and have a look-see around."

Daniel felt lightheaded. "Don't do it, Will. You don't know who you're hunting for."

"Reckon I'll know him when I find him."

"Will—"

"Watch your back, Daniel. It would hit Bailey hard if you didn't come home."

Will hung up. Daniel tried Buck's cell but got only his voice mail. He left a message warning Buck not to return the call. He looked at his watch again. 5:35. He retraced his steps to the visitors' center.

It pained him to throw the bow and remaining arrows into the muddy creek. How many hours had he toiled to fashion them, and how many blisters had he suffered on his hands? Weeks. It had taken weeks to trim the seasoned lengths of pine, to smooth each arrow and glue on the duck feathers and use animal gut and glue to fasten the stone points. He'd worked all one winter on the bow, carefully crafting it and wrapping the grip with leather strips.

Slowly the quiver filled with water and sank out of sight. Tears welled in his eyes as he watched the bow bob and tumble in the tide until finally the black current took it under. It wasn't fair. The bow and arrows were his. He'd made them, and no one had the right to take them from him.

Nothing had gone right for him since the women had come to the island to dig in the old graves. He'd meant the snare for Dr. Knight's girl. That fool Matthew had stumbled into it instead. Maybe it was for the best. Matthew would have had to die, because he never would have learned. The preacher was stupid. He never learned from his mistakes, and he didn't believe in the curse. But he'd stumbled into the snare, and once he was caught, there was nothing to do but finish him.

Maybe this was the way it was supposed to be. Maybe he had to give up his bow and arrow, and Matthew Catlin had to die. Maybe the woman would leave the island and never come back, and he could live in peace again. He didn't like to cause anybody pain and he didn't like killing people. Their screams made him sick. Once they started screaming, he had to shut them up. In his heart, he was a good man, a gentle man. Was it his fault that he'd been born different, that he had to hide the way the Lord made him?

He looked down at his moccasins. He'd made them, too. Not of calf hide, which would have been easier to get, but genuine buckskin. He'd shot the deer himself, tanned the hide in the old way using the animal's brains, and cut and sewn each stitch the way his mother had taught him. Folks on Tawes had it easy, but in the old days, there wasn't money for store-bought shoes. And moccasins, made Indian style, were free for those not too lazy to make them.

He'd made moccasins for each of his special friends, measuring their small feet and sewing them strong and sturdy. The boys had loved them. Not like these city boys. All they wanted was brand-name sneakers from the mall, high-priced shoes. He'd made one pair for a city boy once, but he'd just laughed and said the moccasins were trash. It had made him mad, mad enough to . . . He wouldn't think about that boy anymore. He deserved what he'd gotten.

Sadly, one by one, he pulled off his moccasins and threw them into the creek after his bow and arrow. He could always make more, once the fuss about Matthew's death quieted down. It paid to be safe. Tawes was his home, and it wouldn't do to cause trouble too close to home.

Six o'clock came and went. Bailey and Abbie circled the sunken court again. Mothers walked by, some pushing strollers, others carriages. She saw a dark-haired toddler chasing a ball down the stairs. She rushed toward him, only to discover that the child was a girl and to earn a dirty look from the mother.

She jumped as her cell vibrated. She pulled it from her jeans pocket, dropped it onto the tile floor, and it clattered away. A teenage boy wearing black eyeliner, lipstick, and skin-tight leather pants retrieved it and handed it back to her. "Hello?" she said into the phone.

"Bailey."

"Where is he? Where's Daniel's child?"

"Last chance, Bailey. Three hundred thousand and Daniel never sees him."

"Give him to us, you bastard!"

Two passing Catholic nuns in full gray habit and white starched veils glared at her.

"No reason to be rude. This isn't personal."

"I won't pay you a cent. I—"

"Your choice. Good-bye, Bailey."

The line went dead. Bailey choked back tears. Had she harmed the little boy by refusing? Or had she saved him? She closed her eyes and prayed.

Minutes passed. Still no sign of the child.

Bailey looked at her watch. Quarter past six. She glanced at a woman standing outside a jewelry store drinking a soda. The pretty brunette, with bags on her arm—one bearing a bookstore logo and another a specialty shop—gave no hint that she was an off-duty Maryland state trooper, and neither did the businessman sitting on the steps with his leather attaché case and reading his newspaper. But both of them—cousins of Buck or Forest or Emma, she wasn't sure which—were police officers entrusted with the task of protecting her.

Bailey glanced around nervously. No Lucas, no little boy. Had Lucas lied to them, or had he detected the police and fled before handing over the child?

How long should she wait? She closed her eyes and whispered another prayer for Daniel's safety. Was Lucas watching, taunting her out of spite because of what she'd done to him when he'd broken into her house?

How long should she wait?

* * *

The pay phone rang at 6:18. Daniel seized it and was rewarded by Lucas's voice.

"Good boy."

"What do you want me to do?"

"Wire the five hundred thousand dollars. I'll give you the account number as soon as you're ready."

A red-haired couple with their two redheaded boys walked by and stared at Daniel. He turned his back and opened his laptop. Using his code, he transferred the money from his bank in the Caymans to Lucas's Swiss account. "Done," he said into the phone.

"Very good. It's been a pleasure."

"Is Bailey all right? Did you give her the boy?"

"No questions. But since our business has gone so well, I will give you a bit of advice."

"Yes?"

"Does the name Robert Mellmore mean anything to you?"

Daniel gritted his teeth. The man who didn't exist. The man who'd nearly pulled off a very large land swindle. "Yes, I know the name."

Lucas chuckled. "Don't trust the agency. And don't trust them to provide an airtight identity. If I'd troubled to create Robert myself, instead of leaving it to some G11, no one would have discovered the game."

"You're telling me that the agency was part of that?"

"You're not listening, Daniel. There's no need for this conversation to continue if you're not listening."

"I am."

Lucas laughed again. "You're growing soft on your little island. You've lost your edge."

"Maybe."

"My plan, Daniel. My personal operation. Doubtless you have a drawer full of aliases. Toss them. Trust no one—you'll live longer that way."

He waited.

"Enough of camaraderie. Do you see the trash container?"

"Yes."

"Do exactly as I say."

Daniel forced down his anger. "You're calling the shots."

"Drop your laptop and your cell phone in there and walk away. Leave the museum and return to your boat."

An uneasy feeling stirred the hairs on the nape of Daniel's neck. He looked around, wondering if Lucas was here, or if he had an accomplice. When he was certain none of the tourists were watching, Daniel followed Lucas's instructions. He couldn't help wondering if he'd just handed over $500,000 for nothing . . . wondering why and how Lucas had conceived the scheme to seize the Thomas Sherwood inheritance. Somehow, he felt it had to be more than avarice. Maybe it was simply a twisted game that Lucas had played out of spite.

Daniel turned left as he exited the museum area and walked quickly down a residential street toward the dock where he'd left his boat. He'd have to find a phone to call Bailey. It was after 6:30. Surely she had to have the boy by now. He needed to hear her voice— to know she was all right. He'd go crazy if he didn't reach her.

A two-story house stood vacant next to an empty lot. The grass around the neglected Victorian was high, and a *For Sale* sign stood next to the brick walk leading to the front step. Beside it stood a white, single-car garage with a window. Daniel noticed that the garage needed paint as much as the peeling house.

"Daniel!" a familiar voice shouted. "Get down!"

Daniel hit the ground rolling as gunfire erupted

from the garage window. Bullets plowed furrows into the street around him. Bits of macadam bloodied his face and arms as he scrambled for cover behind a parked SUV, all the while digging for the compact Glock 17 he carried clipped to the inside of his belt.

Glass shattered. Someone screamed.

Then the street was quiet. The silence seemed louder than the gunshots.

"Daniel? Are you all right?"

Buck stepped out from the corner of a house across the way, his Smith and Wesson semiautomatic held at an odd angle.

"Buck?" Daniel rose cautiously from behind the vehicle.

"Get the hell out of the street."

Daniel stared at his cousin. "Buck, are you—"

Buck stopped, staggered, and dropped to his knees, clutching the neat hole in the center of his chest.

CHAPTER TWENTY-ONE

Will knelt by the fireplace and stirred the ashes. The scorched corner of one snapshot remained intact. He picked it out of the hearth, lit a match, and set fire to the picture. The image curled and blackened before becoming indistinguishable as a photograph.

"You owed me one, Matt," Will murmured. He brushed the ashes into a dustpan, carried them outside to the end of his dock, and scattered them on the surface of the water.

Raven nudged Will's knee with his wet nose. Will's other two dogs stood on the lawn sniffing the Newfoundland.

"Feel kind of bad," Will said to Raven. "First thing in my life I ever stole." A crooked smile tilted one corner of his lips. "Well, old boy, I'm bound for hell anyways. Might as well be hanged for the whole hog as for just a slab of bacon."

He went back to the house for his shotgun, whistled up the rest of the pack, and set off for the dig site again. He thought about leaving Buck and Abbie's dog locked in the house, but he'd begun to think of the big animal as a lucky charm. If the animal hadn't disobeyed him and kept digging, he never would have found the gold bracelet. It would have lain there waiting for the next rain to wash it clean of dirt and expose it to whoever came along.

Will had placed calls to Emma and to Daniel before he'd stowed the bracelet under the floor in the cellar hole and before he'd burned the photos of the Irish stuff he'd taken from the church office. It would have been better to start the search right away, but he didn't carry a cell phone, so he'd had to make the calls from his house.

He hated cell phones. Damned things constantly going off and disturbing a man's thoughts. Maybe the Amish had it right. The more a man's home was connected to the outside world, the worse it got.

He'd thought it best that Daniel should hear the news about his brother from him rather than a stranger. And now that he'd told Emma and Daniel about finding Matt's body, he was sure that word was already spreading over the island.

Men would be gathering at the burial ground, and watermen would be searching the shores of Tawes. No need to yell for help from outsiders. The mainland state police would be here soon enough. The way he saw it, the longer it took the uniforms to arrive, the better chances his friends and neighbors would have of settling this the island way.

Island justice, he'd always heard it called. Things were different here on Tawes than on the mainland, maybe better. The United States had its Constitution and Bill of Rights, but the law was supposed to protect the innocent and convict the guilty. It didn't seem to work that way nowadays.

Will might not have a lot of book learning, but he

wasn't uneducated or stupid. This country's laws were based on English common law, where an accused person was judged by a jury of his or her peers. That meant folks who knew them, folks who'd grown up with them and knew a thief or a liar on sight.

Today, lawyers, judges, and other nuts had perverted those laws. Not only was an accused not judged by people who knew them, they had to be judged by total strangers as far away from where the crime was committed as possible. The law was twisted and stretched and squeezed so that the criminals had more rights than the victims. It didn't matter if an accused man had raped and murdered in the past or lived the life of a saint. Nothing counted in the courts but what a jury could be persuaded to believe by slick-talking lawyers. No, the old ways were best. Not fancy, but swift and sure.

A life for a life was what he believed.

By the time Will reached the dig site, other men and a few hardy women were already gathering as he'd supposed they would. Emma was waiting with George, Nate, and Harry. Phillip and Jim were just nosing Jim's flat-bottomed duck boat through the reeds. All the islanders carried guns, and both Jim and Harry had brought their hunting dogs.

Only Emma, Nate, George, and two or three others had the stomach to take a look at poor Matthew. His tongue was swollen, and his face discolored. Insects swarmed around the body, crawling into Matthew's nostrils and open mouth. Emma's face turned a sickly white when she stared into Matthew's vacant eyes, and her freckles stood out like chicken pox. She gagged and barely kept her gorge down, while Nate ran for the reeds and dumped his supper.

The coon dogs had the scent of death in their noses and they milled and whined nervously. The big New-

foundland had made his peace with Will's three, but
he was wary of the strange dogs. He kept close to Will,
sniffing the air and watching from his huge liquid
eyes, alert but without showing aggression.

"Should have left that bear at home," George said.
"Never saw a mainland dog yet was worth the cost of
shootin' him. First step into the marsh, he'll sink out
of sight."

Will smiled. "Not likely. These dogs are bred to water. They've used up north for rescue. Archie might
turn out to be the best tracker in the bunch."

One of Jim's hound bitches snarled at Archie, and
the Newfoundland bared his teeth. Jim curbed his
hound, and she slunk into the midst of the pack with
her tail between her legs.

"Think we should cut Matthew down?" Harry asked.
He was wiping his mouth with the back of his sleeve,
and Will wondered if he'd been sick too.

"It doesn't seem right," Nate said, "just leaving him
hanging like that, him a minister and all."

"No." Jim shook his head. "We have to leave him as
we found him for Buck and the medical examiners.
Don't anybody go near the body. No telling what evidence you could destroy."

"What in God's name could make a man do such a
thing to another?" Emma asked.

"Don't 'spect it had much to do with the good
Lord," George muttered, kicking at the sand. "Devil's
work, if you ask me."

"Looks like moccasin tracks leading away from . . .
from Matthew's remains," Nate said.

Emma looked grim. "Means he's probably one of us."

"Likely," Will agreed. "Not many off this island wear
handmade skin shoes."

"What about that Indian? The stranger?" Phillip

said. "You caught him sneakin' around here the other night, didn't you, Will?"

"Possible," Will answered. "But he was wearing boots when we caught up with him."

"Still . . . an Indian." Phillip looked at Jim. "And from what I hear, husband to the dead doctor."

"Yeah," Harry agreed. "Heard he's a wealthy oil man from out west."

George spat a wad of tobacco onto the grass. "Sounds fishy to me. What's he doin' here on Tawes anyway?"

"Said he was worried about his girl," Will answered.

Phillip whistled at one of his dogs who was nosing around the tents. "Get over here, Nance!" Turning back, he said, "Maybe the oil man came for that, or maybe for other reasons."

"That's fool's talk," Jim argued. "What would Vernon Night Horse have against Matthew? This is bad, as bad as I've ever seen. Why would he string a man up like a deer and then shoot him while he's helpless?"

"Did you come out here to track this murderer or to jabber?" Emma demanded. "I say, let's get on his trail before it gets cold."

Jim brought his hounds forward. "We'll see what the dogs can find. Marsh is hard, even for dogs. Too much water to hold a decent scent."

"Don't take chances, boys," Will said. "He's killed before. He'll think nothing of killing again. We don't want to lose any of you. But don't get foolhardy and pick off Aunt Birdy while she's out gathering mushrooms."

More men arrived as Jim set his dogs on the scent. The pack leader began to bark, and the rest of the hounds streamed after her. Will waited as the men, women, and dogs moved away, until only he and Emma were left with the Newfoundland and Will's three dogs.

"What's on your mind?" Emma asked, hunkering down on the beach. "Usually, you'd take point on a big hunt."

"Figured we might keep looking around here," Will said. "See if there's anything I missed earlier. By morning, it might rain again, and then we'd find nothing."

"Never did care too much to be part of a herd, myself," Emma replied. "Guess I'll stay here and help you out."

"It's a free country."

"That's what I heard, but I've not seen enough of it to tell for certain."

Raven whined, and Will glanced over to see the Newfoundland standing in the pit closest to the tents, the one Matthew had worked on. A cascade of dirt flew as the dog dug excitedly. "Archie! Come up out of there!" he shouted. "Abbie put a lot of work into staking those holes out just so. She won't—"

"She won't like that." Emma pointed.

Archie lumbered up out of the pit, shaggy ears flopping, a human skull clamped between his huge jaws.

"Buck?" Daniel ran to his cousin's side expecting to see a river of blood, expecting to hear a death rasp coming from Buck's throat. He saw neither, but he didn't take time to administer first aid. He caught Buck around the shoulders and half carried, half dragged the bigger man behind the solid bulk of the SUV.

"Damn it, Buck. What are you doing here? You were supposed to be in Annapolis with Bailey."

Already, people were coming down the street. Daniel heard the wail of a police siren. "Was it Lucas? Did you get him?" He ripped off his shirt and balled it up to stop the bleeding.

"Don't know." Buck gasped and pressed his chest.

"Shit, but that hurts." He inhaled and coughed. "He was waiting for you in that garage."

"How bad are you hurt?"

"I think I might have cracked a couple of ribs."

"Ribs?" Daniel drew his hand away and stared at it stupidly. No blood. "You didn't take a bullet to the chest?"

"I sure as hell did." Buck coughed again and leaned against the SUV. "But one of us had sense enough to wear protection."

"You're wearing body armor?"

The wail of the siren grew closer. Excited voices filled the air.

"This could be embarrassing." Buck groaned. "Lots of questions. We'll be tied up here for hours. Anything you can think of to get us out of this wasps' nest?"

"I can try." Daniel looked hard at Buck to assure himself that he wasn't hallucinating . . . that he'd been wrong, and Buck wasn't mortally wounded . . . that the body-armor vest had saved his life. "Wait here. And stay out of sight."

"Wasn't planning on going anywhere until I catch my breath."

Daniel dug his wallet out of a back pocket, rose, and strode toward the approaching men and women. Behind them, a police car turned onto the street, lights flashing.

"Stand back!" Daniel commanded. "Official F.B.I. business! Remain where you are for your own safety!" He flashed ID.

The Maryland state policeman got out of his vehicle and spoke into his radio. "Ten-two." He appeared to be young and uncertain.

Daniel kept both hands in plain view. "Agent Johnson, F.B.I. We have a situation here. Suspected terrorists. My people have the unsubs contained on this block."

"We had reports of shots fired."

"Yes. One of my men was fired on, and he returned fire."

"Are there any injuries? Do you need an ambulance?"

"No injuries," Daniel answered. "We have a possible explosive device planted in a vehicle." Daniel surveyed the gathering crowd of curious onlookers. "I need you to keep these civilians out of this two-block area."

The trooper scanned the vacant street behind Daniel. "Do you have the situation under control?"

"Yes, we do."

"I need to confirm your identification, sir." Daniel tossed his wallet to him. The young trooper frowned. "This appears to be you, Mr. Johnson. But this isn't F.B.I. This says State Department."

"Covert." He gave the cop the *look*. "This is an emergency situation, Officer. There's no time for delay. There may be other operatives in the area. My men's lives are in danger."

"I'll have to contact my desk sergeant—"

"Do it, then!" Daniel snapped. "Our unsubs may be getting away. Give your superior the number on the back. Tell him to ask to speak directly to Agent Evan Mobisy or Agent Anne Pellier. They can verify my identity and the validity of this operation."

Gawking tourists and locals moved closer, pointing at the police car and at Daniel. Someone whipped out a camera, and Daniel threw his hand up to shield his face. "Clear the area for your own safety!" Daniel shouted to them. "There may be a bomb on this block."

The policeman carried on an urgent conversation with his troop sergeant by radio before nodding and saying, "Your story checks out, Agent Johnson. My sergeant has dispatched three more cars. What can I do to help?"

"Control the area. Protect the civilians. Now if you'll excuse me, I have to mop up this scene and try to catch the bad guys."

When Daniel returned to the SUV, he saw no sign of Buck, but he did notice two bullet holes in the door. He circled the vehicle and found Buck on his feet, leaning against the car. He was red-faced and breathing raggedly, but looking more himself.

"Someone will have a hard time explaining those holes to his insurance company," he said, handing Daniel his holstered firearm. "What did you tell them?"

"What I always do. Blame it on the F.B.I."

"I thought you were out of the agency for good."

"I am, but I always carry a fake ID, just for insurance." Buck grinned. "They may not be happy with you."

"They never were."

Together, cautiously they crossed the street and circled the garage. The double wooden doors were open. Buck came around the corner, weapon ready, but nothing stirred in the small building. An '81 Ford pickup truck sat on blocks, windows and paint buried under layers of dust and pigeon droppings. A door hung ajar, but the cab was empty. Together they inspected the garage.

"It's all right," Buck said. He motioned toward the single window facing the street. Lucas lay crumpled on the concrete, a rainbow of shattered window glass on the floor around him, a bullet hole in the center of his forehead.

Daniel nudged one of the dead man's European running shoes.

Lucas didn't move. A stream of sunlight lit his frozen features. Daniel thought his eyes held as much human expression as they ever had.

"Score one for the home team." Buck pried a Glock, almost identical to Daniel's, out of Lucas's lifeless hand.

"I hope to God Bailey got the boy. You were supposed to be guarding her."

"Right, and if I had been, you'd be dead."

"Maybe."

"Maybe, hell, cuz. You owe me." Buck removed the dead man's cell phone and retrieved his laptop from the floor. A quick search of Lucas's pockets showed them empty. "Now what do we do with him?"

"We leave him for the State Department."

Buck looked at him quizzically.

"An inside joke. Most operatives pose as employees of the Department of State. I gave that cop the number of a low-level contact. It won't be long before this place will be swarming with G.S. 14's, intelligence personnel, and real F.B.I. agents. They'll butt heads until one of them comes up with an airtight explanation."

"You think the agency will cover for us?"

"I think they'll have to. After all, Lucas was one of them. He was deep cover. He didn't exist. It will be up to them to tidy up. As he'd put it, 'no loose ends.'"

"Speaking of which, I think you may have left some," Buck reminded him.

"My laptop and cell."

"You go back and get them. I'll bring the boat around to the museum. If I can't get in close to shore, you can swim out. The quicker we put St. Michaels behind us, the better."

Daniel looked down at Lucas. It was ironic, all the operations he'd survived, only to die here in an Eastern Shore town, killed by a good ole boy. "Good shooting, Buck."

"I thought so."

Daniel swallowed. If Lucas hadn't kept his word, there might be no way to discover where he'd kept the boy. They might never find him. He wondered if it would have been better for them all if he'd finished off Lucas last summer when he'd confronted him on the boat. But it was too late for *should haves* and *could haves*. Lucas was dead now, and he'd never threaten Bailey or Daniel's child again. Dead and forever silent. Whatever Lucas knew, he'd taken it with him to the grave. Daniel could summon a lot of regrets, but none for the man on the floor at his feet. He hoped Lucas was bound for the blackest corner of hell.

"Daniel?" Buck's urgent whisper yanked him back from his thoughts. "Are you all right?"

"Yeah, sure. I'm good. How about you? You can walk that far with those ribs?"

"I'll have to, won't I?"

Buck hadn't said anything about Matthew's death, which meant that Will hadn't been able to reach him to tell him about the murder. Daniel would have to tell him, but there would be plenty of time for that on the way back to Tawes. What was important was that Bailey be safe and that they find his son . . . find him alive.

It was dark when Abbie's helicopter touched down in Aunt Birdy's cow pasture. Bailey had hardly spoken on the flight back from Annapolis. She couldn't shake the thought that she'd made a terrible mistake. Even hearing Daniel's voice on Abbie's cell and knowing that he was safe didn't temper her fear that she'd done something that would keep them from recovering Daniel's little boy.

Daniel hadn't told her much, simply that he had Buck with him and they were on their way back to the island. Bailey had wanted to confess that she'd failed him, that Lucas had double-crossed them and hadn't delivered the child, but she'd said nothing. That much caution she'd learned from him. Never trust the phones. She would have to hold off until they were face to face. The waiting was agony.

"They said to meet them at Emma's," Abbie said. "Buck was adamant that we stay there, keep the doors locked, and not go out to your farm or the cabin."

But as they were leaving the aircraft to walk to Emma's, Forest came across the field from Aunt Birdy's house. He was carrying a flashlight, and he was armed with a shotgun.

"Ladies. Don't be alarmed. I'm your escort."

Bailey looked at the gun. "What's wrong?"

"It's Matthew. He's been murdered."

At 10:45 P.M., Buck and Daniel reached Emma's dock. Abbie and Bailey rushed out to meet them, and Bailey threw herself into Daniel's arms. "Are you all right?" she asked. "Did Lucas contact you?"

Buck glanced toward the house and tapped Daniel's arm.

Abbie heard the screen door slam, glanced back, and saw her father step out on the back porch.

"Later," Daniel said to Bailey.

He was bare-chested, and Buck was wearing a shirt she'd seen on Daniel earlier. Buck's posture was stiff, and he seemed to be walking on eggs. Both of them had bruises on their faces. A long bloody scrape ran down Daniel's right arm.

"What happened?" Abbie demanded of Buck. "We waited at the mall, but no one came with the child."

"I may have ruined everything." Bailey was weeping. "Lucas called me. He wanted more money, but I refused. I couldn't. I couldn't take the chance that he'd kill the boy." She clung to Daniel.

"What's wrong with you?" Abbie caught Buck's arm. "You've been hurt, haven't you?"

He shrugged off her touch. "Nothing much."

"No?" Abbie yanked up his shirt. Even by moonlight she could see that Buck's chest was a mass of bruises.

"You look like you've been shot," her father said, quietly coming up behind her.

"Not quite." Buck yanked the shirt down. "Listen, Abbie, I've got to visit the murder scene. I want you and your father to remain here."

"I'll come with you," she said.

"You can't."

"Why not? Forest told us that the body was found at the dig site."

"You aren't coming because I'm not taking civilians into a crime scene."

"May as well," Emma called. She, Jim, and Phillip came around the corner of the house. "Half the island's already there. A few more shouldn't matter."

Buck swore. "Couldn't you keep them away until I got there?"

"Tried." Emma shrugged. "You know folks on Tawes. Nothing's private, least of all death."

"Where's Will?"

"Still out at the burial ground with Nate and Harry." Emma lowered her voice to keep Daniel from hearing. "No one touched Matthew's body, but they're keeping watch over it."

"I'm on my way now," Buck said. "Anybody notified the medical examiner's office?"

"Nope." Emma shook her head. "We thought that was your department, seeing as how you're the law on Tawes. A pity to leave Matthew like that, but nobody wanted to take a chance on destroying evidence."

"I appreciate that."

"Give me a chance to change my clothes," Abbie said. "I'm coming."

Buck glared at her. "Out of the question."

"It's my dig site."

"Not tonight it isn't. And not tomorrow. Not until we find whoever killed Matthew."

"Bull. You're not being fair."

"What's not fair is risking your life. I think you're right, Abbie. I think that whoever killed your mother may have killed Matthew and the Gilbert boy. And until I find that person, you're not going to set foot in that marsh."

"No? Who says?"

"I do." He glanced at her father. "Sir, I'll have to ask you to make certain she stays away. We can't risk her life for a few old bones."

"More than a few," Emma said. "That big dog you gave Abbie . . . he dug into one of the pits. We covered it right back up, Will and me."

"Covered up what?" Abbie demanded.

"A skull."

"The dog dug up a skull?" she repeated. "An Indian skull?"

Emma shrugged. "Don't rightly know what kind it was. I expect it must have been. No white folks ever buried out there so far as I know. You, Phillip?"

"No, none I hear tell of," Phillip said. "All our people are right here in town, in the churchyard. Oh, some of the early settlers buried their kin on their land grants, I suppose. But nobody's been buried anywhere but the town cemetery in my lifetime."

"All the same, I need to see the skull," Abbie replied. "I'll be able to tell if it is Native American or white—at least I think I will."

"Not now you don't." Vernon moved to put an arm around his daughter's shoulders. "I agree with Chief Davis. It's not safe for you out there. I've lost your mother to some madman. I've no intention of losing you, too."

"I'm going—with you or without you."

Buck scowled at her. "I said *no*, Abbie. I mean it. You—"

Her eyes flashed. "You don't know me very well if you think you can keep me away from that site now. Either of you."

CHAPTER TWENTY-TWO

Abbie stared at Matthew's dangling body. She'd
thought she'd prepared herself for the sight. She'd
imagined that since she hadn't particularly cared for
the man, it might be easier to scientifically detach herself from the scene, to look at the corpse without being terrified or disgusted.

She'd been wrong.

No horror flick had ever been as frightening as this
white figure slowly swaying in the salt-tinged night
wind. She wasn't physically sick, but spiritually, she felt
stricken to the core.

Her repulsion was quickly replaced by a surge of
compassion for the dead pastor . . . for the agony and
fear he must have suffered in the last moments of his
life. And oddly, she felt compassion for the sick creature who had done this and thus severed the last
bonds of his own humanity.

Grandmother Willow's words came back to her. "*I feel
a twisted spirit . . . powerful . . . evil. He hunts the night.*"

And then, as clearly as if she'd heard the old woman speaking aloud: "*Three. Three more will die.*"

"Abbie." Buck put an arm around her. "You okay?"

"Yes," she answered. His embrace was warm, but she was chilled to the bone. She couldn't turn away from Matthew Catlin's body. Mentally she counted the dead. Lucas. Did he count as one? Lucas, Matthew . . . And who? Who would make the third? Grandmother Willow was a holy woman, one who had the far sight. If she saw *three* more violent deaths, three there would be. But if Lucas wasn't a part of this . . . would two more die?

Would Buck be one of them? Would she?

She exhaled. "This was worse than I expected."

"Abbie. I'm sorry. It's why I tried to—"

"No," she interrupted softly. "I need to look at the skull. I needed to be here." Still staring at the gently swaying corpse, she rested her cheek against his chest. "I need to see what you see."

He was quiet for a moment. "I guess that makes sense. If we're going to marry—if you're going to a cop's wife—you may have to face death again. I've never seen a body in this condition, but it's not as bad for me as seeing dead children. Leaving the mainland behind meant no more picking kids up off the highway in pieces."

She looked up at him. She couldn't see his eyes in the darkness, but she knew they'd reveal what he tried so hard to hide, that he cared so much for the ones under his protection. . . . the ones he might have saved. "He deserves respect," she said. "They all do. The dead."

He nodded.

"And you give them that."

He motioned toward the tents, where someone had set gas lanterns on her worktable. "Why don't you go on?" he said. "I've got to stay here, to maintain what's left of the scene. Until the medical examiner arrives. He's coming in by' copter from Baltimore. I told them to land, in the field at Bailey's farm. Harry's waiting there to lead them in."

"They're not coming by boat?"

"Not at night. The marsh guts can be tricky at night. Even Jim wanted his boat out of here before dark, and he knows this swamp as well as anyone."

"Will Tawes appears to be at home here."

"Yeah, Will. Will's a special sort of man. One of the old-timers. Will's better in the woods or marsh than even Jim or Emma." He squeezed her shoulders. "Go on, now."

In an attempt to prove to herself that her imagination wasn't running away with her, that it wasn't as awful as she thought, she allowed herself a final glimpse of the pastor.

She was certain that Matthew Catlin's grotesque and frozen image would remain with her forever, lurking in that shadowy place between dreams and reality.

Abbie shuddered. Grasping her mother's turquoise ring, she twisted it on her finger. And touching the silver that had lain next to her mother's warm flesh for so long, she felt a small measure of comfort.

"Can I bring you coffee?" she said.

"Yeah," Buck said. "That would be nice. Black."

"Good choice," she said lightly, walking away. "I didn't think to bring sugar or cream."

She fetched him the insulated mug of coffee, drank a cup herself, and then pulled on gloves to check out Emma's reported Indian skull. Buck's dog lay fastened by a length of rope to a tent pole, just out of reach of the pit. "You," she admonished, "are a troublemaker, and you can forget any idea you have of staying with me."

The black, shaggy dog tilted his head and thumped his tail.

"No, no tricks, no endearing tail-wagging. You stay on this island. I go to Greece. Is that clear?"

Archie didn't answer, but she had the feeling that he didn't need to. Somehow, she suspected, she'd never have a chance of getting free of him.

George came to the edge of the pit carrying a lantern in one hand and a cup of coffee in the other. "Not diggin' bones in the middle of the night, are you?"

"Emma said the dog dug up a human skull. If it's Native American, it can't be as old as the other material I've been finding. Bone decays quickly in this type of soil."

"Dead's dead," George said. He sipped his coffee. "Strong stuff. You wouldn't have any sugar, would you?"

"Sorry, I forgot."

"I can make do." He lifted the lantern higher. "It don't seem right, disturbing the dead."

Abbie knelt in the mud and began to brush aside the disturbed dirt that had obviously been pressed back into place. "A lot of people agree with you, Mr. Williams. But I need—" A jolt of excitement shot through her as her fingers brushed something solid. Carefully she lifted the egg-shaped object.

"Ah, hell." She stared at the skull in the wavering lantern light.

George's eyes widened.

"Call Buck," she said. "Call him, now."

The badly preserved skull was small and fragile, a child's skull. Not old in the context of archaeology, and definitely not Indian.

George stood dumbly, still gazing at the skull.

"Buck!" she yelled. "I need you! Now!"

Three days after Lucas died, Daniel got the call he'd been expecting from a man who'd once been his senior officer at the C.I.A. He and Bailey had been crabbing with hand lines off her dock. They'd netted nearly a dozen fat jimmies, and Puzzle was running up and down barking at the bushel basket that held their catch. "I've got to go to Kent Island to meet someone," he said to Bailey. "The agency has questions about what happened in St. Michaels."

"Can I come?"

He smiled at her. "You know better than that. But it's all right. You don't need to worry. I'll be fine."

"How do I know I'll ever see you again?"

"You have to understand. It cost a fortune to train me, and while I was on staff, I was part of a family. They may not like what I'm doing now, and they may want to lure me back. But they won't use torture and they won't make me disappear." He caught her chin in his hand and kissed her tenderly. "They'll probably offer me a big bonus and first-class plane tickets to Paris."

"You're certain this isn't a trap to—"

"No, honey. It's no trap. Lucas jumped the fence, but he used to work for them. Someone killed him, and they need to know who and why."

She sat down on the deck and let her legs hang over the side. "It scares me. It all scares me. I'm not sleeping well at night."

"You think I don't know that?" He groaned and ruffled her hair. "I'll be fine. We'll be fine. And maybe, if we're lucky, they'll have some idea where Lucas put the boy."

"If there is a boy."

"I think there is, and I don't think either of us will sleep well again until we find him and bring him home." He looked at her meaningfully. "You're all right with that?"

"Yes. Hell, yes. I feel terrible about what happened. I keep wondering if I should have promised Lucas more money."

Daniel shook his head. "And if you had and he still hadn't produced the child? What then? You would have gone the rest of your life believing you'd killed him."

"When? When do you have to go?"

"Now. Right away. But I won't leave you here alone. I've been thinking, this might be a good time for you to fly out to California to see your father."

Her Tawes-blue eyes narrowed. "Fly out to California. Without you? You've lost your mind."

"No, I haven't. It would free me up to help Buck with this investigation."

"You're not a police officer."

"No, I'm not. But I am very good at collecting information. It's what I was trained to do. And good detective work is usually sifting through paperwork. If I don't have to worry about protecting you day and night, it would ease my mind."

"How long?" She looked thoughtful. "It's true my father isn't getting any younger. But school starts the first week of September."

"Then go for two weeks."

"I don't know if I could stand two weeks in my stepmother's house."

"So, stay with your dad a week, and spend the second week doing whatever you like. Get away from all this stress. Shop. Rent a car and sightsee. Don't you have a girlfriend out there?"

"Yes, but—"

"Please, Bailey. Do this for me. You know Will is worried sick about you. He spends the nights circling the house with his shotgun. I don't know when he sleeps."

"I'll think about it."

"No, I want you to get on the Internet and buy a first-class ticket this afternoon."

"First-class? Do you know what first-class tickets cost? When you just lost half a million dollars?"

He sighed. "Not exactly."

"What do you mean, not exactly? Puzzle, stop!" she scolded the corgi. "Come here, and stop that fool barking." She pursed her lips. "And if I went to California for two weeks, what would I do with Puzzle?"

"Emma. Emma promised to watch her."

"So you told Emma before you asked me?"

He shrugged. "I knew you'd use Puzzle as an excuse."

"So what does *not exactly* mean?"

"I checked my Cayman Islands account this morning."

"And?"

"The money I gave to Lucas—the money I wired to his Swiss—"

"I know what money you mean. What about it?"

"It's back."

"It can't be. There must be some mistake. You said—"

"I said it was gone, and it was. But now it's back." What he didn't tell her was that more than the half million had been deposited to his account. The total now stood at $3,700,028. American.

"How? Why?" she demanded.

"I don't know, Bailey. I don't know how or why it got there in the first place, only what Lucas told me, and that's dubious. In any case, I can afford to buy you a first-class ticket. Round trip."

"Two weeks," she bargained. "And I'm not making the reservations until you're safely back on Tawes."

"Deal," he said, offering his hand. "So long as you throw in some hot sex in the shower and a back massage to boot."

* * *

"Buck!" Eight days later, Abbie, her face flushed and eyes spitting fire, confronted him in his office. "Why have you been asking questions about my father's financial affairs?"

Buck laid the pen he'd been doodling with on the desk and rose to his feet. He met her obvious ire with quiet strength. "Did you know he's the beneficiary of a million-dollar insurance policy on your mother?"

"First you insinuate that Daddy wanted to be rid of her, and now you think he killed her for the insurance?"

"I never said that, Abbie." He reached out to touch her, but she moved away.

"The insurance was meant to protect me, to guarantee my education, and my future, if anything happened to either of them. If you know that he was the beneficiary, then you must have discovered that Ànati held an identical policy on him. And she was the beneficiary. Not to mention the policies were taken out years ago."

"I'm only doing my job."

"That's an excuse. You know what my dad thinks? He believes you're asking questions to find out how much I'm worth."

"Do you think that?"

"I don't know what I believe. I told you that this was happening too fast between us. I never wanted a serious—"

"And you believe I did? If I didn't love her—if I wasn't nuts over her—why would I tie myself to a spoiled, egotistical brat who intends to spend half her life jetting back and forth to Greece?"

"Spoiled brat?" She was trembling now, her hands balled into fists at her sides. "I thought we'd get around to that sooner or later. I'm sorry if my father isn't a penniless reservation Indian. But he didn't get where he is financially by luck. He's worked hard for what he has, and he deserves it."

Buck seized her shoulders and held her. "Listen to what you're saying. You asked me to try to find out who murdered your mother and why. That's what I'm doing."

She struggled to jerk free, but he held her. "Not by investigating my father. Daddy didn't kill her. He loved her."

Buck looked into her eyes. "The old saying is that love and hate aren't far apart. Emotions can get out of control. People do bad things to their loved ones, things they don't mean to do."

"He wants me to go back to Oklahoma with him. To-morrow. Daddy's been away from home too long."

"He wants you off Tawes and away from me."

"Apparently, he's a good judge of character, maybe better than I am."

"Are you going?"

"I don't know. I haven't decided yet."

"God, but you're a sight when you're all fired up." He leaned close and kissed her. At first, she struggled, but then she put her arms around him and kissed him back with as much passion as he'd expressed. Need flashed under his skin. They hadn't made love since the night on the boat, and it had been too long. "I love you, Abbie," he said hoarsely.

She drew in a ragged breath and moistened her bottom lip with her tongue. "I hate you."

"I'll take that as an affirmative."

"I'm serious, Buck." Her dark Indian eyes smoldered with resentment. "You're wrong to suspect my father. You don't know him."

"You're right. I don't. But I'd be a poor cop if I let my feelings for you keep me from investigating every lead . . . which is all my questioning is."

He picked up a thick folder from the desk behind him. "I was going to look for you. This just came in.

You were right when you said that skull wasn't a Native American child. The medical examiner's office identified it and the other partial remains found in the same pit as African-American. Three individuals—a child, probably male, approximately seven years old, and a male and female adult."

"How long ago were they buried there?" she asked, thumbing through the papers.

"Putting an exact age on bones in that condition will take a while. My source at the medical examiner's office says they guess twenty-five to thirty-five years."

"That recent?"

Buck nodded. "That recent. The child had a fractured femur, but the other two showed signs of violent death. The male's skull, radius, and ribs were shattered, and what bones remain had cut marks consistent with a thick blade, maybe an ax. There was less of the female to process, but she had broken bones as well as a fractured skull."

"From what I saw, the bodies had been dumped in, not laid out in a normal burial pattern," Abbie said. "In other words—"

"They were murdered, and their bodies hidden in the last place anyone would look."

"Which means that our killer may have murdered my mother to stop her from excavating that grave site." She leaned over the desk and scanned the death report. "So Reverend Catlin's death is linked to Ànati's."

"And to Sean Gilbert's. The stone ax that was used to bludgeon your mother to death had traces of Sean's blood on it."

"But who? Who killed them and why?" She raised her head to look at him. "You can't think my father is guilty. These people died three decades ago."

"Exactly. Which I would have explained, if you had

you I was one of the good guys, didn't I?"

She pushed his hands away. "Can you please concentrate on the murders? How hard is it to identify
these people? There can't be five hundred people on
Tawes, and twenty-five years ago, there were probably

"More, actually. But you're assuming that our victims lived on the island. Someone might have murdered them elsewhere and dumped them here."

"But the killer must have been someone familiar
with the burial ground. It's not likely to be the results
of a Philly drug deal gone bad."

"So now I start asking questions. People on this island have long memories. If a couple and a child went
missing, someone will remember."

"Can I help?" she offered.

"Certain you want to? It's time-consuming work."

"Field work," she said. "I was trained to do it by one
of the best, my mother. And if she taught me anything
about science, it's that you take good notes and no de-

"You're not going to Oklahoma?"

"One of these days, but not yet."

Buck had been to see him today, asking questions
about the bodies Dr. Knight's daughter had uncovered. He admitted he'd known them, had to, because
one of his neighbors might have seen him with the

It was bad, as bad as he'd been afraid it would be.
He'd thought they'd be safe there, had been certain
they would. But Matthew wouldn't stay away from the
burial ground, and had brought in the doctor and her

All these years he'd protected the graves. He'd been so proud of himself. After he'd taken care of the preacher, he'd slept soundly at night. But no more. Now his hands sweated and he saw the faces of his special friends . . . heard them calling out to him . . . begging him not to fail them. He knew what he had to do to make it right.

He had to finish it.

He had to make Dr. Knight's daughter pay for what she'd done.

Maybe then he could sleep. Maybe then they'd understand that he hadn't meant to fail them, that it wasn't his fault.

She had to be taught a lesson.

"You have no idea why Mr. McCready wants to see you?" Abbie asked as she and Buck approached Forest's front porch. "He didn't mention me. I don't know why I couldn't have remained at Emma's. I still haven't finished the paper I'm writing—"

"Spare me, woman. You talk as much as you eat." Buck hugged her. "We still have a killer on the loose. Daniel sent Bailey off to California, where he knew she'd be safe. I'm not leaving you alone at Emma's or anywhere else, not until I find who's responsible for these murders."

Abbie rolled her eyes.

"I care too much about you, darlin'."

She didn't want to admit it, but secretly she was glad Buck hadn't left her tonight. Working at the site as she had been since Matthew was murdered, walking through the marsh—even with Buck's brothers, or Will, or George to guard her—suddenly gave her the creeps.

She wasn't easily frightened, but as each day passed, she felt more at risk. She wasn't sleeping well, not even when she lay in Buck's arms after they'd made love. Strange dreams troubled her, and twice she'd heard an owl hoot in the daytime.

She wondered if she wouldn't do better to go back to Philly and get an early start on the school year. She wondered, but she hadn't done it. She didn't know how she felt about Buck, or if what her father had suggested was true. And how in the hell was she supposed to finish her studies if her personal life was in such turmoil?

"I hardly think anyone's going to break into the house to get me."

"They might," Buck said. "I'm not giving them the opportunity."

He was wearing his pistol. Having him beside her, big and strong and confident, eased Abbie's fears. She didn't want to think about what her life would be like if she decided to go on without him.

Forest's sister opened the door.

"Evening, Miss Margaret," Buck said. "You know Abbie."

"Come in," the older woman called cheerfully. "Daniel's already here." She smiled at Abbie. "I'm so sorry about the loss of your mother."

"Thank you. I miss her."

"And of course you would." She caught Abbie's arm. "You just come into the kitchen with me, dear. I've made lemonade and some lovely scones with lemon curd."

Abbie glanced at Buck.

"Forest and Daniel are in the front parlor. You gentlemen just go on and tend to your business," Margaret said. "If I know Forest, he'll have some single-malt Scotch already poured."

Buck shrugged helplessly as Margaret tugged her

down the center hall, presumably where she could question Abbie at length.

Forest rose and smiled as Buck pushed open the study door. Daniel stood by the window, a pewter cup between his hands. Forest's two dogs lay sprawled on the rug near the empty fireplace. "Come in, come in," the lawyer said.

Buck nodded to Daniel and accepted a drink.

"After hours, a drop of spirits can't hurt," Forest said, waving Buck to a comfortable chair. "I understand you two were up to no good in St. Michaels a bit ago."

Buck glanced at Daniel, who shrugged. "It's Tawes. Nothing much stays a secret."

"I'm sure that whatever you did, you had good reason," Forest said.

"Truer words were never spoken," Buck replied. He tasted the Scotch. It was excellent. Peaty, rich, full-bodied.

Forest closed the heavy door. "I hope Miss Night Horse doesn't feel slighted, but what I have to ask you can't leave this room. Ever."

Buck waited.

"The two of you are aware of the Island Fund and its charitable purposes here on Tawes."

Daniel nodded. "Known about it all my life."

"It's been my responsibility for years, and I'm not getting any younger."

Neither he nor Daniel commented on that.

"To be frank, what I want is for you two to assume management of the fund and its monies. What do you say?"

"I can understand why you'd want Daniel," Buck said, "but—"

Forest poured himself another measure of Scotch. "You two are blood kin. You're honest and levelheaded."

"Daniel?" Buck glanced at his cousin.

"I've already agreed."

"He came a little early, so I felt free to discuss the matter. Plus, Daniel has suggested using interest from the fund to open a private school, open to every child on the island without cost. It might ease the concerns of parents who are afraid our public school will close."

"I know that will please Bailey," Daniel said.

"Daniel's made a donation to the fund. A most generous donation."

"I don't know what to say." Buck looked from Daniel to Forest.

"Say yes," Daniel urged.

"All right." Buck raised his cup. "To the Island Fund," he said. "May it last as long as the blue crabs."

"One more thing," Forest said. "You know I've been tracing the family trees to find the real heirs to the Sherwood—" The doorbell rang. "That must be Emma."

Buck glanced at his watch. Emma was always late.

Forest went to the door and returned with Emma. "You're just in time," he said. "Will you join us in a drink?"

"I'm partial to brandy."

"This is a celebration," Forest said. "I was just about to share some good news with the boys."

Emma smiled. "It's about time we had some good news around here."

"Now that we know Thomas Sherwood's grandfather never owned the land that the realty company wanted for a marina, it goes to the descendants of the last legal owner. You, Buck and his brothers, and Daniel."

"No shit?" Emma gulped her brandy.

Forest laughed. "No shit."

"And no marina," Buck added. "Not now. Not ever."

* * *

Under the glow of an orange moon, Will carried flowers to his daughter's grave as he had so many times in the last thirty-odd years. It was night, but daylight or darkness never made much difference to him. All his life, he'd roamed the island in all kinds of weather. Anyone who saw him passing through the streets after midnight wouldn't give it a second thought.

Once he reached the church cemetery, he found his way unerringly to Beth's resting place beside that of his sister Elizabeth. Sometimes he brought flowers for her as well, but not tonight. She wouldn't approve of what he was doing. Lots of what he'd done in his lifetime, Elizabeth had disapproved of. He supposed it was that way with brothers and sisters.

Somehow, he felt that Beth would have understood. She'd loved Tawes as he had, and she'd know why he had to protect it as long as he could . . . protect it for Bailey and the babe she carried in her womb. The wild places were vanishing. The birds, the fish and crabs, the oysters, and the animals. Too many people crowded them out, left no places for them to feed and raise their young. Soon the fox squirrels would follow the red knots into extinction along with the passenger pigeons that his father had shot by the hundreds and thousands.

Using a garden trowel, he dug into the mound beneath the shadow of Beth's tombstone, pushing aside the damp earth until the hole was as deep as a man's arm could reach. When he was satisfied, he pulled a small package from inside his shirt and unwrapped it.

The Irish gold glittered in the moonlight, and Will turned the artifacts over in his hands, marveling at the artists who had crafted these beautiful objects so long ago. Often and again, he'd wondered about them and the men who'd carried them across a wide sea to this bay country. He was sorry they couldn't lie where they'd been placed, as grave goods for those who'd worn them so proudly.

With a sigh, Will thrust the golden torque, the beads, and the rest of the treasure into the bottom of the hole. "Rest in peace," he murmured as he pushed the soft dirt over them and tamped it down with the handle of the trowel. Lastly, he planted the flowering bulbs he'd brought with him. In spring, jonquils would bloom on Beth's grave.

"Yep," he whispered. "You'd understand me, darling. And I'm afraid no one else could."

CHAPTER TWENTY-THREE

"And we've got what?" Daniel asked. He stood near the double stack of filing cabinets against the back wall of the one-room Tawes police office. Buck sat at his desk, drinking bottled green tea and eating crab cake sandwiches that Emma had sent over with Daniel to stave off starvation.

Buck swallowed and wiped his mouth with a napkin. "We've got a likely identification on the three dead bodies that Archie dug up. The child was probably Le'ron Brown, age nine. I suspect the adults were his parents, Patsy and Sam Brown. The adult male, mid-forties, the female in her thirties."

"Abbie thought the child was younger."

"People remember him as unusually small for his age, so he'd match the partial skeleton we found. Le'ron attended Tawes Elementary School sporadically in the spring before the family moved on. We know they returned to the island that fall, because Le'ron shows up registered from September 22nd through mid February. There's a photograph in his file. No district ever requested the boy's records, so they remained here on Tawes." Buck dug through a stack of folders and produced a faded Polaroid snapshot.

"A nice-looking kid." Daniel felt a stab of sorrow as he handed back the picture. There'd been no news on his own son since Lucas had died, and no one at the agency admitted knowledge of the boy's existence. He hoped to God that Mallalai's son wouldn't end up in a muddy grave like little Le'ron Brown. "Anyone remember the father?"

"Some. Sam apparently hired on as a crabber for several of the local watermen. The wife, Patsy, worked here in town in the packing house. Mary Love thinks she remembers her as a tall, skinny woman who never spoke much. A hard worker."

"Anyone know where they came from?"

"No. The family was so poor they camped out in a tent on Creed Somers' farm for a while. Phillip thinks somebody rented a house to them when winter came on, but he can't recall who."

Daniel opened the refrigerator and helped himself to an iced tea. "Who did the father work for?"

"Creed, George, Jim's father, Joe. Creed's dead. Joe's got Alzheimer's, but he claims Sam crabbed with him for years. Said Sam had red hair and was his cousin from Chestertown."

Daniel smiled. His Uncle Joe had recently told him that he'd gone to grammar school with Teddy Roosevelt, that before he'd led the Rough Riders to Cuba, Teddy crabbed with him in Queen's Sound.

"George remembered Sam, but didn't know just when he'd worked for him. He thought it was a year or two after Will got out of prison. George thinks Sam had a family, but couldn't recollect any details, other than that the man had never stolen from him."

"That's it? That's all you've been able to find out?"

"Aunt Birdy remembers Le'ron. According to her, he was thin, almost frail, but clean and well-mannered. Big beautiful eyes. Pretty as a girl, she said. And shy. She recalls that Le'ron rarely spoke above a whisper. She said she used to send hot lunches to the school for him because he came without even a sandwich. She remembers him going fishing with Emma a few times, but Le'ron's mother was distrustful of white people and put an end to it. Elizabeth was the boy's teacher. She told Emma that Le'ron came to class with shoes tied with bailing twine. She ordered a pair of sneakers for him from a catalog, but the father wouldn't let Le'ron keep them."

Daniel leaned back against the refrigerator. "But none of this tells how or why the three of them ended up in that grave with their heads smashed in."

"No, it doesn't, but identifying them puts me one step closer to finding who killed them. And we know now why the killer wanted to keep people from digging in that Indian burial ground."

"It might tie Sean Gilbert's death to Karen Knight's, and eliminate Abbie's father as a suspect. The Brown family died more than twenty-five years ago."

Buck nodded. "If Vernon had anything to do with his wife's death, which I doubt, he didn't kill the Browns."

"So our killer is a lot closer to home."

"I'm afraid so." Buck finished his second sandwich, dropped the empty bottle in his recycle bin, and carried the plate to the sink to rinse it. "I appreciate your keeping an eye on Abbie for me. She was bound and determined to sink a few more holes out there. I think she's looking for Irish gold."

"Will, Emma, and Harry have been taking turns with me guarding the site since I put Bailey on the plane. I doubt our killer wants to take on that bunch."

"What does Bailey think of California?"

"She says it's noisy. And busy. I think this trip was good for her. She and her father have never been close, but he *is* her father."

"Adopted."

"He raised her. That should count for something."

"You're right," Buck agreed. "I just think of her as a Tawes. She's got Will's eyes, and she's the spitting image of her Aunt Elizabeth. I know Will thinks she hung the moon."

"Yeah, Bailey's been the saving of Will. He can't wait until this new baby is born. You know, Will always liked kids, even when he shied away from adults."

"You used to spend a lot of time with Will when you were young, didn't you?" Buck asked. "I know you were always out in the woods or hanging out at his house."

Daniel stiffened. "Why bring that up?"

"Just remembering."

"You know Will's as decent a man as ever lived."

Buck's gaze locked with his. "Didn't say otherwise." He clapped a hand on Daniel's shoulder. "I'm glad Bailey's off the island, cuz. You did the right thing, sending her to California."

"Yeah," Daniel agreed. "But she'll be home next week. I just hope you can catch this murderer before she gets back."

"Me too," Buck answered. "Me too."

An hour later, out at the archaeological site, Buck reined in his horse and waved at Abbie. Buck's younger brother Harry was raking dirt into a pit, and George was scattering grass seed over the mound where another pit had been filled in. Archie rose from the shade of Abbie's tent and trotted over, great tongue lolling from his wide mouth.

Buck dismounted, tied the reins to a tent stake, and patted the Newfoundland's head. "Looks like you're about finished out here, darlin'."

Abbie dusted the sand off her hands onto her dirty jeans and came to meet him. "Three more pits. Nada. A few pieces of a soapstone bowl, a little hearth charcoal, and some fragments of projectile points— Broadspear variants."

"Nothing special?"

"Nothing special. I don't believe this was ever a burial ground. More of a summer fishing camp."

He kissed her. "Other than the massacre. The story is that a lot of people were buried here after the killings."

"Stories. Unsubstantiated tall tales."

"Maybe, but folks on Tawes put a lot of store in oral tradition. You'd be surprised at how accurate some of these family histories can be. Before literacy was common, spoken words were held to be a man's bond."

"Among my people too," she admitted. "But as a scientist, I can't accept what I can't prove."

"Fair enough." He held her in the circle of his arms. It was a good feeling. She was as prickly as a stickerbush, but he liked her that way. He didn't want to think of her leaving Tawes. She'd be returning to Philly and her doctorate studies in a week or two, and he didn't know what would happen between them after that.

She looked up into his eyes and sighed. "We didn't find anything significant of Native American origin, and nothing from Bronze Age Europe."

"I didn't think you would."

"Whatever Matthew possessed, the objects are lost now. Probably melted down and sold for the weight of the gold."

He kissed the crown of her head. She had sand in

her hair, but he didn't give a damn. He liked the way her hair smelled. He liked the way *she* smelled. "Did I ever tell you that you're special?"

She put both hands on his chest and pushed him away. "Save that for later. I have to finish closing up the final pit."

"You're coming back to Emma's tonight?"

"Yes." She glanced around. "After Matthew, I don't care much to spend the night out here."

"Not even if you have company?"

"Nope," she said, giving a good imitation of his voice. "It's a hot shower and a soft mattress for me."

He gave her one more squeeze and released her. Emma's bedroom was at the far end of the house, and now that Abbie's dad had returned to Oklahoma, he and Abbie shared a bed after the lights went out. It wasn't that he feared Emma's disapproval or damaging Abbie's reputation. What he didn't want was Emma spreading the word over Tawes that the two of them were sleeping together. What people thought was one thing—what they knew for fact, another.

Buck had come out to the site to check on Abbie, to be sure she was all right, but he'd also hoped to catch Will. There were some questions he wanted to ask him. Will had been quieter than usual since he'd discovered Matthew's body, and although Buck had always liked and respected Will, he'd learned to listen to his intuition.

"Do you want me to hang around here while you close shop?" he asked her.

"No. George, Harry, and I can finish up. Harry's got his boat. He and George have offered to escort me back out of the marsh. I have my helicopter parked in Bailey's field. Then Harry will hike back to the site and carry my tent, the supplies, and Archie out by water."

"What about my tent?"

She made a face. "We're burning that."

"Ouch."

Harry joined them. "About done, Abbie. Hey, Buck. You want to grab a shovel and help me with that last hole?"

"I'd love to, but I need to catch up with Will. I was hoping he'd be out here."

"He was, earlier," Abbie said. "But when George arrived, Will remembered something he needed to take care of." She looked around the clearing. "I feel foolish, Buck. We had armed soldiers guarding our site in Turkey, but I never expected to need protection here in my own country."

"All the same, stay close to Harry and George. I wouldn't expect trouble in daylight, but anything's possible. And if I'm wrong, I don't want to gamble with your life."

"Yes, Officer," she said. "Now go, do your thing and let us do ours." He kissed her again and swung up onto Toby's back. Abbie patted the horse's withers. "See you back at Emma's."

"Be careful, Abbie. Remember what happened to Matthew."

She looked at him. "Do you think I could forget? Ever?"

She watched him as he rode away, wishing she could think of a good excuse to keep him here . . . wishing she could swing up on the horse behind him and lock her arms around his waist as she had the night they'd gone to the town dock together.

She'd never felt as uneasy on that wild mountain site in Turkey as she did today. She wasn't a coward, and she had faith in George and Harry. But she couldn't shake the feeling that Buck was in danger.

"*Three more will die,*" Grandmother Willow had said.

Abbie hoped it was just an old woman's babbling.

She tried to convince herself that it was foolish to pay heed to such superstitious nonsense. But all the same, she was afraid. Not for herself so much, but for the big man who had become such a part of her life.

Will wasn't at Bailey's farm and he wasn't at his own home. Buck knew the man could be anywhere on Tawes. Since Will's boat was moored to his dock, it was a good bet he was on the island, and Buck figured he had nothing better to do than to look for him.

He rode back across the fields to the low, woody area where the marsh path to the burial site began and retraced his tracks in the hope that Will had returned to the camp. It was hot and humid, and biting sheep flies buzzed around him and the horse. There were rumblings to the west, and he thought they were in for a thunderstorm.

Buck smashed a fly the size of a small blackbird on Toby's neck, then rubbed his blood-stained palm on his jeans. Mosquitoes hovered and whined. He'd sprayed both himself and the animal before he'd left the office, but he wished he'd tucked the repellent into his saddlebag.

As he and Toby neared the cutoff that led to George's farm, the horse splashed through a fetlock-high puddle. Just beyond the mudhole, Buck noticed the print of a dog's foot. The track was fresh, and he was sure he would have seen it if it had been there when he'd passed earlier. The print was exactly the right size for one of Will's Chesapeake Bay retrievers. Buck got down out of the saddle, examined the imprint, and then searched the sodden grass and earth for another.

A few yards down the overgrown prong, he found what he was looking for. He mounted Toby and rode to George's house. It had been a long time since he'd been there, and he was shocked at the state of the place. The porch sagged, the roof was lacking shutters, and crumbling bricks were noticeably missing from one end chimney.

"Will!" he called. "Will! Are you here?" The wind was rising off the water, and heavy clouds scudded over the bay. They were definitely in for rain by evening. "Will!"

Nothing. No answer.

Buck rode around the house. The fence surrounding the overgrown garden was half down. Chickens scratched for bugs between the rails of the rusty metal gate that lay on the ground. The only sound was the clack-clack-clack of the windmill near the back porch. Buck shouted again, but got no answer. If Will had been here, he decided, he'd moved on. But just to be certain, Buck dismounted and tried the side door.

It was unlocked, but he really hadn't expected anything different. George was a tough old waterman, and he didn't scare easily. Buck looked into the kitchen. It was neat but shabby, and the refrigerator was one of the old rounded-top models that must have dated from the fifties. George didn't have electricity out here, but the windmill pumped his water and powered a generator to keep his appliances going. He used oil or gas lamps, heated with a woodstove, as he had when Buck was a kid and hunted rabbits out here with his father. George had been one of the few people Buck knew on Tawes who still had a working outhouse.

The house felt empty. Pale ribbons of late-afternoon sun threaded through a small window, illuminating the small, metal-topped kitchen table, set for one. No cats or dogs stretched on the worn linoleum floor. A mantel clock ticked, but nothing else stirred. Buck closed the door and went back to his horse.

He found Will a quarter of a mile away coming out

of an old barn that had once been the pride of Albert
Hopkins's farm. The house had been struck by lightning and burned before Buck had been born, and the
outbuildings had all fallen in and been overrun by
greenbriers and rot, all but the stable. Albert's father
had built the barn of chestnut and cedar, and he'd
built it to stand. The barn's roof was sagging and the
loft door hung awry, creaking in the wind. The struc-
ture had clearly seen better days, but it had survived.

The barn was no more than thirty feet from the
road, across the way from where the house had been.
Despite the weeds and wild rose bushes that surrounded the building, he and Will caught sight of
each other at the same instant.

"Buck! Found something you should take a look at."

He dismounted, but when he was on the far side of
the horse, where Will couldn't see him, he unsnapped
the leather guard that held his pistol in place. He
didn't draw it, and he felt ashamed of himself for even
taking the precaution, but he did it all the same.

He fastened Toby's reins to an old fencepost. It was
locust and as twisted as a marsh creek, but enough of
the stone-hard wood remained to hold the horse se-
curely. A few drops of rain splattered on his face as he
threaded his way through the brush to where the
older man stood holding a tin container about the size
of a man's domed lunchbox.

"I got to thinking about those moccasin tracks we
found near Matthew's body," Will said. "I wear moccasins. Emma does too. And so do quite a few other
old-timers I know on Tawes. But when folks sew their
own footwear, it's distinctive, different from every
other pair. I kept musing on where I'd seen those
prints before, and it seemed to me the shape might
match George's feet."

"You went to his house," Buck said. It wasn't a question. He'd known Will had been there. He'd felt it in his gut.

"Did. Barged in and searched the place. Keeps a tidy house for a bachelor, does old George. I didn't find any moccasins, not even a single pair. Boots, work shoes, but no moccasins, and I know he favors them for the marsh and woods, like I do."

"Why would you suspect George of killing Matthew and the others?"

Daniel studied him with narrowed eyes. "You ever know George to have a woman? Sit with one in church, dance with one at a gathering?"

"No, but neither do you."

"I courted Beth's mother a long time ago, hot and heavy. And there were a lot of other girls I danced with and kissed, and did far worse. But not George. If I was as much a gossip as Emma, I'd say George didn't care for the ladies."

"I don't see how George's sexuality matters."

"Who was the last waterman on this island to lay eyes on Sam Brown? Or the last one to admit Sam worked for him? George. And you've only got George's word that Sam vanished. Left without taking his leave, according to George."

"I don't know. That was a long time ago. It would be easy for anyone to forget—"

"No," Will said. "George always struck me as a little strange."

"And Emma isn't?"

"True," Will agreed. "Emma's unnatural, but she's a clean kind of unnatural. Not like George. Emma would never kill anyone that didn't need killing."

"Emma's not a suspect."

"She should be. We all should be until we find who's doing these killings. You can't rule out people because you like them."

"So I should include you, too?"

"Why not? But it's got to be George. Think about it. The Williamses have Nanticoke blood. I've heard George bragging about how good his grandfather was with a bow and arrow, and how he was as much Indian in his heart as African."

Buck folded his arms and tried not to over react. Abbie was with George, but so was Harry. She'd been with George, off and on, since she'd first come to Tawes, and he'd never harmed a hair of her head. "Half the people on the island have Indian blood. You're grasping at straws, Will."

"Am I?" Will gave a sound of bitter amusement. "After I searched George's house and found nothing—not his old bow or any of that arrowhead collection he was so proud of—I started wondering why. Then I thought of this barn. What's the closest place to it?"

"George's farm, I suppose, but you can't blame him for—"

"Me and the dogs, we just walked down here and thought we'd take a look-see. I found where someone had come from the back of the barn. The rain washed away any footprints, but there were greenbriers snapped off, crushed underfoot. And when I went inside, what do you think I found?"

"Don't know, Will, but I think you're going to tell me."

"Take a look." He led the way inside and pointed to the ladder that led to the loft. "Notice what bad shape those rungs are in? All but one?"

"Somebody's taken the trouble to repair one of them." Buck glanced at Will. "And you wondered why."

"I did. I climbed up into the loft, kicked a little moldy hay, and came up with a plastic box. This was inside." He held out the tin box. "Look in it. Bring it back out where it's light enough to get a good look."

Buck lifted the lid. Nestled in a bed of crumpled

plastic wrap was a heavy metal object about six inches long. He removed it and swore softly. There was no mistaking the bronze cloak pin with the geometric pattern. "Matthew's Irish piece."

"The one that Karen Knight's killer stole. Keep looking, boy."

Wrapped in still more plastic were six photographs, all pictures of children, all roughly eight or nine years of age. Four of them were African-American boys, and two were Caucasian. "These look like school pictures," Buck said.

"That's what I thought. My Beth used to come home every year with ones just like this. Had phony bookshelves or the American flag in the background."

Buck turned the photos over. Hand-printed on the first one was the name *Jonah*. The second was labeled *Kwasi*. When he flipped the third picture, Buck suddenly felt sick. It read *Daniel*. He raised his eyes to meet Will's hard look.

"Yeah," Will said, "it's our Daniel." He picked up his shotgun where it rested against the barn wall.

"But I don't see how these pictures tie in," Buck said, not wanting to understand . . . not wanting to believe the crazy possibilities that were surfacing in his mind.

Hadn't he found Will coming out of the barn with the box? Will was casting the blame on George, but it could just as easily be him. Who wanted to keep the marina off Tawes more than Will? And who had been closer to Daniel when he was a kid than Will?

As if he'd read his mind, Will snatched Daniel's picture out of Buck's hand. "You don't need this. Nobody needs it. Look at the other two, Buck," the older man said.

"That could be evidence. You can't—" But Will was already shredding the small photograph and tossing the fragments into the wind.

"Look at the damned name on the back!"

Buck didn't have to. Staring down at the picture, he recognized the thin face and huge eyes of Le'ron Brown.

"George is some kind of pervert who likes little boys," Will said harshly. "He did something to Le'ron and got caught. Then he had to kill them all to hide what he'd done."

CHAPTER TWENTY-FOUR

"By the time we walk to Bailey's farm and you come all the way back here to launch the boat, it will be getting dark," George said as he dumped the tools on the beach near Harry's sixteen-foot aluminum boat. "It don't make sense to me for you to do all this comin' and goin'. Why don't you jest take the boat with the stuff and I'll see Miss Abbie safe out of the marsh?"

"I don't know." Harry glanced at Abbie. "Buck won't like it. He said that two of us had to be watching over her all the time." He kicked the sand. "Wish my boat was big enough to carry us, the dog, and the tent."

"It's not," Abbie said. "But we'll be fine. George has his trusty shotgun, and I've got these." She tapped the knives at her waist. "Go ahead. Take the boat. You don't have lights and you might get lost in the marsh if you don't go now."

"Storm's comin' in," George said. "I wouldn't want to be in that marsh in bad weather. Them guts swell up and burst over the banks. You can't tell creek from swamp. And if you're stuck out there all night, the skeeters will eat you alive."

"Take the dog and go," Abbie urged. "I can't fit Archie in the helicopter anyway." She wanted to be off this site, to put it and the memories of Matthew's hanging body behind her. And she didn't want to be responsible for Harry having to return alone to this beach, hundred-pound bear-dog for protection or not.

"All right," Harry said, "but if Buck gives me hell—'scuse me—if Buck gives me heck, I'll tell him you ordered me to do it."

Abbie laughed. "Sure, blame me. Everyone always does." She glanced around the clearing. All of the pits had been closed and leveled. George had sprinkled grass seed on top. The tents were down, folded, and stacked on the beach with the cooler, her tools, and the folding table. She had her laptop in her backpack and a canteen of water for the hike out. "See you back in Tawes," she said to Harry. "Are you ready, George?"

"Yep, ready as I'll ever be."

"And keep Archie on the leash," Abbie told Harry. "I don't want him coming after us." She hoped that the rain would hold off until she got back to town. If there was wind, she might decide to stay at Bailey's until the weather cleared. She'd flown the helicopter under dicey conditions, and it had handled beautifully. Still, it didn't pay to be reckless with her life or the expensive aircraft. Contrary to whatever Buck might think, she was careful with her father's money.

For the first quarter mile of the hike out, neither she nor George spoke. It would have been difficult to hear each other in any case, because the wind was kicking up. The path was too narrow and slippery to walk two abreast in some places, and the marsh grass rustled and snapped as it bent and swayed overhead.

Abbie could hear the low boom of thunder to the west.

"Watch out." George, who'd been leading the way with his shotgun cradled in his arms, stopped short. "There. You don't want to step on him."

Abbie looked into the muddy grass, and her heartbeat quickened. There, only a few feet in front of George, a three-foot, mottled brown snake with dark irregular bands slithered across the track. She shuddered. "Yuck. What kind is it?"

"Just a water snake, not poison." He peered at her from under his sweat-stained felt hat. "That one won't bite, not if you don't bother him. But some . . ." He looked off into the reeds for emphasis. "But some of these snakes are bad."

She shrugged. "No rattlesnakes around the Chesapeake. Out West, there are lots of them." She'd seen her share on far-flung archaeological digs, and she'd learned to listen for the telltale rattle and not to poke around in spots where they might be lurking, but she'd never learned to shed her repulsion for them.

"Nope, not around here. I hear tell they got plenty of them copperheads out in the mountains. Here, we got other kinds of snakes. Kings, milk snakes, garters, all manner of water snakes, and more black snakes than you can count."

"I don't like snakes," Abbie admitted.

"The only poison one we got on this island is a water moccasin. They're mean, and they'll come after you," George said. "You see a snake, any color at all, what rears up and gapes its mouth at you—and that mouth's all white inside like a ball of cotton—you scoot. That's a moccasin, and they'll kill a man or a dog quicker than you can say Jack Robinson."

"I'll take your word for it."

The snake vanished into the reeds, and George held a clump of phragmites up so she could pass under.

"Thanks." She moved on, stepping cautiously as the trail dipped into a low spot and water seeped up over the edges of her shoes.

Drops of rain were hitting her cheeks and arms and blurring her vision. She removed her sunglasses and tucked them into her shirt pocket as she walked.

"Turn off there," George said.

"No, I'm sure that's not the main path," she said. "That's just a—"

"I said, turn off!"

At his gruff tone, she turned to stare at him. Her mouth went dry. George had the strangest expression on his face, and he held the shotgun level, the barrel pointed at her midsection.

"You heard me. That way!" He motioned to the game trail that led into the reeds.

"George . . ." Her skin suddenly felt hot, and black specks danced in front of her eyes. "You don't want to do anything—"

"Do as I say! Do it or I'll shoot you here. This shell is loaded with buckshot. You know what a twelve-gauge will do to a deer?"

She raised her hands. "George, think about what you're doing. We're friends. We—"

He shook his head. "We're not friends," he said. "You're stupid. You didn't have sense enough to leave things be."

"I came here because I was asked to come," she pleaded. "Because my mother—"

"Drop those knives. Slow. Pull them out with your fingers. That's right. Now toss them into the reeds. Both of them."

He smiled, and the smile terrified her more than the gun.

"I'm one of them," he said. "All these years, I protected them, watched over them. Until you and her came. You disturbed the dead. You should have let them rest."

"You killed her, didn't you?" Abbie asked. "You killed my mother?"

He gestured with the gun barrel. "Git movin'. And don't think about runnin'. You can't run faster than a load of buckshot."

The water level was higher along this track. Soon she was wading through mud and muck that rose over her ankles.

Throw that pack into the pond," George said. "You won't have no more need for it."

"Why?" she asked him. "Why did you have to kill her?"

"She wouldn't listen," he answered hoarsely. "She had to be taught a lesson."

"You won't get away with this. Harry knows you're with me. If you hurt me, they'll find out. They'll put you in jail."

"They won't know it was me. They'll think it was the curse. All I got to do is cut myself with a knife. Or whack myself on the head. I'll tell them that something came out of the swamp and jumped me. You won't be able to tell 'em anything different."

Rain was falling harder now. Wind whistled across the marsh, flattening the phragmites and bending the tangles of stunted cedar trees that clung to grassy hummocks. A great blue heron burst up almost at Abbie's feet and flew off over the whipping grass. She slipped and staggered in an attempt to keep from falling. George jammed the shotgun into her spine, and she cried out in pain.

"Not far now," he said. He'd thought about this a lot, how to do it when he got the chance. He couldn't just shoot her. No matter what he said, that wouldn't be right. He'd thought of putting a knife in her back and scalping her. That would be an Indian way to deal with enemies, the way a blood brother would do it. But he didn't think he had the stomach for that much blood. A cut on the head bled bad, and if he cut off her black hair, there would be a river of blood.

They'd all been scared when they'd seen how he'd done for Matthew. If he'd strung him up sooner and filled him full of arrows, maybe no one would have dug up Le'ron. The boy could have slept there in his mama's arms. But now, it was too late. They'd found Le'ron, and nothing would ever be right again.

Killing Dr. Knight's daughter would be different from the others. He didn't want to do it, but he had to. Otherwise, he would have failed.

Lightning flashed, and he blinked against the sudden bolt of light. It wasn't far now. He'd stay until it was over, until he was certain that she was done for, and then he'd make his way back to the main trail. He wanted them to find him, to find him hurt. It might be a long time before they found her body, but that would be all right, too. It would be finished, and he could sleep easy at night. He slipped a hand into his pants pocket and found the little piece of bone. He rubbed it, and it gave him comfort.

He knew that what he was doing would please them. He knew they'd want him to teach her a lesson, to teach everyone that the curse was real.

Buck reached the dig site and found Harry just pushing off from the beach. "Hey, brother!" He kicked the horse's sides and urged Toby down to the water's edge.

Harry waved and shut off the electric motor. He was close enough to shore that when he turned the rudder, the momentum carried the aluminum pram back into the shallows.

"Where's Abbie?" Buck shouted above the rain.

"She and George walked out. I had the damned dog on a rope. I didn't take it off until I was under way, but you know how bullheaded Archie is. He jumped out of the boat and swam back to shore."

"You were supposed to stay with her!"

"I know. I'm sorry, but Abbie—"

"How long ago did they leave?" Buck demanded. Lightning arced across the sky, and the Tennessee walker shied and tossed his head. "Was George with her?"

"Yeah. He said they'd be fine. He'd see her to the helicopter." Harry stood up in the boat. "I looked for the damned dog but—"

"Leave the boat!" Buck shouted. "I need you here! It's George! George is the killer!" Thunder spooked the horse and he reared. Swearing, Buck leaned forward and forced the animal down. "Follow me!" he told Harry, once he had Toby under control.

Eyes wide, Harry leaped out of the boat and splashed ashore through the driving rain, rifle in hand. "I'm sorry, Buck. I'm sorry! I didn't know it was George. You want me to call for help?"

"No need. I've already contacted Daniel and told him to gather men. Will's coming with his dogs. He's somewhere between George's place and the marsh trail. Don't shoot Will by mistake!" Buck pulled the horse's head around and raced him back across the barren site and down the narrow track.

Buck ducked his head as the horse plunged under a low-hanging branch. Thunder cracked and Toby shied again, nearly spilling Buck into the sodden phrag-mites that closed in on either side of the trail. The skies opened, and a deluge of rain poured down on the island.

Buck had ridden only a short way when he heard a dog bark. It was a deep, full-throated bellow that could only belong to Archie. The sound came from the right, off in the marsh. Buck pulled Toby up short, threw himself out of the saddle, and set off on foot down the nearest game trail.

Abbie heard the dog behind them, and her heart surged with hope. Archie had been with Harry, but if he wasn't, if he was coming after her, she had a chance. "They know about you!" she cried at George. "Run while you can!"

"You keep moving," George answered brusquely. "Up ahead there."

Abbie climbed over a rotting log and sank to her knees in the muddy water. Something loomed out of the rain. As she struggled closer, she saw that it was an old wooden boat, but how it had gotten this far into the swamp, she couldn't imagine.

"Nor'easter flooded the island," George said, as if reading her mind. "Pushed this old hull up here. God carried it here. No way a man could get it out." He gestured toward it. "Somebody used it for a duck blind," he said. "Tarred it all inside. Made it waterproof. Snake-proof too."

Abbie looked at the boat. It was rotting, but someone had nailed a crude ladder to the side.

"Get up there," George said.

Abbie heard Archie's booming bark. Closer now. She prayed to God that Buck was with him. That someone would come.

"That's it," George urged. "Climb right up on the deck. Now open that cabin hatch."

Abbie shivered as she tugged at the door.

"Hurry up!"

Abbie yanked at the rusty handle. She could see that someone had fastened a slide bolt to the outside. George meant to lock her in here.

The door gave way. Abbie shielded her eyes against the rain. The interior of the boat was dim, and tar or not, water six inches deep had flooded it. A few beer cans and an empty shotgun shell bobbed in the water. The faded remains of a pinup calendar hung precariously from the far wall, but it wasn't the image of the scantily clad girl on the Harley that drew her attention.

Curled on the rotting table was a thick, dark snake longer than a man's arm. As she stared in speechless horror, the snake drew back and opened its mouth wide. Teeth gleamed. The interior of the snake's mouth flashed white—as white as cotton.

"Thought you might like company." George laughed. "Go on in. Make yourself at home."

Abbie dashed for the far side of the boat. The shotgun roared. She scrambled over the side and jumped. Cursing, George came around the boat after her, but she had already clawed herself out of the mud and was splashing through the undergrowth toward a narrow creek that lay perhaps fifty feet from the boat.

She didn't look back. She knew George would have more shotgun shells, that he'd reload, that she couldn't outrun the range of the gun. But he'd have to hunt her down. She wasn't going to stand there and wait to be murdered.

George's second shot pinged through the branches over her head and rained around her. Something sharp and hot jabbed the back of her thigh and one arm, but she kept running. She dove into the water, went under, and came up kicking.

The creek was no more than ten feet wide, and the far bank was a wall of sheer mud. She tried to climb it, but slid down. She heard a ferocious growl, looked back, and saw George swing the barrel of the shotgun at Archie. The Newfoundland yipped in pain, but lunged at the man again. George clipped him on the head and the dog slumped to the ground.

Abbie half ran, half swam down the creek, desperately seeking a place where she could get out of the water. The storm raged directly overhead. Lightning flashed, and thunder cracked and boomed. The torrent of rain made it difficult for her to see more than a few yards ahead.

If she could reach the tall reeds, hide in them, George might not find her. Help might reach her before he did. Around a bend, she saw a flat meadow of grass. The bank here was lower, and she managed to climb up. The growth wasn't tall enough to hide in, but she couldn't turn back. She waded and crawled through the muck.

The burning in her thigh nagged at her, but fear drove her on. Then another shot rang out. It sounded different from George's shotgun, but she couldn't be sure.

"Abbie!"

She turned to see Buck standing on the far bank. "Abbie, get down!"

She threw herself flat in the mud. Seconds later, lightning shattered a pine a few hundred yards away. Flames shot from branches, to be quickly drenched by the pouring rain. The smell of brimstone filled her nostrils.

She raised her head. George was plunging across the mud flat toward her. She scrambled up, but Buck shouted again. "Stay there!"

Abbie could make out George plainly through the rain. His hat was gone. His eyes were wild. His mud-covered face was twisted in rage so that he didn't appear human. She crouched there, trembling, too frightened to scream.

Suddenly George stepped into a grassy pool and sank waist-deep into the mud, shotgun held over his head.

Abbie began to inch away.

"Stay where you are!" Buck yelled.

George was struggling now. The water rose to his chest. He threw the shotgun aside and clawed at the water and clumps of grass, pulling great handfuls loose. He was near enough that she could see his terrified eyes. He was sinking deeper and deeper.

"Help!" he screamed. "Help me!"

Abbie couldn't move. Her heart thudded erratically against her ribs.

Lightning struck again, closer.

George was blubbering now. Crying out, "Mama! Mama! Help me!" The black water closed over his shoulders.

"Abbie!" Buck had circled around the mud flat and now moved toward her from the opposite direction George had come. Buck was stepping cautiously from grass hummock to hummock. "Don't move, babe," he called to her. "If you move, you'll go under. It's quicksand."

"Please!" George howled. "Please!" The muddy water reached his chin, and he choked and thrashed. He scratched and clawed at the air. "Help me! Help . . ."

Abbie closed her eyes and tried not to think of the cold muck filling George's eyes and ears . . . of the thick mud pouring down his throat and choking off his breath. She tried not to think of the cold, silent water closing over him.

And then Buck's strong arms were around her, and she stopped thinking, clung to him, and wept with joy.

A week later, Daniel and Bailey moored the skiff at his dock and walked up the lawn to the cabin. Archie, lying in the shade of the porch, raised his massive head—swathed in bandages—and bellowed a welcome.

Abbie opened the kitchen door. "Hey!" she cried. "Buck! Come here."

He filled the doorway behind her and laughed. "What's that you've got, cuz?"

Bailey smiled and looked at the dark-haired child Daniel was holding in his arms. "This is Rafi," she said, beaming at the little boy dressed in bright red shorts, new sneakers, and a matching red dinosaur T-shirt. "This is Daniel's—this is *our* son, Rafi."

Abbie and Buck came out onto the porch. "Hello, there." Abbie smiled at the toddler. "Aren't you a handsome boy?"

Buck looked into his cousin's eyes. "You found him?"

"Daniel was coming to the airport to pick me up," Bailey supplied, "and someone from the agency called him."

"They said they had a package for me," Daniel said. "It seems our mutual friend wasn't all bad. Rafi got sick, and Lucas left him in the emergency room in Easton with his passport, his birth certificate, and a State Department phone number. Child services got involved, but eventually, the agency straightened it all out and contacted me."

"So he's yours?" Buck asked.

Bailey caught the small hand and squeezed it. "All ours. Rafi Daniel Catlin. He doesn't speak much English. *Bunny* and *Coke* are about it, but he seems very bright."

"That's wonderful," Abbie said.

"Yeah," Daniel agreed. "It is." He put his free arm around Bailey. "And Emma tells me that congratulations are in order for you two."

"No," Abbie said. "They are not."

"Yep," Buck said. "I asked her to marry me, and she said *maybe*."

Bailey laughed. "*Maybe? Maybe* means *congratulations?*"

"At least she didn't say, 'Hell, no!'," Buck said. "Come on in. Spaghetti sauce is ready, and I'm about to put the noodles on."

"I helped," Abbie said. "I added the hot peppers."

"*Really* hot," Buck said. "I've convinced her to stay a few more days. Then she has to be in Philadelphia to start classes."

Daniel stood Rafi on the floor. The little boy seized Bailey's hand and stared at Archie with large dark eyes.

"He loves animals," Bailey said. "Don't you, Rafi? He and Puzzle are already friends."

"Maybe he'd like Archie for his very own," Abbie teased.

"No way," Buck said. "Archie's going nowhere. If it wasn't for him, I never would have caught up with you and George in time."

"Bad business, that." Daniel glanced at Abbie. "But over now."

"Yeah, over. Once and for all." Buck smiled. "I appreciate your letting me use this cabin until you can get the Sherwood house in shape for me. I'd be glad to pay rent."

"No rent," Bailey said. "We don't need two houses anymore. We're glad we can help." She looked at Abbie. "I'm starved, and that spaghetti sauce smells delicious. Can I do anything?"

"Maybe talk some sense into Buck," Abbie replied. "He's still trying to convince me that we can work out something permanent. My doctorate will take a few years, and I'll have to be in Greece summers for—"

"Small details," Buck said.

"And when I get my degree, I'll have to look for a position at a university."

Daniel shrugged. "You can commute."

"That's what I tell her. It's not as though she doesn't have transportation."

"That's true," Bailey agreed. "And I can't think of anyone we'd rather have as a neighbor."

"Besides," Buck said, going to stand beside Abbie and draping an arm around her shoulders, "we can't fight when we're not together."

"I keep telling him it will never work," Abbie insisted.

"Quiet, woman, and pour the wine."

She rolled her eyes. "Ignore him. He's playing macho cop again."

Buck grinned. "She knows all about that. Ask her about the handcuffs."

Abbie laughed and poured the wine.

When they all had drinks, Buck raised a glass, "To Rafi and your new baby."

"To Rafi and Betsy," Daniel touched his glass to Buck's.

"It's a girl," Bailey informed them. "Rafi will be a big brother. We're naming her Elizabeth Emma Tawes Catlin."

"That's a mouthful," Buck said.

Abbie smiled. "I think it's beautiful." She looked at Rafi. "And he's beautiful. But . . . why did the C.I.A. go to the trouble to find your son and deliver him to you?"

"Simple," Daniel answered. "The agency considers itself a family. They take care of each other, even the black sheep, like me."

"Like the people on Tawes," Bailey said.

"Exactly," Buck agreed. "And you know how it is with family, babe. We may squabble among ourselves, but when the wind blows and the tide rises, we always look after our own."

BLOOD
KIN
JUDITH E.
FRENCH

Hidden behind the deceptive beauty of Tawes Island, secrets remain unspoken, waiting to be brought to light.

Bailey Elliot arrives on Tawes to look into her own past, but its wary residents don't take to outsiders digging up long-buried scandal. Her great uncle warns her she's not safe, and despite the sizzling attraction between her and Daniel Catlin, he tells her, "The sooner you leave, the better."

Now Bailey discovers a diary no one wants her to read, Daniel gives in to temptation, and a decades-old crime of passion is about to be reenacted....

- -

51

2961

BLOOD
KIN
JUDITH E. FRENCH

Hidden behind the deceptive beauty of Tawes Island, secrets remain unspoken, waiting to be brought to light.

Bailey Elliot arrives on Tawes to look into her own past, but its wary residents don't take to outsiders digging up long-buried scandal. Her great uncle warns her she's not safe, and despite the sizzling attraction between her and Daniel Catlin, he tells her, "The sooner you leave, the better."

Now Bailey discovers a diary no one wants her to read, Daniel gives in to temptation, and a decades-old crime of passion is about to be reenacted....

Dorchester Publishing Co., Inc.
P.O. Box 6640
Wayne, PA 19087-8640

___52685-9
$6.99 US/$8.99 CAN

Please add $2.50 for shipping and handling for the first book and $.75 for each additional book. NY and PA residents, add appropriate sales tax. No cash, stamps, or CODs. Canadian orders require an extra $2.00 for shipping and handling and must be paid in U.S. dollars. Prices and availability subject to change. **Payment must accompany all orders.**

Name: _____

Address: _____

City: _____ State: _____ Zip: _____

E-mail: _____

I have enclosed $_____ in payment for the checked book(s).

CHECK OUT OUR WEBSITE! www.dorchesterpub.com
____ Please send me a free catalog.

A KILLING
TIDE

P. J. ALDERMAN

Kaz Jorgensen is used to fear—the anxiety of negotiating treacherous currents as she captains her family's fishing trawlers, the terrifying nightmares of the day she almost lost her life on the river. But now a man is dead, an arsonist has set the *Anna Marie* ablaze and her brother is missing, accused of both crimes. How much more can she take?

Michael Chapman knows how to take the heat—as fire chief he's dealt with more than his share. No way can he afford to get involved with the sister of a suspect. But the scorching attraction between him and Kaz burns out of control. Whatever happens, he can't allow another woman to die because of him.

HEAT LIGHTNING

COLLEEN THOMPSON

An unidentified man is terrorizing Luz Maria Montoya. Almost strangled to death outside a deserted parking lot, she has no idea who is the perpetrator of this very personal hate crime. Investigator Grant Holcomb has been assigned to find her attacker, but he makes no secret of his conflicting feelings. As Luz Maria receives threatening phone calls and grisly warnings, part of him wants to protect the sultry Latina, while the other half hopes the escalating tension between them will explode in an electrifying burst of . . . *HEAT LIGHTNING*.

KILLER *in* HIGH HEELS

Gemma Halliday

L.A. shoe designer Maddie Springer hasn't seen her father since he reportedly ran off to Las Vegas with a showgirl named Lola. So she's shocked when he leaves a desperate plea for help on her answering machine—ending in a loud bang. Never one to leave her curiosity unsatisfied, Maddie straps on her stilettos and heads for Sin City.

There she finds not only her dad, but also a handful of aging drag queens, an organized crime ring smuggling fake Prada pumps, and one relentless killer. Plus, it seems the LAPD's sexiest cop is doing a little Vegas moonlighting of his own.

REMEMBER THE ALIMONY

BETHANY TRUE

Tips from Delaney Davis-Daniels, former Miss Texas:

Avoid sleeping with the enemy. Even if your ex's attorney is the most luscious man ever and you had no idea who he was when he gave you the most incredible night of your life.

Never let 'em catch you crying. When your slimeball former husband turns up dead and you're suspect #1, stay strong. After all, you have a gorgeous lawyer willing to do anything to help you prove your innocence—as long as he doesn't get disbarred first.

And remember: *Love never follows the rules.*